THE END

Slavering at the mouth and panting, Hogspit cleaved down, holding the cutlass with both paws. The blade tanged off a rock, sending a shock through him. He spat at his enemy, snarling, "I'll carve yer guts inter frogmeat an' dance on 'em!"

Log-a-Log wiped the weasel's spit from his headband, eyes flat with menace. "Nobeast ever spat on me an' lived. I could've slain ye a dozen times. Here! There! Left! Right! Up 'n' down!" Whirling about he pricked Hogspit each time he spoke, showing him the truth of the statement. Halting, the shrew curled his lip scornfully at the Rapscour and turned his back on him, saying, "Gerrout o' my sight, vermin, you've done yoreself no honor here today!"

Swinging the cutlass high, Hogspit charged at the shrew's unprotected back. At the last possible second Log-a-Log turned and ran him through, gritting up into the coward's shocked face, "No skill, no sense, and no honor, now y've got no life!"

THE REDWALL BOOKS

OTHER BOOKS

WITHDRAWN

A tale of

REDWALL

The Long Patrol

BRIAN JACQUES

Illustrated by Allan Curless

FIREBIRD

AN IMPRINT OF PENGUIN GROUP (USA) INC.

*This book is dedicated to the memory of a nine-year-old boy,
Jimmy Casey—the bravest warrior of all who never gave up,
and who will live on in the hearts of all who knew him.*
BRIAN JACQUES

FIREBIRD
Published by the Penguin Group
Penguin Group (USA) Inc., 345 Hudson Street, New York, New York 10014, U.S.A.
Penguin Group (Canada), 90 Eglinton Avenue East, Suite 700, Toronto, Ontario, Canada M4P 2Y3
(a division of Pearson Penguin Canada Inc.)
Penguin Books Ltd, 80 Strand, London WC2R 0RL, England
Penguin Ireland, 25 St Stephen's Green, Dublin 2, Ireland (a division of Penguin Books Ltd)
Penguin Group (Australia), 250 Camberwell Road, Camberwell, Victoria 3124, Australia
(a division of Pearson Australia Group Pty Ltd)
Penguin Books India Pvt Ltd, 11 Community Centre, Panchsheel Park, New Delhi - 110 017, India
Penguin Group (NZ), 67 Apollo Drive, Rosedale, North Shore 0632, New Zealand
(a division of Pearson New Zealand Ltd)
Penguin Books (South Africa) (Pty) Ltd, 24 Sturdee Avenue,
Rosebank, Johannesburg 2196, South Africa

Registered Offices: Penguin Books Ltd, 80 Strand, London WC2R 0RL, England

Originally published in Great Britain, by Hutchinson Children's Books Ltd, London, 1997
First published in the United States of America by Philomel,
a division of the Putnam & Grosset Group, 1998
Published by Firebird, an imprint of Penguin Group (USA) Inc., 2004

5 7 9 10 8 6

Text copyright © The Redwall Abbey Company Ltd, 1997
Illustrations copyright © Allan Curless, 1997
All rights reserved

THE LIBRARY OF CONGRESS HAS CATALOGED THE PHILOMEL EDITION AS FOLLOWS:
Jacques, Brian.
The long patrol: a tale from Redwall / Brian Jacques;
illustrated by Allan Curless.—1st American ed.

p. cm.
Summary: Tammo, a daring young hare hungry for adventure,
is sent with Russa Nodrey, the wandering red squirrel, to join the Long Patrol
and defend Salamandastron against the Rapscallion horde.
ISBN 978-0-399-23165-0 (hc)
[1. Animals—Fiction. 2. Fantasy.]   I. Curless, Allan, ill.   II. Title.
PZ7.J15317Lo   1998   [Fic]—dc21   97-15508   CIP   AC

ISBN 978-0-14-240245-0
Printed in the United States of America

Except in the United States of America, this book is sold subject to the condition that
it shall not, by way of trade or otherwise, be lent, re-sold, hired out, or otherwise
circulated without the publisher's prior consent in any form of binding or cover
other than that in which it is published and without a similar condition
including this condition being imposed on the subsequent purchaser.

The publisher does not have any control over and does not assume
any responsibility for author or third-party Web sites or their content.

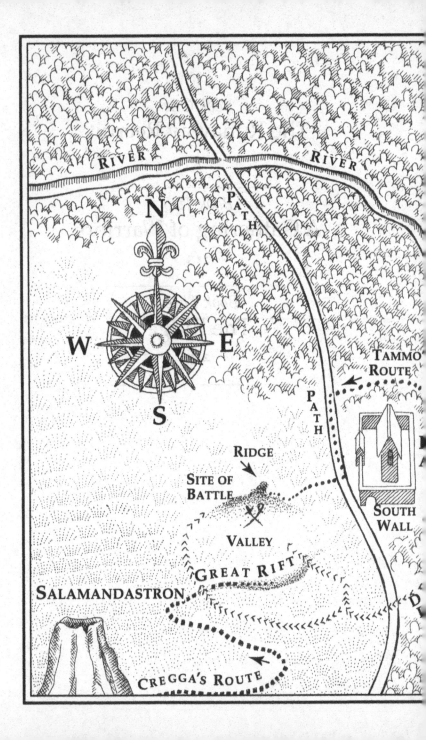

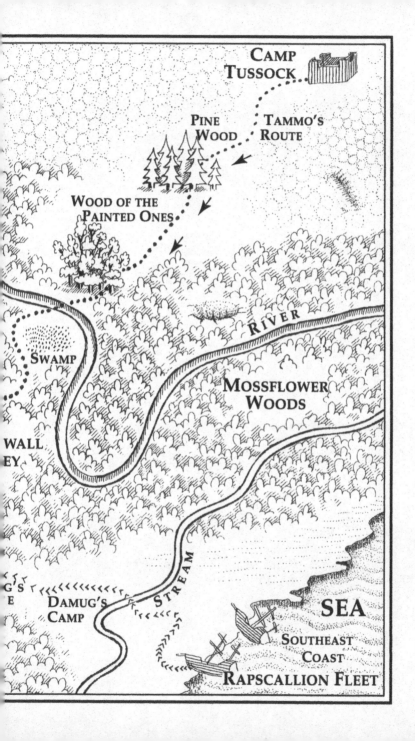

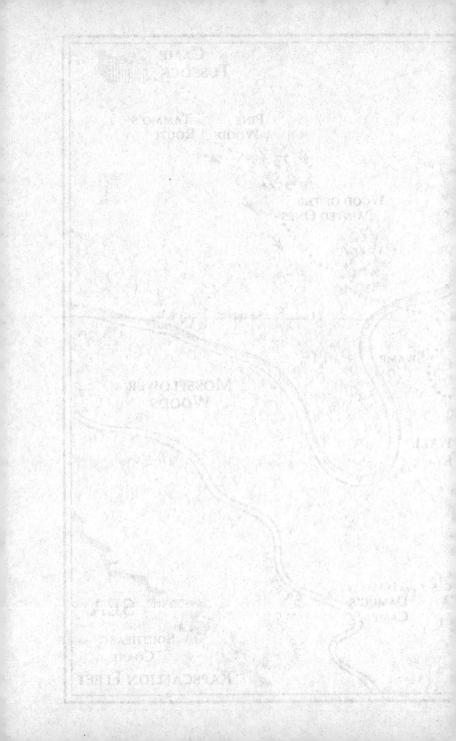

Sometimes I sit here through the night,
Dreaming of those far-flung days.
I'll gaze into the fire's warm light,
As if into some sunlit haze.
And here they come, those comrades mine,
Laughing, happy, brave to see,
Untarnished by the dust of time,
Forever fresh in memory.
The way we marched, the feasts so grand,
I'll tell you of them all,
From Salamandastron's west strand,
And north up to Redwall.
Of high adventures each new dawn,
As side by side we stood in war,
This tale is told that you may learn,
Just what true friends are for.

The Ballad of Tammo

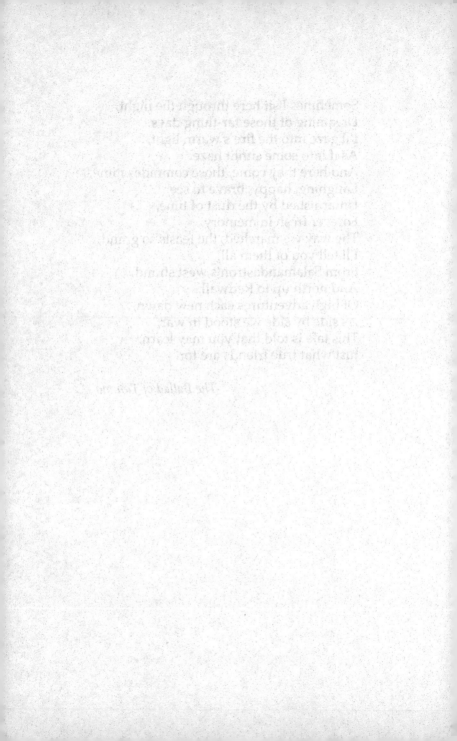

BOOK ONE

The Runaway Recruit

1

Melting snowdrifts with grassy knolls poking through made a patchwork of the far east lands as winter surrendered its icy grip of the earth to oncoming spring. Snowdrop, chickweed, and shepherd's purse nodded gratefully beneath a bright mid-morning sun, which beamed through small islands of breeze-chased clouds. Carrying half-melted icicles along, a tinkling, chuckling stream bounded from rocky cliff ledges, meandering around fir and pine groves toward broad open plains. Already a few hardy wood ants and honeybees were abroad in the copse fringes. Clamoring and gaggling, a skein of barnacle geese in wavering formation winged their way overhead toward the coastline. All around, the land was wakening to springtime, and it promised to be a fair season.

It is often said that a madness takes possession of certain hares in spring, and anybeast watching the performance of one such creature would have had his worst fears confirmed. Tamello De Fformelo Tussock, to give this young hare his full title, was doing battle with imaginary enemies. Armed with stick and slingshot, he flung himself recklessly from a rock ledge, whirling the stone-loaded sling and thwacking left and right with his stick, yelling, "Eulaliaaaa! Have at you, villainous vermin, 'tis m'self, Captain Tammo of the Long Patrol! Take that, y'wicked weasel! Hah! Thought you'd sneak up behind a chap, eh? Well, have some o' this, you ratten rot, beg pardon, rotten rat!"

Hurling himself down in the snow, he lashed out powerfully with his long back legs. "What ho! That'll give you a bellyache to last out the season, m'laddo. Want some more? Hahah! Thought y'didn't, go on, run f'your lives, you cowardly crew! It'd take more'n five hundred of you t'bring down Cap'n Tammo, by the left it would!"

Satisfied that he had given a justly deserved thrashing to half a thousand fictitious foebeasts, Tammo sat up in the snow, eating a few pawfuls to cool himself down.

"Just let 'em come back, I'll show the blighters, wot! There ain't a foebeast in the blinkin' land can defeat me . . . Yaaagh, gerroff!" He felt himself hauled roughly upright by both ears. Lynum and Saithe, Tammo's elder brother and sister, had sneaked up and grabbed him.

"Playing soldiers again?" Lynum's firm grip indicated that there would be no chance of escape.

Tammo's embarrassment at being caught at his game made him even more indignant. "Unhand me at once, m'laddo, if you know what's good for you," he said, struggling. "I can walk by myself."

Saithe gave Tammo's ear an extra tweak as she admonished him: "Colonel wants a word with you, wretch, about his battle-ax!"

Tammo finally struggled free and reluctantly marched off between the two hulking hares, muttering rebelliously to himself, "Huh! I can tell you what he's goin' t'say, same thing as usual."

The young hare imitated his father perfectly, bowing his legs, sticking out his stomach, puffing both cheeks up, and pulling his lips down at the corners as he spoke: "Wot wot, stap me whiskers, if it ain't the bold Tammo.

4

Now then, laddie buck, what've y'got to say for y'self, eh? Speak up, sah!"

Lynum cuffed Tammo lightly to silence him. "Enough of that. Colonel'd have your tail if he saw you makin' mock of him. Step lively now!"

Entering the largest of the conifer groves, they headed for a telltale spiral of smoke that denoted Camp Tussock. It was a rambling stockade, the outer walls fashioned from tree trunks with a big dwelling house built of rock, timber, moss, and mud chinking. This was known as the Barracks. Moles, squirrels, hedgehogs, and a few wood mice wandered in and out of the homely place, living there by kind permission of the Colonel and his wife, Mem Divinia. Some of them shook their heads and tut-tutted at the sight of Tammo being led in to answer for his latest escapade.

Seated close to the fire in his armchair, Colonel Cornspurrey De Fformelo Tussock was a formidable sight. He was immaculately attired in a buff-colored campaign jacket covered with rows of jangling medals, his heavy-jowled face shadowed by the peak of a brown-bark forage helmet. The Colonel had one eye permanently closed, while the other glared through a monocle of polished crystal with a silken cord dangling from it. His wattled throat wobbled pendulously as he jabbed his pace stick pointedly at the miscreant standing before him.

"Wot wot, stap me whiskers, if it ain't the bold Tammo. Now then, laddie buck, what've y'got to say for y'self, eh? Speak up, sah!"

Tammo remained silent, staring at the floor as if to find inspiration there. Grunting laboriously, the Colonel leaned forward, lifting Tammo's chin with the pace stick until they were eye to eye.

" 'S matter, sah, frogs got y'tongue? C'mon now, speak y'piece, somethin' about me battle-ax, wot wot?"

Tammo did what was expected of him and came smartly to attention. Chin up, chest out, he gazed fixedly at a point above his father's head and barked out in true military fashion: "Colonel, sah! 'Pologies about y'battle-ax, only used it to play with. Promise upon me honor, won't do it again. Sah!"

The old hare's great head quivered with furious disbelief, and the monocle fell from his eye to dangle upon its string. He lifted the pace stick, and for a moment it looked as though he were about to strike his son. When the colonel could find it, his voice rose several octaves to shrill indignation.

"*Playin'*? You've got the brass nerve t'stand there an' tell me you've been usin' my battle-ax as a *toy!* Outrage, sir, outrage! Y're a pollywoggle and a ripscutt! Hah, that's it, a scruff-furred, lollop-eared, blather-pawed, doodle-tailed, jumped-up-never-t'come-down bogwhumper! What are yeh?"

Tammo's mother, Mem Divinia, had been hovering in the background, tending a batch of barleyscones on the griddle. Wiping floury paws upon an apron corner, she bustled forward, placing herself firmly between husband and son.

"That's quite enough o' that, Corney Fformelo, I'll not have language like that under my roof. Where d'you think y'are, in the middle of a battlefield? I won't have you roaring at my Tammo in such a manner."

Instead of calming the Colonel's wrath, his wife's remarks had the opposite effect. Suffused with blood, his ears went bright pink and stood up like spearpoints. He flung down the pace stick and stamped so hard upon it that he hurt his footpaw.

"Eulalia'n'blood'n'fur'n'vinegar, marm!"

Mem countered by drawing herself up regally as she grabbed Tammo's head and buried it in the floury folds of her apron. "Keep y'voice down, sir, no sense in settin' a bad example to your son an' makin' yourself ill over some battle-ax!"

The Colonel knew better than to ignore his wife.

Rubbing ruefully at his footpaw, he retrieved the pace stick. Then, fixing his monocle straight, he sat upright, struggling to moderate his tone.

"*Some* battle-ax indeed, m'dear! I'm discussin' one *particular* weapon. *My* battle-ax! *This* battle-ax! D'y'know, that young rip took a chip out o' the blade, prob'ly hackin' away at some boulder. A chip off my blade, marm! The same battle-ax that was the pride of the old Fifty-first Paw'n'fur Platoon of the Long Patrol. 'Twas a blade that separated Searats from their gizzards'n' garters, flayed ferrets out o' their fur, whacked weasels, an' shortened stoats into stumps! An' who was it chipped the blade? That layabout of a leveret, that's who. Hmph!"

Tammo struggled free of Mem's apron, his face thickened with white flour dust. He sneezed twice before speaking. "I ain't a leveret any longer, sir. If y'let me join the jolly ol' Long Patrol, then I wouldn't have t'get up to all sorts o' mischief, 'specially with your ax, sah."

The Colonel sighed and shook his head, the monocle falling to one side as he settled back wearily into his armchair. "I've told you a hundred times, m'laddo, you're far too young, too wild'n'wayward, not got the seasons under y'belt yet. You speak to him, Mem, m'dear, the rogue's got me worn out. Join the Long Patrol indeed. Hmph! No self-respectin' Badger Lord would tolerate a green b'hind the ears little pestilence like you, laddie buck. Run along an' play now, you've given me enough gray fur, go an' bother some otherbeast. Be off, you're dismissed, sah. Matter closed!"

Tammo saluted smartly and hurried off, blinking back unshed tears at his father's brusque command. Mem took the pace stick from her husband's lap and slapped it down hard into his paw.

"Shame on you, Cornspurrey," she cried, "you're nought but a heartless old bodger. How could y'talk to your own son like that?"

The Colonel replaced his monocle and squinted

challengingly. "Bodger y'self, marm! I'd give me permission for Lynum or Saithe t'join up with the Long Patrol, they're both of a right age. Stap me, though, neither of 'em's interested, both want t'be bally soil-pawed farmbeasts, I think." He smiled slightly and stroked his curled mustache. "Young Tammo, now, there's a wild 'un, full of fire'n'vinegar like I was in me green seasons. Hah! He'll grow t'be a dangerous an' perilous beast one day, mark m'words, Mem!"

Mem Divinia spoke up on Tammo's behalf: "Then why not let him join up? You know 'tis all he's wanted since he was a babe listenin' to your tales around the fire. Poor Tammo, he lives, eats, an' breathes Long Patrol. Let him go, Corney, give him his chance."

But the Colonel was resolute; he never went back on a decision. "Tammo's far too young by half. Said all I'm goin' t'say, m'dear. Matter closed!"

Popping out his monocle with a wink, Cornspurrey De Fformelo Tussock settled back into the armchair and closed his good eye, indicating that this was his prelunch naptime. Mem Divinia knew further talk was pointless. She sighed wearily and went back to her friend Osmunda the molewife, who was assisting with the cooking.

Osmunda shook her head knowingly, muttering away in the curious molespeech, "Burr aye, you'm roight, Mem, ee be nought but an ole bodger. Oi wuddent be surproised if'n maister Tamm up'n runned aways one morn. Hurr hurr, ee faither can't stop Tamm furrever."

Mem added sprigs of young mint to the golden crust of a carrot, mushroom, and onion hotpot she had taken from the oven. "That's true, Osmunda, Tammo *will* run away, same as his father did at his age. He was a wayward one too, y'know. His father never forgave him for running away, called him a deserter and never spoke his name again—but I think he was secretly very proud of Cornspurrey and the reputation he gained as a fighting hare with the Long Patrol. He died long before his son retired from service and brought me back here to Camp Tussock. I was always very sorry that they were never reconciled. I hope the Colonel isn't as stubborn as his father, for Tammo's sake."

Osmunda was spooning honey into the scooped-out tops of the hot barley scones. She blinked curiously at Mem. "Whoi do ee say that?"

Mem Divinia began mixing a batter of greensap milk, hazelnut, and almond flour to make pancakes. She kept her eyes on the mix as she explained: "Because I'm going to help Tammo to run away and join the Long Patrol. If I don't he'll only hang around here gettin' into trouble an' arguin' with his father until they become enemies. Now don't mention what I've just said to anybeast, Osmunda."

The faithful molewife's friendly face crinkled into a deep grin. "Moi snout be sealed, Mem! Ee be a doin' the roight thing, oi knows et, even tho' ee Colonel won't 'ave 'is temper improved boi et an' you'll miss maister Tamm gurtly."

A tear fell into the pancake mix. Tammo's mother wiped her eyes hastily on her apron hem. "Oh, I'll miss the rascal, all right, never you fear, Osmunda. But Tammo will do well away from here. He's got a good heart, he's not short of courage, and, like the Colonel said, he'll grow to be a wild an' perilous beast. What more could any creature say of a hare? One day my son will make us proud of him!"

2

Several leagues away from Camp Tussock, down the far
southeast coast, Damug Warfang turned his face to the
wind. Before him on the tide line of a shingled beach lay
the wave-washed and tattered remnants of a battered
ship fleet. Behind him sprawled myriad crazy hovels,
built from dunnage and flotsam. Black and gray smoke
wisped off the cooking fires among them.

The drums began to beat. Gormad Tunn, Firstblade of
all Rapscallions, was dying.

The drums beat louder, making the very air thrum to
their deep insistent throbbing. Damug Warfang watched
the sea, pounding, hissing among the pebbles as it clawed
its way up the shore. Soon Gormad Tunn's spirit would
be at the gates of Dark Forest.

Only a Greatrat could become Firstblade of all
Rapscallions. Damug cast a sideways glance at Byral
standing farther along the beach, and smiled thinly.
Gormad would have company at Dark Forest gates
before the sun set.

Gormad Tunn, Firstblade of all Rapscallions, was close
to death.

Greatrats were a strange breed, twice the size of any

normal rat. Gormad had been the greatest. Now his sun was setting, and one of his two sons would rule as Firstblade when he was gone. The two sons, Damug Warfang and Byral Fleetclaw, stood with their backs to the death tent where their father lay, in accordance with the Law of the Rapscallion vermin. Neither would rest, eat, or drink until the great Firstblade breathed his last. Then would come the combat between them. Only one would remain alive as Firstblade of the mighty army.

The day wore on; Gormad Tunn's flame burned lower.

A small pebble struck Damug lightly on his back. "Lugworm, is everything ready?" he whispered, lips scarcely moving.

The stoat murmured low from his hiding place behind a rock, "Never readier . . . O Firstblade."

Damug kept his eyes riveted on the sea as he replied, "Don't call me Firstblade yet, 'tis bad luck!"

A confident chuckle came from the stoat. "Luck has nothin' to do with it. Everythin' has been taken care of."

The drums began to pound louder, booming and banging, small drums competing with larger ones until the entire shoreline reverberated to their beat.

Gormad Tunn's eyelids flickered once, and a harsh rattle of breath escaped from his dry lips. The Firstblade was dead!

An old ferret who had been attending Gormad left the death tent. He threw up his paws and howled in a high keening tone:

"Gormad has left us for Dark Forest's shade,
And the wind cannot lead Rapscallions.
Let the beast stand forth who would be Firstblade,
To rule all these wild battalions!"

The drums stopped. Silence flooded the coast like a sudden tide. Both brothers turned to face the speaker, answering the challenge.

"I, Byral Fleetclaw, claim the right. The blood of Greatrats runs in my veins, and I would fight to the death him who opposes me!"

"I, Damug Warfang, challenge that right. My blood is pure Greatrat, and I will prove it over your dead carcass!"

A mighty roar arose from the Rapscallion army, then the hordes rushed forward like autumn leaves upon the gale, surrounding the two brothers as they strode to the place of combat.

A ring had been marked out higher up on the shore. There the contestants stood, facing each other. Damug smiled wolfishly at his brother, Byral, who smirked and spat upon the ground between them. Wagers of food and weapons, plunder and strong drink were being yelled out between supporters of one or the other.

Two seconds entered the circle and prepared both brothers for the strange combat that would settle the leadership of the Rapscallion hordes. A short length of tough vinerope was tied around both rats' left footpaws, attaching them one to the other, so they could not run away. They were issued their weapons: a short, stout hardwood club and a cord apiece. The cords were about two swordblades' length, each with a boulder twice the size of a good apple attached to its end.

Damug and Byral drew back from each other, stretching the footpaw rope tight. Gripping their clubs firmly, they glared fiercely at each other, winding the cords around their paws a few turns so they would not lose them.

Now all eyes were on the old ferret who had announced Gormad Tunn's death, as he drew forth a scrap of red silk and threw it upward. Caught on the breeze for a moment, it seemed to float in midair, then it dropped to the floor of the ring. A wild cheer arose from a thousand throats as the fight started. Brandishing their clubs and whirling the boulder-laden cords, the two Greatrats circled, each seeking an opening, while the bloodthirsty onlookers roared encouragement.

"Crack 'is skull, Byral—go on, you kin do it!"

"Go fer 'is ribs wid yer club, Damug! Belt 'im a good 'un!"

"Swing up wid yer stone, smash 'is jaw!"

"Fling the club straight betwixt 'is eyes!"

Being fairly equally matched, each gave as good as he got. Soon Byral and Damug were both aching from hefty blows dealt by their clubs, but as yet neither had room to bring cord and boulder into play. Circling, tugging, tripping, and stumbling, they scattered sand and pebbles widespread, biting and kicking when they got the opportunity, each knowing that only one would walk away alive from the encounter. Then Byral saw his chance. Hopping nimbly back, he stretched the footpaw rope to its limits and swung at Damug's head with the boulder-loaded cord. It was just what Damug was waiting for. Grabbing his club in both paws, he ducked, allowing the cord to twirl itself around his club until the rock clacked against it. Then Damug gave a sharp tug and the cord snapped off short close to Byral's paw.

A gasp went up from the spectators. Nobeast had expected the cord to snap—except Lugworm. Byral hesitated a fatal second, gaping at the broken cord—and that was all Damug needed. He let go of his club, tossed a swift pawful of sand into his opponent's face, and swung hard with his cord and boulder. The noise was like a bar of iron smacking into a wet side of meat. Byral looked surprised before his eyes rolled backward and he sank slowly onto all fours. Damug swung twice more, though there was little need to; he had slain his brother with the first blow.

A silence descended on the watchers. Damug held out his paw, and Lugworm passed him a knife. With one quick slash he severed the rope holding his footpaw to Byral's. Without a word he strode through the crowd, and the massed ranks fell apart before him. Straight into

13

his father's death tent he went, emerging a moment later holding aloft a sword. It had a curious blade: one edge was wavy, the other straight, representing land and sea.

The drums beat out loud and frenzied as the vast Rapscallion army roared their tribute to a new Leader: "Damug Warfang! Firstblade! Firstblade! Firstblade!"

3

Some creatures said that Russa came from the deep south, others thought she was from the west coast, but even Russa could not say with any degree of certainty where she had come from. The red female squirrel had neither family nor tribe, nor any place to call home: she was a wanderer who just loved to travel. Russa Nodrey, she was often called, owing to the fact that squirrels' homes were called dreys and she did not have one, hence, no drey.

Nobeast knew more about country ways than Russa. She could live where others would starve, she knew the way in woods and field when many would be hopelessly lost. Neither old- nor young-looking, quite small and lean, Russa carried no great traveler's haversack or intricate equipment. A small pouch at the back of the rough green tunic she always wore was sufficient for her needs. The only other thing she possessed was a stick, which she had picked up from the flotsam of a tide line. It was about walking-stick size and must have come from far away, because it was hard and dark and had a luster of its own—even seawater could not rot or warp it.

Russa liked her stick. There was no piece of wood like it in all the land, nor any tree that produced such wood. It was also a good weapon, because besides being a lone wanderer, Russa Nodrey was also an expert fighter and a very dangerous warrior, in her own quiet way.

Off again on her latest odyssey, Russa stopped to rest among the cliff ledges not far from Camp Tussock. Happy with her own company, she sat by the stream's edge, drank her fill of the sweet cold water, and settled down to enjoy the late-afternoon sun in a nook protected from the wind. The sound of another creature nearby did not bother Russa unduly; she knew it was a mole and therefore friendly. With both eyes closed, as if napping, Russa waited until the creature was right up close, then she spoke in perfect molespeech to it.

"Hurr, gudd day to ee, zurr, wot you'm be a doin' yurrabouts?"

Roolee, the husband of Osmunda, was taken aback, though he did not show it. He sat down next to Russa and raised a hefty digging claw in greeting. "Gudd day to ee, marm, noice weather us'n's be 'avin', burr aye!"

Russa answered in normal speech, "Aye, a pity that somebeasts blunder along to disturb a body's rest when all she craves is peace an' quiet."

"Yurr, so 'tis, marm, so 'tis." Roolee nodded agreement. "Tho' if ee be who oi think ee be, marm Mem at Camp Tussock will be pleased to see ee. May'ap you'm koindly drop boi furr vittles?"

Russa was up on her paws immediately. "Why didn't you just say that instead of yappin' about the weather? I'd travel three rough leagues 'fore breakfast if I knew me old friend Mem Divinia was still cookin' those pancakes an' hotpots of hers!"

Roolee led the way, his velvety head nodding. "Burr aye, marm, ee Mem still be ee gurtest cook yurrabouts, she'm doin' pannycakes, ottenpots, an' all manner o' gudd vittles!"

Russa ran several steps ahead of Roolee coming into Camp Tussock. Lynum was doing sentry duty at the stockade entrance. In the fading twilight he saw the strange squirrel approaching and decided to exercise his authority.

Barring the way with a long oak quarterstaff, he called officiously, "Halt an' be recognized, who goes there, stranger at the gate!"

Russa was hungry, and she had little time for such foolishness. She gave the husky hare a smart rap across his footpaw with her stick. "Hmm, you've grown since I last saw ye," she commented as she stepped over him. "Y'were only a fuzzy babe then—fine big hare now though, eh? Pity your wits never grew up like your limbs, y'were far nicer as a little 'un."

Mem Divinia wiped floury paws on her apron hem and rushed to meet the visitor, her face alight with joy. "Well, fortunes smile on us! Russa Nodrey, you roamin' rascal, how *are* you?"

Russa avoided Mem's flour-dusted hug and made for the corner seat at the table, as she remembered it was the most comfortable and best for access to the food. She winked at Mem.

"Oh, I'm same as I always was, Mem. When I'm not travelin' up an' down the country, I'm roamin' sideways across the land."

Mem winked back at Russa and whispered, "Your visit is very timely, friend. I have something to ask of you." Then, on seeing the Colonel approaching the table, she quickly mouthed the word "later." Russa understood.

Colonel Cornspurrey De Fformelo Tussock viewed the guest with a jaundiced eye and a snort. "Hmph! Respects to ye, marm, I see you've installed y'self in my flippin' seat! Comfortable are ye, wot?"

Russa managed a rare smile. "Aye, one seat's as good as another. How are ye, y'old fogey, still grouchin' an' throwin' orders around like they're goin' out of style? I've seen boulders that've changed faster than you!"

The conversation was cut short by Osmunda

thwacking a hollow gourd with a ladle, summoning the inhabitants of Camp Tussock to their evening meal.

Mem Divinia and her helpers always provided the best of victuals. There was steaming hot, early-spring vegetable soup with flat, crisp oatmeal bannocks, followed by the famous Tussock hotpot. In a huge earthenware basin coated with a golden piecrust was a delicious medley of corn, carrots, mushrooms, turnips, winter cabbage, and onions, in a thick, rich gravy full of Mem's secret herbs. This was followed by a hefty apple, blackberry, and plum crumble topped with Osmunda's greensap and maple sauce. Hot mint and comfrey tea was served, along with horse-chestnut beer and red-currant cordial. Afterward there were honeyed barleyscones, white hazelnut cheese, and elderflower bread, for those still wanting to nibble.

Tammo sat quietly, still out of favor with his father, the Colonel, since the battle-ax incident. He listened as Russa related the latest news she had gathered in her wandering.

"Last autumn a great storm in the west country sent the waves tearing up the cliffs, and a good part of 'em collapsed into the sea."

The Colonel reached for cheese and bread with a grunt. "Hmph! Used to patrol down that way, y'know, lots of toads, nasty slimy types, murderous blighters, hope the cliffs fell on them, wot! Anythin' happenin' at Salamandastron of late?"

Tammo leaned forward eagerly at the name: Salamandastron, mountain of the Badger Lords, the mysterious place that was the headquarters of the Long Patrol.

Unfortunately Russa dismissed the subject. "Hah, the badger mountain, haven't been there in many a long season. Place is still standin', I suppose . . ."

The Colonel's monocle dropped from his eye in righteous indignation. "You *suppose*, marm? Tchah! I should

18

jolly well hope so! Why, if Salamandastron weren't there, the entire land would be overrun with Searats, Corsairs, vermin, Rapscallions, an' … an' … whatever!"

Russa leaned forward as if remembering something. "Spoke to an owl last winter. He said a whole fleet of Rapscallions had taken a right good thrashin' on the shores near Salamandastron. Wotsisname, the old Warlord or Firstblade or whatever they call him? Tunn! Gormad Tunn! He was wounded near to death. Anyhow, seems they've vanished into thin air to lick their wounds since then. I've seen no signs of Rapscallions, but if I were you I'd sleep with one eye open, y'can never tell where they'll turn up next. Cruelest pack o' slayers ever to draw breath, that lot!"

"I don't think we need worry too much about Rapscallions," Mem interrupted her friend. "They only plunder the coasts in their ships. Strange how they never sail the open seas like Searats an' Corsairs. Who's the Badger Lord at Salamandastron now, have y'heard?"

Russa poured herself a beaker of tea. "Big female, they say, madder than midwinter, stronger than a four-topped oak, temper like lightnin', full o' the Bloodwrath. She's called Cregga Rose Eyes, wields a pike that four otters couldn't lift!"

Osmunda nodded in admiration. "Hurr, she'm got'n a purty name, awright."

Russa laughed mirthlessly. "There's nought pretty about it! That one's called Rose Eyes because her eyes are blood red with battle light. I'd hate to be the vermin that tried standin' in her path."

All eyes turned on Tammo as the question slipped from his mouth: "What's a Rapscallion?"

The Colonel glared at his son. "Barbarian-type vermin, too idle t'work, too stupid t'build a decent home. Like y'mother says, they only raid the coastlines, nothin' for you t'worry your head over. Mind y'manners at table, young 'un, speak when y'spoken to an' not before, sah!"

Russa shook her head at the Colonel's statement. "You an' Mem are both wrong. Rapscallions are unpredictable, they can raid inland as easily as on the coast. I saw their Chief's sword once when I was young. It's got two edges, one all wavy for the sea, an' the other straight for the land. There's an old Rapscallion sayin': 'Travel whither blade goes, anyside the sword shows.'"

The Colonel cut himself a wedge of cheese. "Huh! What's all that fol-de-rol s'posed t'mean, wot?"

"Have we not had enough of this kind of talk, swords-'n'vermin an' war?" cried Mem Divinia, banging her beaker down on the table. "Change the subject, please. Roolee, what d'you make of this weather?"

The mole changed the conversation to suit Mem, who could see by the light in her husband's eye that he was spoiling for an argument with Russa.

"Ho urr, ee weather, marm . . . Hurr . . . umm . . . Well, ee burds be a tellin' us'n's 'twill be a foine springtoid, aye. May'ap missie Whinn'll sing ee song abowt et."

Mem coaxed a young hedgehog called Whinn to get on her paws and sing. Whinn had a good voice, clear and pretty; she liked to sing and did not need much urging.

"Blow cobwebs out of corners, the corners, the
    corners,
Throw open all your windows
To welcome in the spring.
Now icicles are shorter,
And turning fast to water,
Out yonder o'er the meadow,
I hear a skylark sing.

All through the earth a showing, a showing, a
    showing,
The green grass is a growing,
So fresh is everything.
Around the flow'rs and heather,

The bees do hum together,
Their honey will be sweeter
When 'tis made in spring."

Tammo and the other creatures at the table joined in as Whinn sang the song once more, and there was much tapping and clapping of paws. The evening wore on, with everybeast getting up to do his bit, singing, dancing, reciting, or playing simple instruments, mainly small drums or reed flutes.

Owing to the amount of food he had eaten and the warmth of the oven fire, Colonel Cornspurrey had great difficulty keeping awake. With a deep sigh he heaved himself up and took a final draught of chestnut beer, then, swaying a little he peered sleepily at Russa Nodrey, and said, "Hmph, I take it you'll be off travelin' again in the mornin', marm?"

Russa looked as fresh as a daisy as she nodded to him. "Crack o' dawn'll be early enough for me. Thank ye for your hospitality—Camp Tussock vittles were as good as ever."

Shuffling off to the dormitory, Cornspurrey called back, "Indeed 'twill, keep the noise down when y'go, I'll bid ye g'night now. An' you others, don't sit up too bally late, work t'be done on the morrow."

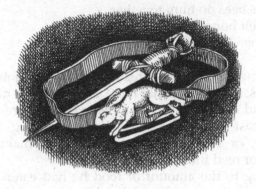

4

When his father had gone to bed, Tammo watched his mother and Russa conversing earnestly in low voices. He knew they were discussing something important, but could catch only snatches of their conversation.

"Nay, 'tis impossible, Mem. I travel alone, y'know that!"

"Well, there's a round score o' pancakes to take along if you'll help me, Russa."

"But I might not be goin' anywhere near Salamandastron!"

"Well then, take him as far as Redwall Abbey. He'll meet other warriors there, and the Long Patrol visits regularly. He won't be any trouble, I promise you. The Colonel's forbidden him t'go, but there'll only be trouble 'twixt the two of 'em if he has to stay."

"A score o' pancakes you say, Mem?"

"Make it thirty if y'like! He'll keep up with you an' obey every word you say, I know he will. Do it as a favor to me an' you'll always be welcome to a meal at Camp Tussock!"

"Hmm, thirty pancakes, eh, hah! And it'd be one in the monocle for that old waffler, somebeast disobeyin' his orders. Right then, I'll do it, but we'd best leave tonight an' be well away from here by the morn. I'll wait outside in the copse. Send him out when he's ready."

Russa departed, muttering something about preferring to sleep out under the stars. Mem Divinia started clearing the table.

"Come on now, all of you, off t'bed, mind what the Colonel said, work t'be done tomorrow. Tammo, you stay here an' help me to clear away. Good night all, peaceful dreams!"

One by one they drifted off to the big dormitory cellar, which had been built beneath the stockade.

Osmunda nodded to Mem. "They'm all gone abed now, marm."

Mem took a haversack from her wall cupboard and began adding pancakes to its contents. "Tammo, put those dishes down and come here. Hurry, son, there's not much time."

Mystified, Tammo came to sit on the table edge near his mother. "What'n the name o' seasons is goin' on, marm?"

Osmunda smacked his paw lightly with a ladle. "Do ee be 'ushed now, maister, an' lissen to ee muther."

Mem kept her eyes averted, fussing over the haversack. "Lackaday, I'm not sure whether I'm doin' the right or the wrong thing now, Tammo, but I'm givin' you a chance to see a bit o' life out in the world. I think 'tis time you grew up an' joined the Long Patrol."

Tammo slid off the table edge, disbelief shrill in his voice. "Me, join the jolly ol' Long Patrol? Oh, marm!"

Mem pulled the haversack drawstrings tight. "Keep y'voice down or you'll waken the entire camp. Our friend Russa has agreed to take you in tow. She'll keep you safe. Now don't be a nuisance to that old squirrel, keep up, and don't dare cheek her. Russa ain't as lenient as me an' she's a lot quicker on her paws than your father, so mind your manners. There's enough food in the haversack to keep you going for a good while, also thirty of my pancakes for Russa. Come over here, Tamm, stand still while I put this on you."

Mem Divinia took from the cupboard a twine and linen belt, strong and very skillfully woven. It had a silver buckle fashioned in the image of a running hare. Attached to the belt was a weapon that was neither sword nor dagger, being about half the length of the former and twice the size of the latter. Tammo cast admiring glances at the beautiful thing as his mother set the belt sash fashion, running over his shoulder and across his chest, so that the buckle hung at his side.

The long knife had no sheath, but fitted neatly through a slot in the belt buckle. Carefully, the young hare drew the weapon from its holder. Double edged and keenly pointed, its blue steel blade was chased with curious designs. The cross hilt was of silver, set with green gems. Bound tightly with tough, red, braided twine, the handle seemed made for his paw. A highly polished piece of rock crystal formed the pommel stone.

Mem tapped it lovingly, saying, "This was made by a Badger Lord in the forge at Salamandastron; 'tis called a dirk. No weapon ever served me better in the days when I ran with the Long Patrol. Your father always preferred the battle-ax, but the dirk was the weapon that I loved specially. It is the best gift I can give you, my son. Take it and use it to defend yourself and those weaker than you. Never surrender it to a foebeast or let any creature take it from you. Time is running short, and you must leave now. Don't look back. Go, make Camp Tussock proud of you. Promise me you'll return here someday, your father loves you as much as I do. Fate and fortune go with you, Tamello De Fformelo Tussock—do honor to our name!"

Osmunda patted his ears fondly. "Furr ee well, maister Tamm, oi'll miss ee!"

Seconds later Tammo was rushing out into the night, his face streaked with tears and covered in white flour dust from his mother's good-bye embrace. Russa Nodrey materialized out of the pine shadows like a wraith.

"I hope my pancakes aren't gettin' squashed in that

there bag. Looks like you've brought enough vittles with ye to feed a regiment for seven seasons. Right, come on, young 'un, let's see if those paws o' yours are any good after all the soft livin' you've been brought up with. Shift y'self now. Move!"

The young hare shot forward like an arrow from a bow, dashing away from his birthplace to face the unknown.

5

The new Firstblade of all Rapscallions sat alone on the creaking, weather-beaten stern of his late father's vessel, which lay heeled half over on the southeast shore. Damug Warfang had watched dawn break over the horizon, a red glow at first, changing rapidly as the sun rose in a bloom of scarlet and gold. A few seabirds wheeled and called to one another, dipping toward the gentle swell of the placid sea. Hardly a wave showed on the face of the deep, pale-green waters inshore, ranging out to mid-blue and aquamarine. A bank of fine cloud shone with pearl-like opalescence as the sunrays reflected off it. Now the wide vault of sky became blue, as only a fresh spring morn can make it; scarlet tinges of sun wisped away to become a faint rose thread where sea met sky as the great orb ascended, golden as a buttercup.

All this beauty was lost on Damug as the ebb tide hissed and whispered its secrets to the shingled beach. Probing with his swordpoint, he dug moodily at the vessel's timbers. They were rotten, waterlogged, barnacle-crusted, and coated with a sheen of green slime. Damug's pale eyes registered anger and disgust. A bristletail crawled slowly out of the damp woodwork. With its antennae waving and gray, armor-plated back undulating, the insect lumbered close to Damug's footclaw. With a swift, light thrust he impaled it on his swordpoint and sat watching it wriggle its life away.

Behind him breakfast fires were being lit and drums were beginning their remorseless throb again as the Rapscallion armies wakened to face the day. Damug sensed the presence of Lugworm at his back, and did not bother turning as the stoat spoke.

"Empty cookin' pots cause rebellion, O Firstblade. You must throw the sword quickly, today!"

Damug flicked the swordblade sideways, sending the dying insect into the ebbing sea. Then he stood and turned to face Lugworm. The Greatrat's jaw was so tight with anger that it made his voice a harsh grate.

"I know what I've got to do, slopbrain, but supposing the sword falls wave side up? How could I take all of those back there out to sea in a fleet of rotten, water-logged ships? We'd go straight to the bottom. There's not a seaworthy vessel on this shore. So unless you've got a foolproof solution, don't come around here with that idiotic grin on your stupid face, telling me what I already know!"

Before Lugworm could answer, Damug whipped the swordpoint up under his chin. He jabbed a little, causing the blade to nick skin. Lugworm was forced to stand tip-pawed as Damug snarled, "Enjoying yourself now, cleversnout? I'll teach you to come grinning at my predicament. Come on, let's see you smile that silly smile you had plastered on your useless face a moment ago."

The stoat's throat bobbed as he gulped visibly, and his words came out in a rush as the blade of the unpredictably tempered Warlord dug a bit deeper. "Damug, Firstblade, I've got the answer, I know what t'do, that's why I came to see you!"

The swordpoint flicked downward, biting into the deck between Lugworm's footpaws. Damug was smiling sweetly, his swift mood swing and calm tone indicating that his servant was out of danger, for the moment.

"Lugworm, my trusty friend, I knew you'd come up with a solution to my problem. Pray tell me what I must do."

Rubbing beneath his chin, where a thin trickle of blood showed, Lugworm sat upon the deck. From his belt pouch he dug out a small, heavy brass clip. "Your father used this because he favored sailin', always said it was better'n paw sloggin' a horde over 'ill'n'dale. If y'll allow me, Chief, I'll show ye 'ow it works."

Damug gave his sword to the stoat, who stood up to demonstrate.

"Y'see, the Rapscallions foller this sword. The Firstblade tosses it in the air, an' they go whichever way it falls, but it's gotta fall wid one o' these crosspieces stickin' in the ground. Wave side of the blade up means we sail, smooth side o' the blade showing upward means we go by land."

"I know that, you fool, get on with it!"

Lugworm heeded the danger in Damug's terse voice. He attached the brass clip to the wave-side crosspiece and tossed the sword up. It was not a hard throw; the flick of Lugworm's paw caused the weapon to turn once, almost lazily, as morning sunlight glimmered across the blade. With a soft thud it fell to the deck, the straight, sharp blade edge upward.

"Y'see, Chief, it works every time 'cos the added weight on the wavy side hits the ground first. But don't fling it 'igh in the air, toss it up jus' like I did, slow like, wid a twist o' yer paw. 'Tis easy, try it."

Damug Warfang was not one to leave anything to luck. He tried the trick several times, each time with the same result. The sword always landed smooth edge upward. Damug removed the brass clip and attached it to a bracelet he wore.

"Good! You're not as thick as you look, friend Lugworm."

The stoat bowed his head respectfully to the new Firstblade, saying, "I served your father, Gormad Tunn, but he became old and strange in the brain and would not listen to my advice. Heed my counsel, Chief, and I will make the name Damug Warfang feared by all on land and sea. You will become the greatest Firstblade that Rapscallions have ever known."

Damug nodded. "So be it. You are my adviser and as such will be at my side to reap the benefit of all my triumphs."

Before Lugworm could voice his thanks, the blade was in his face, its point almost tickling his right eyeball. The smile on Damug's lips was cold enough to freeze water.

"Sly little Lugworm, eh? Counselor to mighty ones! Listen, stoat, if you even think about crossing me I'll make you scream half a season before you die!"

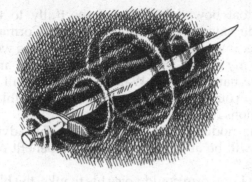

6

The rats Sneezewort and Lousewort were merely two common, low-ranked Rapscallions in the Firstblade's great army. The pair scrabbled for position on a clump of boulders at the rear of massed hordes of vermin warriors, who had all gathered to witness the Throwing of the Sword ceremony. They jostled and pushed, trying to catch a glimpse of what was going on in the stone circle where the duel had taken place. High-ranking officers called Rapmarks occupied the immediate edge of the ring, as was their right. The ordinary rank and file struggled, standing tip-pawed to get a view of the proceedings.

Sneezewort hauled himself up on Lousewort's back, and the dull, stolid Lousewort staggered forward under the added weight, muttering, "Er, er, wot's goin' on down there, mate?"

Sneezewort flicked his companion's ear with a grimy claw. "Straighten up, jellyback, I can't see much from 'ere. 'Ang on, I think ole Firstblade's gonna say sumpin'."

Lousewort flinched as his ear was flicked harder. "Ouchouch! Stoppit, that's me wounded ear!"

Staggering farther forward he bumped into a big, fat, nasty-looking weasel, who turned on them with a snarl. "Hoi! If you two boggletops don't stop bangin' inter me

30

an' shoutin' like that y'll 'ave more'n wounded ears ter worry about. I'll stuff yore tails up yore snotty noses an' rip 'em off, so back off an' shut yer gobs!"

Damug's voice rang harsh and clear across the savage crowd of vermin gathered on the shore.

"The spirit of my father, the great Gormad Tunn, appeared to me in my dreams. He said that the sword will fall land side up and seasons of glory will reward all who follow Damug Warfang. Plunder, slaves, land, and wealth for even the lowest paw soldier of the mighty army of Rapscallions. I, your Firstblade, pass the words of my beloved father on to you, my loyal comrades!"

Sneezewort could not resist a snigger as a thought occurred to him. "Yeeheehee! 'Beloved father'? They couldn't stan' the sight o' each other. Huh, Damug'll be in trouble if'n the sword lands wavy side up after shootin' 'is mouth off like that, I tell yer, mate!"

The big weasel turned 'round, testing the tip of a rusty iron hook. "Damug won't be in 'arf the trouble you'll be in if'n yer don't put a stopper on that blatherin' jaw o' yourn, snipenose!" He turned back in time to see the sword rise above the crowd. There was a vast silence, followed by a rousing cheer.

"Land up! Land up!"

Lousewort thrust a stained claw into his wounded ear and wiggled it. "Stand up? Wot's that supposed ter mean?"

The big nasty weasel whirled around and dealt two swift punches, one to Lousewort's stomach, the other to Sneezewort's nose. They both collapsed to the ground in a jumbled heap, and the weasel stood, paws akimbo, sneering at them. "It means you need yer ears washin' out an' yer mate needs his lip buttoned! Any more questions, dimwits?"

Clutching his injured nose, Sneezewort managed to gasp out, "No thir, it'th all quite clear, thank yew, thir!"

Damug gave his orders to the ten Rapmarks, each the commander of a hundred beasts.

"Our seasons of petty coast raids are over. We march straight up the center of the land, taking all before us. Scouts must be continuously sent out on both sides to report any area that is ripe for plundering. Leave the ships to rot where they lie, burn your dwellings, let the army eat the last of our old supplies here today. We march at first light tomorrow. Now bring me the armor of the Firstblade!"

That night Damug stood garbed in his barbaric regalia, the swirling orange cloak of his father blowing open to reveal a highly polished breastplate of silver, a short kilt of snake-skin, and a belt fashioned from many small links of beaten gold, set with twinkling gemstones. On his head he wore a burnished brass helmet surmounted by a spike, with iron mesh hanging from it to protect his neck. The front dipped almost to his muzzle tip; it had two narrow eye slits.

Oily smoke swirled to the moonless skies as the lights of myriad dwellings going up in flames glimmered off the armor of Damug Warfang, Firstblade. Roaring, drinking, singing, and eating their last supplies, the Rapscallion regiments celebrated their final night on the southeast shores. They gambled and stole from one another, fought, argued, and tore the waterlogged fleet apart in their search for any last bits of booty to be had.

Damug leaned on his sword, watching them. Beside him, Lugworm cooked a fish over glowing charcoal for his Chief's supper. He looked up at the Firstblade's question.

"Are they all ready to follow and obey me, Lugworm?"

"Aye sirrah, they are."

"All?"

"Save two, Chief. Borumm the weasel and Vendace the fox. Those two were allies of your brother, Byral, so watch your back whilst they're about."

Smiling humorlessly, Damug patted his adviser's head.

"Well answered, Lugworm. I already knew of Borumm

and Vendace. Also I knew that you were aware of them, so you have just saved your own life by not staying silent."

Lugworm swallowed hard as he turned the fish over on the embers.

Lousewort staggered up over the tide line under the weight of a large circular ship's steering wheel. It was a great heavy piece of work, solid oak, decorated with copper studding, now moldy and green.

Sneezewort stood tending their fire, over which he was roasting some old roots and the dried frame of a long-dead seabird. He shook his head in despair. "Ahoy, puddenbum, where d'yer think yore goin' wid that thing?"

Smiling happily, Lousewort stood the wheel on its edge. "Er, er, looka this, it's a beauty, izzenit, mate? I'll wager 'tis worth a lot, thing like this. . . ."

Sneezewort snorted at his slow-witted companion. "Oh, it's a beauty, all right, and it will be worth somethin'. After you've carried it back an' forth across the country fer seven seasons an' found a new ship to match up wirrit. Great ole useless chunk o' rubbish, wot do we need wid that thing? Get rid of it afore ye cripple yerself carryin' it!"

He gave the wheel a hearty push, sending it rolling crazily off into the darkness. There was a crash, followed by the outraged roar of the big nasty weasel.

"Belay, who threw that? Ooh, me footpaw! I'll carve the blackguard up inter fishbait an' 'ang 'im from me 'ook!"

In their panic the two dithering rats ran slap into each other twice before tearing off to hide in the darkness.

Damug tossed the remnants of the fish to Lugworm and wiped his lips upon the orange cloak.

"Keep an eye open whilst I sleep. Oh, and pass the word around: I want every Rapscallion painted red for war when we march tomorrow, fully armed and ready for slaughter!"

7

Tammo had never been so tired in all his young life. It was three hours after dawn and they were still running. His footpaws felt heavy as two millstones, and the weight of the haversack on his back, which had been fairly light at first, was now like carrying another beast.

Those open plains that had always looked smooth and slightly undulating from a distance, what had happened to them? Suddenly they had become a series of steep hills and deep valleys, with small sharp rocks hidden by the grass, areas of thorny thistle and slopes of treacherous gravelly scree. The welcome sunlight of dawn was now a burning eye that blinded him and added to the discomfort of his already overheated body.

Staggering and gasping for breath, Tammo slumped down on the summit of a hill, unable to go another pace forward. Russa Nodrey was already there, still upright, breathing calmly as she viewed the prospect to the south. From the corner of her eye she watched the young hare with a tinge of admiration, which she kept well hidden from him.

"Nothin' like a brisk trot, eh, Tamm? How d'you feel?"

Tammo was on all fours, head bent as he tried to regulate his breath. He spoke still facing the ground, unable to look up. "Not too blinkin' chipper, marm. Need water, somethin' to eat, and sleep. Give anythin' for a jolly good snooze, marm!"

Russa crouched down beside him. "Lissen, young 'un, call me Russa, pal, matey, anythin' you like. But stop callin' me marm. It makes me feel like some fat ole mother duck!"

Tammo glanced sideways at her, mischief dancing in his eyes. "I'll do that, matey, but you stop callin' me young 'un or I'll *start* callin' you mother duck!"

Standing behind him, Russa smiled as she pulled the haversack from his back. Despite her initial reluctance, she was beginning, if a little grudgingly, to enjoy Tammo's company.

"Let's have this thing off ye, Tamm. We can't stop here, got to press on a bit afore we make camp."

Tammo flexed his shoulders and moved to a sitting position. "Why's that? This looks like a jolly good spot, wot?"

The squirrel pointed south, indicating another two hilly tors. "We've got to land up across there by midday. Right, here's where yore eddication starts, young 'un . . . er, pal. Tell me, why should we make camp there instead o' here?"

Tammo pondered the question a moment. "Haven't a bally clue, old pal. Tell me."

Russa began shouldering the haversack. "Well, for a start, 'tis too open up here, we c'n be seen for miles. A good camp should be sheltered for two reasons: one, in case o' the weather; two, t'stay hidden. Doesn't do t'let everybeast know where ye are in open country."

The young hare stood up slowly. "Hmm, makes sense I suppose."

"You can bet yore life it does." The squirrel winked at him. "But afore y'go harin' off, let me tell you the rest. At midday it'll be hottest, that's when we should sleep a few hours an' save energy. We can eat'n'drink too afore we nap, sleep's good fer the digestion. If we ate an' drank now, we'd be travelin' on full bellies. It'd take us twice as long to get there in that state. All right, matey, let's be on our way. I'll carry this 'avvysack fer a while—'tis only fair."

Tammo started down into the valley, digging his paws in against a shale drift. He felt much lighter and better for the brief rest. "Indeed 'tis only fair, considerin' the weight of your pancakes, old pal!" he called back.

Russa caught up and quickly took the lead. "Less of the old, young scallywag, or I'll put on a turn of speed that'll have ye eatin' me dust fer a full day!"

Tammo pulled a wry face at the squirrel's back. "What ho, young Russa, point taken. Lead on, but not too fast."

Russa shook her head as she skirted a patch of mossy grass, still wet and slippery with morning dew. "Rest yore jaws an' let the paws do the work, Tamm, seasons o' gabble! I never did so much talkin' in all me life. Save yore breath fer travelin', that's another lesson y've got to learn."

"Right you are, O wise one, the jolly old lips are sealed!"

"Good! Then shut up an' keep up!"

"To hear is to obey, O sagacious squirrel!"

"You've gotta have the last word, haven't yer?"

"Only because you're the strong silent type, great leader."

"I'll great leader you, y'cheeky-faced rogue!"

"Bad form f'r a Commander to insult the other ranks, y'know. Whoops! Yowch!"

Not looking where he was going, Tammo trotted into the area of mossy grass and slipped, landing flat on his back. Because of the steep incline, he rolled a good way downhill, until he was halted by a boulder.

Russa went by him, looking straight ahead, a smile playing 'round her lips. "Tut tut, I've already told ye, matey, y'can't lie down fer a nap until we make camp!"

Tammo learned a lot that first morning. By midday they

were standing on top of the hill overlooking the spot Russa had chosen for a campsite. Down in the valley a little stream tumbled over a rock ledge, forming a tiny waterfall. There were wild privets and dogwood to one side, making a shady bower.

Hot and dusty, Tammo wiped a paw across his mouth at the sight of fresh water. He saluted smartly at Russa and said, "Permission t'go down an' chuck m'self in yonder cool water!"

The canny squirrel shrugged. "Suit y'self, matey, if'n that's what y'feel like doin'."

The young hare let out a joyful whoop and sped off downhill.

Russa backed off and, dropping out of sight, cut off at a tangent, approaching the glade from a different angle.

Ducking out of his shoulder belt and dirk, Tammo cast both aside and leapt into the water. It was ice cold and crystal clear. The sudden shock robbed him of his breath for a moment; then he gave vent to a yell of sheer delight. It was good to be alive on such a day. Gulping down the sweet fresh water, Tammo stood beneath the cascade with his mouth wide open, falling backward and splashing playfully with all four paws.

"Yerrah! Now dat's wot I likes ter see, Skulka, a young critter fulla the joys o' spring!"

Rubbing both eyes and snorting water from his nostrils, Tammo floundered upright to see who had spoken.

Two ferrets, big and lean and clad in tattered rags, stood on the bank, one with an arrow half drawn on her bowstring, the other with a spear stuck in the ground as he tried on Tammo's belt and dirk for size.

The young hare knew he was in deep trouble. Glancing around to see if he could spot Russa, Tammo pointed at his property. "Good day, friends! I say, that's my belt an' dirk you're jolly well tryin' on, y'know!"

The female kept her arrow centered on Tammo. Turning to her partner, she revealed a row of snaggled, discolored teeth in a grin. "Lah de dah, Gromal, ain't 'e got nice manners? Didyer know that's 'is jolly ole dirk'n' belt yore tryin' on?"

Gromal had fastened the belt around his waist, and now he was stroking the dirk handle and admiring the fine blade. "Ho, is it now? Well 'ere's the way I sees it, Skulka. That beast flung 'isself in our water widout so much as a by yer leave. Lookat 'im there, drinkin' away an' sportin' about as if it belonged to 'im!"

Tammo stood quite still in the stream and managed to force a friendly smile at the evil pair. "Accept my apologies, you chaps. Sorry, I didn't know the stream belonged to you. I'll just hop right out."

Gromal pulled his spear from the ground. "Aye, that's the ticket, me young bucko. You jus' 'op right up 'ere on the bank so's we kin search yer. Yore gonna pay fer the use of our water. Keep that shaft aimed at 'im, Skulka. If'n 'e makes one false move, shoot 'im atween the eyes an' slay 'im!"

Skulka drew her bowstring tight, sniggering. "If 'e don't 'ave no more val'ables, then mebbe we c'n use 'im as a slave fer a few seasons."

A hardwood stick came whirling in a blur from the tree cover and struck the arrow, snapping it clean in two pieces. Russa hurtled out like a lightning bolt, shoving Skulka into the water and launching herself at Gromal. She caught him a terrific headbutt to the stomach, and he crumpled to the ground, mouth open as he fought for air. Tammo waded swiftly to the shallows, and as Skulka staggered upright, he dealt her a powerful kick with both footpaws. She fell back in the water, and he sat upon her, applying all his weight.

Russa had relieved Gromal of the dirk; now she grabbed her hardwood stick and stood waiting for him to rise. He came up fast, seizing his spear and charging her. Almost casually she stepped to one side, dealing him three quick hard blows to the back of his head as he rushed by her. The ferret dropped like a log.

Ignoring him, she turned to Tammo and said, "Best let that'n up afore ye drown her, mate."

Tammo hauled Skulka dripping and spluttering from the stream. He shook water from his eyes, peering indignantly at Russa. "I say, y'might've told me about these two before you let me flippin' well dash down here an' dive in the water, wot?"

The squirrel kicked Skulka flat, trapping her across the throat with the hardwood stick. Then she shrugged indifferently. "I didn't know they were down there. Besides, you couldn't wait to dash into the water. I never approach a campsite without checkin' it out first, mate, and so should you."

Tammo heaved a sigh as he took his belt from the fallen ferret. "Another jolly old lesson learned, I suppose?"

Russa patted his back heartily. "You jolly well suppose right, me ol' pal!"

While the two ferrets sat on the bank recovering from their drubbing, Russa paced around them. She glanced across at Tammo, who was carrying the haversack out of the shrubbery where she had left it. "What d'you think we should do with these vermin, Tamm, kill 'em, or let 'em go?"

The young hare was shocked at the suggestion of cold-blooded slaying. "Russa Nodrey!" he cried, his voice almost shrill with outrage. "You can't just kill them! You wouldn't!"

The squirrel's face was impassive. "D'you know why I'm alive today? 'Cos my enemies are all dead. Make no mistake about it, Tamm, these two scum would've slain you just fer fun if I hadn't been here."

The ferrets began to wail imploringly.

"No no, we was just sportin' wid yer, young sir!"

"We ain't killers, we're pore beasts fallen on 'ard times!"

Russa curled her lip scornfully. "Aye, an' I'm a blue-bird wid a frog for an uncle!"

Tammo placed himself between Russa and the ferrets. "You're not goin' to slay them. I'll stop you, Russa!"

The squirrel sat down and, unfastening the haversack, began selecting a few of Mem Divinia's pancakes. "Huh! No need t'fall out over a pair of nogoods like them. Please yoreself, mate, do what y'like with 'em."

Tammo flung Skulka and Gromal's weapons into the water, then he drew his dirk and pointed it at the cringing duo. "Get up an' get goin', you chaps. I never want to see your ugly faces again. Quick now, or I'll let Russa loose on you!"

Without a backward glance, the pair sped off as if pursued by a flight of eagles. Tammo put up his dirk. "There, that's settled!"

Russa filled a beaker with water from the stream. "So you say, me ole mate."

"What d'you mean, so I say?"

"Ah, you'll learn one day. I thought you were starvin'. Come an' get some o' these vittles down yer face."

They dined on pancakes spread with honey, beakers of stream water, and a wedge of cold turnip and carrot pie apiece. The sun was unusually hot for early spring, and Tammo felt rather giddy after their adventure. Finding a soft shady spot beneath the hedgerow, he was asleep in a trice. Russa sat with her back against a dogwood trunk and napped with one eye open.

8

When the sun was past its zenith, Russa woke Tammo. He felt marvelously refreshed and immediately shouldered the haversack, saying, "My turn to carry this awhile. Come on, pal, where to now?"

Still traveling south, the squirrel took him to the top of the next rise and pointed with her stick. "Little patch of woodland yonder, we should make it at twilight."

The going was much easier for Tammo. He enjoyed the sight of new places and fresh scenery, learning from his experienced traveling companion all the time. Russa seemed to come out of her normally taciturn self and was much more verbose than usual.

"Skirt 'round this patch, Tamm, don't want to disturb that curlew sittin' on 'er nest, do we?"

"Of course not, jolly thoughtful of you. Leave the poor bird in peace to sit on her eggs, wot?"

"Nothin' of the sort. If'n we crossed there that'd upset 'er, and she'd fly up kickin' a racket to warn us off. That'd give our position away to anybeast who was trackin' us."

"Oh, right. I say, d'you suppose there is somebeast after us?"

Russa's reply was cryptic. "I dunno, what d'you think?"

*

41

The squirrel was as good as her word. Long shadows were gone and twilight was shading the skies as they arrived at the woodland patch, which was considerably bigger than it had seemed from afar. Russa allowed Tammo to pick their campsite, and he chose an ancient fallen beech with part of its vast root system poking into the air.

Russa nodded approval. "Hmm, this looks all right. Want a fire?"

Tammo shrugged off his belt and weapon. "If you say so. Spring nights can be jolly cold, and besides, I'd like to have a hot supper, if y'have no objections."

Russa shook her head vigorously. "None at all, matey. There's plenty o' deadwood an' dry bark about. I'll see t'the fire, you unpack the vittles."

Flint and steel from Russa's pouch soon had dry tinder alight. Clearing a firespace around it, she added fragrant dead pine twigs, old brown ferns, and some stout billets of beech. Tammo found a flagon of elderberry wine in the pack. He warmed pancakes before spreading them with honey, and set two moist-looking chunks of plum cake near the flames to heat through. They sat with their backs against the beech, pleasantly tired, eating, drinking, and chatting.

Russa picked up Tammo's dirk and inspected it closely. "This is a rare weapon, mate. Is it your father's?"

"No, it was my mother's. She was a Long Patrol fighter, y'know. She said a Badger Lord made it for her in the forge at Salamandastron, the great mountain fortress. Can you tell me anythin' of the mountain, Russa? I've never seen it."

Reflectively the squirrel balanced the blade in her paw, then she threw it skillfully. It whizzed across the clearing and thudded point first into a sycamore trunk.

"Sometimes a thrown blade can save your life," she said. "I'll teach you how to sling it properly before long."

Tammo had to tug hard to pull the dirk from the tree trunk. "I'd be rather obliged if y'did. Now what about

42

Salamandastron?"

Russa took a sip of wine and settled back comfortably. "Oh, that place, hmm, let me see. Well, a mountain's a mountain, much like any other, but I can give you the chant I heard the Long Patrol hares sayin' last time I was over that way."

Tammo piled a bit more wood on the fire. "You know the Long Patrol hares? Tell me, what do they chant?"

The squirrel closed her eyes. "Far as I can recall it went somethin' like this:

"O vermin if you dare, come and visit us someday,
Bring all your friends and weapons with you too.
You'll find a good warm welcome, let nobeast
    living say
That cold steel was never good enough for you.

You won't find poor helpless beasts all undefended,
Like the old ones, babes, and mothers that you've
    slain,
And you'll find that when your pleasant visit's
    ended,
You'll never ever leave our shores again.

All you cowards of the land and you flotsam of the
    sea,
Who murder, pillage, loot whene'er you please,
There's a Long Patrol a waitin', we'll greet you
    cheerfully,
You'll hear us cry 'Eulalia' on the breeze.

"Tis a welcome to the bullies who slay without a
    care,
All those good and peaceful creatures who can't
    fight,
But perilous and dangerous the beast they call the
    hare,

43

Who stands for nought but honor and the right.

Eulalia! Eulalia! Come bring your vermin horde,
The Long Patrol awaits you, led by a Badger Lord!"

Tammo shook his head in admiration. "By golly, that's some chant! Are they really that brave and fearless, these Long Patrol hares?"

Russa threw a burning log end back into the fire. "Ruthless, they can be, but they keep the shores defended and the land safe fer peaceful creatures t'live in. C'mon now, mate, y'need yore sleep for tomorrow's trekkin'. Stow y'self over there in the dark, away from the flames."

Tammo pulled a wry face at this suggestion. "But I'm nice'n'warm here, why've I got to move?"

The squirrel's face grew stern. "Because I says so, now stop askin' silly questions an' shift!"

Tammo retreated into the surrounding bushes, muttering, "Nice warm fire an' I've got t'sleep back here, a chap could catch his death o' cold on a night like this, 'taint fair!"

Sometime during the night, Tammo was awakened by a bloodcurdling scream. He leapt up, grabbing for his dirk, which he had left within paw's reach. It was not there.

He stood in the firelight and looked around. His friend was missing too. Cupping paws around his mouth, the young hare yelled into the night-darkened woodlands, "Russa, where are you?"

With a bound the squirrel cleared the fallen beech trunk and was at his side, wiping the dirk blade on the grass. "I'm here. Keep y'voice down an' get back under cover!"

Together they crouched in the bushes. Tammo was bursting to question Russa, but he held his silence, watching the squirrel's eyes flick back and forth as she craned her head forward, listening.

From somewhere in the midst of the trees there came a

shriek of rage. Russa stood erect and shouted in the direction whence it had come, "Yore mate's dead, ferret! Take warnin' an' clear off, 'cos I'm comin' after you next an' I don't take prisoners!"

Skulka's answering call came back, thick with rage: "It ain't over, old one, we'll get you an' yer liddle pal! Jus' wait'n'see!"

This was followed by the sound of Skulka crashing off through the ferns. Then there was silence. Russa gave Tammo back his dirk, saying, "It was those two ferrets we tangled with earlier today, mate. I knew they'd be back, 'specially after they saw you take our 'avvysack o' vittles out o' the bushes back there."

Tammo felt weak with shock. "Russa, I'm sorry. If I hadn't let them see the haversack they would've gone off none the wiser."

The wily squirrel shook her head. "Wrong, matey, they would've tried to get us whether or not. I knew they was followin' us all day. 'Twas logical they'd make their move tonight when they thought we'd be asleep. So I took off into the trees wid yore blade an' bumped straight into the one called Gromal, armed wid a long sharpened stake, if y'please. So I had to finish it then an' there, 'twas him or me. But I'm a bit worried, Tamm."

Tammo was puzzled by this statement. "What's worryin' you, Russa?"

"Well, did y'hear the other ferret shoutin', she said *we'll* get you. We. It's like I thought, there must be a band of 'em somewheres about. I had a feeling I knowed them two from long ago, they always run with a robber band."

Tammo gripped his blade resolutely. "Right, mate, what's t'be done?"

Russa ruffled Tammo's ears rather fondly. "Sleep's to be done. Shouldn't think they'll be back tonight, but we'll take turns standin' guard. More likely they'll try an' ambush us out in the open tomorrow, so get y'sleep— you'll need it."

Night closed in on the little camp. The fire dimmed from burning flame to glowing embers, trees murmured and rustled, their foliage stirred by a westering wind. Tammo dreamed of his home, Camp Tussock. He saw the faces of his family, and Osmunda and Roolee, together with the young creatures with whom he had played. Elusive aromas of Mem Divinia's cooking, mingled with songs and music around the fire of a winter's night, assailed his senses. A great sadness weighed upon him, as though he might never see or feel it all again.

Russa climbed into a tree and slept the way she had for many seasons, with one eye open.

9

Extract from the writings of Craklyn squirrel, Recorder of Redwall Abbey in Mossflower Country.

Great Seasons! Now I know I am old. A beautiful spring afternoon, the sun smiling warmly over Mossflower Wood and our Abbey, and almost everybeast, from the smallest Dibbun baby to the Mother Abbess herself, is out in the grounds at play. While here am I, sitting by the kitchen ovens, a cloak about me, scratching away with this confounded quill pen. Ah well, somebeast has to do it, I suppose. Though I never thought that one day I would be old, but that is the way of the world, the young never do.

Let me see now, out of the Redwallers of my early seasons there are only a few left: Abbess Tansy, my dear friend, the first hedgehog ever to be Mother of Redwall; Viola Bankvole, our fussy Infirmary Sister; and who else? Oh, yes, Foremole Diggum and Gurrbowl the Cellar Keeper, two of the most loyal moles ever to inhabit Redwall Abbey. Counting the squirrel Arven and myself, that is everybeast accounted for. Arven is our Abbey Warrior. Who would have thought that such a mischievous little rip would grow up to be so big and reliable, respected throughout Mossflower?

Alas, the seasons caught up with all the old crew who were our elders, and they have gone happily to the sunny meadows. Though they are always alive in our memories, those good creatures and the knowledge and joy they imparted to all. Sad, is it not, though, that our Abbey has lacked a badger and a hare for many a long season now? But I beg your indulgence, I am getting old and maudlin, I've become the same ancient fogey my friends and I would laugh at in our youth. Enough of all this! If I sit here much longer I'll be baked to a turn like the oatfarls in the oven. If my creaking joints will allow me, I'm going out to play with the others. After all, it is springtime, isn't it?

Abbess Tansy ducked as a ball made from soft moss and twine flew over her head. She wrinkled her nose at the tiny mouse who had thrown it. "Yah, missed me, Sloey bunglepaws!"

The mousebabe stamped her footpaw and grimaced fiercely. "A not 'uppose t'duck you 'ead, Muvver Tansy, you stannup straight!"

Behind Tansy a Dibbun mole picked up the ball and was about to throw it clumsily when Craklyn sneaked up. She took the ball from him and threw it hard, hitting Tansy on the back of her head.

With the soft ball sticking to her headspikes, the Abbess whirled around, a look of comic fury upon her face. "Who threw that ball? Come on, own up!"

Craklyn's expression was one of simple innocence. "It wasn't me, Mother Abbess!"

Tansy glared at the little ones playing the game. "Well, who was it, one of you rascals?"

The Dibbuns fell about laughing as a small mole named Gubbio pointed to Craklyn. "Yurr, et wurr ee flung yon ball, marm!"

Craklyn looked horrified. She pointed to Gubbio, saying, "No, it wasn't! You were the one who threw the ball! We saw him, didn't we?"

This caused more hilarity among the babes. The sight of the Recorder fibbing like a naughty Dibbun was too much for them. They skipped about giggling, pointing to Craklyn.

" 'Twas marm Craklyn, 'twas 'er!"

Abbess Tansy pulled the ball from her headspikes and pretended to lecture the Recorder severely: "You naughty creature, fancy throwing things at your Abbess! Right, no supper for you tonight. Straight up to bed, m'lady!"

It all proved too much for the Dibbuns, who threw themselves down on the grass, chuckling fit to burst.

Foremole Diggum in company with Arven the squirrel Warrior and several other moles passed by, headed for the south wall. They had been talking earnestly together as they went, but on seeing Abbess Tansy they stopped conversing and nodded to her as they hurried on their way.

"Afternoon, marm, an' you too, marm!"

Craklyn exchanged glances with Tansy. "They're up to something. Hi, Arven! What's the rush, where are you all off to?"

"Nothin' for you t'be concerned with, marm," Arven called back to her. "Just out for a stroll."

Immediately, Tansy took Craklyn's paw and began to follow them. "You're right, they are up to something. Out for a stroll, eh? Well, come on, friend, let's join 'em! Carry on with the game, you little 'uns, and no cheating!"

Behind the shrubbery that bordered the outer wall of the ramparts on their south side, Diggum Foremole and the rest were questioning a mole called Drubb.

"Whurr do ee say 'twas, Drubb?"

He pointed with a heavy digging claw in several places as he brushed hazel and rhododendron shrubs aside.

"Yurr see, an' yurr, yonder too, roight along ee wall if'n you'm look close. Hurr, see!"

Craklyn and Tansy arrived on the scene. Straight away the Abbess started to interrogate Arven: "What's going on? There's something you aren't telling me about. What is it, Arven—I demand to know!"

The squirrel had crouched low at the wallbase, probing the joints of massive red sandstone blocks with a small quill knife. He looked up at Tansy, keeping his voice deceptively calm. "Oh, it's something and nothing, really. Drubb here says he thinks the wall is sinking, but he may not be right. We didn't say anything to you, Tansy, because you've enough to do as Abbess . . ."

He was cut short by Tansy's indignant outburst. "The south outer wall of my Abbey is sinking and you didn't consider it serious enough to let your Abbess know? Who in the name of stricken oaks do you think I am, sir— Mother Abbess of Redwall, or a little fuzzbrained Dibbun playing ball?"

Diggum Foremole touched his brow respectfully. "You'm forgive oi fer sayin', marm, but ee lukked just loik a fuzzybrain Dibbun a playin' ball when us'n's passed ee but a moment back, hurr aye."

Tansy drew herself up grandly, spikes abristle and eyes alight. "Nonsense! Show me the wall this instant!"

The group wandered up and down the length of the high battlemented south wall for the remainder of the afternoon, talking and debating and pointing earnestly. The final conclusion was inescapable. The wall was sinking, bellying inward too. They probed the mortar between the stone joints, stood on top of the wall, and swung a weighted plumb line from top to bottom. Then, placing their faces flat to the wall surface and each one squinting with one eye, they gauged the extent of the stone warp. Whichever way they looked at it there was only one thing all were agreed upon. The south wall was crumbling!

10

Darkness was stealing over Redwall Abbey, and the lights of Great Hall shone through long, stained-glass windows, laying columns of rainbow colors across the lawn. Buttressed and arched, the ancient building towered against a backdrop of Mossflower woodlands. From bell tower to high roof ridge, it was the symbol of safety, comfort, and achievement to all the Redwallers who called it home.

Sister Viola Bankvole had never adopted the simple habit worn by most Abbey creatures. She favored flounces and ruffles, supported by more petticoats than enough. She made her way out of the Abbey's main door, holding up a lantern and tutting fussily as playful night breezes tugged at her cloak and bonnet. Brazen and slow, Redwall's twin bells boomed out sonorously, calling everybeast to table for the evening meal.

Abbess Tansy and her party were at the north wall gable, completing an exhaustive inspection of the entire outer walls.

Foremole Diggum patted the stones fondly. "Burr! Thank ee, season'n'fates, thurr b'aint nuthen wrong with ee rest of'n our walls, marm, boi 'okey thurr b'aint!"

Arven held up his lantern, watching Abbess Tansy's

face anxiously. "He's right, Tansy. The east, north, and west walls, including the gatehouse, stairs, ramparts, and main gates, are all sound as the day they were built!"

The Abbess rubbed a paw across her tired eyes. "So they are, but that's little comfort when the whole south wall could topple at a moment's notice."

Viola came bustling up, bonnet ribbons streaming out behind her. "Mother Abbess! There's a full evening meal waiting inside that cannot start without your presence! My word, just look at yourselves, dusty paws, thorns and teazels sticking to your clothing, what a sight! Craklyn, I thought you were supposed to be helping with the Dibbuns' bedtime. Goodness knows what time those babes will get up to the dormitory tonight when they haven't even been fed yet! Oh, and another thing . . ."

Arven's voice cut strongly across the bankvole's tirade: "Enough! That will do, Sister Viola!"

Tansy took advantage of Viola's huffy silence to say, "Thank you, Sister, we will be in to dine shortly. Meanwhile, would you be good enough to take my chair and order the meal to start in my absence? But do not send the Dibbuns to bed. I have something to say for all Redwallers to hear."

Viola seemed to swell up with the importance of her mission. Nothing she could think of pleased her more than taking the Abbess's place, albeit only for a short time. The bankvole swept off back to the Abbey, cloak aswirl with the wind.

Craklyn watched her go as they made their way toward the Abbey pond to wash. "Hmph! That bankvole, sometimes I think a swift kick in the bustle would do her the world of good."

Tansy stifled a smile as she reproved her friend. "Sister Viola is a good and dutiful creature, and she can't help being a bit overzealous at times. Mayhap we could all take a little lesson from her devotion to detail."

The bustle and chatter of good company was always a

keynote to Redwall dining. Great Hall was packed with Redwallers, eating and conversing across well-laden tables. Golden and brown crusts of batch loaves, nut-bread, and oatfarl shone in the candlelight; tureens of steaming barley and beet soup, filled with corn dumplings, were placed at intervals, between hot cheese and mushroom flans and fresh spring salads. Flagons of spiced fruit cordial and dandelion tea vied for place with pear and chestnut turnovers, apple and cream puddings, and two huge wild cherry and almond cakes. Many of the elders sat Dibbuns on their laps, sharing their plates with the Abbeybabes. The young ones were jubilant at the chance to stay up late.

Arven and the moles came to the table in Tansy's wake. The good Abbess signaled Viola to stay where she was, in the big chair at the head of the table. Shoving Sloey the mousebabe and Gubbio the Dibbun mole playfully apart, Tansy placed herself between them on the low bench, saying, "Move aside there, you two great fatties, let a poorbeast in!"

Sloey looked up from her soup as she moved to make room. "Big fatty y'self, marm. Wot you be late for?"

Gubbio spoke for his Abbess as he munched a large slice of cake. "Apportant bizness, oi surpose."

Tansy ladled soup for herself, winking at the molebabe. "Aye, mate, apportant bizness it was!"

The meal continued in no great hurry, a low buzz of conversation accompanying it. Time was never a factor when victuals were being taken at Redwall. When Tansy judged the moment was right, she stood up and nodded to Viola. The bankvole rang a small pawbell which was on the table near where she sat. Talk died away and Dibbuns were shushed as Tansy addressed her creatures.

"My friends, listen carefully. As your Mother Abbess I have something to tell you. Now there is no cause for alarm, but Foremole Diggum, Arven, Craklyn, some other good moles, and myself have inspected the

53

structure of our Abbey's outer walls today. For some reason as yet unknown to us, the south wall is in a dangerous state."

Shad, a big otter who occupied the gatehouse as Keeper, was immediately up on his paws. "What's t'be done, marm?"

Tansy gestured to Diggum, and the Foremole answered for her: "Hurr, furstly us'n's needs to foind out whoi ee be unsafe, on'y then'll us be able to fixen ee wall."

With Tansy's permission, Arven was next to speak. "There's no need for anybeast to worry, but we must set a few sensible rules for the safety of all. From tomorrow we will fence off an area isolatin' the entire south wall. Please do not hang about near it. Carry on with your chores and pleasures as normal, and see that none of our little 'uns try to play in the area, because it will be dangerous for a while. Lots of stone and rubble are bound to be lying about when the wall is demolished."

An incredulous murmur arose 'round Great Hall.

"They're going to knock down the south wall, demolish it!"

Shad the Gatekeeper thwacked the table with his thick tail, silencing the talkers. "Hearken t'me! Wot's all the bother about? Stands t'sense that a wobbly wall 'as t'be knocked down afore y'can build it back right. You 'eard Abbess Tansy, there ain't no cause to worry!"

Pellit, a fat dormouse kitchen helper, shook his head knowingly. "Huh, just wait until the first vermin comin' up the path spots the wall knocked down. That'll be the time to start worryin'!"

A loud hubbub broke out as a result of the dormouse's observation, and argument and dispute took over until Great Hall was in uproar. Many of the Abbeybabes, upset by the noise, began wailing with fright.

Without warning, Viola Bankvole leapt up onto the table. Seizing a big empty earthenware basin, she raised it high and sent it crashing to the floorstones. The noise of it smashing to fragments caused a momentary silence. That was enough for Viola; she was in, her voice ringing out sternly: "Silence! Be quiet, I say! Have you no manners at all? You there, Brother Sedum, and you, Pellit, take these babes off to bed right now! The rest of you, stop behaving like a pack of wild vermin. Shame on you! Arven, you are Abbey Warrior, tell these silly creatures of your plans!"

Arven had made no plans at all, but he took the center floor and made them up boldly as he went along, his voice ringing with confidence to reassure the listeners.

"My plans, yes—I was just coming to that before all the shouting started. Foremole Diggum and his moles will take care of the demolition and rebuilding, together with any of you he chooses to assist him. The work will be carried out in shifts, so that the job will be completed as soon as possible. Meanwhile I'm sure our friend Shad will contact the Skipper of Otters and his crew, and together with our own stout creatures they will form a force to guard and patrol the immediate area. Really, friends, there is no cause to worry at all. Many seasons have passed since any vermin bands were seen in this part of Mossflower Country."

Tansy clapped her paws in appreciation of Arven's fine speech, and soon the other Redwallers joined in, heartened by his words.

Late that night when most other creatures were abed, Tansy presided over a meeting of the Abbey elders in Cavern Hole, a smaller, more comfortable venue. While they were gathering she took the opportunity to murmur to Craklyn, "What price a swift kick in the bustle now, marm? I think Viola behaved magnificently tonight in Great Hall. There's a lot more to our Infirmary Sister than mostbeasts would think, d'you agree?"

The squirrel Recorder nodded vigorously. "Indeed there is, she can be a proper little firebrand when she wants. All right, Mother Abbess, I'll eat my words. I'd sooner shake her by the paw than kick her in the bustle!"

Deep into the small hours they sat debating the issue of the south wall, its possibilities and its perils. The meeting ended with Diggum's irrefutable mole logic.

"Hurr well, so be't. Us'n's caint do ennythin' 'til we foinds out wot maked ee wall go all of awobble. Oi'm thinkin' us'n's won't be able t'do that proper lest us gets a gudd noight's sleep."

Arven tossed and turned in his bed, the question of the wall troubling him greatly, until finally sleep took over and he settled down. In his dreams he was visited by Martin the Warrior, the guiding spirit of Redwall Abbey. Martin was the Warrior who had been instrumental in founding Redwall long ages before. The dust of countless seasons had blown over his grave, though his image was still fresh on the wall tapestry of Great Hall. It was often in times of trouble and crisis that he would appear in dreams to one or another Redwaller of his choosing, comforting and counseling them.

On this night, however, his words carried a warning to Arven. Looming through the mists of slumber the warriormouse strode, armored and carrying his legendary sword. Arven instinctively knew there would be a message for both him and the Abbey, and as he watched Martin draw near, a great sense of peace and well-being swept over him. He felt like some small creature folded within the security of a figure that was old, wise, compassionate, and above all, safe.

The Warrior spoke:

"Watch you ever the southlands,
And beware when summertide falls,
A price will be paid for these stones we hold dear,
Though war must not touch our walls."

Arven had no recollection of his dream the next day.

56

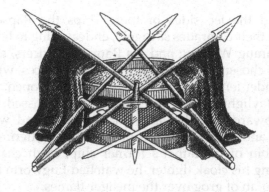

11

On the southeast coastline the mighty Rapscallion army crouched, saturated, cold, and hungry, amid the wreckage of their ships. Gray-black and bruised though it was, dawn proved a welcome sight for the dispirited vermin masses. Nobeast could have known that after they had burned their dwellings a storm would arrive in the night.

It came from the southeast, tearing across the seas with a vengeance, without warning. Battering torrents of rain sheeted down to drown the campfires 'round which the vermin were sleeping. Hailstones big as pigeon eggs were mixed with the deluge, while a gale-force wind drove the downpour sideways over the beach.

Shrieking and roaring, rats, ferrets, stoats, weasels, and foxes dashed about on the shingle, seeking shelter as the storm's intensity grew. Ships beached on the immediate tide line were seized upon by the mountainous seas and heaved out upon the waves, where they were smashed like eggshells as they crashed into one another. Rigging and timbers, ratlines and gallery rails flew through the air, slaying several unfortunates who were running panicked on the shore.

Only four vessels, beached high above the tide line, their hulls half buried by sand and shingle, were safe.

Around the lee sides of these ships the Rapscallions fought their comrades savagely, endeavoring to find shelter. Damug Warfang and his Rapmark officers, together with a chosen few, occupied the cabin spaces, while the remainder fended for themselves out in the open.

By daylight the rain and hailstones had passed, sweeping upward into the land, though the wind was still strong and wild. Damug crouched over a guttering fire in the cabin of his father's former ship, teeth chattering. Drawing his cloak tighter, he watched Lugworm heating a pannikin of grog over the meager flames.

"That looks ready as it'll ever be. Give it here!"

With his teeth rattling like castanets against the container, the Greatrat sipped gingerly at the scalding concoction. When he had drunk enough the Firstblade gave the remainder to Lugworm, who choked it down before Damug could change his mind. Peering through the broken timbers, Damug cast his eye over the low-spirited Rapscallions roaming the shore.

"We'll move right away, get inland where the weather's a touch milder. First grove o' woodland we find will do for a camp; fire, water, whatever food we can forage, then they'll be ready to gear up and march."

Lugworm fussed around his Chief, brushing dirt and splinters from Damug's cloak. "Aye, sir, they'll be fine then, fightin' fit fer a journey o'er to the west, ter pay that badger back for yore father."

Whack!

The Greatrat's mailed paw caught Lugworm alongside his jaw, sending him crashing into a shattered bunk. Damug was like a madbeast: flinging himself upon the hapless stoat he beat him unmercifully, punctuating each word with a blow or kick.

"Don't you ever mention that beast within my hearing again! We stay away from that cursed mountain! Aye, and that rose-eyed destroyer, that blood-crazed badger! That ... That ..." He grabbed Lugworm by the throat and shook him like a rag. "That . . . *badger!* You even *think* about her again and I'll kill you stone dead!"

Damug Warfang hurled the half-conscious Lugworm from himself, slammed the door clean off its hinges, and strode quivering with rage out of the cabin. Grabbing a ferret called Skaup, he bellowed right into his face, "Get the drums rolling, and tell my Rapmarks to line up their companies. We march north. Now!"

Within a very short time the Rapscallion soldiers were formed up into columns five wide and marching away from the hostile coast.

Damug strode at the head of his army; on either side of him, six rats pounded their big drums. Ragged banners flapped wildly in the wind, their poles ornamented with the tails of dead foebeasts. The poles' tops were crowned with the skulls of enemies, and their long pennants bore the sign of Rapscallion, the two-edged sword.

Borumm the weasel and Vendace the fox were scouts, known by the title Rapscour. They marched to the left flank of the main body with twoscore trained trackers each. Borumm glanced back at the receding shoreline and the sea, saying, "Take yer last peep o' the briny, mate, this lot won't be goin' nowheres by water anymore. 'Is Lordship Damug don't like sailin'."

Vendace narrowed his eyes against the driving wind. "That's a fact, cully, an' I'll wager an acorn to an oak that 'e won't be 'eadin' over Salamandastron way neither. "Taint only ships Damug's afeared of."

Borumm let his paw stray to the cutlass at his side. "A proper Firstblade shouldn't be afeared o' nought. But we'll frighten 'im one dark night, eh, mate?"

Vendace grinned wolfishly at his companion. "Aye, when 'e's least expectin' it, we'll find space atwixt 'is ribs fer a couple o' sharp blades. Then we'll be the Firstblades."

Borumm closed his eyes longingly for a moment.

"Harr, we'll turn this lot right 'round an' make fer the soft sunny south coast an' rule it like a pair o' kings."

Lugworm stumbled along behind the last column, clasping a damp strip of blanket to his bruised throat. Being a Firstblade's counselor had its drawbacks. It would take him a day or two to get back into his Chief's favor, and meanwhile he decided to stay as far away from Damug as possible.

Lousewort and Sneezewort marched just ahead of him, being in the back five of the last contingent. Lousewort caught sight of Lugworm and called back to him, "G'mornin', Luggy, wot sorta mood's the boss in t'day?"

Lugworm tried to speak, but could manage only a painful gurgle.

Sneezewort looked quizzically at Lousewort. "Wot did 'e say, mate?"

The stolid Lousewort shook his head. "Er, er, 'e jus' said 'Gloggle oggle ogg,' or sumthin', I dunno."

Sneezewort prodded his mate. " 'Gloggle oggle ogg,' eh? That's wot you'd a bin sayin' right now if'n you was totin' that stoopid big wheel along wid yer."

The big nasty-looking weasel's voice reached them from the rank marching in front. "Wot stoopid big wheel's that yer talkin' about?"

"Oh, the one I chucked awa—Wot wheel are ye talkin' about, comrade? I don't know nothin' about any wheel, d'you, matey?"

Lousewort nodded obliviously. "Oh yep, you remember, Sneezy, my nice big wheel wot you throwed away. Owow! Wot are ye kickin' me for, mate?"

All morning the wind continued to blow, right until midnoon, when a drizzle started. Damug Warfang rapped out commands to the drummers.

"Speed up that beat to double march, there's a woodland up ahead."

The two Rapscours and their scouts dashed ahead of

the Rapscallions to reconnoiter the spot. It was a prime campsite, with a small pond containing fish, and lots of fat woodpigeons roosting in the trees. By late noon the army was completely sheltered from the weather: rocky ledges, heavy tree trunks, and overhead foliage sealed them off from cold, wind-driven rain. A feeling of well-being pervaded the camp, now they were in a fresh location. This was luxury, after an entire winter spent on the hostile and hungry southeast shore.

Borumm and Vendace were snugly settled in, having spread an old sail canvas over the low curving limb of a buckthorn, with a rocky outcrop at their back. They sat cooking a quail over their campfire. Lugworm was with them, hiding behind a flap of the overhanging canvas, glancing nervously around at the passing Rapscallions.

Borumm chuckled at the stoat's apprehensive manner. Shoving him playfully, he said, "Wot's the matter, matey? You ain't doin' no 'arm jus' sittin' 'ere sharin' a bird with two ole pals."

Lugworm averted his face as a Rapmark walked by. "What'd Damug say if'n somebeast told 'im I was sittin' 'ere talkin' wid you two?"

Vendace shrugged as he tended the roasting quail. "We won't tell 'im if you don't. Stop frettin' an' 'ave some o' this bird. All you gotta do is tell us where ole Firstblade'll be sleepin' tonight an' how many guards'll be around, an' anythin' else y'think we should know. Leave the rest to us, matey."

Borumm whetted a curved dagger against the rock. "Aye, by tomorrer it shouldn't make any difference who saw yer talkin' to us. Damug won't be around to throttle yer again, 'e'll be searchin' for 'is daddy in Dark Forest!"

Sneezewort had a good fire going. He stirred the half-burned wood hopefully, watching Lousewort returning from the pond. He noticed that his companion looked very damp.

"Yore lookin' a bit soggy, mate. Didyer catch any-thin'?" he called.

Lousewort slumped by the fire, waving away the cloud of steam rising from his ragged garments. "Er, er, I nearly did, but I got pushed inter the water."

Sneezewort picked up a small log and brandished it angrily. "Pushed in? Huh, show me the slab-sided black-guard wot pushed yer!"

"Er, er, it was that big nasty-lookin' weasel."

Sneezewort threw the log on the fire, sighing resignedly. "Ah well, that one's got 'is lumps comin' someday. So, you didn't bring any vittles back at all?"

Lousewort produced a pile of dripping pondweed. "Er, er, only this. May'aps we can make soup out of it."

His companion turned up a lip in disgust. "Yurgh, dirty smelly stuff, chuck it away!"

Lousewort was about to carry out his friend's order when his paw was stayed. Sneezewort stared unhappily at the mess of dripping vegetation, shaking his head, and said, "Take my ole helmet an' fill it wid water. Pondweed soup's better'n nothin' when yer belly thinks yore throat's cut!"

Damug belched loudly and settled back to suck upon the bones of the tench he had just devoured. From the shelter of an ash nearby he heard his title whispered.

"Firstblade!"

The Greatrat lay still, lips hardly moving as he answered, "Gribble, is that you?"

From his hiding place, the rat Gribble called in a low voice, "Aye, 'tis me. Lugworm's gone over to Borumm an' Vendace. From wot I 'eard they'll make their move tonight, Chief."

Damug Warfang smiled and closed his eyes. "Good work, Gribble. It always pays to have watchers watching watchers. I'll be ready. Go now, keep your eyes and ears open."

12

Russa Nodrey added twigs to the fire embers, peering upward at slatey skies that showed between treetops that morning. "Hmm, doesn't look too good out there t'day. No point in leavin' camp awhile, those vermin'd probably ambush us afore we got out o' these trees."

Tammo looked up from the beaker of hot mint tea he was sipping. "Y'mean the rotten ol' vermin are hiding in these woodlands? I thought you said they'd ambush us out on the flatland."

The wily squirrel pointed a paw at the sky. "So they would if it were fine weather, but put y'self in their place, mate. You wouldn't stand out in the open soakin' an' freezin', waitin' fer us to come out of a nice dry camp like this. No, if'n you'd any sense at all you'd get under cover, out of the weather. They're probably creepin' through the trees toward us right now."

The young hare dropped low, drawing his dirk. "Are you sure that's what the rascals are up to?"

Russa added more wood to the fire. "Sure as liddle apples, if I know anythin' about vermin!"

Tammo was amazed at his companion's calm manner. "Then what're you standin' there loadin' more bally wood on the fire for? Shouldn't we be doin' somethin' about the situation?"

Russa hid the haversack away beneath some bushes, then rummaged about in her back pouch. She tossed Tammo a sling and a bag of flat pebbles. "Here, I take it y'can use that."

Tammo loaded a pebble into the tough sinewy weapon, and swung it. "Rather! I was the best slingshot chucker at Camp Tussock!"

Russa twirled her hardwood stick expertly. "Right, here's what we'll do. I'll take to the trees an' pick 'em off as you draw 'em out. Use the sling, leave yore blade where 'tis unless they get too close, then don't fool about, use it fer keeps. Move now, I c'n hear 'em comin'— sounds like there's enough o' the scum. We'll have our work well cut out, mate."

Tammo heard a twig snap some distance away and heard a harsh cry.

"There's one of 'em, come on!"

He turned to answer Russa, but she was not there.

Suddenly a rat came leaping over the fallen beech at him. Tammo reacted swiftly. Swinging the loaded sling, he brought it cracking down between his assailant's eyes. The rat fell poleaxed by the force of the blow. For a second Tammo froze, almost paralyzed at the sight of the rat's broken body, half shocked, half exhilarated at this victory and escape. But there was no time to think. Instinctively he began whirling his sling. Leaping backward a few paces, he centered on a shadowy form in the shrubbery and let fly. He was rewarded by a sharp agonized cry as the slingstone smashed home. The young hare turned and ran a short distance. He was stopping to load up his sling when a sharp-clawed paw gripped the back of his neck.

"Haharr, gotcha!"

There was a heavy clunking noise, and the vermin collapsed limply. Russa leaned out of the foliage of an oak, directly over where Tammo stood. She waved the piece of hardwood at him.

"Best weapon a beast ever had, this 'un! Get goin', Tamm, there's more of 'em than I reckoned!"

The woodlands became alive with vermin war cries. An arrow zipped past Tammo, grazing his ear before it quivered in the oakwood. Then they came pounding through the woodlands toward him, a score or more of snarling savages, brandishing an ugly and lethal array of weapons. Whipping a slingstone at them, Tammo took off at a run, only to find he was headed straight in the direction of another group.

Whichever way he wheeled there were vermin coming at him. Foliage rustled overhead, and Russa came sailing out of a tree to land beside him, her jaw set grimly.

"I never figgered on this many, mate. The villains've got us surrounded. Pity it had to happen yore first time out, Tamm. Still, there's one consolation—if'n we go together, I won't be left t'carry the news back to yore mum."

Tammo felt no fear, only rage. Drawing his blade, he gritted his teeth and swung the loaded sling like a flexible club. "Stand back t'back with me, pal. If we've got to go, then let's give 'em somethin' to jolly well remember us by. Eulaliaaaaaaa!"

The vermin rushed them but were swiftly repulsed, such was the ferocity with which the two friends fought. Four rats went down from blade thrust, sling, and stick. Whirling to meet a second onslaught, following hard on the heels of the first, Russa stunned a weasel with the butt of her stick, grabbing him close to her so that he took the spear thrust of a ferret behind him. Tammo whipped the loaded sling into the face of another and slashed out to the side with his dirk, catching a rat who was sneaking in on him.

A big, wicked-looking fox swung out with an immense pike. The heavy iron blade thudded flat down on Russa's head, stunning the squirrel and knocking her flat. Tammo tripped over a wounded rat and stumbled awkwardly.

The vermin pack flung themselves on the pair. Tammo managed to slay one and wound another, then he went under, completely engulfed by weight of numbers. Stars and comets rattled about in his head as the butt end of the fox's pike flattened him.

Waves of throbbing pain crashed through the young hare's skull. He struggled to lift his paws to his head but found he was unable to. Noise followed, lots of noise, then an agonizing pain across his shoulders. Opening his eyes slowly, Tammo found himself facing Skulka. She was swinging the thorn-covered wild rose branch that she had just struck him with.

"Hah! I thought that'd waken 'im! Would yer like another taste o' this, me bold young warrior?"

Tammo's paws were tightly bound, but that did not stop him bulling forward and up, catching the ferret hard beneath her chin with a resounding headbutt. Her jaws cracked together like a window slamming as she fell backward.

A rat ran forward swinging a sword, shouting, "I'll finish 'im!"

Russa had recovered sufficiently to kick out at the rat with her tightly lashed footpaws, and he was knocked sideways, striking his back sharply against a tree trunk.

Rubbing furiously at his spine, the rat came at Russa, sword held straight for her throat. "I'll show ye the color o' yer insides fer that, bushtail!"

He was stopped in his tracks by the big fox's pike handle. "No, y'won't, cully. I want some sport wid these two afore we put paid to 'em. Now then, young 'un, where'd yer 'ide that bagful o' vittles you two've bin totin' around?"

Tammo glanced down at the pikepoint pricking his chest. He smiled contemptuously at his tormentor, and said, "Actually I stuffed 'em down your ears while you were asleep last night, figurin' that owing to the lack of brains there'd be plenty o' room inside your thick head, old chap."

The fox quivered with anger but held his temper. "You've just cost yer comrade 'er tail, and when I've chopped it off I'm gonna ask yer again. We'll see 'ow smart yer mouth is then, bucko. Skulka, Gaduss, grab 'old o' that squirrel ..."

Suddenly the fox stopped talking and stared dumbly at the javelin that appeared to be growing out of his middle. A blood-curdling cry rang through the trees.

"Eulaliaaaaaa! Give 'em blood'n'vinegar!"

This was followed by a veritable rain of arrows, javelins, and slingstones. Taken by surprise, the vermin scattered. One or two who were a bit slow were cut down where they stood. From somewhere a drum began beating and the wild war cry resounded louder: " 'S death on the wind! Eulaliaaaa! Eulaliaaaaaa!"

The vermin had obviously heard the call before. Whimpering with terror they fled, many of them falling to the rain of missiles pursuing the retreat.

Tammo was busily trying to sever his bonds on the fallen fox's pikeblade, when the drums sounded close. He looked up to see a very fat hare striding toward him. Amazingly, the creature was making the drum sounds with his mouth.

"Babumm babumm barabumpitybumpitybumm! Drrrrrrubbity dubbity rump ta tump! Barraboom-boomboom!"

A tall elegant hare with drooping mustachios, carrying a long saber over one shoulder of his bemedaled green velvet jacket, stepped languidly out of the tree cover.

"Good show, Corporal Rubbadub, compliments to y'sah. Now d'you mind awfully if one asks y'to give those infernal drums a rest?"

With a smile that was like the sun coming out, the fat hare threw up a smart salute and brought both footpaws down hard as he gave two final drum noises.

"Boom boom!"

The tall hare's saber whistled through the air as he spoke to Tammo and Russa. "Stay quite still, chaps, that's the ticket!"

The two friends winced and closed their eyes tightly as the saber whipped around them like an angry wasp. In a trice the cords that had bound them were lying slashed on the ground.

Russa smiled one of her rare smiles. "Captain Perigord Habile Sinistra to the rescue, eh!"

The hare made an elegant leg and bowed. "At y'service, marm, though I'm known as Major Perigord nowadays, promotion y'know. Hmm, Russa Nodrey, thought you'd have perished from vermin attack or old age seasons ago. Who's this chap, if I may make so bold as t'ask?"

Standing upright, Tammo returned the Major's bow courteously. "Tamello De Fformelo Tussock, sah."

"Indeed! Any relation to Colonel Cornspurrey De Fformelo Tussock?"

"I should say so, sah, he's my pater!"

"You don't say! Well, there's a thing. I served under your old pa when I was about your seasons. By m'life! Then you'll be Mem Divinia's young 'un!"

"I have that honor, sah."

Major Perigord walked in a circle around Tammo, shaking his head and smiling. "Mem Divinia, eh, great seasons o' salt, the prettiest hare ever t'slay vermin. I worshiped her, y'know, from afar of course, she was ever the Colonel's, and me? Pish tush! I was nought but a young Galloper. Ah for the golden days o' youth, wot!"

He broke off to listen to the screams of the fleeing vermin growing fainter, then turned to Corporal Rubbadub and said, "Be s'good as to call the chaps'n'chappesses back, will you, there's a good creature."

Still smiling from ear to ear, Rubbadub marched off in the direction of the retreat, his drum noises echoing and rolling throughout the small woodland.

"Barraboom! Barraboom! Barraboomdiddyboomdiddy boomboom!"

The Major perched gracefully on the fallen beech trunk. "Complete March Hare, ol' Rubbadub, took too many head wounds in battle, doncha know. Never speaks, but the chap makes better drum noises than a real drum, or four real drums f'that matter. Brave as a badger and fearless as a fried frog, though, a perilous creature t'have on your side in a pinch."

Tammo remembered the term "perilous hare," so he gave the polite rejoinder, "As you say, sah, a perilous creature, an' what more could one ask of a hare?"

Perigord nodded his head and winked broadly at the younger beast. "Rather! 'Tis easy t'see you're the Colonel's offspring, though I think that fortunately you favor your mother more."

Tammo touched his aching head and leaned back against the beech.

Major Perigord was immediately apologetic. "Oh, my dear fellow, what a beauty of a lump they gave you on the old beezer—you too, Russa. Forgive me, chattin' away here like a sea gull at suppertime. We must get y'some medical attention. At ease in the ranks there, sit down an' rest until Pasque gets back. She's our healer—have y'right as rain in two ticks, wot! You're with the Long Patrol now, y'know, no expense spared!"

Despite his headache, Tammo managed a bright smile. "Did you hear that, Russa? We're with the Long Patrol!"

13

To Tammo's utter amazement, when all the hares returned to camp, he counted only eleven, including Perigord and Rubbadub. The Major was amused by the look on his new friend's face.

"I can see what you're thinkin', laddie buck. Well, let me tell you, the Long Patrol counts quality high above quantity, wot! Here, let me introduce y'to our happy band. This is our Galloper, Riffle, fleet of paw and faster'n the wind. Sergeant Torgoch, a walkin' armory, collects weapons, 'specially blades. These two're Tare'n'Turry the terrible twins, can't tell 'em apart, eh, never mind, neither c'n I. Lieutenant Morio, our Quartermaster, can steal a nut from a squirrel's mouth an' make him think he's jolly well eaten it. My sister, Captain Twayblade, charming singer but rather perilous with that long rapier she carries. The delightful Pasque Valerian, best young medico t'come off the mountain, I've seen her fix a butter-fly's wing. That chap there's Midge Manycoats. He's our spy, master o' disguise an' deadly with a noose. Then there's Rockjaw Grang, Giant o' the North, bet y've never seen a hare that size in a season's march. That leaves m'self, whom y've met, an' Corporal Rubbadub, the droll drummer."

Rubbadub smiled widely, clapping his ears together twice and issuing a drum sound so that it looked as if the ears, and not his mouth, had made the noise.

"Boomboom!"

Russa nudged Tammo and, nodding toward Torgoch, murmured, "That 'un's carryin' yore blade, mate!"

Amid the array of daggers, swords, and knives bristling from Torgoch's belt, the young hare identified his own weapon, its shoulder belt wound 'round the blade.

Tammo braced himself and faced the hare. "Beg pardon, old lad, but I rather think that's my dirk you've got."

The Sergeant took Tammo's weapon from his belt. Balancing it deftly on his paw, he smiled ruefully. "I 'oped it wouldn't be, young sir, 'tis a luvverly blade. I took it orf a vermin oo didn't look as if 'e'd be usin' it agin. You'd best 'ave it back, y'don't see knives like this'n a lyin' about every day. A proper officer's weapon 'tis, I'd say a Badger Lord could've made it."

Tammo was about to put on the belt when he suddenly sat down hard on the ground and began shivering. The ache in his head had become overwhelming. The tall saturnine Lieutenant Morio nodded gloomily at Pasque Valerian and said, "I'll light a fire an' heat some water. You'd best see to that young 'un, he's got a touch o' battle shock. I recall m'self bein' like that first time I saw serious action."

Pasque sat alongside Tammo, rummaging in her herbalist's pouch. "Lie back now, easy does it. Here, chew on this—don't swallow it, though. Spit it out when you've had enough."

It was a sort of sticky moss, bound together by some type of vegetable gum, with a taste reminiscent of mint and roses. Tammo chewed slowly, and through half-closed lids he watched Pasque mixing herbs by the fire. She was the prettiest, most gentle creature he had ever encountered. Tammo resolved that he would get to know her better, then his thoughts became muddled as he drifted away into warm dark seas of slumber.

Night had fallen when he awakened, and a delicious aroma of cooking reminded him he was very hungry.

Perigord's sister, Twayblade, patted the log beside her. "Feelin' better now, young 'un? Come an' perch here. Rubbadub, bring this beast somethin' to eat, wot."

Instinctively, Tammo reached to touch his injured head. A massive paw engulfed his, and he found himself staring upward into the fearsome face of the giant hare, Rockjaw Grang.

"Nay, lad, th'art not to touch thy 'ead yet awhile. Best leave alone what our little lass 'as patched up. Sithee, coom an' set by t'fire."

Rockjaw picked Tammo up as if he were a babe and sat him down between Twayblade and Pasque, who smiled quietly at him and said, "I hope you're feeling better this evening."

Tammo flushed to his eartips and muttered incoherently, feeling completely awkward and embarrassed for the first time in his life. He wanted so much to talk with Pasque, yet his tongue would not obey his brain. Rubbadub saved the situation by marching up with a bowl of hot pea and celery soup with fresh-baked bread to dip in it.

He winked and grinned broadly. "Drrrrrrrr tish boom!"

Russa raised her eyebrows. "Oh, he does cymbals too?"

The young Galloper Riffle refilled the squirrel's beaker. "Aye, marm, bugles also, an' flutes when he's a mind to. Ol' Rubbadub's a full band when the mood takes him."

Major Perigord turned to his troop good-humoredly. "Stripe me, but you're a dull bunch o' ditchwallopers! We ain't welcomed our guests with the anthem yet."

Tammo looked up from his soup. "The anthem?"

Midge Manycoats took out a tiny flute and got the right key. "Humm, humm, fa, sol la te, fa, fa, fa, that's it. Right, troop, the 'Song of the Long Patrol.' Like to hear it, Tammo?"

72

The young hare nodded eagerly. "Rather, I'd love to!"

With Midge acting as conductor and choirmaster, the little woodland camp with its flickering fire shadows, echoed to the famous marching air of the Salamandastron fighters.

"O it's hard and dry when the sun is high
And dust is in your throat,
When the rain pours down, near fit to drown,
It soaks right through your coat.
But the hares of the Long Patrol, my lads,
Stout hearts they walk with me
Over hill and plain and back again
To the shores of the wide blue sea.

Through mud and mire to a warm campfire,
I'll trek with you, old friend,
O'er lea and dale in a roaring gale,
Right to our journey's end.
Aye, the hares of the Long Patrol, my lads,
Love friendship more than gold.
We'll share long days and tread hard ways,
Good comrades, brave and bold!"

Rubbadub completed the anthem with a long drumroll and a double boom as Tammo and Russa thumped out their applause on the tree trunk.

The terrible twins, Tare and Turry, called out to Tammo, "Come on, come on, you've got to jolly well sing us one back!"

"Aye, so y'have, sing up, Tamm, you look as if y'could belt out a good ditty!"

Russa Nodrey noted the horrified look on Tammo's face, and smiled wryly at Perigord. "Hah! Look at 'im, that'n would sooner be boiled in the soup than sing wid yore pretty Pasque sittin' next to 'im!"

She spared Tammo further embarrassment by

volunteering herself. "Ye can't expect that hare t'sing whilst 'e's recoverin' from an injury. I'll do my anthem for you, 'tis called 'The Song of the Stick.' Though I usually sings it when I'm alone."

Leaping up, Russa began twirling her small hardwood staff, tossing it in the air, catching it on her tail, flicking it back overhead into her paws, and spinning it until it became a blur as she sang:

> "This ain't a sword, it ain't a spear,
> An arrow, nor a bow,
> 'Tis just a thing I carries 'round
> With me where e'er I go.
> It cannot talk or grumble,
> And never answers back,
> But it can sniff out vermin
> An' land 'em such a crack!
>
> O my liddle stick o' wood, my liddle stick o' wood,
> Whacks here'n'there an' everywhere,
> No weapon's half so good,
> An' I am tellin' you,
> My friend so stout'n'true,
> This liddle piece o' timber
> Has always seen me through.
>
> It'll wallop a weasel, sock a stoat,
> Or fling a ferret from 'is coat,
> 'Twould knock a fox clean out his socks,
> My liddle stick o' wood!"

The hares gathered 'round, applauding Russa, who was still performing tricks with the hardwood, which seemed as though it had a life of its own.

Tammo waved at her. "Thanks, matey, that was great!"

Russa came over to whisper in his ear. "I wouldn't do it fer any otherbeast, Tamm, performin' in public ain't my thing. So remember, you owe me one, pal."

When the meal and the entertainment were over, Major Perigord gave out his orders.

"Heads down now, chaps, we move out at dawn. Rockjaw, take first watch. Riffle, Midge, recky 'round a bit, see if y'can pick up the vermin trail for the mornin'. Compliments an' g'night, troop."

Russa and Perigord sat by the fire, long after the rest were asleep, conversing in low tones.

"What brings you an' the Patrol over thisways, friend?"

"Rapscallions an' Lady Cregga Rose Eyes's commands. We travel on her orders, Russa. Last winter we did battle with old Gormad Tunn an' his army, never seen so many vermin in me life, wot! Well, we gave 'em the drubbin' they richly deserved an' sent the scum packin'. Great loss o' life on both sides, but Rapscallions got the worst of it, by m'left paw they did! Our Badger Lady was like a pack o' wolves rolled into onebeast when the Bloodwrath came upon her. They took off like scalded crabs an' we pursued 'em almost into deep water, hackin' an' smashin' at their fleet, did a fair part of damage to it. Hah, off they sailed, screamin' an' cursin' something dreadful!"

Russa stared into the fire. "Evil murderin' beasts, 'twas all they deserved!"

The elegant Major stroked his mustachios reflectively. "Trouble is, nobeast seems t'know where the blighters went. We know Rapscallions don't sail out on the open seas, they hug the coasts an' make raids from their ships. So we're certain they can't have had their fleet sunk out at sea an' got themselves drowned, worst luck. Lady Rose Eyes is extremely worried, y'see they've dropped completely out of sight, over a thousand Rapscallions, with Gormad Tunn and those two evil sons of his, Damug an' Byral. Our Badger Lady figures that the cads are layin' up someplace, plannin' a major comeback. Huh, they won't come near Salamandastron again, but she's of the

75

opinion, an' rightly so, that the great Rapscallion army'll find a target easier than our mountain. Russa, I tell you, with a mob o' that magnitude they could create a veritable bloodbath anyplace!"

Russa nodded her agreement. "So she sent you an' yore troop out to track 'em down?"

Perigord stirred the embers with his sabertip. "That she did, old friend, and we searched most o' the winter until we located today's gang. But they're only a blinkin' fraction of the main band, must've had their ship blown off course an' wrecked. I think they're travelin' overland to join up with the others, that's why we're trailin' 'em. Pity we had to show our paws by attackin' them today, but I couldn't let you an' young Tammo be slain by those foul blackguards."

Russa patted the Major's left paw gratefully. "Thanks, Perigord. I wasn't greatly bothered, but it'd be a shame t'see a fine young hare like Tammo butchered by vermin. I brought him along with me because 'tis his life's ambition to join the Long Patrol. 'E idolizes you lot."

The hare squinted along the length of his saberblade. "I could see that. Bear in mind, both Tammo's mater'n'pater ran with the Patrol once. He comes of good fightin' stock, that young 'un. Officer material, I shouldn't wonder, wot?"

Both beasts sat silently, watching the flames die to embers. Russa finally stretched out in the shelter of the beech log and said, "If you take him with yer I'll come along for the trip. Promised his ma I'd look out fer 'im. Wot's yore next move?"

The Major unbuttoned his tunic and lay down. "Sleep what's left o' the night, I s'pose, then carry on trailin' the vermin an' see where they go. Though if they persist in travelin' south I'll have to stop 'em permanent—can't have those killers wanderin' up the path to Redwall Abbey. Lady Cregga'd have an absolute fit if she knew we'd let a gang o' bloodthirsty thieves anywhere near the Abbey."

Russa rolled over so that her back was warmed by the embers. "Fits right in with my plans. I was plannin' on visitin' ole Abbess Tansy, an' of course there's always the famous Redwall kitchens, no grub better in the land!"

Major Perigord Habile Sinistra licked his lips dreamily. "I'm right with you there, old sport!"

14

Arven was jerked into wakefulness by Shad the otter Gatekeeper. The burly creature was cloaked and carrying a lantern. "All paws on deck, mate, yore needed at the wall!"

Wordlessly, the squirrel donned his tunic and grabbed a cloak, then the pair stole out of the dormitory silently, loath to waken young Redwallers still sleeping.

Descending the spiral stairs to the ground floor, Shad explained what had taken place. "I was asleep in the gatehouse not an hour back when Skipper an' his otter crew arrived. Funny, I sez, I was comin' over t'see you today, messmate. Was you now, sez 'e t'me, well that *is* funny, Shad, 'cos I couldn't sleep fer dreamin' that summat was amiss at the Abbey, so I roused the crew an' set course for 'ere right away! Well, there's a stroke o' luck, sez I to 'im, you saved me a journey, matey, y'better come an' look at our south wall."

By then Shad and Arven were at the main door of the Abbey building. Pale stormlit dawn was breaking. A gale-force wind tore the breath from their mouths, buffeting both creatures sideways, and hissing rain glistened off the grass in the cold half-light.

Sheltering the lantern beneath his flapping cloak, Shad

shouted at Arven, "Come an' see for yoreself!"

Leaning into the tempest, heads down and cloaks drawn tight, both beasts made their way to the south wall.

Skipper of Otters stood at the southeast end of the wall, he and his crew sheltering beneath a monstrous jumble of branches, limbs, twigs, leaves, and stone blocks. Arven nodded briefly to the otters, then, launching himself into the mass of foliage, he shed his cloak and climbed nimbly upward into the tangle. No squirrel could climb like the Champion of Redwall; in a short time Arven was vaulting out of the foliage onto the battlemented walkway that formed the walltop. Bracing himself against the stormy onslaught, he surveyed the damage and its cause.

Mossflower woodlands grew practically right up to the east wall, curving slightly at the south corner and petering out to give way to gently sloping grassland. Directly at the curve a great beech tree had fallen upon the end of the south wall. The ancient forest giant had stood there for untold seasons in high and wide-girthed splendor, only to be felled during the night by the irresistible force sent by weather's wildness.

Near the beech base, Arven could see where the top-heavy tree had broken. Long, thick wood splinters shone white in the rain like the bone fragments and shards of some dreadful wound. In its crashing fall the trunk had hit the wall, scattering battlements, walkway, and sandstone blocks, the tremendous weight hewing a large V shape into Redwall's outer defenses.

As Arven came springing back down to ground, Skipper draped the squirrel's cloak about his shoulders. "Much damage, mate?" he asked.

Arven nodded. "Much!"

Skipper indicated his sturdy crew with a wave. "Well, much or little, it don't bother us, matey, we're 'ere to lend a paw in any way y'need otters. Where d'you want us t' start?"

Arven patted the faithful creature's back. "You're a good 'un, Skip, you and your crew. This Abbey only stands by the goodness and loyalty of its friends. But there's nothin' we can do whilst the weather keeps up like this. Come on, let's get you lot inside and find you some breakfast by the fire."

Skipper's craggy face broke into a smile. "Lead us to it, me ole mate!"

Mother Buscol was official Redwall Friar, and the small fat squirrel liked nothing better in life than to cook. She watched the hungry otter crew poking their heads around her kitchen doorway and hid her pleasure by scowling at them.

"Indeed to goodness, an' what do all you great rough beasts want, hangin' around my kitchens like a flock of gannets?"

Skipper winked roguishly at her. "Feedin', marm!"

Narrowing her eyes, she shook a ladle at him. "Hot oatmeal an' mint tea's all you're gettin' out o' me this morn."

Skipper came bounding in and swept Mother Buscol off her paws, planting several hearty kisses on her chubby cheeks. "Oatmeal an' mint tea is fer Dibbuns, me beauty. Where's the good October Ale an' a pan of shrimp'n'hotroot soup, aye, an' some o' those shortycakes fer afters? Cummon, tell me afore I kisses you 'til sundown. Haharr!"

Her slippered paws kicked the air as she beat the otter playfully with her ladle. "Lackaday, put me down, you great wiry whiskered oaf, or I'll clap you in a boiler an' make riverdog pudden of you!"

Behind her back, Shad had purloined a batch of hot scones, and now he slid past Mother Buscol, chuckling. "Where's yore manners, mate? Put the pore creature down an' we'll wait in Cavern 'Ole 'til brekkfist's ready."

Laughing, Mother Buscol went about her business. "Indeed to goodness look you, shrimp'n'hotroot soup with the best October Ale an' my good shortybreads. Whatever next?"

Dibbuns hastily finished their meal and trundled into Cavern Hole to sport with the playful otters.

"Skipper, Skipper, it me, Sloey, I jump offa table an' you catch me!"

"Burr, 'old ee still, zurr h'otter, oi wants to ride on ee back!"

"Teehee! We tella Muvver Buscol you steal 'er scones!"

Otters rolled and wrestled happily about the floor with the babes, tickling, swinging, and playfighting. Abbess Tansy and Craklyn came to see what all the noise was about, and Tansy shook her head at Skipper and his crew, sprawled on the floor.

"Really, sir, I don't know who's the worse, you or these babes. Come on, Dibbuns, be off with you. The elders need to talk with Skipper while he has his breakfast."

Foremole Diggum scratched his head as he inspected the plans Craklyn had drawn up on a parchment. "Umm, can ee go through et all agin, marm, then may'ap oi'll unnerstan' wot ee wants a doin'!"

The Redwall Recorder outlined her scheme for the second time. "As I said, the tree falling has started demolition on the wall, so it's not all bad. But how to move the tree so we can continue with the job? Here's my idea. First we need axes and saws to lop off all the top foliage of the beech, then, if it is not already broken clean of its stump, we must sever it. Once that job is done the tree must be supported by struts, to make sure it doesn't fall any further. Then the remaining wall can be removed, the tree trunk dropped and rolled out of the way. Clear?"

Diggum continued scratching his head. "Hurr, 'tis a pity oi be such a simplebeast, oi'm still all aswoggled with ee plan, marm."

Arven stood up decisively. "Oh, you'll get the hang of it as we go along, Diggum. What's the state of the weather outdoors now?"

Gurrbowl the Cellar Keeper and Viola Bankvole went outside. They were back shortly to report. "The rain has stopped, though it's still quite windy; sky over to the south is clearing. If the wind dies down 'twill be a fine afternoon."

Skipper quaffed his beaker of October Ale. "Right y'are, marm, then let's get those axes an' saws out o' the toolstore an' sharpen 'em up. We'll start work after lunch!"

Still mystified by the plan, Foremole Diggum decided to inspect the job from a different angle. He gathered together a few of his trusty moles for the task. "Yurr, Drubb, Bunto, Wuller, an' ee Truggle, oi figger et's toime us'n's taked a lukk at ee wall proper loik!"

Skipper was greasing a double-pawed saw when he noticed the moles leaving, carrying nothing but a few coiled ropes. "Ahoy, where d'you suppose they're bound?"

Arven glanced up from the axblade he was whetting. "Leave them be, Skip. I could see Diggum wasn't too happy with Craklyn's plan, so I suppose he's going to take a look for himself. You know moles, they always look at things in a different way from otherbeasts, and quite often theirs is the most sensible way. Maybe they'll find out something we don't know."

Foremole Diggum moved slowly along the wallbase on all fours, sniffing the ground, scratching the stone, and probing the soil with his strong digging claws. About midway along the south wall he stopped and, pointing to a spot on the sandstone blocks three courses up, addressed Truggle: "Roight thurr, marm!"

The other moles nodded wisely; their Foremole had made a good choice. Truggle produced a small wooden mallet and began striking the place Diggum had indicated. Diggum placed an ear against the ground, directly below where she was hitting, and listened carefully, ignoring the wind and the wet grass. When he had heard enough, the Foremole signaled Truggle to stop and straightened up.

Drubb blinked earnestly at Diggum. "Boi 'okey, gaffer, oi can tell by ee face you'm founded summat."

Foremole Diggum took a twig and stuck it into the ground on the place where his ear had been.

"Ho oi found summat sure enuff, doant know 'ow oi missed et afore. Wot caused ee wall to sink'n'wobble? Ee answer's daown thurr, 'tis a cave or may'ap summ sort o' chamber!"

Bunto shook his Foremole by the paw. "Hurr! Oi knowed ee'd foind ee answer. Wot now, Diggum, zurr?"

Foremole Diggum's homely face wrinkled into a cheery smile. "Us'n's got some diggin' t'do!"

Five sets of digging claws met over the twig.

"Who'm dig deep'n'make best 'oles?
Only us'n's, we be moles!"

83

15

Lugworm had done his work well. The two rat sentries guarding Damug Warfang's shelter of brush and canvas sat upright with four empty grog flasks between them. The crafty stoat had known that the strong drink would be irresistible to beasts standing guard through the cold lonely night hours. Lugworm watched them from his hiding place until he was sure the pair were sleeping soundly. Slipping away he found Borumm and Vendace waiting at the place he had arranged to meet them.

Borumm drew his curved dagger, impatient to go about his business. "Everythin' ready, mate, coast clear?"

Lugworm nodded fearfully, wishing he had never been drawn into the conspiracy to slay the Firstblade. "Aye, 'tis ready, but go carefully, Damug's a light sleeper."

Vendace drew his blade, suppressing a snigger. "Light sleeper, eh? Well 'e won't be after tonight!"

Lugworm edged away from the would-be assassins nervously. "There, I've done me bit, the rest's up to youse two. But remember, if yer fail an' get caught, then not a word about me!"

Borumm the weasel kicked out, sending Lugworm sprawling.

Vendace stood over him, snarling scornfully. "Garn, git outta my sight, stoat, yore in this up to yer slimy neck. The only consolation you've got is that we don't intend ter fail, or git caught. Now beat it an' keep yer gob shut!"

As Lugworm scrambled away whimpering, the fox winked at his cohort. "We'll deal wid him tomorrer, no use leavin' loose ends lyin' about. If Lugworm can betray Damug 'e'd do the same fer us someday. Come on, let's pay the Firstblade a liddle visit."

Damug perched in the branches of the ash tree near his shelter, the rat Gribble crouching by his side. Together they watched the weasel and the fox as, daggers drawn, the pair slid by the two sleeping sentries, silent as night shadows. The Greatrat waited a moment, until he heard blades grating against the sack of stones he'd wrapped in his cloak and laid by the fire. Then he nodded to Gribble.

The rat blew two sharp blasts upon a bone whistle.

Pheep! Pheep!

Ten heavily armed Rapmark officers broke cover, rushed in, and surrounded Borumm and Vendace.

It was fine and sunny next morning, a perfect spring day. Damug allowed Gribble to dress him in his splendid armor; choosing a cloak that did not have dagger slits in it, draped it loosely across one shoulder, and strolled out to the woodland's edge. The entire Rapscallion army was marshaled there, awaiting him, each beast fully armed and ready to march, their faces painted bright red. The face paint served a double purpose: it instilled fear into those they chose to attack, and marked them so they would not strike one another down in the heat of battle.

Damug took up position on a knoll where he could be seen and heard. Whipping out the sword that was his symbol of office, he shouted, "Rapscallions! Are you well rested and well fed?"

A roar of assent greeted him. "Aye, Lord, aye!"

He smiled approvingly. Now his horde looked like true

Rapscallions. They bore little resemblance to the cringing vermin who had wintered on the cold shores after their defeat at Salamandastron.

Damug yelled another question at them. "And are you ready to conquer and slay with me as your Firstblade?"

Again the wild roars of agreement echoed in his ears. He waited until they died down before saying, "Bring out the prisoners!"

Over a single drumbeat the rattle of chains could be heard. Covered in wounds from the beatings they had received, three pitiful figures, chained together at neck and paw, were led forward. It was Borumm, Vendace, and Lugworm, stumbling painfully against one another as they staggered to stay upright. Spearbutts knocked them down on all fours in front of Damug, and the vast crowd of Rapscallions pressed forward to hear Damug's pronouncement.

"Let these three wretches serve as a lesson to anybeast who thinks Damug Warfang is a fool. They are cowards and traitors, but I am not going to order them slain. No! I will give them a chance to show us all that they are war-riors. At the first opportunity of battle, these three will lead the charge, their only weapons being the chains they wear. Those chains will stay on them, binding them together until death releases them. They will march, eat, and sleep all their lives in chains. Let nobeast feed them or comfort them in any way. I am Firstblade of all Rapscallions. I have spoken!"

The three prisoners were made to kneel facing Damug and thank him for sparing their lives. When they had finished he swept contemptuously by them. Waving his sword at two random vermin, he rapped out, "You there, and you, come here!"

Sneezewort nudged his companion Lousewort. "Git up there, thick'ead, Lord Damug pointed at you, not me!"

Lousewort approached the knoll where Damug stood. Sneezewort breathed a sigh of relief: whatever it was,

Lousewort would be on the receiving end. The other beast Damug had indicated strode up before him. It was the big nasty weasel.

The unpredictable Warlord circled them both. "Give me your names!"

"Hogspit, they calls me Hogspit, Sire."

"Er, er, I'm Lousewort, yore Lordness!"

Damug leaned on his sword and stared at them closely. "Lousewort and Hogspit, eh! And are you both Rapscallions, true and loyal to your Firstblade?"

Both heads bobbed dutifully. "Aye, Sire!"

Damug laughed aloud and clapped their shoulders with his mailed paw. "Good! Then I promote you both to the rank of Rapscour. You two will take the places of Borumm and Vendace, with twoscore each to command. Take your scouts and go now, travel due north, and report back to me every two days on what lies ahead."

Sneezewort was livid. He followed his companion, arguing and shouting at him, "Lord Damug never pointed at you, 'e pointed at me, I'd swear 'e did. Wot would the Firstblade want wid a fleabrain like you as a Rapscour officer?"

Lousewort drew himself up importantly. "Er, er, less o' that, mate, I ain't no fleabrain, I'm a Rapscour now. So don't go tellin' me no more of yer fibs. Lord Damug pointed t'me, you said so yerself, huh, you even shoved me forward!"

Sneezewort was hopping with rage. He ran at Lousewort, shrieking, "I'll shove yer forward an' sideways an' back'ards as well, y'great lump o' lard-bottomed crabmeat!"

But Lousewort was a bit too large and solid to shove. He stood firm, shaking a cautionary paw at his friend. "Er, er, stop that, you, y'can't shove me, I'm an officer now!"

Sneezewort advanced on him, sneering ominously. "So I can't shove yer, eh? Who's gonna stop me, Scrawfonk?"

Lousewort grabbed hold of Sneezewort and held him

firmly. "Ooh, you shouldn't a called me that, that's a bad name to call anybeast! Er, er, I know who'll stop yer, my brother officer. Hoi, Hogspit, there's a low common pawrat 'ere, callin' an officer naughty names an' shovin' 'im too."

The big nasty weasel strode aggressively up and punched Sneezewort hard in the stomach. "Lissen, popguts, don't let me ever catch you givin' cheek to a Rapscour. An' you, blatherbonce, don't let 'im shove yer, see!"

Grabbing them both by the ears, Hogspit banged their heads together resoundingly. He strode off, leaving them both ruefully rubbing their skulls.

Lousewort looked at Sneezewort dazedly. "Er, er, let that be a lesson to yer, matey!" he muttered.

A short while after the Rapscours had left with their scouts, the great army got under way. Drums beating to the pace of their march battered out at a ground-eating rate as the day advanced into warm sunny afternoon. Northward the Rapscallion host tramped, dust rising in a cloud behind their banners and drums—only three days away from the southernmost borders of Mossflower Country.

16

A young female hare named Deodar stood on a hilltop close to the west shore. She nibbled at a fresh-plucked dandelion flower, watching a Runner approaching from the northeast. Deodar knew it was Algador Swiftback, even though he was still a mere dot in the distance. His peculiar long leaping stride marked him out from all the others at Salamandastron.

Now he would appear on a hilltop, then be lost to sight as he descended into the valley, but pop up shortly atop another dune, traveling well, with his graceful extended lope serving to eat up the miles easily. The sun was behind Deodar now, hovering over the immeasurable expanses of sea that lapped the coast right up to the shore in front of the mountain. She waved and was rewarded by the sight of Algador waving back. Deodar sat on the sandy tor, enjoying the heat of the sun on her back.

Algador took the last lap at the same pace he had been running all day. He could run almost as fast as his brother, Riffle, the Galloper of Major Perigord's patrol. Breathing lightly, he sat down next to Deodar.

"Hah! So you're my relief. What'll this be now, miss, your third run o' the season?"

Deodar stood, flexing her limbs. "Fifth, actually. Where did you cover, Algy?"

Algador made a sweep with his paw. "Northeast from there to there. No sign of Perigord returning yet, and no signs of Rapscallions or other vermin."

Deodar closed one eye, squinting along the pawtracks her friend had just made. "Righto, Algy, I'll follow you out along your trail then cut west and come back, coverin' the jolly old shoreline."

Algador rose and turned to face Salamandastron farther down the coastline. Between patches of green vegetation growing on its rocky slopes, the mountain took on a light buff tinge. An extinct volcano crater jutted in a flat-topped pinnacle over the landscape. He nodded in its direction. "How's Rose Eyes, showed herself lately?"

His companion shook her head. " 'Fraid not, you'll have to shout your report through the forge door. Lady Cregga sees nobeast while she's forgin' her new weapon. D'you recall the day she broke her old spear, wot!"

Algador could not resist a chuckle. "Hahaha! Will I ever forget it, missie! Standin' neck high in the sea an' sinkin' two Rapscallion ships, was that ever a flippin' sight. I thought she'd have burst with rage when the spearhaft snapped an' she lost her blade in the water!"

Deodar took off into a loping run, calling back, "Can't stop jawin' with the likes o' you all day, must get goin'!"

Algador waved to her. "Run easy, gel, watch out for those shore toads on the way back, don't take any nonsense off the blighters. Take care!"

The sun's last rays were turning the sea into a sheet of fiery copper as Algador entered the mountain. Without breaking stride he took hallway, stairs, and corridors as though they were hill and flatland, traveling upward from one level to another. Sometimes he swerved around other hares and called out a greeting, other times he caught a glimpse of the setting sun through narrow slitted-rock windows. Arriving at a great oak double door, he halted, waiting until his breathing was normal and mentally going over his report speech. Standing stiffly to attention, he reached out a paw and rapped smartly upon the door. There was no answer, though he could hear noises from inside the forge room. Algador waited a moment, knocked once more, and gave a loud cough to emphasize his presence.

A massively gruff voice boomed out, echoing 'round the forge room and the antechamber outside where the hare stood, "I'm not to be disturbed. What d'you want?"

Algador swallowed nervously before shouting back, "Ninth Spring Runner reportin', marm, relieved nor'west o' here this afternoon!"

There was silence followed by a grunt. "Come in!"

Algador entered the forge room and shut the door carefully behind him. It was only the second time he had been in there. A long unshuttered window, with its sill made into a seat, filtered the last rosy shafts of daylight onto the floor. Massive, rough-hewn rock walls were arrayed with weapons hung everywhere: great bows, quivers of arrows, lances, spears, javelins, daggers, cutlasses, and swords. A blackened stone forge stood in the room's center, its bellows lying idle, the white and yellowy red charcoal fire embers smoking up through a wide copper flue.

The hare's eyes were riveted on a heroic figure standing hammer in paw over a chunk of metal glowing on the anvil. Lady Cregga Rose Eyes, legendary Badger Ruler of Salamandastron.

Her size was impressive: even the big forge hammer in her paw seemed tiny, like a toy. Over a rough homespun tunic she wore a heavy, scarred, metal-studded apron. The glow from the red-hot metal caught her rose-colored eyes, tingeing them scarlet as she glared down at Algador. His long back legs quivered visibly, and he felt like an acorn at the foot of a giant oak tree.

91

The Badger Lady nodded wordlessly, and Algador found himself babbling out his report in a rush.

"Patrolled north by east beyond the dunes for two days, marm, spent one night by the river, saw no signs of anybeast. No track or word of Major Perigord so far, no sign of Rapscallions or vermin. Sighted a few traces of shrews yesterday morn, marm."

Lady Cregga rested the hammerhead on the anvil horn. "You didn't contact the Guosim shrews or speak to them?"

"No, marm, 'fraid I didn't. Traces were at least three days old, campfire ashes an' vegetable peelin's, that was all, marm."

Cregga took tongs and replaced the lump of metal she was working back in the forge. Then she gave the bellows a gentle push, flaring the charcoal and seacoal into flame.

"Hmm, pity you missed the shrews. Their leader, the Log-a-Log, might have had some information for us. Never mind, well done. Ask Colonel Eyebright to come up here, will you?"

"Yes, marm!" The young hare stood motionless to attention.

Lady Cregga watched him for a moment, then unusually she gave a fleeting smile. "If you stand there any longer you'll take root. Go now—you're dismissed."

Algador saluted and wheeled off so quickly he almost tripped over his own footpaws. Lady Cregga heard the door shut as she turned back to her work at the forge.

Cutting straight through the main dining hall, Algador made for the Officers' Mess. He accosted another young hare coming out, carrying tray and beakers. "Evenin', Furgale! I say, is Colonel Eyebright in there? Got a rather important message for him."

Furgale was a jolly type, obliging too. Placing the tray on a window ledge, he waggled an ear at the Runner. "Say no more, old pip, I'll let him know you're here."

Flinging the door open wide, Furgale danced comically to attention. Closing both eyes tightly, he bellowed into the small room, "Ninth Spring Runnah t'see you, Colonel Eyebright. Sah!"

Eyebright was every inch the military hare, of average size, silver gray with long seasons, a smart, spare figure in plain regulation green tunic. Looking up from the scrolls he was studying, Eyebright twitched his bristling mustache at the messenger. "I'm not deaf y'know, young feller. Send the chap in!"

Algador marched smartly into the Officers' Mess. "Lady Cregga sends her compliments an' wishes you to attend her in the forge room, Colonel, sah!"

The Colonel's eyebrows rose momentarily, then, fastening his top tunic button, he rose and put aside the scrolls. "Very good, I'm on m'way!"

He eyed the Runner up and down, a kindly smile creasing his weathered features. "Ninth Spring Runner, eh? Obviously enjoyin' the job, young Algy!"

Algador stood at ease, returning his Commanding Officer's smile. "Very much, thank ye, sah."

Eyebright's silver-tipped pace stick tapped Algador's shoulder approvingly. "Good show, keep it up, won't be long before we have y'out gallopin' for a Long Patrol like that brother o' yours."

Algador swelled with pride as the dapper Colonel marched spryly off.

Cregga nodded her huge striped muzzle to the window seat as she poured pennycloud and dandelion cordial for herself and the Colonel. They sat together, he sipping his drink as he watched the parched badger take a long draught of hers. "Thirsty work at the ol' forge, eh, marm?" he said.

The rose-hued eyes flickered in the forge light. "That's not what I called you up here to talk about, Colonel. I had the Ninth Runner report to me this evening, and the news is still the same—all bad. No sign of Perigord's patrol, no word of Rapscallions, everything's too quiet. My voices tell me that big trouble is brewing somewhere."

Eyebright chose his words carefully. "But we've no proof, marm, mayhap things being quiet is all for the best. No news bein' good news, if y'know what I mean."

The Colonel tried not to jump with fright as Lady Cregga suddenly roared and flung her beaker out of the window. "Gormad Tunn and those two spawn of his are out there getting ready to plunge the land into war. I'm certain of it!"

The old hare kept his voice calm. "Tunn and his army could be anywhere, far north, south coast, wherever. We can only do our best by protecting the west land and the seas in front of us. We can't just go marchin' out an' fightin' all over the place."

Lady Cregga strode to the forge and, seizing a pair of tongs, she rummaged in the fire, pulling out the lump of metal she was working on. Laying it on the anvil she took up her hammer. "Colonel, how many hares would it take to guard Salamandastron and the shores roundabout?"

The Colonel's eyebrows shot up quizzically. "Marm?"

Clang!

Sparks flew as Cregga's hammer smashed down on the glowing metal. "Don't 'marm' me! Answer the question, sir—how many fighting hares could do the job, and are you able to command them?"

Eyebright stood up abruptly. "Half the force would be sufficient to protect this area. As to your second question, marm, of course I am able to command. Are you questioning my ability or merely insulting my competence?"

The Badger Lady let the hammer drop. Leaving the anvil, she came to stand in front of the old hare, towering above him. "My friend, forgive me, you are my strong right paw on this mountain. I did not mean to question your skills as a Commander. I spoke in haste, please accept my sincere apology."

The pace stick rose, pointing directly at Cregga. Eyebright's tone was that of a reproving father to an errant daughter. "I have served you well, Cregga Rose Eyes. Anybeast, no matter what their reputation or size, would be down on the shore now to give satisfaction, had they called my honor into question as you did. I forgive you those words, though I will not forget them. Marm, your trouble is that you are eaten up with hatred of Gormad Tunn, his brood, and their followers. You feel bound to destroy them. Am I not right, wot?"

Cregga hooded her eyes, gazing out of the window at the night seas. "You speak the truth. When I think of the gallant hares we lost on the beach and in the shallows of the tide on those three days and nights—and what for? Because Gormad thought his Rapscallion forces great enough to conquer Salamandastron. Aye, he tried to make cruel sport of us, the same way he has done to other more helpless creatures all his miserable life. It will not go on! Soon I will have made myself a new battlepike. If there is no news by then I intend to take half our warriors and go forth to seek out and destroy the evil that goes by the name Rapscallion. One day they will be nought but a bad memory in the minds of good and honest creatures. You have my oath on it!"

Colonel Eyebright left the forge room in resigned silence. Nobeast could swerve the Lady Rose Eyes from her purpose once her mind was made up.

Down in the dining hall, Algador was taking supper with his friends, all young hares the same age as himself. Furgale tore into a large salad, speaking with his mouth full, as there were no officers present.

"I say, chaps, when d'you suppose the lists'll be posted for new recruits to the jolly ol' Long Patrol?"

Cheeva, a young female, flicked an oatcake crumb at him. "First mornin' o' summer, my pater says. Hope my name's on it. I'll bet Algy's top o' the bloomin' list, wot?"

Algador sliced into a hefty carrot and celery flan. "Do you? I'll pester the life out of Major Perigord until he takes me as Galloper with Riffle. I think I'm old enough to beat the ears off him in a flat run now!"

Suddenly the room echoed with banging clanging noises, the din reverberating off the walls. Cheeva clapped paws to her ears, crying, "Great seasons o' salad, who's makin' all the clatter?"

Algador had to shout to make himself heard. He called to Colonel Eyebright, who was passing through on his way to the mess, "I say, sah, who's creatin' that infernal racket?"

The Colonel stopped by their table, gesturing to them to stay seated. "Some badger or other at her forge, why don't y'go up there an' tell her to stop?" He nodded at the smiling young faces turned toward him. "I've a feelin' that you lot are goin' to find yourselves Long Patrollin' sooner than you think!"

At this announcement the young hares cheered wildly, eyes aglow, fired with hope and desire. Heedless of what lay ahead.

17

"Barradum! Barradum! Barrabubbitybubbityboom!"

Russa peered bad-temperedly from under the edge of a cloak that served her as a blanket. "Hoi, drumface, pack it in, willyer!"

Rubbadub marched over, his fat face wreathed in morning smiles. Placing a plate of hot food in front of the half-awake squirrel, he brought his cheerful features right up to her nose. "Boom! Boom!"

Tammo and the rest of the column laughed, spooning down an early breakfast of barley meal mixed with honey and hazelnuts.

Sergeant Torgoch did a very good imitation of a motherly female. "Come on, sleepyhead, rise an' shine, the mornin's fine, the lark's in the air an' all is fair, the day's begun, look there's the sun!"

Midge Manycoats skipped about like a Dibbun. "Oh, mummy, may I go out an' play? I'll pick some daisies for you!"

Torgoch's voice dropped back to that of a gruff Patrol Sergeant. "Siddown an' finish yer brekkfist, you useless liddle omadorm, or I'll 'ave yore paws pickled for a season's 'ard marchin'!"

Wiping his lips on a spotless white kerchief, Perigord

buckled on his saber, and flexed his footpaws. "Listen up, troop, we're marchin' due south. Exercise extreme caution out on the flatlands, an' keep y'r eyes peeled for vermin. When the blighters have recovered their nerve I wouldn't be surprised if they chance another crack at us, wot!"

Equipment was packed away into haversacks, and weapons brought to the ready as the Sergeant harangued them. "Right, you 'eard the h'officer, form up an' stir yer stumps now!"

Grasshoppers rustled and bees hummed about early flowering saxifrage and heathers, and the sun shone boldly from a sky of cloudless blue. It was a glorious spring morning on the open moorland. Tammo strode along between Russa and Pasque; the squirrel had her stick, and both hares carried loaded slings. Up in front, Perigord conversed easily with Riffle, though his eyes roved restlessly over the landscape. "Pretty clear tracks, eh, wot? Seems they ain't bothered about coverin' their trail, I'd say."

"Aye, sir, mebbe they'll try somethin' when we reach that rocky-lookin' hill up ahead."

The Major kept his eyes front as he answered, "Hmm, or that little outcrop to the left—*Down troop!*"

An arrow zipped by them like an angry hornet as they threw themselves to the ground. Lieutenant Morio bounced up immediately. "Just one of 'em, sah. There he goes!"

The sniper, a rat with bow and quiver, had broken cover and was racing toward the rock-rifted hill. Perigord sat up, his jaw tight with anger as he saw a rip the shaft had torn on the shoulder of his stylish green velvet tunic.

"Just look at that, the blinkin' cad! Drop the blighter, Rock."

Rockjaw Grang set shaft to a longbow that resembled a young tree. He squinted along the arrow, stretching the flexible yew bow into a wide arc, tracking his quarry.

The rat halted, relieved he was not being chased. He

unslung his bow and began coolly choosing an arrow. Rockjaw's shaft took him out like a thunderbolt.

The giant hare shook his head at the fallen rat's foolishness. "Yon vermin should've kept a runnin'. 'Ey up, there's more!"

Four more broke cover to the right from behind a low rise; shooting off a few slingstones at the hares, they began dashing for the hilltop. Regardless of what orders they had been given, the vermin did not want to be caught out alone by the hares.

Perigord turned to Twayblade and Riffle. "Cut 'em off, try an' take one alive! Rockjaw, you an' Midge cover the hill. The rest of you—about face!"

Tammo shot Russa a puzzled glance. "About face?"

Sergeant Torgoch grabbed Tammo and spun him around roughly. "Don't question orders, young 'un, do like the h'officer sez!"

A band of vermin poured out of the woodland toward them. Tammo and Pasque whirled their slings as Perigord called out, "On my command, two slings, arrows, or one javelin, then go at 'em with a will. Steady now, let the blighters get closer ..."

Tammo felt his teeth begin to chatter. He ground them together tightly and caused his head to start shaking. The vermin faces were plainly visible now, painted red with some kind of mineral dye. Yelling, roaring, and brandishing fearsome weapons, they rushed forward, paws pounding the earth. Perigord leveled his saber at them, remarking almost casually, "Let 'em have it, chaps!"

Tammo's first slingshot missed altogether; in his excitement he whipped the sling too high. His second shot took a weasel slap on the paw, causing him to drop his spear with a yelp. Then Tammo found himself charging with the Long Patrol, the war cry of the perilous hares ripping from his throat along with his comrades. Even Russa was shouting.

"Eulaliaaaaa! 'S death on the wind! Eulaliaaaaaa!"

They met with a clash, Perigord slaying the leading pair before they could blink an eye. Tammo thrust out at a stoat and missed; the stoat feinted with his cutlass, and as Tammo backed off his foe skipped forward and tripped him. The young hare fell. He saw the stoat launch himself in a flying leap, cutlass first. Levering himself swiftly aside, Tammo kept his paw outstretched with the dirk pointed upward. The stoat landed heavily on the blade.

Pulling his blade free, Tammo scrambled up, only to find the vermin fleeing with Long Patrol hares hard on their heels.

Major Perigord and Rubbadub came marching up, the former cleaning his saber on a pawful of dried grass. "Well done, young 'un, got y'self one, I see!"

Tammo could not look at the vermin he had slain, and his head began shaking again as he tried to face the Major.

Shrugging off his tunic, Perigord inspected the torn shoulder. "I know how y'feel, Tamm, but he'd have got you if you hadn't got him. Here, see."

He retrieved the stoat's cutlass and pointed to the notches carved into the wooden handle. "Count 'em, tell me how many you make it."

Tammo took the weapon and counted the notches. "Eighteen, sir!"

Perigord took the blade and flung it away with a grimace of distaste. "Aye, eighteen, though they weren't all fightin' beasts like you an' me, laddie buck. Those smaller notches you saw were for the very old or the very young, creatures too weak to defend themselves. Don't waste your sympathy on scum like that one. Come on now, stop shakin' like tadpole jelly an' give us a good ol' De Fformelo Tussock smile. Rubbadub, beat 'em over to that hill yonder, we'll form up there."

Rubbadub's pearly teeth flashed in a huge grin as he marched off drumming the Long Patrol to him.

"Drrrubadubdub drrrubadubdub dubbity dubbity

dub. Baboom!"

Perigord and Tammo stared at each other for a moment, then burst into laughter.

The patrol squatted on the hilltop, Pasque Valerian tending to one or two minor injuries that had been received. Twayblade swished the air regretfully with her long rapier. "Sorry we didn't take any prisoners, Major, but those vermin weren't takin' any prisoners either, the way they were fightin', so me'n'Riffle had to give as good as we jolly well got."

Perigord watched from the hilltop as the remaining vermin grew small in the afternoon distance. "No matter, old gel, we can still track 'em. As long as we cut 'em off before they reach Redwall Abbey. What d'you make o' those villains, Russa, pretty sharp thinkers, wot?"

The squirrel munched on an apple, nodding. "Aye, 'twas a clever move they made. Clear tracks to this hill, then they must've split up a couple of hours afore dawn an' circled back. Leavin' a few to the left'n'right to distract us, the rest of the crafty scum went back to the woodland so they could ambush us from be'ind. Knowin' we'd be expectin' them to be waitin' for us, hidin' about here on this hilltop."

Rockjaw Grang was watching the retreating vermin and counting their numbers. "Sithee, there's still enough o' yon beasts to make a scrap. They must've numbered fifty or more when we first met 'em, sir. By my count they still got'n thirty-two."

"Hardly enough for eleven bold chaps'n'chappesses like us," Riffle snorted scornfully. "Thirteen if y'count Tamm an' Russa. I say, thirteen, is that unlucky?"

Lieutenant Morio stood up, dusting off his paws. "Aye, unlucky for them when we catch up with 'em. Everybeast fit now, Pasque?"

The beautiful young hare was closing up her medicine pouch. "Yes, Midge took a slight cheek wound and Turry nearly lost the tip of an ear. I've seen to them both. Now there's only the Major's jacket, but I can do that this evening."

The twins, Tare and Turry, ragged Tammo unmercifully.

"Heehee! Lookit the long face on ole Tamm!"

"Bet he wishes he'd been wounded, just so's Pasque could bandage him up an' bathe his brow a bit!"

"If I were him I'd chop me nose off, that'd get her attention!"

"Aye, she'd say, 'Goodness nose, what've they done to your handsome hooter?' Hahahaha!"

Pasque joined in the fun. Grabbing Turry she began rebandaging his ear fiercely. "Hello, what's this ear? Goodness knows, your bandage has come loose. Here, let me tie it a bit more snugly!"

Turry squeaked as he tried to get away. "Ow ow! You've cut off all the blood to me ear! Stoppit!"

Sergeant Torgoch loomed over the playful young ones. "Now then, young sirs an' miss, I'll cut off all yore ears an' cook 'em for me supper if yore not all formed up an' ready t'march two ticks from now. Up on yore paws, you idle lot! Where d'you think y'are—on an 'oliday for 'ares? Move y'selves!"

Pasque marched at the rear with Tammo. She smiled and waved to the Sergeant. To Tammo's surprise, he smiled and winked at her.

Tammo scratched his ear, completely puzzled. "Is he always like that, shoutin' one moment an' smiling the next?"

"Sergeants are all the same," the young hare chuckled. "Bark's worse than their bite. Torgoch is my favorite Sergeant, he's always there to look out for you if you get in any trouble."

18

The remainder of the day went smoothly enough, with the patrol following the vermin track steadily. Late afternoon brought them to the banks of quite a sizeable river. Major Perigord halted them within sight of it.

They crouched in a patch of fern, viewing the scene ahead. Through a screen of weeping willow, elder, sycamore, and holm oak, the river made a welcoming sight, with patches of sun-burnished water showing amid cool islands of tree shade. Tammo was wondering why they had halted and concealed themselves, when he heard Perigord and Twayblade discussing their next move.

"Looks very temptin' indeed, eh, gel?"

"Exactly, good spot for an ambush, I'd say."

Tammo remembered the last time he had rushed forward to water. The hares were right, this time he would be on his guard.

The Major issued orders in a whisper. "Sergeant Torgoch, take young Pasque an' scout the terrain downstream. Cap'n Twayblade, do likewise upstream, take one with you."

"Permission t'go with you, Cap'n. *Please*, marm, I'd like a chance t'be a real part of the patrol!"

Twayblade could not help smiling at the eager Tammo. "Stripe me, but you're a bright'n'brisk 'un. Still, one volunteer's worth ten pressed creatures. C'mon then, young Tamm."

Leaving the edge of the fern cover, Twayblade drew her deadly long rapier and stooped low. "Follow me, Tamm, duck an' weave, take advantage of any cover, keep your eyes open an' do as I do. That is until I give you an order, then it's do as I say!"

Tammo enjoyed learning from an expert. He kept low, rolling behind mounds, bellying out to crawl over open spaces swiftly, then stopping dead and remaining motionless, disguised among bushes. Never traversing in a straight line, they headed east, keeping with the outer edge of the tree fringe until Twayblade decided they had gone far enough. She flattened herself against a gnarled dwarf apple tree, and for a moment Tammo lost sight of the Captain. She blended in with the tree bark until she was almost invisible to the casual observer, and only by staring hard could the young hare make her out.

"Great seasons, Cap'n," he chuckled admiringly, "you nearly vanished altogether then! Mayhaps you'll teach me that trick, marm?"

Twayblade shook her head vigorously. "Not me. Little Midge Manycoats is the chap, he'll teach you all about disguise an' concealment, he's the best there is. Righto, let's make our way to the riverbank an' follow it back down t'where we left the patrol. Everythin' seems to be safe enough hereabouts, but let's not get careless, Tamm. Keep that splendid blade o' yours at the ready, wot!"

They took a drink at the river's edge; the water was cold and sweet. Splashing through the shallows, they cooled their footpaws as they went. Tammo noticed a good patch of watercress, fronds streaming out around a limestone rock beneath the water. He did not stop to gather it, but noted the spot and carried on in Twayblade's wake. The rest of the journey back was pleasant and uneventful, and they arrived at the ferns as noontide shadows lengthened.

The Captain made her report: "Well, well, I see you lot've had a nice little nap whilst we were gone, wot! Nothin' to report, the coast's clear up that way."

Torgoch and Pasque returned; the Sergeant threw a brisk salute. "River narrows downstream, sah, lots o' rocks stickin' up. That's where the vermin made their crossin', still wet pawprints on the stones. We'd catch 'em up by midnight if the patrol got under way smartlike, sah."

Perigord judged the sun's angle. "I think we'll make camp here, Sergeant. No sense in chasin' our tails off, wot. Early start tomorrow, good fast march, an' I've little doubt we'll encounter 'em about high noon. Camp down, troop."

Insects skimmed and flitted on the river surface in quiet twilight, and the campfire flickered warmly. Tammo and Russa opened their haversack. The squirrel dug out the last of her pancakes and distributed them, saying, "Warm these over by the fire, toast 'em up a mite, they're good!"

Rockjaw spitted his on a willow twig and held it over the flames. "How's the soup a comin' along, Rubbadub?"

Corporal Rubbadub pulled a wry face as he took a sip from his ladle. "Brrrrumbum dubadub!"

Lieutenant Morio raised an eyebrow. "As bad as that, eh? Nothin' hereabouts we can add to it?"

Tammo rose and winked at them. "Wait there. I spotted some fresh watercress earlier on. Won't be a tick!"

It was slightly eerie being alone in the gathering gloom as Tammo made his way back upriver. Once or twice he thought he heard noises, and each time he drew his blade and halted, listening, but the only sounds he could make out were those of the flowing water. The young hare gripped his weapon tightly, chiding himself aloud, "Not very good form, sah, behavin' like a ditherin' duckwife!"

Squaring his shoulders, he loped onward until the limestone rock showed pale and ghostly through the gloom. Wading out to it he gathered pawfuls of the fresh watercress, lopping it off below the waterline with his dirk. Carrying the delicious treat back to the bank, Tammo stuck his blade in a sycamore trunk and began tying the cress in a bundle, using his shoulder strap to secure it.

Four dark shapes dropped out of the branches overhead, making Tammo their target. Footpaws whamming onto his back, shoulders, and head drove Tammo flat, stunning him. Before he had a chance to recover and fight back, a cruel noose slid over his head, pulling tight about his neck. Cords were whipped skillfully around his paws. Tammo was unable to cry out; groggily he tried to head-butt one of the wraithlike figures, but a heavy stick struck him in the midriff. Doubled up and fighting to suck air through his wide-open mouth, Tammo was shoved roughly into a cradle made from woven vines. In a trice he was hoisted up into the tree foliage, high among the leafy branches. A dirty gag was bound around his mouth, and the noose loosened.

Savage green-black faces came close to his, lots of them—they seemed to be everywhere.

"Mayka move! Goo on, beast, mayka move! Choohakk! Cutcha t'roat an' eatcha iffya mayka move!"

A paw stroked Tammo's long ears, and a deep grating voice chuckled, "Choohoohoo! Dis a nicey wan, dis wan ours!"

19

On the afternoon that the weather cleared and brightened up, there was great activity in Redwall Abbey. Armed with axes, saws, and pruning knives, the creatures set about the task of dismantling the beech tree that had collapsed upon the already unstable south wall. Arven and Shad the Gatekeeper took a long, double-pawed saw, and between them they tackled the heaviest limb they could reach.

Viola Bankvole stood by as Infirmary Sister, with an array of unguents, salves, bandages, and medicines, in case of injuries. Mother Abbess Tansy had given her permission for any willing Redwallers, young or old, to join in. She remarked to her friend Craklyn as they watched the beech being decimated, "Far better to let everybeast take part, don't you think? It makes a heavy chore into more of a social activity."

The squirrel Recorder had her doubts. "We need more organization, Tansy. Look at Sloey and Gubbio—they're sitting perched up on that branch with hammers, knocking away at twigs, the little turnipheads!"

Tansy smiled fondly up at the two Dibbuns. "Oh, leave them, they can't get into much mischief doing that."

Craklyn pointed lower down the same branch. "But

see, Brother Sedum and Sister Egram are trying to saw through the bottom of the same branch. Look out—there it goes!"

The branch snapped with a sharp crack, Sedum and Egram fell backward with a joint yell, and the two Dibbuns squeaked in dismay as they plummeted earthward.

"Haharr gotcha!"

Lithe and brawny, Skipper of Otters dropped his ax and leapt beneath the branch to catch Sloey and Gubbio in his strong paws. Giggling helplessly, the three of them fell into the mass of leafy foliage, the Dibbuns crowing aloud with excitement, "Again! Do it again! More, more!"

Skipper sat up rubbing his head. "Ouch! You liddle coves—watch where yore a wavin' those 'ammers!"

Viola was over like a shot. "I knew it, some creature was bound to get hurt! Come away from there, you naughty babes! And you, call yourself a Skipper of Otters, have you no sense at all? Stop scrabbling about in those leaves with the Dibbuns this instant!"

She swept Sloey up in her paws, and the mousebabe, who was still waving her hammer, which was no more than a small nut mallet, bopped the good Sister an unlucky one between the ears. Viola turned her eyes upward, gave a faint whoop, and sat down hard.

Skipper shook with laughter as he gave orders to some other Dibbuns who had just arrived on the scene. "Ahoy, mates, git bandages an' ointment, fix pore Sister Viola up, she's sore wounded!"

Full of mischief, the Abbeybabes needed no second bidding.

Viola floundered about helplessly on the grass as they poured ointment on her head and dashed 'round and 'round her until she was swathed in bandages. Tansy and Craklyn had to turn away, they were chuckling so hard. Then Tansy caught sight of the cook.

"Mother Buscol, perhaps you and Gurrbowl would

like to set up the evening meal out here? There's lots of deadwood from the tree for a fire. Couldn't we have a chestnut roast and baked parsnips? Craklyn and I will help—I know, we'll make honey and maple apples. Is there any strawberry fizz in the cellars? That would be lovely for our workers!"

Grumbling aloud, the fat old squirrel trundled off to the kitchens for her ingredients. "Lackaday, an' what's wrong with a kitchen oven, may I arsk? Indeed to goodness, look you, a full picnic meal for who knows 'ow many creatures, an' everywhere 'tis nought but bushes an' bangin'. Come on, Gurrbowl, we'll 'ave to see what can be done!"

Goodwife Gurrbowl the Cellar Keeper shook her head severely at Sister Viola as she passed. "Moi dearie me, b'aint you'm gotten no sense, Viola, a playin' wi' ee Dibbuns an' gittin' eeself all messed oop loik that!"

Skipper and his crew, with Arven and the more able-bodied Redwallers, set to with a will, chopping, sawing, and hauling heavy branches. The work went well. They struck up a song as they toiled:

"Oh, seed is in the ground an' up comes a shoot,
Seed is in the soil an' down goes a root,
Here comes a leaf an' there goes a twig,
Seasons turn as the tree grows big!

Saplin' bends with the breeze at dawn,
Wearin' a coat of bark t'keep warm,
Growin' lots o' green leaves 'stead o' fur,
Birds go a nestin' in its hair.

Some gets flow'rs as they spread root,
Some gets berries, some gets fruit,
Trees grow t'gether in a glade,
All through summer that's nice shade.

Lots o' trees do make a wood,
Just the way that good trees should,
Ole dead trees when they expire
Keep my paws warm by the fire!"

They had scarcely finished the song when a voice rapped sternly from the deepest section of the foliage, "That's still no reason to cut down a tree, is it?"

Skipper looked at Arven strangely. "Did you say somethin', mate?"

"No, I thought it was you for a moment, Skip."

The voice sounded out again, quite irritable this time. "Honestly, where there's no feeling there's no sense. I'm trapped in here, you great pair of buffoons. In here!"

Skipper thrust himself into the foliage. "Sounds like an owlbird t'me!"

A deep sigh escaped from the leafy depths. " 'Owlbird?' Did I call you an otterdog? No! Then pray have the goodness to at least get the name of my species right. Owl, say it!"

Skipper shrugged his brawny shoulders. "Owl!"

"Thank you!" the voice continued. "Now are you going to stand about jawing all day or do you think you and your friends can muster up the decency to get me out of here?"

Right at the heart of the foliage was a thick dead limb with a deep weather-spread crack in it, and wedged there was a female of the type known as Little Owls. She had wide gray eyebrows and huge yellow eyes, which were fixed in a permanent frown.

Arven climbed over a limb and nodded amiably at her. "Good day to ye, marm. You'll excuse my sayin', but we never cut down your tree, the storm knocked it down."

The owl moved her head from side to side huffily. "So you say. All I know is that I'm not three days in this nest, hardly settled down, Taunoc gone hunting for beetles, when the whole world collapses in on me. Knocked

110

unconscious, completely out! I've only just regained my senses, due to your infernal banging and knocking, of course!"

Skipper put down his ax guiltily. "An' are ye all right, marm?"

The owl was a very small one, but she puffed herself up until she filled the entire crack, glaring at the otter. "All right? Do I look all right? Clutching on here, half upside down, doing my level best to stop three eggs spilling out and breaking all over the ground. Oh, yes, apart from that and being knocked out, I suppose I'm all right!"

Tansy and Craklyn pushed into the foliage, all concern for the owl's predicament.

"Oh, you poor bird! Three eggs and your home's destroyed!"

"Viola, come quick! Arven, Skipper, hold this branch steady. Stay still, my dear, we'll have you and your eggs out of there safely in no time at all!"

The Redwallers flocked in to help; carefully they extricated the Little Owl from the crack. The nest, with its three eggs intact, was lifted out as gently as possible. Then, chopping away twigs and foliage, they led the bird out into the open.

Tansy found out that the owl's name was Orocca. They brought her to the fire, placing the nest on a pile of blankets. Orocca was small but looked formidably strong and fierce. She ruffled her feathers and sat on her nest, staring aggressively at everybeast, the pupils of her immense golden eyes dilating and contracting in the firelight.

Mother Buscol gave her warm candied chestnuts, hazelnuts crystallized in honey, and some strawberry fizz. "Indeed to goodness, bird, you need sweet food to get over your shock. Eat up now, look you, there's plenty more."

As Orocca ate voraciously, Viola approached her with herbs and medicines. The owl shot her a glare that sent her scuttling. Timidly she stood behind Skipper and called to Orocca, "When will your egg babies be born?"

The answer was terse and irate. "When they're ready, and not a moment before, silly!"

Foremole Diggum and his team arrived at the fire. Diggum clacked his digging claws together in delight. "Hoo arr, lookee, Drubb, 'unny apples an' chesknutters by ee foire! Gurr, us'n's be fair famishered. 'Scuse oi, marm, 'opes you'm doant objeck to molers settin' 'longside ee?"

To everybeast's surprise, Orocca actually smiled at Diggum. "Please be seated, sir, I enjoy the company of moles immensely. I find them wise and sensible creatures, not given to ceaseless chatter and inane questions."

Foremole and his crew sat, heaping their platters with food.

Arven scratched his head in bewilderment. "Orocca doesn't seem too fond of us, yet she took to you straight away. What's your secret, Diggum?"

Foremole's homely face crinkled into a knowing grin. "Hurr, oi 'spect 'tis our 'andsome lukks, zurr!"

Striving to keep a straight face, Arven sat next to Diggum. "Oh, I see. But pray tell me, sir, apart from admiring yourself in a mirror, what else have you been up to this afternoon?"

The mole poured himself a beaker of strawberry fizz. "Us'n's been a diggen, oi'll tell ee wot oi found, zurr!"

Later on Arven sought out Tansy, who was in the dormitory with Mother Buscol, bedding down Dibbuns for the night. Peeping 'round the door, Arven watched in silence, recalling fondly his own Dibbun times. The Abbeybabes lay in their small beds, repeating after Abbess Tansy an ancient poem. Arven had learned it from Auma, an old badgermother, long ago.

He listened, mentally saying the lines along with the little ones.

"Night comes soft, 'tis daylight's end,
Sleep creeping gently o'er all,
Bees go to hive, birds fly to nest,
Whilst pale moon shadows fall.

Silent earth lies cloaked in slumber,
Stars standing guard in the skies,
'Til dawn steals up to banish darkness,
I must close my weary eyes.

Safe dreams, peace unto you, my friend,
Night comes soft, 'tis daylight's end."

Mother Buscol stayed with the yawning Dibbuns while Tansy drifted quietly outside to see what her friend wanted. Together they descended the stairs and strolled out into the beautiful spring night, and Arven related what Diggum Foremole had told him.

"Diggum and his team located the exact spot where the trouble with the south wall began. Today while we were dealing with the tree, he and his moles began excavating. I've arranged with him to show us what he found."

Holding lighted lanterns, Diggum and his stout crew awaited them at the edge of a sloping shaft they had dug into the ground near the wallbase.

Tugging his snout courteously to Tansy, the mole Chieftain greeted her. "Gudd eventoid to ee, marm, thurr be summat yurr oi wanten ee t'cast thy eye ower. Oi'll go afront of ee an' moi moles'll foller, keepen furm 'old o' yon rope."

Sensibly the moles had pegged ropes either side of the shaft walls, forming a strong banister. Gingerly, everyone followed Diggum into the shaft. The earth was moist and slippery underpaw.

Following Diggum's advice, Tansy held tightly to the ropes. By lantern light she saw that the shaft leveled out into a small tunnel, where she was forced to crouch, her gown sweeping its sides.

"Burr, oi'm sorry you'm 'abit be gettin' amuckied oop," Foremole murmured apologetically. " 'Tis only a place fit furr molefolk, marm."

The Abbess patted the broad back in front of her. "Oh, 'tis nothing a washday won't solve, friend. Lead on, I'm dying of curiosity to see what you've discovered."

When she did see it, Tansy was almost lost for words. She stood awestruck at what the flickering lantern light revealed.

"Great seasons o' sun an' showers, *what is it?*"

A Gathering of Warriors

BOOK TWO

A Gathering of Warriors

20

Between them both, Hogspit and Lousewort knew virtually nothing about scouting ahead for the Rapscallion army. Their promotion to the rank of Rapscour was greeted with scorn by the twoscore vermin trackers each had under his command. All day they had trudged steadily north, with the eighty vermin ignoring their commands pointedly. They went their own way, foraging and fooling about, pleasing themselves entirely.

Lousewort was completely bullied and cowed by Hogspit; the big nasty weasel took every available chance to beat or belittle his fellow officer. Lousewort bumbled along in Hogspit's wake like some type of menial lackey.

It was about early noon when they breasted a long rolling hill with a broad stream flowing through the fields below it. Hogspit immediately gave his verdict on the area.

"It'll do fer a camp tonight, I s'pose, good runnin' water an' plenty o' space. Wot more could Damug ask fer 'is army?"

Lousewort gave his opinion, for what it was worth. "Er, er, not much shelter, though. Wot iffen it rains?"

Hogspit fetched him a clip 'round the ear. "Iffen it rains then they'll just 'ave ter get wet, blobberbrain. That's

117

unless you've got ideas of buildin' lots o' nice liddle wooden 'uts t'keep 'em dry."

Lousewort thought about this for a moment. "Er, er, but there ain't no wood around, mate, an' even if there was it'd take too lon—Yowch!" He jumped as the weasel booted him hard on the behind.

"If brains wuz bread you'd a starved to death afore you was born!"

The conversation was ended when a weasel came panting up the hillside and pointed down to where the stream curved 'round the far side of the tor. Throwing a smart salute, he rattled out breathlessly to the two officers, "Boatloads o' scruffy-lookin' mice down that way, sirs!"

Hogspit swelled his chest officiously, sneering at the messenger. "Ho, 'tis 'sirs' now, is it? A lick o' trouble, a coupla foebeasts, an' all of a sudden we're officers agin, eh! Right then, 'ow many o' these scruffy-lookin' mouses is there?"

Lousewort tried hard to look like a commander of twoscore as he parroted Hogspit's last words. "Er, er, aye, 'ow many is there?"

The big weasel silenced him with an ill-tempered stare before turning back to the tracker. "Never mind goin' back t'count 'em. Get the others t'gether quick an' meet us down there. Cummon, dunderpaws, let's take a look!"

Lying in a hollow not far from the stream bank, both Rapscours saw the vessels come 'round the bend. There were six long logboats, each carved from the trunk of a large tree, and seated two abreast at the oars were small creatures, their fur wiry and sticking out at odd angles. Each of them wore a brightly colored cloth headband and a kilt, held up by a broad belt, through which was thrust a little rapier. Others of them sat at prow and stern atop supply sacks, and all of them seemed extremely short-tempered, for they argued and jabbered ceaselessly with one another. Only an older creature, slightly bigger than the rest, remained aloof, standing on the prow of the lead boat surveying the river ahead. In all, there were about seventy of them crewing the long logboats.

Hogspit rubbed his paws together. Grinning wickedly, he glanced back to see the tracker leading thirty vermin into the defile. The weasel sniggered with delight. Thirty Rapscallions would be more than enough to take care of a gang of scruffy-looking mice. He stuck a grimy claw under Lousewort's nose, issuing orders to him.

"Huh, this'll be simple as shellin' peas. You stay 'ere with this lot, I'll go out there an' scare the livin' daylights out of those mouses. Be ready t'come runnin' when I shouts yer!"

Swaggering out onto the stream bank, Hogspit called out to the oldish creature in the prow of the first craft as it drew level, "Hoi, graybeard! Git them boats pulled in 'ere. I wants ter see wot you've got aboard—an' move lively if y'know wot's good for yer!"

For a small beast, the leader had extremely dangerous eyes. He held up a paw and the crews ceased rowing. Steering the prow 'round with a long pole, he waited until his craft was close enough, then vaulted to dry land on the pole.

One paw on his rapier, the other tucked into his belt, he looked the weasel up and down. His voice, when he spoke, was deep and gruff.

"Lissen, swampguts, I know wot's good fer me, an' what's aboard these boats is none o' yore business—so back off!"

Hogspit was amazed at the small beast's insolence. Swelling out his chest, he laid paw to his cutlass handle. "Do you know who yer talkin' to? I'm Rapscour Hogspit of Damug Warfang's mighty Rapscallion army!"

The creature drew his small rapier coolly, quite unimpressed. "Then clean the mud out yore ears an' lissen t'me, Spit'og, or whatever name y'call yoreself. I wouldn't know Damug wotsisname or his army if they fell on me out of a tree! I'm Log-a-Log, Chieftain o' the

Guosim shrews. So pull steel if y'fancy dyin'!"

Hogspit whipped out his cutlass and charged with a roar.

In the hollow, Lousewort felt his belt tugged urgently by a rat, who squealed, "Is that it, do we charge too?"

Lousewort pulled free of the rat's tugging paw. "Er, er, no, I want t'see wot 'appens."

Log-a-Log faced the oncoming Rapscour until he was almost on top of him, then, stepping neatly aside, he tripped Hogspit, lashing his back smartly with the rapier blade as the big weasel went down.

The shrew circled him teasingly. "Up on yore paws, y'great pudden, or I'll finish ye where you lie!"

His face ugly with rage, Hogspit scrambled up and began taking huge swings at the shrew with his cutlass. Each time the blade came down it was either on the ground or thin air. The shrews in the boats sat impassively watching their leader making a fool of the bigger creature.

Turning aside the bludgeoning cutlass with a flick of his rapier, Log-a-Log mocked his opponent. "It must be a poor outlook fer this Damug cove if'n this is the way he teaches his officers t'handle a blade. Can't yer do any better, bucketbum?"

Slavering at the mouth and panting, Hogspit cleaved down, holding the cutlass with both paws. The blade tanged off a rock, sending a shock through him. He spat at his enemy, snarling, "I'll carve yer guts inter frogmeat an' dance on em!"

Log-a-Log wiped the weasel's spit from his headband, eyes flat with menace. "Nobeast ever spat on me an' lived. I could've slain ye a dozen times. Here! There! Left! Right! Up'n'down!" Whirling about he pricked Hogspit each time he spoke, showing him the truth of the statement. Halting, the shrew curled his lip scornfully at the Rapscour and turned his back on him, saying, "Gerrout o' my sight, vermin, you've done yoreself no honor here today!"

Swinging the cutlass high, Hogspit charged at the shrew's unprotected back. At the last possible second Log-a-Log turned and ran him through, gritting up into the coward's shocked face, "No skill, no sense, and no honor, now y've got no life!"

21

When the drumbeats ceased that evening, Damug Warfang was standing on the stream bank with the entire Rapscallion horde spread wide around the valley behind him. He sat down on the head of a drum the rat Gribble had provided. Facing him in three ranks stood the remains of the trackers, with Lousewort at the front.

The Firstblade shook his head in disbelief at the tale he had heard. "Three hundred shrews in twenty big boats, are you sure?"

Lousewort nodded vigorously—his life depended on it. The others nodded too, backing him up.

"Let me get this clear," Damug continued, "they ambushed you, slew thirty of my trackers and a Rapscour, then got clean away?"

The nodding continued dumbly.

"And not one, not a single one, was slain or taken prisoner?"

More nods. The Greatrat closed his eyes and massaged their corners slowly. He was tired. Four times he had been over the same ground with them, and still they stuck firmly to their story. He glanced at the carcasses of the thirty-one vermin lying half in, half out of the stream shallows, creatures he could ill afford to lose, slow and stupid as they had been.

Turning his gaze back to Lousewort and the living, he sighed wearily. "Three hundred shrews, twenty big boats, eh? Well take my word, I'll find the truth of all this sooner or later, and when I do, if the answer is what I think, there'll be some here begging me for a swift death before I'm finished with them. Understood?"

The nodders' necks were sore, but still they bobbed up and down wordlessly.

Damug indicated the slain. "You will dig a pit twelve times as deep as the length of my sword, and when you have buried these bodies you will stand in the water all night up to your necks. Nor will you eat or drink again until I give the order. Gribble, detail two officers to stand watch on them."

Dying campfires burned small red blossoms into the night all around the valley, throwing slivers of scarlet across the swift-flowing stream. Stars pierced moonless skies, and a wispy breeze played about the sleeping Rapscallion camp.

Vendace gritted his teeth as the file scraped his neck. "Keep yer 'ead still," Borumm hissed at him impatiently as he worked on the fetters binding them together. "It won't take long now!"

Lugworm was already free—it was he who had managed to steal the file. Fearfully, the stoat whispered to the fox and the weasel, "You'll 'ave ter work faster, we ain't got all night!"

Borumm stifled the rattle of the neckband with both paws. The chains chinked softly as they fell from Vendace's body. The fox massaged his neck, eyes glittering furtively in the darkness. "Shut yer snivelin' face, stoat. C'mon, let's get movin'. We need t'be across that stream an' long gone by dawn."

Clinging to the rocks in midstream, Lousewort and forty-odd trackers struggled to keep their chins up above water, sobbing and cursing as the cold numbed their limbs and the icy flow threatened to sweep them away. Already some of their number, the weaker ones, had been drowned by others trampling them under in their efforts to stay alive.

Two Rapmark Captains sat hunched in sleep over a small fire on the bank. A ferret ground his chattering teeth as he glared in their direction. "Look at 'em, snoozin' all nice'n'warm there, while we're freezin' an' drownin' out 'ere. It ain't right, I tell yer!"

Lousewort hugged a weed-covered nub of rock, coughing water from both nostrils miserably. "Er, er, mebbe they'll let us come ashore when it's light."

Snorting mirthlessly, a sodden rat pulled himself higher to speak. "Who are you tryna fool, mate? 'Ow many of us d'yer think'll be *left* by tomorrer? Whether 'e knew it or not, Damug sentenced us to die by pullin' this liddle trick!"

The two sleeping Rapmark Captains were fated never to see dawn. They kicked briefly when the chains of Borumm and Vendace tightened about their necks. As the officers slumped lifeless, the escapers relieved them of their cloaks and weapons. Then, grabbing a coil of rope, Borumm plunged into the stream and waded out to where the wretched vermin clutched feebly at the rocks.

Securing the rope to a jagged rut, Borumm held it tight, and hissed, "You know me'n' Vendace—we're your ole Rapscours. We're gettin' out of 'ere, and anybeast feels like quittin' Damug an' his army can come along. That one ain't the Firstblade his father was!"

A ferret took hold of the rope as Vendace and Lugworm waded up. "I'm wid yer, mate! An' so would you lot be if y've got any sense. Warfang treats 'is own army worse'n 'is enemies. Lead on, Borumm!"

Vendace silenced the general murmur of approval. "Keep the noise down there. I'll make it to the other bank wid this rope an' lash it tight 'round a rock. Y'can grab on to it an' make yore way over, but be quick, there's no time ter lose!"

Pulling themselves paw over paw along the taut line, the escapers made their way to the opposite side of the stream. Borumm perched on a rock with the last few, but when it was Lugworm's turn to take the rope, Borumm pushed him aside.

"Where d'yer think yore off to, slimeface?" he snarled.

The stoat's voice was shrill with surprise. "It was all part o' the plan, we escape together, mate!"

There was nowhere to run. Borumm grinned wolfishly at him. "I ain't yore mate, an' I just changed the plan. We don't take no backstabbers an' traitors wid us. You stay 'ere!"

Borumm swung the bunched chains savagely, and Lugworm fell lifeless into the stream before he even had a chance to protest about the new arrangements. Lousewort was shocked by the weasel's action. "Ooh! Wot didyer do that for? The pore beast wasn't doin' you no 'arm, mate!"

Borumm was not prepared to argue. There was only himself and Lousewort left on the rock. He swung the chains once more, laying Lousewort senseless on the damp stones. Swinging off on to the rope, the weasel hauled himself along, muttering, "Sorry about that, mate, but if'n you ain't for us yore agin us!"

22

Bubbling and hissing furiously, the tank in Sala-mandastron's forge room received a red-hot chunk of metal. Lady Cregga Rose Eyes held the piece there until she was sure it was sufficiently cooled. Then, slowly, she withdrew the wet gray steel. It was an axpike head, the top a straight-tipped, double-bladed spearpoint. Below that was a single battle-ax blade, thick at the stub, sweeping out smoothly to a broad flat edge, the other side of which was balanced by a down-curving pike hook.

The Badger Warrior turned it this way and that, letting it rise and fall as she tested the heft of her new weapon. Satisfied that everything about the lethal object suited her, Cregga began reheating it in the fires of her forge. The next job was to put edges to the spear, ax, and hook blades—not sharpened edges, but beaten ones that would never need to be honed on any stone.

She straightened up as the long-awaited knock sounded upon the door, followed by Deodar's voice.

"Tenth Spring Runner reportin', marm, relieved on the western tide line this afternoon!"

The rose-eyed badger had waited two days to hear a Runner's voice. She recognized it as female and roared out a gruff reply, "Well, don't hang about out there,

126

missie. Come in, come in!"

The young haremaid entered boldly, slamming the door behind her and throwing a very elegant salute. "Patrolled north by west, marm, returnin' along the coast. No signs of vermin or foebeast activity; still no sign or news of Major Perigord's patrol whatsoever. Spotted a few shore toads but they kept their distance. Nothin' else to report, marm!"

Cregga put aside her work, great striped head nodding resolutely. "Well done, Runner, that's all I needed to know. Stand easy."

Deodar took up the at-ease position and waited. The Badger Lady picked up her red-hot axpike head with a pair of tongs. "What d'you think, missie? 'Tis to be my new weapon."

The hare gazed round-eyed at the fearsome object. "Perilous, marm, a real destroyer!"

Setting it to rest on the anvil, Cregga squinted at the Runner. "Answer me truly, young 'un, d'you think you're about ready to join the Long Patrol?"

Deodar sprang quivering to attention. "Oh, I say! Rather! I mean, yes, marm!"

A formidable paw patted Deodar's shoulder lightly. "Hmm, I think you are too. Do you own a weapon?"

"A weapon, 'fraid not, marm, outside o' sling or short dagger. Colonel Eyebright ain't fussy on Runners goin' heavy-armed."

Cregga's big paw waved at the weapons ranged in rows on the walls. "Right, then let's see you choose yourself something."

She checked Deodar's instinctive rush to the weaponry. "No hurry, miss, take care, what you decide upon may have to last you a lifetime. Go ahead now, but choose wisely."

The young hare wandered 'round the array, letting her paw run over hilts and handles as she spoke her mind aloud. "Let me see now, marm, nothin' too heavy for me,

I'll never be as big as Rockjaw Grang or some others. Somethin' simple to carry, quick to reach, and light to the paw. Aha! I think this'd jolly well fit the bill, a fencing saber!"

Cregga smiled approvingly. "I'd have picked that for you myself. Go on, take it down and try it, see how it feels!"

Reverently, Deodar took the saber from its peg and held it, feeling the fine balance of the long, slightly curving single-edged blade. It had a cord-whipped handle, with a basket hilt to protect the paw. So keen was its edge that it whistled menacingly when she swung it sideways.

Suddenly Lady Cregga was in front of her, brandishing a poker as if it were a sword. "On guard, miss, have at ye!"

Steel clanged upon steel as they fenced around the glowing forge, Cregga calling out encouragement to her pupil as she parried blows and thrusts with the poker.

"That's the way, miss! Step step, swing counter! Now step step step, thrust! Backstep sideswing! Keep that paw up! Remember, the blade is an extension of the paw, keep it flexible! And one and two and thrust and parry! Counter, step step, figure of eight at shoulder level! Footpaws never flat, up up!"

With a quick skirmishing movement the badger disarmed her pupil, sending the saber quivering point first into the door. "Enough! Enough! Where did you learn saber fighting, young 'un?"

Deodar looked disappointed that she had been disarmed. "From my uncle, Lieutenant Morio, but evidently I didn't learn too well, marm."

Cregga pulled the saber from the door, presenting it back to Deodar hilt first. "Nonsense! If you'd learned any better I'd have been slain. What d'you want to do, beat the Ruler of Salamandastron on your first practice?"

The young Runner took the saber back, smiling gratefully. "No, marm! Thank you for this saber—and the lesson too."

That same night the list of new recruits was posted at the entrance to the Dining Hall, and everyone clamored around it to see who had been promoted to the Long Patrol. Drill Sergeant Clubrush, who was responsible for day-to-day discipline among the younger set, sat near the doorway of the Officers' Mess with Colonel Eyebright. The hares were old friends, being of the same age and having served together many long seasons.

Eyebright tapped his pace stick gently against the table edge. "Stap me, but I wish Lady Cregga hadn't ordered me t'post that confounded list. Just look at 'em, burstin' their britches to be Patrollers, all afire with the stories they've heard, an' not a mother's babe o' them knows what they're really in for, wot?"

The Sergeant sipped his small beaker of mountain beer. "Aye, sir, 'taint the same as when we was young. You didn't get t'be a Patroller then 'til you 'ad t'duck yore 'ead to get through the doorway. I recall my ole pa sayin' you had t'be long enough t'be picked for Long Patrol. I'd 'ave gived those young 'uns another season yet, two mebbe, 'tis a shame really, sir."

The Colonel turned his eyes upward to the direction of the forge. "Mark m'words, Sarge, 'tis all Rose Eyes's doin'. I've never known or heard of a badger sufferin' from the Bloodwrath so badly. I've had it from her own blinkin' mouth that she's bound to march off from here with half the garrison strength to destroy Tunn an' his Rapscallions. Have y'ever heard the like? A Ruler of Salamandastron leavin' our mountain t'do battle goodness knows how far off. She'd have had us *all* go if I hadn't dug me paws in!"

Clubrush finished his drink and rose stiffly. "Beggin' y'pardon, sir, I'd best get 'em organized afore supper. Oh buttons'n'brass, willyer lookit, there's young Cheeva sobbin' 'er 'eart out 'cos she wasn't posted on the list."

Eyebright nodded sadly. "She was far too young, her pa an' I decided we'd leave her a while yet. Better Cheeva cryin' now than me an' her father weepin' when Cregga's bloodlust brings back sad results. You go about y'business now, Sarge, I'll see to her."

Drill Sergeant Clubrush marched smartly into the midst of the successful candidates, bellowing out orders.

"Keep y'fur on now, young sirs an' missies! Silence in the ranks there an' lissen up please! Right, anybeast whose name's bin posted up 'ere—in double file an' foller me. We're goin' up to Lady Cregga's forge room where I'll h'issue you wid weapons I thinks best suited to gentlebeasts. No foolin' about while yore up there ... Are you lissenin', Trowbaggs, I'll 'ave my beady eye on you, laddie buck! Keep silence in the ranks, show proper respect to the Badger marm, an' mind yore manners. Tenshun! By the right ... Wait for it, Trowbaggs ... By the right quick march!"

As they marched eagerly off, Colonel Eyebright went to sit next to the young hare Cheeva, who was sobbing uncontrollably in a corner. The kindly old officer passed her his own red-spotted kerchief.

"Now, now, missie, this won't do, you'll flood the place out. Come on now, tell me all about it, wot?"

Cheeva rocked back and forth, her face buried in the kerchief. "Waahahhh! M ... m ... my n ... n ... name wasn't p ... p ... posted on th' r ... r ... rotten ole li ... li ... list! Boohoohoo!"

Eyebright straightened his shoulders, adopting a stern tone. "Well I should hope not! It was the unanimous verdict of the officers who made out that list that you be kept back. D'you know why?"

" 'Co ... co ... cos I'm t ... too yu ... yu ... young! Waaahahaaarr!"

The Colonel's trim mustache bristled. "Balderdash, m'gel, who told y'that? The reason is that we decided you were real officer material, needed sorely on this mountain, doncha know! Suppose Searats or Corsairs launched an attack on us whilst that lot were off gallivantin'. Who

130

d'you suppose we'd be lookin' for to take up a trainee commandin' position, eh, tell me that? Long Patrol isn't the be all an' end all of young hares like y'self who want t'make somethin' of themselves. Ain't that right, young Deodar?"

Without Cheeva seeing him, the Colonel winked broadly at Deodar, seated nearby. She had had no need to go to the forge room for a weapon; she was polishing her saber blade with a rag. Deodar caught on to the officer's little ruse right away.

"Oh, right you are, sah, I'd have been rather chuffed if I was picked t'be a trainee officer at the garrison here."

Cheeva looked up, red-eyed and tear-stained. "Would you really?"

Deodar snorted as if the question was totally ridiculous. "Hah! Would I ever? How's about swappin' places—I'll stay here for officer trainin' an' you go bally well harin' off with that other cracked bunch?"

Colonel Eyebright shook his head sternly. "Sorry, miss, orders've been posted, you've got to go. Soon as I've got you lot out o' my whiskers I'm goin' to start Cheeva's officer trainin'. First task, nip off an' wash that face in cold water, miss. Can't have the troops seein' anybeast of officer material boohooin' all over the place, can we, wot?"

Cheeva gave back the kerchief and ran off half laughing and half weeping. " 'Course not, Colonel, sah, thank you very much!"

Eyebright wrung out the spotted kerchief, smiling at Deodar. "Good form, gel, thanks for your help. And don't polish that saber away now, will ye!"

After supper the new recruits laid their paws upon the table and began drumming loudly until the dining hall reverberated to the noise. This was the prelude to a bit of fun traditional to Long Patrol.

Colonel Eyebright played his part well. Striding from the Officers' Mess, he held up his pace stick for silence.

131

When it was quiet he began the ritual with a short rhyme.

"Who are these strange creatures, pray,
Say who are you all,
Stirring up a din an' clatter
In our dining hall?"

Young Furgale rose in answer in time-honored manner.

"We are no strange creatures, sah,
But perilous one an' all,
Tell Sergeant we're the Long Patrol,
We've come to pay a call!"

The Colonel bowed stiffly and marched back to the Mess, where he could be heard announcing to the waiting Clubrush:

"Wake up from your slumbers, Sergeant, dear,
I think your new recruits are here."

Wild cheering and unbridled laughter greeted the appearance of Clubrush. He dashed out of the Officers' Mess, roaring and glaring fiercely like the Drill Sergeant of every recruit's nightmares. On these occasions a Sergeant always wore certain things, and Clubrush had dressed accordingly. 'Round his waist he wore a belt with dried and faded dock leaves hanging from it—these were supposed to be the ears of recruits that he had collected. 'Round his footpaws he trailed soft white roots—recruits' guts. Over one shoulder was a banderole of cotton thistles representing tails. All over the Sergeant's uniform were pinned bits and pieces of herb and fauna, supposedly the gruesome bits he had collected from sloppy recruits.

Scowling savagely, he paced the tables, singing in a ter-rifyingly gruff voice as he went:

"You 'orrible lollopy sloppy lot,
You idle scruffy bunch!
I'll 'ave yore tails off like a shot
An' boil 'em for me lunch!

You lazy loafin' layabouts,
'Ere's wot I'll do fer starters
If you don't lissen when I shouts,
I'll 'ave yore guts fer garters!

O mamma's darlin's, don't you cry,
Yore dear ole Sergeant's 'ere,
Those foebeasts, why, they're just small fry,
'Tis *me* you'll learn to fear!

I'll 'ave yore ears'n'elbows,
You sweepin's o' the floors,
An' long before the dawn shows,
You'll 'ave marched ten leagues outdoors.

O dreadful 'alf-baked dozy crowd,
I'll stake me oath 'tis true,
Long Patrol Warriors, tall'n'proud,
Is wot I'll make of you!"

Sergeant Clubrush's fierce demeanor changed instantly as he patted backs and shook paws of the young hares crowding 'round him.

"Welcome to the Patrol, buckoes, you'll do us proud!"

Cregga Rose Eyes had a handle for her axpike—a thick pole, taller than herself. The wood was dark, hard, and sea-washed, like that of Russa's stick. Long summers gone, somebeast had found it among the flotsam of the tide line. Now the Badger Lady rediscovered it, lying with a pile of other timber at the back of her forge. She worked furiously, far into the night, shaping, binding,

133

fixing the awesome steel headpiece to its haft, speaking aloud her thoughts as she bored holes through wood and metal for three heavy copper rivets.

"Sleep well, Gormad Tunn, sleep on, Damug, Byral, and all your Rapscallion scum! I am coming, death is on the wind! On the day when you see my face, you and all of your evil followers will sleep the sleep from which there is no awakening!"

23

Tammo had been gone too long for Russa Nodrey's liking. She caught Perigord's glance as she took up her stick. "Nobeast takes this long t'gather a few pawfuls of 'cress, Major. Somethin's wrong—I'm goin' to take a look!"

Perigord buckled on his saber. "Tare, Turry, Rubbadub, guard the camp an' supplies, the rest o' you chaps, off y'hunkers an' come with us!"

Traveling swiftly and silently they spread out, covering trees, riverbank, and shallows carefully. It was not long before they picked up Tammo's trail. Captain Twayblade found the rock where she too had noted watercress growing underwater.

Pasque waved wordlessly from a short distance up the bank. Keeping voices to a barely audible murmur, they gathered 'round her. "A bundle o' watercress. He was here—see, 'tis tied up with his shoulder belt."

Midge Manycoats inspected the trunk of a nearby sycamore. "There's a knifepoint mark here. Looks like Tammo stuck his blade in this tree!"

A pebble struck Rockjaw Grang on the side of his neck. "Owch! 'Ey up, somebeast's chuckin' stones!"

Out of the darkness above, a volley of small stones peppered Perigord's troop, followed by rustling in the high foliage, sniggering laughs, and reedy voices calling, "Tammo! Tammo! Choohakka choohak! Where poor Tammo?"

Russa shouted aloud at Perigord, "Let's get out o' here!"

The Major shot her a puzzled look. "Wot, you mean retreat, run away?"

Shielding herself from the stones with an upraised paw, the squirrel winked several times at him. "Aye, let's run fer it afore we're battered t'death!"

Perigord suddenly caught on; he cut and ran into the shallows. "Retreat, troop, everybeast out o' here, quick as y'like. Retreat!"

The Long Patrol were not used to running from anything, but they obeyed the command. Pounding upstream through the shallows, they halted out of range of the rain of pebbles.

Then Twayblade turned on Perigord, her long rapier flicking angrily at the air. "Retreat from a few stones'n'pebbles, what are we, pray—a flight of startled swallows?"

Perigord laid the blame firmly at Russa's paws. "Ask her!"

The squirrel looked from one to the other. "Well, if y'stop lookin' all noble an' outraged for a tick I'll tell ye. Really 'twas my fault. I've traveled this riverbank afore, an' if'n I'd been thinkin' clear I'd have stopped you pitchin' camp where the Painted Ones roam."

Twayblade ceased twitching her rapier. "Painted Ones?"

Russa's bushy tail stood up angrily. "Aye, Painted Ones. Tribes o' little tree rats is all they are, though they paints their fur black'n'green an' lives in the boughs an' leaves 'igh up. Huh! Some o' the villains even attaches bushtails to themselves an' masquerades as squirrels, the liddle blackguards, not fit t'lick a decent squirrel's paws! But they're savage an' dangerous, almost invisible when they're among the treetops. Young Tammo's in a bad fix if y'ask me!"

The saturnine Lieutenant Morio nodded his agreement. "But no doubt you've got a plan, marm?"

Russa had. She explained her strategy then slid off among the trees, leaving the hares to carry out their part of the scheme.

Sheathing his blade, Perigord began gathering flat heavy pebbles. "Slings out, chaps, load up an' give 'em stones for supper!"

Meanwhile, Tammo lay bound and gagged. The leader of the Painted Ones was digging teasingly at him with the point of his captured dirk, giggling wickedly each time his prisoner flinched.

"Ch'hakka hak! 'Ear you friends, alla gone now, soon dissa one cutcha up wirra you own knife. Den we eatcha! Hakkachook!"

Tammo had heard Russa and the hares and felt a mixture of anger and sadness when Perigord shouted retreat and they ran off. Now he felt alone and deserted, certain too that something horrible was about to be inflicted upon him by the sadistic little tree creatures, who seemed very confident and contemptuous of landbeasts.

Then Tammo's heart leapt as he heard the night air ring with a familiar war cry:

"Eulalia! 'Tis death on the wind! Eulalia! *Charge!*"

Whacking, cracking, whizzing all around him, a veritable load of slingstones tore upward into the foliage. One rock big as a miniature boulder whipped by him, snapping off branches in its path. Good old Rockjaw Grang!

Turning his head to one side, Tammo peered into the gloom and saw small black and green figures retaliating, loosing pebbles from their own slings at the bold enemy below.

Russa had reached the far side of the trees. She skipped nimbly up into a stately elm and turned toward the distant din of battle. Thrusting the hardwood stick into her mouth she bit down on it and took off like a fish skimming through water, building up her speed as she raced through the treetops. Bright eyes cut through the darkness as she traveled even faster, the limbs and leaves passing in a blur, knowing that swiftness was the key to her mission. Sighting the back of the first Painted One, Russa grabbed her stick in one paw, still hurtling through the top terraces of foliage at a breakneck pace. She cracked the hardwood stick down between the rat's ears, then, changing her angle at the same time and shooting in a downward curve, she battered mercilessly at anybeast in her path.

The hardwood stick was like a living thing in her paws, whacking heads and paws and cracking limbs. Overhead Russa spotted a glint of steel as a stream of orders was shouted down through the treetops. "Chakkachook! Killa! Killa!" Swooping upward, she disposed of two more rats with a quick side-to-side jab to their faces. Bulling into the leader of the Painted Ones, she laid him senseless with a single rap to his skull.

Russa grabbed the dirk and slashed through Tammo's bonds. "Quick, get behind me an' lock y'paws 'round my waist!"

With a swift kick she sent the Painted Ones' leader from the bough they were standing on. As soon as he started to fall, Russa leapt after him, with Tammo holding grimly on to her and shouting, "We're comin' dooooooooown!"

Leaves, twigs, branches, limbs tore madly by in a rushing kaleidoscope of brown, black, and green. Tammo's heart seemed to fly up into his mouth as all three plummeted earthward, Russa's footpaws practically resting on the back of the rat as his body smashed a path down to the ground for them. They landed with a thrashing crashing sound, flattening an osier bush as the three bodies hit it.

Major Perigord whirled a slingstone upward, remarking as he let the pebble fly, "Just dropped in to join the jolly old scrap, wot? Bravo!"

Letting go of Russa, Tammo flopped awkwardly onto the ground. Apart from various scratches he was surprised to find himself unharmed. Russa yanked the battered and unconscious tree rat leader upright and pushed him into Rockjaw's open paws.

"Make light, get me a lantern, somebeast, 'urry!" she cried.

Tinder and flint hastily fired a lantern Riffle had brought. Bidding Riffle hold the light close to their captive, Russa grabbed the leader by one ear, hauling his head upright. Then she pressed the dirkpoint under his chin and called upward, imitating the tree rats' speech, "Chakkachook! Dis beast a dead'n, we cuttim 'ead off, you chukka more rocks. Dissa beast tellya true, chahakachah!"

The slingstones stopped and a mass wail went up from the foliage.

"Yaaahaaaagg! Norra kill Shavvakamalla! Yaaahaaaagg!"

Rockjaw Grang slung the senseless leader over his shoulder. "Shavvakawot? Sithee, 'tis a big name for a lickle rat!"

Sergeant Torgoch smiled at his friend's broad accent. "Take 'im back t'camp. We'll get a good night's sleep with their Chief as 'ostage, wot d'ye say, sah?"

Drawing his saber, Perigord began backing his troop out of the area. "Capital idea! But we'd best keep up the threats, just t'make sure they know we mean business. I say, are you hurt, old lad?"

Tammo was limping on his right footpaw. "Little sprain, sah, I'll be right as rain in a bit."

The hares backed off, shouting horrible threats into the trees. "I say, you rips up there, leave us alone or we'll scoff your jolly old leader. I'm quite serious, y'know.

Chop chop, yum yum, eatim alla up, as you blighters say, savvy?"

"Yaaaaahaaaag! No eata Shavvakamalla! Yaaahaaa-haaagghh!"

"Hah! Y'don't like that, do you? Well keep your bally distance or it's fricassee of tree rat for brekkers!"

"Aye, an' we'll use the leftovers t'make tree rat turnover fer lunch, it'll go nice with a bit o' salad!"

"Actually I'd rather fancy a slice of tree rat tart. D'you think there'd be enough of him left t'make one, eh, Rockjaw?"

"By 'eck, goo an' get thy own tree rat, Cap'n. I'm doin' all the carryin', so this 'un's mine. Bah goom, 'e'll make a grand tree rat 'otpot with a crust o'er 'is 'ead!"

"Yaaaahaggaaaah! Nono tree rats 'otpot, yerra no eatim!"

Major Perigord called a halt to the teasing. "Quite enough now, pack it in, chaps—those rotters've got the message, I think. I say, Rockjaw, I hope you were jokin' about tree rat hotpot. We're not really goin' to eat the blighter, y'know."

Rockjaw Grang plodded along with his burden, muttering a single word:

"Spoilsport!"

24

The remainder of the night passed uneventfully, though Perigord's troop knew they were being watched from the treetops by the Painted Ones. Pairing off, the hares took turns to guard the camp and keep an eye on the still-unconscious prisoner.

Tammo and Pasque were on second watch. They sat together, keeping the fire fed with twigs and dried moss.

Tammo eyed the captive's slumped figure uneasily. "I say, d'you think the rascal will come 'round before mornin'? He looks pretty much of a heap, maybe the fall finished him off?"

Pasque felt the pulse on the rat's neck and checked his breathing by holding a thin blade of grass close to his mouth and nostrils. "Not t'worry, he'll live, though whether or not he'll ever be the same after you an' Russa landin' atop of him remains t'be seen. Now—I'd best take a look at that footpaw you've been hobblin' about on."

Tammo dismissed the idea airily. "Oh, that? Hah! 'Twas nothin' really, I'm fine, thanks!"

Pasque Valerian began pulling herbs and dressing from her bag. "Sorry, but I've got to fix it up, Major's orders. If you have to travel on that paw all day tomorrow it'd become worse an' you'd slow us all up. So hold still."

Pasque damped warm water on dock leaves and crushed gentian stems, binding the poultice to Tammo's right footpaw with a thin brown cloth strip. When she was done, Tammo was pleased with the result. The bandage was firm but not tight, and he could use the footpaw quite freely without twingeing pains.

"Golly, that feels like a new paw now. My thanks to you, marm!"

Pasque fluttered her long lashes comically. "Why, thank ye, young sir, though if you had any of your mother's pancakes left I'd charge you two of 'em for my services!"

The leader of the Painted Ones stirred. "Whuuchakka huunhh! Whuuurrg! Shavvakamalla hurtened much lotsa!"

Pasque reopened her medicine bag, showing open disdain for the creature as she treated him. "Hmph! Hurtened much lotsa, is it? Y'wicked little runt, I'd have hurted you much lotsa more if I could've got a clear shot at you. Here, sit up'n'drink this!"

Averting his head, the rat tried to push away Pasque's medicine. Tammo came to her aid. Grabbing the protesting vermin's jaws he forced them open, pushing the rat's head back.

"Carry on, chum, pour it down the filthy ol' throat, an' I hope it tastes jolly awful. Give the bounder a bigger dose if he tries spittin' it out!"

Between them they fixed up the rat's injuries. Tammo, working under Pasque's directions, proved capable with bandage and splint, though whenever his friend was not watching, he would give the bindings an extra sharp tug, causing the rat to groan. Pasque took the groans as a sign that more medicine was needed, and she dosed him well.

"Oh, do stop moanin' an' whinin', you cowardly little bully. Thank the fates you're still alive an' bein' treated by civilized hares!"

Morning dawned warm, with the promise of a hot sunny day. Steam rose in drifting tendrils from the mossy riverbank as Corporal Rubbadub marched about, sounding reveille.

"Rubbadubdub, dubbadubbity dub, baboom baboom baboom!"

The Painted Ones' leader clapped both bandaged paws to his aching head and glared pleadingly at Rubbadub, who merely smiled and leaned close to the rat's ear, to give him the full benefit of his skills.

"Boompity boompity boom!"

Major Perigord stretched languidly, issuing morning orders as he did. "Rise'n'shine, troop. 'Fraid we can't take the chance of breakin' our fast hereabouts, what with the flippin' forces o' darkness up there in the arboreal verdance, waitin' to take a crack at us an' rescue ol' Shavvaka wotsisface. We'll cross the river lower down an' don the nosebag when we're well away from here. Those painted chaps can have their boss wallah back once we've crossed the river. Break camp, Sergeant."

Torgoch, looking fresh as a daisy, saluted stiffly. "Right y'are, sah! Midge, Riffle, move y'selves. Tare'n'Turry, make sure that fire's well doused before y'leave. Rockjaw, sling that h'injured vermin over y'shoulder. Officers lead off, other ranks bringin' up the rear!"

Rockjaw threw the rat over one shoulder, chatting to Lieutenant Morio as he did.

"Wot does the Major mean by 'arboreal verdance,' sah?"

"Hmm, arboreal verdance, lemme see, I rather think it means treetops, leafy green ones."

"Oh! Then why didn't 'e say treetops?"

"Why should he when he knows how t'say words like arboreal verdance?"

Rockjaw cuffed the moaning rat lightly. "Hush thy noise, or I'll give thee summat to moan about an y'won't see your arboreal verdance again!"

They crossed the river at the ford, which was littered

143

with huge rocks, providing good stepping-stones. Behind them the foliage rustled and trembled as the Painted Ones followed, anxious as to the fate of their Chieftain. Perigord soon dispelled their fears by frog-hopping the hobbled rat back to the last stepping-stone, where he left him to be rescued by his own kind. But not without a severe warning.

Fearlessly the Major drew his saber and pointed it at the swaying tree cover. "Listen up now, every slackjawed one o' ye! My name is Major Perigord Habile Sinistra, but don't for a moment think that 'cos I'm left-pawed I can't use this blade! If y'don't improve your ways I'll return here, me an' my warriors, an' we'll chop y'all up an' eatcha, got that! We didn't eat your leader simply because he's a coward an' a bully an' that'd make him taste bad. If I were you chaps I'd set about findin' a new commander today! Now if you've understood all that, an' you prob-ably haven't if you're as dense as ol' Shavvachops here, then take heed because I'm perilous an' don't make idle threats. I bid ye good morn!"

Throwing up an elegant front salute with his saber, Perigord wheeled on one paw and marched back to his patrol.

Torgoch nodded admiringly. "Does yore 'eart good t'see a h'officer with steel in 'is backbone layin' down the law to vermin, don't it, Rock!"

The giant hare dusted off his shoulder as if he had been carrying some unspeakable bundle of garbage there. "Aye, by 'ecky thump! But if'n I'd a been him I'd 'ave told 'em I'd chop off their arboreal verdancy. Sithee, that'd make yon vermin sit up straight!"

Breakfast time slipped by unnoticed. Having picked up the vermin trail, the patrol marched swiftly onward over the grasslands in the fine spring morning. Between them, the twins Tare and Turry struck up a lively marching chant.

"As I marched out one sunny day,
O lairo lairo lay!
I met a hare upon the way,
O lairo lairo laydee!
With ears like silk, and eyes so brown,
And fur as soft as thistledown,
She smiled at me an' that was that,
My poor young heart went pitter pat!

O pitter pat an' eyes of brown,
She looked me up an' looked me down,
I ask you now, what could I do,
I said, 'Please, may I walk with you?'
We walked together all that day,
O lairo lairo lay!
As laughingly I heard her say,
O lairo lairo laydee!

'Pray tell to me, O brave young sir,
Are you a wild an' perilous hare
Who thinks of nought from morn 'til night
But march an' sing an' charge an' fight?'
O march an' sing, O perilous hare,
So I said to this creature fair,
'To march an' fight is my intent,
The Long Patrol's my regiment!'

And then upon that sunny day,
O lairo lairo lay!
She turned from me an' skipped away,
O lairo lairo laydee!
She said, 'I fear that we must part,
Sir, I would not give you my heart,
That Long Patrol, alas alack,
Those hares march off an' ne'er come back!'

O ne'er come back an' Long Patrol,

145

While rivers flow an' hills do roll,
I'll march along my merry way,
An' look for pretty hares each day!"

Two hours into noon, woodlands were sighted. However, this was no copse but vast expanses of mighty trees.

Russa picked up the pace, smiling fondly. "Yonder lies Mossflower, an' the Abbey of Redwall within a few days. What d'yer think o' that, young Tamm?"

Before Tammo could answer, Perigord interrupted sharply: "Only a few days to the Abbey, you say? By the left! We'd best put on a stride an' catch up with those vermin!"

Doubling the pace to a swift lope, they headed toward the shady green vastness of the sprawling woodlands. The first thing Tammo noticed on entering Mossflower was the silence. It was complete and absolute. The sudden call of a cuckoo nearby made him start momentarily. Overawed by the ancient wide-girthed splendor of oak, beech, elm, sycamore, and other towering giants, the young hare found himself whispering to Russa, "Why is it so bally quiet in here?"

The squirrel shrugged. "Dunno, I've never given it a thought. May'aps because out in the open y'can hear the wind, an' distant sounds travel on the breeze, but in 'ere, well, 'tis sort o' closed in like."

Stirring the moist carpet of dead vegetation with his sabertip, the Major commented, "Cap'n Twayblade, let 'em rest their paws awhile here and scrape up a quick snack—no cookin' fire. Russa, you come with me and we'll track ahead. They've left plenty o' trail in this loam."

When the pair had left, Tammo sat with his friends in dappled sunlit shadows. They munched dried apples, nuts, and oatcake, washed down with beakers of water.

"I've never been to Redwall Abbey, what's it like?" he whispered to Pasque.

"Can't help you there, chum. I haven't either. Neither has Riffle, Tare'n'Turry, or any of us younger ones. Cap'n Twayblade has."

The Captain put aside her beaker. "Well, I'll tell you, chaps, I don't wish to appear disloyal to Salamandastron, but Redwall Abbey, by m'life, there's a place an' a half! I was only there once, with Torgoch an' Rockjaw, we were carryin' dispatches from Lady Cregga to the ol' Mother Abbess, congratulatin' her on a onescore season Jubilee, as I recall. Anyhow, we arrived at Redwall in time for the feast. Remember that, eh, Rock?"

The burly Rockjaw Grang grinned and nodded, speaking in his odd way. "Bah gum, that were a do I'll not forget! Sithee, I've ne'er clapped eyes on so much luvly grub in one place: puddens'n'pies, cakes, turnovers, pasties, tarts, you name it an' it were there. Trifles, cream, cheeses, soups, an' more kinds o' fresh-baked breads than y'could twitch an ear at! But by 'ecky thump, I've tasted nought like that October Ale they brew at yon Abbey. . . ."

He sat with a dreamy look on his craggy face as the Sergeant contributed his reminiscences. "Ho yerss, they 'ad all manner o' fizzy cordials an' berry wines too. We sang an' danced an' feasted for more'n three days. I declare, you ain't never met such obligin' creatures as those Redwallers, 'omely an' friendly as the season's long, they was. If'n I'm still around when I gets too old to patrol, I'd like nothin' better than to retire meself to Redwall Abbey, 'tis the 'appiest place I've ever seen in all me seasons!"

Riffle could not resist rubbing his paws together gleefully. "Good egg! An' we're going to be there in a few days, wot!"

Faint but urgent a faraway cry echoed through the woodlands.

"Eulaliaaa! Rally the troops! Death on the wind! Eulaliaaaaa!"

Food and talk were instantly forgotten; weapons appeared as the Patrol leapt to the alert.

"Rally the troops! Eulaliaaaaaa!"

Captain Twayblade's long rapier thrust toward the cries. "Over that way, I reckon! Eulaliaaaaaa! Chaaaaaaarge!"

They took off like a sheet of lightning, blades and slings whirling, roaring aloud the war cry to let Perigord know help was on its way.

"Eulaliaaa! 'S death on the wind! Eulaliaaaaa!"

Despite his bandaged paw, Tammo was up with the front-runners, Twayblade, Riffle, and Midge. Straight on they raced, through bush and shrub, loam flying, leaves swirling, twigs cracking, and startled birds whirring off through the trees. Pawsounds thrummed fast against the earth like frenzied, muted drumbeats. Sunlight and shadow wove together as they hurtled onward, bellowing and baying like wolves to the hunt.

25

Bursting over the brow of a humpbacked ridge, the wild charging hares crashed through a grove of rowans down into a narrow rocky defile and flung themselves like madbeasts into the fray. Major Perigord was backed into a small cave; beset by yelling vermin, he held the entrance gallantly. A broken javelin tip protruded from his right shoulder, and he was slashed in several places, but still he wielded his saber like a drum major's staff, fighting gamely against overwhelming odds, which threatened to bring him down and get at whoever was behind him inside the cave. Smashing into the rear of the vermin and scattering them like ninepins, the Long Patrol hares arrived to their officer's rescue.

"Eulaliaaaa! Give 'em blood'n'vinegar! Eulaliaaaa!"

Tammo's dirk, Twayblade's rapier, and Riffle's dagger claimed the first three foebeasts. Rockjaw Grang slew two with ferocious kicks from his mighty hindpaws. Lieutenant Morio had his face laid open by a cutlass slash as he brought down another with his lance. Perigord flung his saber after the remainder, who were scrabbling off up the far side of the small ravine. He fell on all fours, shouting hoarsely, "Run 'em to earth, keep after the scum!"

More than a score of the remaining vermin ran off through the woodlands, with the hares hard on their heels. Sergeant Torgoch ran alongside Twayblade, trying to keep his eye on the escapers as they fled into the deep tree cover. "They're splittin' up, Cap'n. What now, marm?" he shouted.

Twayblade kept running, watching the vermin starting to fan out, issuing orders as she went. "Lieutenant Morio stayed behind with the Major, so with Russa that makes us eleven. Torgoch, you take Rubbadub and Midge ..."

Tammo interrupted, his face full of concern. "But where *is* Russa?" he said. "Has anyone seen her?"

"Probably off somewheres finishing off a few dozen vermin with that stick of hers," said Twayblade, sounding more confident than she felt. "Torgoch, Rubbadub, Midge, keep after those to the left. Riffle, go after those who've gone right—Tare'n'Turry, go with him. Tammo, Pasque, Rockjaw, stay with me, there's about ten of 'em bunched together keepin' straight ahead. We'll stick with them, and everyone keep your eyes skinned for Russa."

Knowing they were running for their lives, the fleeing vermin dashed helter-skelter, south into Mossflower. Tammo was beginning to feel weariness weighting his paws, owing to the headlong dash to the defile and the subsequent fighting. However, he was running with the famed Long Patrol, so he tried hard not to show signs of fatigue. Keeping his mouth closed, he breathed hard through his nostrils and whacked both footpaws down resolutely.

As Twayblade shot ahead, a rat tripped over some protruding tree roots in front of her. Before the creature could recover, she was upon him, dispatching him as he tried to rise. Tammo noted a weasel breaking off from the main body and slipping behind a hornbeam. Shooting off to one side, he watched the tree as his companions raced past it. Slowing his pace, Tammo came around the hornbeam. The weasel was smiling, thinking he had shaken off his pursuers. Turning to head east, he ran straight into Tammo. A look of surprise crossed the vermin's ugly face and he grabbed for the hatchet shoved through his belt, but too late. Tammo slew him with a single thrust. The chilling feeling took control of Tammo as he dashed to join the others, teeth chattering and limbs trembling uncontrollably. He sighted them up ahead; they were halted, retreating slowly. Rockjaw Grang saw him and called, "Stay where thee are, Tamm, 'tis bad swampland 'ereabouts!"

Tammo walked forward another few paces until the ground became squishy, where he joined his companions. Farther out in the swamp the remaining vermin had rushed heedlessly into a dangerous quagmire.

Twayblade nodded in their direction. "Nothin' we can do about 'em now, chaps. Put up y'weapons."

Horrified, Tammo stood watching. Nearly all eight of the vermin were in over their waists. They shrieked and struggled, making the position worse for themselves, grabbing at one another as the bottomless ooze sucked them remorselessly down. One, a nimble ferret, pulled himself up onto a rotting log and managed to scramble along its length as his weight pushed it down. Behind him, his comrades, who had only their heads showing above the treacherous surface, yelled piteously to him.

"Rinkul, 'elp us, mate, do somethin', 'elp us!"

But the ferret was intent on saving only his own skin. Hauling himself upright, he streaked the length of the sinking trunk, flinging his body forward in an amazing leap. He landed in some bushes where the ground became firmer and ran off, hop-skipping wildly until he was clear of the main swamp. Turning, he watched, as did the hares, the remaining vermin gurgle horribly as the muddy depths claimed them for its own. Seconds later there was nought but a smooth gray-brown patch amid the green rotting vegetation to indicate where they had gone down. The ferret, Rinkul, turned and shrugged.

As he squelched his way off over the swamp's far side, Tammo noticed that he was twirling something.

A sick feeling swept over the already trembling young hare, and he fell down on all fours. Pasque was right beside him, wiping his face with some damp grass. "Tamm, what is it? Are you wounded?"

Tammo's face seemed to have aged several seasons as he fought to stop shaking, muttering words at the ground in front of him.

Captain Twayblade assisted Pasque to pull the shivering hare upright. She cocked an eyebrow at the younger creature. "I say, can y'make out what he's chunnerin' on about, wot?"

Tears began brimming in Pasque Valerian's soft brown eyes. "Oh, Cap'n, he said that the ferret was carryin' Russa's stick!"

Twayblade sheathed her rapier, grim-faced. "Come on, Rock, we'd best get back to the Major, post haste. Stay with Tammo, young gel, take y'time bringin' him back, we'll go ahead. If y'see the others, tell 'em where we are."

The kindly Rockjaw Grang took off his tunic and draped it about Tammo's quivering shoulders. It was so large that it lapped his footpaws, but it was thick and warm. "There thou goes, sunshine, thee tek it easy now!" he said, patting Tammo's face.

It was full noontide when Pasque and Tammo made it back to the defile, accompanied by Sergeant Torgoch, Rubbadub, and Midge, whom they had met up with on the way. Perigord was seated in front of a fire, his right paw in a sling that held a large herbal pad to the shoulder. On seeing the Major, Tammo was able to say only one word.

"Russa?"

Perigord's normally languid face was pale and drawn as he nodded toward the cave. Breaking free of Torgoch and Pasque, the young hare staggered into the little

152

chamber. A strange scene confronted him. Lieutenant Morio, with a bandage 'round his face that ran beneath his chin and ended in a bow between his ears, was nursing a tiny badger. Looking for all the world like an old harewife, he placed a paw to his lips.

"Sshh! I've just got him t'sleep!"

In a corner there was a still form, covered by a ragged homespun blanket. Close to it, Russa, also wrapped in a cloak, was sitting with her back against the sandstone wall. Tammo gave a deep sigh as he sat down next to his squirrel friend.

"Whew! Thank the seasons you're alive, mate!"

Russa blinked slowly through clouded eyes. "Not for long, young 'un. They hit me good this time—two arrows an' a spear. But I gave good as I got, sent a few of 'em along in front t'pave the way for me."

Tammo put a paw around the squirrel's narrow shoulders. "Russa, don't talk like that. You'll be all right, honest, you will!"

Russa Nodrey smiled, coughed a little, then swallowed as if clearing her throat. She took Tammo's free paw, saying, "None o' your nonsense now, sit still an' lissen t'me, Tamm. Tell yore mama I did the best I could, an' if y'see Osmunda again, tell 'er I sent my regards. Make yore family proud of you, Tamello De Fformelo Tussock, never do anythin' you'd be ashamed to tell 'em. One other thing: you don't 'ave to be a Long Patroller if'n y'don't want to. Mebbe there's other things y'do better."

Russa stayed Tammo's reply by squeezing his paw feebly. "Oh, I've seen you fight, Tamm, yore one o' the best, but you've 'ad a different upbringin'. You ain't no slayer like those hares out there—at Salamandastron they're brought up to it."

Tammo tried to choke back the tears that fell on Russa's paw. "You'll be fine, matey. I'll tell Pasque to get all her medicines an' herbs an' we'll ..."

Russa managed to wink at him. "Medicines an' herbs

153

won't do me no good now, Tamm. I wish you'd stop soakin' me paws an' carryin' on like that. I've got other places t'go, I've always been a wanderer, so I wants t'see what 'tis like on the sunny hillsides by the still meadows. . . ."

Outside the hares sat listening as Major Perigord related what had happened.

"Russa an' meself were scoutin' ahead when we heard roarin' an' screamin'. Of course it wasn't the vermin doin' the noisemakin'. We reckoned 'twould be innocent creatures captured by those villains, so we'd no choice except to try an' rescue 'em. On m'word, we ran straight into it! Thirty-odd assorted blackguards, tormentin' an' torturin' an old badgerwife an' a babe. Scoundrels! We gave 'em a taste or two o' their own medicine, I can tell you! Trouble was that we were outnumbered by about eighteen t'one—they'd slain the old badger. Well, we fought 'em off best as we could an' I pulled the poor dead ol' badger into the cave with the little 'un still clinging to her. Russa was protectin' my back, that's when she took two arrows. Then we turned and tried to hold 'em off, shoutin' Eulalias like nobeast's business, hopin' you chaps'd hear us. Sadly Russa took a spear through her middle, so I bundled her in the cave with the badgers. That's when I got the lance in me shoulder, took another few slashes too. Just look at me best green velvet tunic. Good job you arrived when y'did. I was about ready to go under. By the by, did y'get 'em all?"

Twayblade took the tunic from her brother's shoulders and inspected it. "Ripped t'bits, be a long time before you get another like it. Ah, the vermin. Yes, they split up, but so did we, got 'em all barring one, a ferret, he escaped through a swamp. I shouldn't think a lone villain would bother the Redwallers a good deal, wot?"

Sergeant Torgoch poured himself hot mint tea from the canteen by the fire. "Don't think 'e would, marm. Some o' those big otters that 'angs about the Abbey'd be only too glad to accommodate 'im, if'n 'e showed 'is nose 'round there."

Tammo came walking from the cave, dry-eyed and stone-faced.

"Russa Nodrey has just died, sah." His voice trembled as he tried to be a soldier worthy of the Long Patrol, but tears streamed down his face.

Perigord closed his eyes tightly and stood, head bowed.

That night they sealed up the cave with earth and rock. On the front of the pile, Rockjaw Grang placed a huge flat slab, which Tammo and Pasque had worked on, scraping deep into the sandstone with knifepoints a simple message:

Russa Nodrey and an unknown badger lie within.
They died fighting for freedom against cruelty.
Seasons may pass, but we will remember them.

The baby badger slept on, between Pasque and Tammo, wriggling in his slumbers to get closer to them. Tammo had never seen a badger before; he stroked the infant, glad to have a creature near who knew nothing of killing and war before that day.

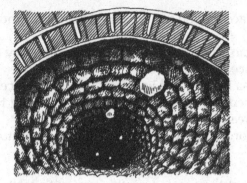

26

Beneath the Abbey's south wall, Foremole Diggum and his team held the lanterns out over the underground cavern. Holding on to the moles' digging claws, Tansy and Arven leaned out at the edge of the shored-up timber platform that the moles had built at the end of the small tunnel down which they had come. They peered down into the shadowy depths of what appeared to be a huge abyss, wide, dark, and mysterious.

Far below them water could be heard. Foremole tossed a turnip-sized boulder into the yawning chasm. They listened, but only silence followed.

Tansy turned to the solemn-faced mole leader. "Where has that rock gone to?" she asked.

Her question was followed by an echoing distant splash. Foremole shook his head gravely. "Daown thurr summwhurrs, marm, hurr, that'n be's a gurt deep 'ole."

They stood awhile, then Tansy backed off the platform gingerly. "Dear me, that's enough of that! It's like looking down from a high building and not seeing the ground. I was beginning to feel quite woozy!"

Foremole Diggum and his crew assisted her back to the surface, offering his irrefutable mole logic as he lit their way. "Urr, 'tis better feelin' woozed up on furm ground for gennel beasts such as ee, marm. Oi thinks us'n's be 'appier talkin' abowt et all in ee Abbey, thurr be things oi've gotter say regardin' yon gurt 'ole!"

Intrigued by Foremole's words, they all followed him indoors.

On entering the Abbey, Tansy walked straight into a dispute that had broken out in the kitchens. Amid much paw-wagging and whisker-twitching, the Abbess placed herself between the dormouse Pellit and a sturdy squirrel called Butty, whom Mother Buscol was training in the ways of the kitchen. Both creatures argued fiercely, glaring truculently at each other.

"I won't be able to get on with me work, she'll be in the way!"

"Work? Huh, when did *you* ever work? You spend half y'time sleepin' on empty veggible sacks by the back oven!"

"You young skipwaggle, keep a civil tongue in yer head when yore talkin' to elders'n'betters!"

"Listen, you might be older'n me, but we'll soon find out who's better if you call me a skipwaggle again!"

Tansy grabbed a copper ladle and struck it on a cooking pot with a resounding clang. "Silence, please, this instant! Now, one at a time. What's this all about? Pellit, you first."

The dormouse adopted an air of injured innocence. "Mother Abbess, all I said was that the bird shouldn't be allowed to live in our kitchens, 'taint right. For one thing, we need the space in that cupboard for storage, there's little enough room fer that down 'ere as it is . . ."

Tansy's hard stare and upraised paw halted Pellit. "You're speaking in riddles, sir. Butty, begin at the beginning!"

The young squirrel explained as best he could: "Well, marm, 'tis the owl Orocca. She's been lookin' 'round the Abbey for somewheres t'put her nest an' eggs. She searched high'n'low but nowheres suited her until she discovered our kitchens an' that big corner cupboard where we store apples. Anyhow, me an' Shad shifted her in there, owl, eggs'n'nest. Then before y'know it, old whinin' whiskers Pellit is moanin' an' complainin' an' reportin' the matter to Sister Viola."

Redwallers gave way as Tansy swept regally across to the cupboard. She opened the door and was confronted by the great golden eyes of Orocca. The owl snuggled down righteously atop her nest on the middle shelf, and said, "Hmph! You've already wrecked one homesite where I lived, now I suppose you're going to eject me from this one?"

With a wry smile hovering on her lips, Tansy turned to Pellit. "D'you know where an auger or a drill can be found?"

The dormouse answered her hesitantly, "Er, yes, marm, Gurrbowl an' Foremole Diggum keeps 'em in the wine cellars for borin' bungholes in barrels, marm."

Tansy tapped the cupboard door. "Good! Then go and get some form of drilling tool from them and bore lots of holes in this door, so that our guest has plenty of fresh air to breathe in her new home. Well, don't stand staring, Pellit, hurry along now!"

Turning back to the owl, Tansy bobbed a small curtsy. "I hope you'll be comfortable here. If you need anything at all, just ask. I'll detail Mother Buscol to take care of you; should you want to leave your nest, I'm sure you'll be able to trust her to keep an eye on the eggs until you return."

Orocca blinked rapidly, her head bobbing up and down. "My thanks to you, Abbess. This will be a good warm home for my eggchicks when they break shell. If any of your creatures sees my husband, Taunoc, perhaps they would tell him where I am."

Craklyn, who had witnessed the quarrel, patted Tansy's paw admiringly as they made their way down to Cavern Hole. "Well, you took care of that wonderfully, but poor old Pellit's got a face on him like a fractured tail. Did you see him?"

Tansy folded both paws into her wide habit sleeves. "Actually I'm glad Orocca caused that disturbance. For some time now I've been thinking of making certain changes in the kitchens. Mother Buscol is a bit old to be in charge of all the cooking, and young Butty is a good hard-working creature and a fine cook. I think he'll make an excellent Friar given the chance."

Craklyn agreed with Tansy, though she had reservations. "What about Pellit? He's older and has worked in the kitchens longer than Butty. Won't it cause bad feelings if you promote the young squirrel over the dor-mouse's head?"

But like a wise Mother Abbess, Tansy had a reason for everything she did concerning her beloved Redwall. "I don't think so, Craklyn. The trouble with Pellit is that he's fat, getting on in seasons, and of course he's a dormouse. That's why he's always nodding off in the warmth from the ovens. If I left him in the kitchen he'd injure himself someday. So I've decided that he shall be Viola Bankvole's new assistant—he's always chatting to her and hanging about the Infirmary, and the job's an easy one, so he'll have plenty of time to rest. Mother Buscol can look after Orocca and the eggchicks when they arrive. That way she'll be in the kitchens a lot to keep an eye on our new Friar, Butty."

Tansy spoke to Mother Buscol and Viola, and then to Butty and Pellit, before taking her seat in Cavern Hole. Everyone seemed happy with the new arrangements. Craklyn sat with the other creatures, very impressed with the know-how and wisdom the seasons had bestowed upon her old friend.

Word had passed around regarding the chasm beneath the outer south wall, and now everybeast was familiar with the news. Arven opened the discussion.

"So now we know what was causing the wall to collapse. I suppose the continuous action of the water wore the ground away and formed the big hole. What d'you think, Diggum?"

"Well, zurr, oi thought the same as ee at furst. But me'n'moi moles, we h'explored ee sides o' the gurt 'ole, an' guess wot? Us'n's found that part o' ee sides o' yon pit wurr square stones. Aye, they'm been builded thataway boi summbeasts long gone, hurr!"

This announcement caused a buzz of speculation. Tansy hid her surprise and silenced the gossip.

"One moment, please! Thank you. I was about to say that this casts a whole new light on things, but it only seems to deepen the puzzle. Let us not get carried away with wild speculation, friends. Has anybeast a sensible suggestion to offer?"

Skipper of Otters ventured an idea. "Supposin' me'n'my crew put some long ropes together an' went down there tomorrer, marm. We might find where all that water's flowin' to, an' who knows wot else?"

The mole Bunto scratched his nosetip with a hefty digging claw. "Gudd idea, zurr, an' may'ap ee'll take a lukk at ee carvens on yon stones."

Foremole Diggum donned a tiny pair of glasses and peered over the top of them at Bunto. "Yurr, ee never told oi abowt no carven on walls!"

Bunto smiled disarmingly, saying, "Probberly 'cos you'm never arsked oi, zurr!"

Foremole took Bunto's answer quite logically. "Hurr, silly o' me. No matter, next toim oi'll arsk ee!"

That seemed to settle the matter. Tansy looked around the assembly. "Right then, Skipper and his crew will look into it tomorrow. Any more questions, suggestions, or business? Good, then I'm off to my bed. It's been a long day."

An amazingly cultured voice rang out from the doorway: "Excuse me, I do beg your pardon for interrupting,

160

but does anybeast know the whereabouts of an owl named Orocca, last seen perched on a nest containing three eggs?"

A trim and very dignified-looking male Little Owl opened the door wide and bowed courteously to the Redwallers. Tansy had long ago given up being surprised by anything; she simply returned his bow with a polite nod of her head.

"Ah, I take it your name is Taunoc, sir. Welcome to Redwall Abbey. This is our Foremole, Diggum, he will take you to your wife. Main kitchen, far corner, right in the apple cupboard. You'll probably find a dormouse there drilling holes. If he disturbs you, then please send him away."

The Little Owl bowed once more. "My thanks to you, marm. I bid you a pleasant good night!"

When he had departed with Foremole, there was a moment's silence. Then both Tansy and Craklyn burst into helpless laughter. "Whoohoohoo! Oh, hahahaha! Great seasons, did you see the face on him, and such beautiful manners. Heeheehee! Oh, dear, what next?"

Craklyn widened her eyes and did a perfect imitation of Taunoc. " 'Last seen perched on a nest containing three eggs?' Hahahaha!"

Tansy rose, supporting herself weakly on the chair arm. "Heeheehee! No more business! No more questions! No more anything, please! I need my bed! Oh, whoohoohoohaha! Sorry!"

Leaning against each other, Recorder and Abbess left Cavern Hole, tears streaming down their faces as they giggled and whooped.

Bunto looked blankly at Drubb. "Hurr, oi'm glad they'm 'appy, b'aint you?"

"Burr aye, but wot they'm a larfin' anna chucklen at oi doant know. 'Twas on'y summ owlybird a looken furr 'is missus."

Gradually the spring night cast its spell over Redwall. Lanterns flickered, fires guttered, and a stray draft moved the tapestry in Great Hall before passing on. All was peaceful, calm, from dormitory to cellars.

Beneath the south wall, far down in the stygian gloom of the chasm, something moved. Something cold, slippery, and long . . . Something moved.

27

Dawn's half-light was barely peeping over windowsills when the young squirrel Butty pounded on Tansy's bedroom door. Pulling the coverlet over her head, Tansy complained in a sleep-muffled moan, "Go 'way, 'taint light yet, I've only just closed my eyes!"

But the new Friar persisted, thumping the door and shouting, "Mother Abbess, marm, new owlbabes have arrived in our kitchens! Oh, please come quick, I dunno what t'do!"

Tansy's footpaws found her old slippers as she threw on a dressing gown and dashed to the door.

"Rouse Sister Viola, Mother Buscol, and Craklyn, and bring 'em straight down to the kitchens. Go quickly and try not to waken the others!"

Completely in a dither, Butty raced off, yelling aloud, "Owl babies! Just arrived in the kitchens! New little 'uns!"

Abbess Tansy peered around the half-open cupboard door. From beneath Orocca's fearsome talons, three sets of massive golden eyes stared unblinkingly back at her. All of Redwall, clad in a variety of nightshirts, tasseled caps, dressing gowns, old sandals, and slippers, packed into the kitchens, hopping up and down eagerly to catch a glimpse of the new arrivals.

Mother Buscol complimented the owl on her eggchicks: "My my, wot beautiful liddle birds. They've got yore eyes, too!"

A brief smile flitted across Orocca's solemn features. "Thank you, Buscol. These are my first brood, and I'm glad they're all fit and well. My husband, Taunoc, will be pleased, when he eventually gets to see them."

Craklyn raised her eyebrows in surprise. "Taunoc hasn't seen his babes yet? Where is he?"

Orocca lifted her talons, allowing the chicks to stumble forward. "Poor Taunoc was in a worse tizz than that young squirrel of yours. The moment he heard eggshells cracking he took off in a fluster, muttering about hunting to feed five beaks now. He'll be back."

The Little Owls were mere fuzzballs, with eyes practically larger than their bodies. When they were not dumbling and stumbling to stay upright, they were huddling together to keep their balance. Orocca knocked the door open wide with a sweep of her wing.

Now all the Redwallers could see the three chicks clearly, there were exclamations of delight, particularly from the Dibbuns, whom Skipper and his otters had lifted onto their shoulders so they could get a clear view.

"Burr, can they'm owlyburds coom out t'play with us'n's?"

"Why don't they say noffink yet?"

" 'Ello, likkle owlyburds, d'you want some brekkfist?"

Viola Bankvole, keeping a safe distance from Orocca, took charge. "A sensible idea, why don't we all go in to breakfast and leave Orocca to clean up her nest?"

Viola and Tansy ushered the crowd out, while Mother Buscol and Gurrbowl Cellarmole stayed behind to help the owls.

Skipper of Otters whacked his tail down hard upon the tabletop. "Stow the gab now, mateys, yore Abbess wants a word!"

164

Nodding thanks to Skipper, the Abbess tucked paws into her dressing-gown sleeves and stood to address the Redwallers. "Listen carefully now—this won't take long. Summer's nearly here, 'tis a beautiful day outside, so here's my plan. I say we cancel all work and worries until tomorrow, and let today be one of feasting and celebration for the three little lives that have arrived into our Abbey. A triple birthday party out in the orchard!"

Cheers of joy rang to the rafters of Great Hall.

Brother Ginko was Redwall's Bellringer. Today he didn't stand below and pull on the ropes; instead, he climbed the stairs to the steepletop chamber, stood on the beams between the two bells, and operated them by pushing with both paws. The warm brazen sounds rang out over Mossflower.

Larks took to the meadow air, and woodland birds fluttered out over the green tree canopy, adding their morning songs to the bell tones rising into a bright sunlit sky.

Below in the line of trees skirting the east ramparts, a furtive figure slunk close to the wall's edge. Rinkul the ferret, last of the vermin band being pursued by the hares, fled south along the woodland edge. Dried swamp mud clung to his matted fur as he hurried on, chewing roots and berries and casting fearful glances backward. Rinkul hoped the bells were not ringing to denote that he had been spotted—he could see the figure of Brother Ginko framed against the open arches of the steeple chamber. He held still awhile, then, satisfied he had not been detected, Rinkul left the shelter of the Abbey wall to cut off over the south common lands, where he could see a stream that would provide him with drinking water.

With the sun warm upon his back and the bells booming in his ears, the ferret lay flat on his stomach, drinking greedily of the fresh stream water. After a while he rose into a crouch, checking that he was still alone. He stared hard and long at what he saw. It seemed incredible, but he trusted the evidence of his own keen sight. Redwall's battlemented south ramparts were collapsing. The line of high, thick masonry had been breached by the fall of a massive tree, and farther along, the wall dipped and leaned inward, as if messed about by some colossal paw.

Rinkul backed into the shallows, still staring at the fractured outer wall. Following the stream course southeast to hide his tracks, he tucked Russa Nodrey's hardwood stick into his belt.

"Got to find the Rapscallion armies," he muttered delightedly to himself. "This information'll make me an officer, a Rapmark!"

Brother Ginko had his back to the fleeing ferret. He shielded his eyes and stared hard at the two figures loping steadily down the path from the north toward the Abbey. Hares—it was two hares!

Halting the toll of one bell, he continued ringing the other singly, warning of creatures approaching. Skipper and Shad came racing out of the Abbey, hard on the heels of Arven, who was belting on the great sword of Martin the Warrior.

The squirrel Champion cupped both paws around his mouth and yelled upward, "Strangebeasts on the path, Ginko?"

The Bellringer leaned outward, pointing. "Aye, two hares come out o' the north!"

The look of concern melted from Skipper's tough face, to be replaced by one of comic dismay. "Did you say 'ares, messmate? Lock up the vittles an' stan' by fer a famine, prepare to be eaten outta 'ouse'n'ome!"

Breaking cover from the woodlands, Tammo stared excitedly at the soaring towers and gables of the red sandstone building farther down the path. Pasque's voice at his side echoed both their thoughts.

"Golly, is that Redwall Abbey? 'Tis even bigger'n I thought it'd jolly well be. What a beautiful sight!"

Sergeant Torgoch kept his eyes ahead as he said, "None

more luvverly, miss! Right, fall inter twos an' let's see us marchin' up there like Long Patrol an' not a bunch o' waddlin' ducks on daisy day! Chins up, chests out, shoulders back, tails twitchin' smartly! Keep up at the back there, Grang!"

The giant hare Rockjaw Grang was carrying the baby badger in a sling across his chest. He frowned at the Sergeant. "Beggin' thy pardon, Sarge, but could y'keep thy voice down? Sithee, ah've just gotten yon tyke asleep for his mornin' nap!"

Major Perigord, who was marching at the head of the column, smiled whimsically at the thought of Rockjaw as a nursemaid. "Don't fret, Rock. If Galloper Riffle an' Turry are already there, they'll have no shortage of blinkin' badgerminders t'take the little 'un off y'paws, then you can sit down to a good ol' tuck-in with the rest o' the chaps, wot?"

A dreamy look crossed Rockjaw's face as he wiped a paw across his lips. "Redwall Abbey vittles, by 'eck, lead me to 'em!"

28

Abbess Tansy and Arven, with a deputation of otters and elders, stood in the open gateway to greet the Long Patrol. Captain Twayblade broke ranks to embrace the Abbess warmly.

"Mother Abbess, so good t'see you, old friend. You look wonderful!"

"Twayblade, what a lovely surprise. Welcome to our Abbey again!"

Old friends met old friends, and new ones were made as introductions flew thick and fast. The dashing hares of the Long Patrol were much admired by the Redwallers as they stood there chatting in the Abbey gateway, leaning on their weapons, smartly clad in their tunics, with medals and ribbons on display. Secretly, even the most humble Abbeydwellers wished they too could present such a picture—jolly, courteous, and kind, but feared by their enemies and totally perilous.

Major Perigord winked at Skipper. "What d'ye say, old lad, d'ye think everybeast here would like to march in with us, make a jolly good entrance, wot!"

Skipper stood smartly to attention at the Major's side. "Good idea, matey. Ahoy, form up in a line o' fours, let's bring our guests 'ome in style. Arven, Shad, up front 'ere with me'n'the Major. Great seasons, I wish we 'ad a band!"

Perigord drew his saber with a flourish and a rattle. "Your word is my command, sah. Rubbadub, beat us in with your best drums, if y'would!"

Dibbuns whooped in delight and amazement as Corporal Rubbadub milled about, waving his paws and setting up a dust and a din.

"Baboom! Baboom! Baboombiddy boombiddy boom! Drrrrrapadapdap! Drrrubbadubdub! Bababoom! Bababoom! Bababoom!"

Cheering aloud and stamping their paws in time to the beat, the cavalcade marched across the lawns to the Abbey in fine military style. Tammo and Pasque strode alongside Friar Butty and the molebabe Gubbio, chatting animatedly. The young squirrel Friar had excellent news for them.

"You've arrived at a good time, friends. Today we're havin' a great feast to celebrate the birth of three liddle owlchicks."

Pasque's normally soft voice was shrill with excitement. "I say! Y'mean we're actually goin' t'be guests at a famous Redwall feast?"

Gubbio grabbed her paw as he hop-skipped to Rubbadub's drums. "Ho aye, marm, ee'll 'ave such vittles'n'fun as ne'er afore!"

As soon as they were inside the Abbey, those hares who had never visited Redwall were led off on a grand tour by a gang of eager Dibbuns. Other Redwallers went about their tasks to prepare for the festivities, while Abbess Tansy and her elders retired to Cavern Hole with Perigord, Twayblade, Rockjaw, and Torgoch.

The hares were offered light refreshments of candied fruits and red-currant cordial as they exchanged news and information with their hosts. Tansy listened carefully to the account of the skirmish in the defile, shaking her head in sorrowful bewilderment at the death of Russa Nodrey, who had visited Redwall many times in bygone seasons. When the tale was told, Rockjaw opened the sling, which he had held easily concealed beneath his tunic, and presented the Abbess with his precious burden.

"Sithee, marm, this is the babby. A grand likkle male an' good as gold for company on a march, 'e is!"

Tansy could not wait to hold the tiny bundle. She placed a cushion in her lap and laid him on it. He was no more than a season old, hardly any age at all. Lying flat on his back, the babe yawned and opened his soft dark eyes as the Abbess inspected him. The badger's back was silver gray, and his chest and paws were velvety black. He had a moist brown nose and a snow-white head, sectioned by two thick black stripes running either side of the muzzle from whiskers to ears, covering both eyes.

Craklyn touched the upturned footpads. "Seasons of winter! Just look at the size of these paws! He's goin' to be big as an oak when he grows to full size!"

Tansy chuckled fondly as she tickled the babe's tiny white-tipped ears. "Welcome to Redwall Abbey, little sir, and pray, what name do you go by?"

The baby badger held out his paws to her, growling, "Nunnee! Nunnee!"

"The little chap's said that several times," Major Perigord explained, "only word he seems t'know. We've surmised that it means Nanny, the old badger he was with. She was prob'ly his grandmother or nurse—'fraid we haven't a clue as to who his parents are. There was certainly no sign of them where we found him. Had there been two grown badgers with him, those vermin would've given the place a wide berth, wot!"

Foremole Diggum placed a honeyed hazelnut in the babe's paws, and immediately he began chewing the nut hungrily.

"Burr," said Diggum, " 'ee may be a h'orphan, but thurr b'aint nuthin' amiss wi' ee appetoit, no zurr!"

A bowl of creamy mushroom soup was sent for, and

Tansy fed the babe while other matters were discussed. The Redwallers knew nothing of Rapscallions, nor had any other vermin been sighted in the region of late. Arven related the dangerous position of the Abbey's outer south wall and their plans to rebuild it.

By the time the discussions were near their close, the little badger had licked the soup bowl clean and gone back to sleep in the Abbess's lap. Major Perigord had listened pensively to the problems faced by Redwall and its creatures. He stood abruptly, having reached a decision.

"Well, chaps, my duty as Commanding Officer, Long Patrol, is pretty clear. Until your wall is rebuilt and the Abbey safe'n'secure once more, me an' my hares will guard Redwall an' patrol the area night and day. Couldn't do any less, wot! Lady Cregga'd have me ears'n'tail if I didn't. So, marm, if you are willin' to accept us, me an' my troop are at y'service!"

Bowing low, Perigord presented his saber hilt-first to the Abbess. Abbess Tansy touched the handle, signifying her approval.

"My humble thanks to you, Major. I am sure that I speak for all Redwallers when I say that we are assured of safety by your presence, and your gallant offer is warmly accepted!"

Foremole Diggum threw in a gem of mole logic: "Gudd! Then if you'n's be afinished usin' gurt long apportant words, may'ap us'n's best go an' get ee feast ready, ho urr aye!"

Midge Manycoats sucked his paw ruefully. "Huh, I've just been pecked by perishin' owlbabes!"

Chuckling, Friar Butty replaced the lid on a steaming pan. "You must taste good to 'em, Midge. Come over 'ere an' lend a paw. I'm showin' Tammo an' Missie Pasque how t'make Mossflower Wedge."

Both hares were intrigued by the goings-on in Redwall's kitchens; it made such a pleasant change from marching and fighting. Pasque had lined a rectangular earthenware dish with pastry, which Butty was viewing approvingly.

"Well done, missie, we'll make cooks of you hares yet. Tammo, are you ready with the first layer?"

Tammo wielded a ladle, enjoying himself immensely. "Wot? I'll say I am. Now don't tell me, Butty, just watch this!" He spread the chopped button mushroom and grated carrot mixture on its pastry base, making sure it was level.

"There! Righto, Pasque, you an' Midge chuck in the next layer!"

Watched by the Friar, the two hares spread sliced white turnip and chopped leeks as a second layer. Then Butty placed a third layer of diced potato and slivered white cabbage.

He winked at Tammo and stood back, wiping his paws on a cloth. "Go on then, Tamm, I'm not tellin' you what's next, 'tis up t'you."

Tammo took the lid off a panful of dark rich gravy. "Mmm, smells absolutely super duper! Stand clear, please!" He poured the gravy over the layered vegetables evenly, watching it soak through, pulling his paw back swiftly to avoid a slap with Butty's damp cloth.

"No takin' secret licks at the pan, or I'll tell yore Sergeant an' he'll have yore tail for supper, or wotever it is he does. C'mon now, take an end o' this cover each."

Gingerly they lifted a big pastry top between them and flopped it gently over the dish. Butty took a knife and trimmed it while Tammo and Midge crimped the edges. Pasque borrowed Butty's knife to cut a series of arrowhead slits in the center, then she brushed the top with a mixture of light vegetable oil and finely chopped spring onions.

The squirrel Friar shook their paws. "Well done, good effort for y'first Mossflower Wedge. Now, how long does it stand in the oven?"

Pasque and Tammo spoke out together, "Until it tells you it's done!"

"Right! And when's that?"

"When the crust is golden brown an' shiny, an' there's no more steam coming out of the slits in the middle!"

"Correct! See, I told you I'd make Redwall cooks out of you. Now, let's see how good y'are at makin' Abbey Trifle. . . ."

A single lantern had been left burning at the platform dug by the moles beneath the south outer wall. The pale light flickered, sending its radiance down into the depths of the darkened chasm, where it shone feebly on the spray-drenched stones by the rushing water. In the dim light, bunched wet scales glistened, savage rows of ivory-hued teeth showed briefly, and two slitted eyes filmed over. The creature had heard the furry creatures above, it had seen them, so it waited hungrily, knowing that sooner or later they would be descending into the gloomy rift. Coiling its sinister length around a rock to prevent it being swept away . . . it waited.

29

Sneezewort sat on the hillslope enjoying the mid-morning sunshine. In an old upturned helmet he was boiling up a broth of frogspawn and some stream vegetation on his fire. The rat watched his companion approaching, then turned his gaze upon the helmet, pretending to be engrossed with the task of cooking.

Lousewort came damp-furred and shivering. An enormous lump showed between his ears as he squatted by the fire to dry his shivering body.

Sneezewort spoke to his former companion without looking up. "Thought yew was supposed ter be an officer gettin' punished."

Lousewort peered hungrily at the mess bubbling in the helmet. "Er, er, well, I ain't a ossifer no more, mate. Er, er, that looks good. I'm starvin'."

Sneezewort stirred the broth with his dagger. "Don't you 'mate' me, I ain't yore mate no more. Why aren't yer still stannin' up t'yer neck in chains inna river?"

The other rat shrugged noncommittally. "Er, er, they all escaped durin' the night, with Borumm an' Vendace, but I got left be'ind."

"Left be'ind? Didn't yer wanna go wid 'em? Better'n freezin' yore tail off inna stream, I woulda thought."

174

"Er, well, I got knocked over me 'ead an' left senseless."

"Harr harr! Wouldn't take much t'leave *you* senseless. Wot 'appened then?"

"Er, er, well, I woke up an' shouted the alarm. Lord Damug sent Skaup the ferret out wirra 'undred or more, to 'unt 'em down. Er, Lord Damug said t'me that at least I was loyal, stoopid but loyal 'e called me, an' 'e said that I wasn't fit ter be an ossifer an' told me I'd got me ole job back, servin' in the ranks. So 'ere I am, mate, we're back together, jus' me'n'you."

Sneezewort snorted as he picked the helmet off the flames between two sticks and set it down by the fireside. "Hah! So y'think yer can come crawlin' back t'me, eh? Where's all yer brother officers now, tell me that? An' anudder thing, don't think yore sharin' my vittles, slobberchops! Go an' get yore own, y'big useless gully-wumper!"

Lousewort sulked by the fire, looking hurt and touching the lump between his ears tenderly. Then, as if remembering something, he reached into his sodden garments and drew out a big dead gudgeon, its scales glistening damply in the morning sunlight.

"Er, er, I stood on this an' killed it when I jumped off the rock in the stream. D'yer think it'll be all right to eat?"

Sneezewort nearly knocked the helmet over as he grabbed the fish. "Course it will, me ole mate. Tell yer wot I'll do, I'll shove it in wid this soup an' cook it up a bit on the fire, while you scout for more firewood, mate. You kin 'ave the 'ead'n'tail, those are the best bits, I'll 'ave the middle 'cos yew prob'ly damaged that part by jumpin' on it, mate!"

Lousewort rose, smiling happily. "Er, er, then we're still mates?"

Sneezewort's snaggle-toothed grin smiled back at him. "I was only kiddin' yer a moment back. We wuz always mates, me'n'you, true'n'blue! If yer can't find a spot by yer fire an' a bit t'spare for yer ole mate, then wot sorta mate are yer, that's wot I always says. You nip along now an' get the wood!"

Damug squatted at the water's edge, honing his sword-blade against a flat piece of stone as he conveyed his orders to the Rapmark Captains.

"There's plenty of food and water here. We'll camp by this stream until they bring back Borumm and Vendace and the others. When they do I'll make such an example of them that no Rapscallion will ever even think of disobeying me again. Gaduss, we've got no scouts at present, so you take fifty with you and go north. I want you to do a two-day search in that direction, but if you find anything of interest before that, report back immediately."

The weasel Gaduss saluted with his spear. "It shall be done, Firstblade!"

Nearly a full day's journey up the same stream bank, the water broadened, running through two hills whose tops were fringed with pine and spruce trees. Log-a-Log, Chieftain of the Guosim shrews, was busily cleaning moss from the bottom of a beached and upturned log-boat, assisted by another shrew called Frackle.

They paused to watch the other shrews fishing. Frackle wiped moss from her rapier blade, nodding toward them. "Lots o' freshwater shrimp in that landlocked stretch o' water," she said.

Log-a-Log ran his paw along a section of hull he had cleaned off. "Aye, freshwater mussels, too. Minnow an' stickleback were there in plenty last time I fished that part. Take a stroll over there, Frackle, easy like—an' don't look up at yonder hill on the other bank, we're bein' watched by some o' those thick-'eaded Rapscallion vermin who tried attackin' us yesterday."

Frackle sauntered away, murmuring casually, "Aye, I see the glint o' the sun on blades up in those trees at the 'illtop, Chief. What d'ye want me to do?"

The shrew Chieftain went back to cleaning his boat. "Just take things easy, mate. Tell the crews not t'look suspicious, pass the word to the archers t'drift back to their boats an' git their bows'n'arrers ready. We'll give those vermin a warm welcome if they comes down offa that 'ill an' tries crossin' the stream."

Panting and breathing heavily after their long run, Vendace, Borumm, and forty-odd Rapscallion fugitives lay flat among the trees on the hilltop, watching the shrews below.

Borumm stared at the packs that had been unloaded from the boats. "There ain't time fer us t'stop an' forage in this country. We needs those packs o' vittles if'n we're gonna circle an' make fer the sunny south."

One of the fugitives crawled up alongside the weasel. "Cap'n Borumm, those are the beasts that set on us. They kin fight like wolves wid those liddle swords o' theirs. Huh, you shoulda seen the way that ole Chief one finished off Hogspit!"

Vendace curled his lip at the vermin in a scornful sneer. "Stow that kinda talk, lunk'ead, yore with real officers now. Huh, 'Ogspit? I coulda put paid to 'im wid both paws tied be'ind me back. Bunch o' river shrews don't bother me'n'Borumm none, do they, mate? Phwaw! They're bakin' sumthin' down there, I kin smell it from 'ere. Mmmm! Biscuits, or is it cake?"

Borumm smiled wickedly at the fox. "Wotever it is we'll soon be samplin' it. Right, let's make a move. Keep 'idden climbin' down the 'illside, play it slow. I'll give the word ter charge if they spots us."

The shrewboats were all cleaned and anchored in the shallows. Log-a-Log and his shrews stood around the cooking fire, all acting relaxed, but keyed up for action.

"Scubbi, Shalla, take the archers an' use our boats fer cover. Spykel, Preese, get be'ind those big rocks wid yore sling team. Lead paddlers, stay back 'ere with me an' Frackle, ready to jump in the boats an' launch 'em. Those vermin are startin' downhill, too far out o' range yet. If we 'ave to make a run fer it, stay out o' midstream and use the current close t'this bank."

A rat named Henbit came running to the hilltop. His eyes took in the situation at one quick glance. Turning, he dashed back pell-mell to where the ferret Skaup was leading the main party at a run, hot on the tracks of the fugitives.

Henbit dashed up and threw a hasty salute. "Borumm an' Vendace straight ahead, Cap'n! They've jus' left that 'illtop to cross the stream an' attack those shrews!"

Skaup acted quickly. "You there, Dropear, take fifty an' run on ahead. Don't go up the 'ill, go 'round it—come at 'em along the shore. I'll take the rest an' make for the shore from 'ere, that way we'll get 'em between us. Never mind the shrews, we're 'ere to bring those traitors back, not to fight wid a gang o' boatmice. Get goin'!"

Vendace and Borumm were almost down the hill when the fox whispered to his partner, "D'yer think they've seen us? I coulda swore I saw the ole one lookin' over this way once or twice."

Borumm waved his paw to the vermin scrabbling downhill, urging them to move a bit faster. "Nah, if'n they'd seen us we'd 'ave known by now, mate. Best stop our lot when we reach the stream bank, that way we can all charge together. That water looks pretty shallow t'me."

It took more time than Vendace liked for the last vermin to get down off the hill onto the shore. He fidgeted impatiently, conveying his anxiety to Borumm. "All of a sudden I don't like this, mate. Those shrews gotta be blind if they ain't seen us by now. Lookit our lot too, barrin' for me an' you an' a couple o' others, there's scarce a

178

decent blade between us—they're mostly armed wid chunks o' wood or stones."

The weasel glared bad-temperedly at the fox. "Fine time ter be tellin' me you've got the jitters. Wot's the matter, mate, don't you think we kin take a pack o' scruffy shrews? Straighten yerself up! Come on, you lot. *Chaaaaaarge!*"

Bellowing and roaring, they made it into the shallows—then they were besieged on three sides. Log-a-Log and his Guosim loosed arrows and slingstones across the water. The charging line faltered a second under the salvo, then they were hit by the forces of Dropear and Skaup coming at them from both sides. It was a complete defeat for Vendace and Borumm's vermin.

"Stay yore weapons, Guosim," Log-a-Log called to his shrews, "this isn't our fight no more. But stand ready to bring down any vermin tryin' to cross the stream!"

The fugitives could run neither forward nor sideways. Some tried running back uphill, where they made easy targets for arrow and lance. The remainder, knowing what fate would await them at the paws of Damug Warfang, fought desperately, trying to break free and run anyplace.

Across the stream the shrews sat in their logboats, paddles poised as they watched the awful carnage.

Frackle averted her eyes, as if she could not bear to watch. "They're from the same band. Some of those creatures must've fought together side by side. How can they do that to one another?"

Log-a-Log watched the slaughter through narrowed eyes. "They're vermin, they'd kill their own families for a crust!"

There were only ten of the original fugitive band left alive—the rest lay floating in the stream or draped on the hillside. Skaup grinned evilly at Borumm as he noosed his neck to the others, forming them into a line. "Firstblade Damug'll be well pleased to see you an' the fox safe back under 'is paw, weasel."

Bound paw and neck, the prisoners tottered painfully along the shore, driven by spearbutts and whipped with bowstrings. Skaup turned to stare across the stream at the Guosim sitting in their logboats. "You got off light t'day, but you've slain Rapscallions. We'll settle with you another day!"

Log-a-Log's face was impassive as he picked up a bow and sent an arrow thudding into Skaup's outstretched paw. "Aye, we've slain Rapscallions, an' we'll slay a lot more unless you get gone from this place. I warn ye, scum, next time I draw this bowstring the arrow won't be aimed at yore paw. Archers ready!"

Guosim bowbeasts stood up in the logboats, setting shafts to bowstrings, awaiting their Chieftain's next command.

Skaup's face was rigid with agony. He looked at the shrew shaft transfixing his paw and the Guosim with bows stretched, and slunk off, his voice strained with pain and anger as he yelled, "We'll meet again someday, I swear it!"

A ribald comment echoed across the stream waters at his back: "Be sure t'bring that arrow with ye, 'twas a good shaft!"

Skaup was close to collapse when he made it back to his party. Dropear threw a paw of support around his shoulders. "Siddown, Cap'n, an' I'll dig that thing outta yore paw."

The ferret pushed him roughly aside and staggered onward. "Not here, fool. Let's get out o' sight farther down the bank!"

Log-a-Log and his shrews stood watching them until they were behind a curve in the stream course. The shrew leader stroked his short gray beard. "Hmm, what we saw 'ere t'day tells me somethin', mates. If they could afford to slay more'n thirty o' their own kind, then there must be more of 'em than I thought—a whole lot more! Right, let's get these craft under way midstream, where the current runs swift. Watch out for a weepin' willow grove on yore port sides. We'll take the back waterways an' sidecut off to Redwall Abbey. I think I'd best warn 'em there's trouble comin'."

30

Algador Swiftback cast a fleeting glance backward as he marched on into the gathering evening. "Whew! I say, we've covered a fair old stretch today. Salamandastron's completely out o' sight!"

Drill Sergeant Clubrush's voice growled close to his ear. "The mountain might be out o' sight, laddie buck, but I'm not! No talkin' in the ranks there, keep pickin' those paws up an' puttin' 'em down. Left right, left right, left right . . ."

More than five hundred hares of the Long Patrol, some veterans but mainly new recruits, tramped eastward into the dusk, with Lady Cregga Rose Eyes, axpike on shoulder, always far ahead.

The lolloping young hare named Trowbaggs still had difficulty in learning to march properly. He put his left paw down when everybeast was on their right, and vice versa, and for the umpteenth time that day he stumbled, treading on the footpaws of the hare marching in front.

"Oops! Sorry, old chap, the blinkin' footpaws y'know, gettin' themselves mixed up again, right left, right left . . ."

Deodar shook her head in despair as she watched him. "Trowbaggs, y'great puddenhead, it's left right, not right left!"

Clubrush's stentorian voice rang out over the marchers:

"Long Patrol—halt! Stand still everybeast—that means you too, Trowbaggs, you 'orrible liddle beast!"

Thankfully, the marching lines halted, standing to attention until the order was given.

"First Regiment, stand at ease! Water an' wood foragers fall out! Duty cooks, take up chores! Lance Corporal Ellbrig, pick out yore sentries for first watch! The remainder of you, lay out y'packs an' groundsheets, check all weapons an' arms! Four neat rows now, clear away any nettles an' prickles over there—that's yore campsite for tonight, you lucky lot!"

Hares dashed hither and thither on their various duties as Sergeant and Lance Corporal roared out orders. In a short time, military precision resulted in camp being set up.

Algador sat with his companions by the shallows of a small pond, everybeast cooling off their footpaws and resting on their packs.

Furgale lay flat on his back, complaining to the stars: "Oh, my auntie's bonnet! I thought ol' Clubrush was goin' to march us all bally night. Look, there's steam risin' out of the water where I'm dippin' me pore old paws!"

The Sergeant's tone was almost an outraged squeal. "Get those dirty great sweaty dustridden paws out o' that water! It's for drinkin', not sloshin' about in. Trowbaggs, what'n the name o' seasons are you up to, bucko?"

"Wrappin' m'self up in me groundsheet, Sarge. Good night!"

Veins stood out on the Sergeant's brow as he roared at the hapless blunderer, "Sleepin'? Who said you could sleep, sah? Get that equipment cleaned, lay out yore mess kit, line up for supper! Forget sleep, Trowbaggs, stay awake! Yore on second watch!"

Trowbaggs groaned aloud as he searched in the dark for his mess kit. "Somebeast's pinched me flippin' spoon. Oh, mother, I want to go home. Save me from all this, I wasn't cut out for it, wot!"

"Never mind, scout," a kindly older hare named Shangle Widepad whispered to him, "it gets worse before it gets jolly well better. Here, I'll swap with you. I'm on first watch. You do it and I'll take second sentry for you, that way you'll be able t'get a full night's sleep."

When the camp had quieted down and was running smoothly, Clubrush went to sit beside Lady Cregga at the pond's far side. She looked up from polishing her axhead and asked, "How are they doing, Sergeant?"

"Oh, they'll shape up, marm, never fear. First day's always the longest for the green ones. P'raps if we don't march 'em as 'ard an' far tomorrer . . ."

The rose eyes glinted dangerously. "They'll learn to march twice as hard and fast, aye, and fight like they never imagined before I'm done with them. I never brought them along on any picnic, and the sooner they realize that the better. Dismissed, Sergeant Clubrush!"

The Sergeant stood to attention and saluted. "Aye, marm, thank ye, marm!"

Clubrush went to where his equipment was neatly laid out. Somebeast had carefully folded his groundsheet so that he could retire immediately without making it up into a sleeping bag. Being an old campaigner, the Sergeant upset the sheet with his pace stick. A pile of nettles and some soggy bank sand flopped out on the ground.

He lay down on the clean dry part of the sheet and shouted, "Oowow! Who put this lot in me bed? You 'orrible rotten lot, I'll march yore blatherin' paws to a frazzle in the mornin'!"

Smothered giggles sounded from the recruits' area. Sergeant Clubrush smiled as he settled down. They were good young 'uns; he'd do all he could to help them make the grade.

Obeying Damug's orders, Gaduss the weasel had scouted north with his patrol all day, reaching the southern edge of Mossflower Wood by nightfall. He allowed no fires to be lit in the small camp set up at the outer tree fringe. The night passed uneventfully.

In the hour before dawn, the scouts broke camp and pressed on. They had not been traveling long when the weasel gave a signal. Dropping flat in a patch of ferns, the vermin patrol watched Gaduss wriggle forward. Through the mist-wreathed tree trunks a silent figure moved, seeking shadows between shafts of dawn light.

Gaduss unlooped from his belt a greased strangling noose fashioned from animal sinew. Winding it around both paws, he inched forward until he was shielded by an ash tree, directly in the traveler's path. Timing it just right, he leapt out behind the unwary creature and whipped the noose over his head and 'round his neck.

Rinkul was fortunate in that it also looped over the stick he was carrying. In panic, he pushed outward with the piece of polished hardwood, preventing the sinew from biting into his windpipe.

Both beasts went down, rolling over and over in the loam, kicking, snapping, and scratching at each other. The vermin broke cover and dashed to assist their officer, tearing the fighting duo apart. Seconds later the two were face-to-face, Gaduss wide-eyed with surprise.

"Rinkul, wot'n the name o' blood'n'claws are you doin' 'ere?"

The ferret massaged his neck where the noose had bruised it. "Findin' me way back ter Gormad Tunn an' the army. Nice reception yer gave me, mate, 'arf choked me ter death!"

Gaduss stuffed the noose back into his belt. "You 'aven't 'eard, then. Gormad's dead, so is Byral, 'tis Damug Warfang who's Firstblade of Rapscallions now. Where've y'been?"

Rinkul sat down on a rotting stump. "Been? That's a long story, mate. Our ship was driven off course an' wrecked up near the northeast coast. I've been through a lot o' things an' I'm the onlybeast left alive out o' a shipload. But that's by the by. Get me ter Damug Warfang, I've got news fer 'is ears alone—urgent news!"

31

In the orchard of Redwall Abbey the tables for the owlchicks' feast had been laid. Friar Butty supervised his helpers 'round a firepit, over which the hot dishes were being kept at a good temperature. Apple, pear, and plum blossoms were shedding their petals thickly on the heads of the feasters. It was a joyous sight.

The three owlchicks sat on cushions inside an empty barrel alongside their mother's place at the table; the badgerbabe lay in an old vegetable basket lined with sweet-smelling dried mosses. Tammo and Pasque sat together, with Arven and Diggum Foremole on either side of them. Mother Abbess Tansy occupied her big chair, which had been specially carried out. She looked very happy, clad in a new cream-colored habit, belted with a pale green girdle cord. The Dibbuns had made her a tiara of daisies and kingcups, which she wore proudly, if a little lopsidedly, on her headspikes.

Good Redwall food had the tables almost bent with its weight. Rockjaw Grang grabbed spoon and fork in a businesslike way. Gurrbowl Cellarmole nodded to him as she and Drubb rolled a barrel of October Ale up to its trestle. "Hurr, ee lukk ready t'do a speck o' dammidge to yon vittles, zurr!"

Sergeant Torgoch eyed a large spring salad longingly. "You'll 'scuse me sayin', marm, but 'e ain't the only one 'ereabouts who's lived on camp rations fer a season, eh, Rubbadub?"

The fat hare's smile matched the sun in the sky. "Rubbity dubdub boomboom!"

Abbess Tansy nodded politely to the Major. "As our guest, sir, perhaps you'd like to say the grace?"

Perigord's mouth was watering furiously, but he wiped his lips on a kerchief and drooped an elegant ear in Tansy's direction. "Quite, er, thank ye, marm!"

"Thanks to seasons an' jolly good luck,
We've all got a sword an' a head,
An' the way we'll tuck into these vittles
Will show that we're living, not dead."

"Haharrharr!" Shad the Gatekeeper chortled. "Short'n'sweet, that's 'ow I likes it, mate. Dig in!"

Everybeast did so with a will. Redwallers had no strict rules about dining: sweet was as good as salad to start, stew as acceptable as cake, and all shared the feast with one another.

"Here, mate, try some o' this plum slice with black-currant sauce!"

"Whoi thankee, zurr mate, may'ap you'm aven summ o' moi deeper'n ever turnip'n'tater'n'beetroot pie. Hurr—that be th'stuff!"

"Mmmm! Well, what d'you think of our Mossflower Wedge, eh, Pasque?"

"Excellent. I never knew I was such a jolly good cook, wot!"

"I say, this Abbey Trifle is absoballylutely top hole!"

"Just give me good ol' fresh crusty bread an' ripe yellow cheese, oh, with some o' these tangy pickles, an' a plate o' salad, an' maybe some stuffed mushrooms. Put that fruitcake on the side, I'll deal with it later. More

188

October Ale, please!"

"Damson an' gooseberry pudden with meadowcream, that's f'me!"

"Ahoy, Dibbun, drink any more o' that strawberry fizz an' you'll go bang!"

"Awright den, me go bang. Ooh, likkle berryfruit tarts, me like 'em!"

Taunoc dropped in and peered at the owlchicks in their barrel, saying, "Goodness, what handsome chicks. I think they resemble me strongly."

"Wot a pity," a raucous voice called out. "Shame they don't look more like yore missus, hahaha!"

The Little Owl sniffed pityingly. "There speaks a beast with all his taste in his mouth."

"Have you decided on names for the little ones yet, marm?" the Abbess called across to Orocca.

Orocca took her beak out of a hazelnut turnover long enough to reply, "Owls never name their eggchicks. They'll tell us their own names once they are ready to speak."

Tansy gave her a charming nod and a smile, then, pulling a wry face, she turned to Craklyn. "Oops, excuse me for asking, but what about our badgerbabe? We're going to need a name for him soon. Anybeast come up with a good idea yet?"

Craklyn paused from her rhubarb and maple crumble. "D'you see the giant hare over there, the one they call Rockjaw? Well, I think he's thought up a name for the little fellow."

At their request, Rockjaw emerged from behind a pair of platters piled high with salad, bread, cheese, cake, and pasties and wiped his mouth daintily on the tablecloth hem. "By 'ecky thump, marms, there's only one thing better'n food—*more* food! Sithee, I've dubbed yon likkle tyke well. "E's to be named Russano."

Captain Twayblade nodded her agreement. "Aye, 'tis a good strong name. Russa Nodrey saved his life, so her name'll live on in the badger. 'Twas clever of ol' Rock, really, he took Russa's first name an' the first two letters of her second. Russano, I like it. Here's to Russano!"

Everybeast raised their drinks to toast the babe's new name.

"Russano! Good health, long seasons!"

"May he always remember his pretty ol' nurse, Rockjaw Grang!" Lieutenant Morio added, then ducked quickly beneath the table as Rockjaw picked up a pie.

"Ah've never struck a h'officer wi' an apple an' red-currant pie afore, but there's allus a first time, 'tenant Morio!"

Amid the general laughter, Craklyn got up and sang an old Abbey birthing song.

> "O here's to the little ones,
> Sunshine on all,
> As we grow old'n'small,
> May they grow tall,
> Not knowing hunger or winter's cold bite,
> Fearing no living thing, by day or night,
> Strong in the heart, and sturdy of limb,
> Making us proud to know of her or him.
> Here's to the life we love, honest and new,
> Grant all these hopes and dreams come true,
> With each fresh dawn may joy never cease,
> Long seasons of happiness and peace!"

Perigord thumped the tabletop with his tankard. "Splendid, well sung, marm! Long Patrol, let us honor little Russano in Salamandastron style. Draw steel!"

Tammo was not sure what to do, though he felt privileged to be part of the hares' brief ceremony. Pulling forth his blade, he held it flat over the vegetable basket like the rest. Gazing solemnly up through a crisscross of deadly steel, the badgerbabe watched Major Perigord as he intoned:

"We are the Long Patrol, these are our perilous
    blades,
Pledged to your protection across all the seasons,
Our lives are yours, your life is ours.
    Eulaliaaaaaaaaaa!"

"Blister me barnacles, mate," Skipper of Otters whispered to Arven. "I felt the fur rise all along me back when
those warriors shouted their battle cry!"

The Champion of Redwall smiled. "Aye, me too, but
did y'see the little Russano? He never batted an eyelid.
He'll grow to be a cool 'un, I wager."

"I've heard that hares can't sing," Ginko the Bellringer
called out. "Is that right?"

Pasque Valerian threw a paw across Rubbadub's
shoulders. "An' where pray did y'hear that, sir?
Everybeast up on y'paws an' form two rings, one inside
the other. One ring goes left, the other circles right.
Midge, Riffle, you show 'em. Rubbadub, you beat time
an' I'll do the singin'. 'Hares on the Mountain.'"

Whooping and leaping, the hares gripped their
Redwall partners' paws.

"'Hares on the Mountain,' beat it out good'n'fast!"

Rubbadub grinned massively, striking up his drum
noises. "Rubbity dubbity dumbaradum, rubbity dubbity
dumbaradum . . ."

Both circles began moving counter to each other with
the beat, at every third step banging both paws down
hard and doing a double clap. Soon the Redwallers had
the hang of it. When the circles were moving to Pasque's
satisfaction, she sang out loud and speedy:

"'O mother, dear mother, O mother come quick,
Calamity lackaday bring a stout stick,
There's hares on the mountain, they're all
    rough'n'big,
A cuttin' up capers an' dancin' a jig!

They wear rusty medals an' raggy old clothes,
There's one with an apple stuck fast to his nose,
Another's got seashells all tied to his back,
There's hares on the mountain alas an' alack!'

'O daughter, my daughter, now listen to me,
Such rowdy wild pawsteps I never did see,
Run into the house quick an' cover your eyes,
An' I'll give those ruffians such a surprise!'

A hare in a frock coat so fine an' so long
Scraped on a small fiddle an' banged a big gong,
He seized the poor mother an' gave a loud cry,
'Let's warm up our paws with a reel, you an' I!'

'O mother, sweet mother, oh may I look now?'
'Come stir y'stumps, daughter, an' look anyhow,'
As she whirled around the good mother did call,
'There's a handsome one here with no partner at all!

'So batter that drum well an' kick up your paws,
I'm reelin with mine an yore jiggin' with yours,
A leapin' an' twirlin' as cares fly away,
Those hares on the mountain can call any day!' "

All through the grounds of the Abbey, the warm sunny afternoon resounded with the joyous sounds of feasting and laughter. Sloey the mousebabe filled her apron pockets with candied nuts and dashed off with the other Dibbuns to play hide-and-seek.

Gubbio and the rest drew straws to see who would be denkeeper. A tiny hedgehog named Twingle drew the short straw. Covering his eyes with a dock leaf, he began counting aloud in baby fashion.

"One, three, two an' a bit, four, sixty, eight, three again, an' a five-seventy-nine . . ."

Squealing and giggling with excitement, the little

creatures dashed off to hide before Twingle finished counting.

"Four, two an' a twelve, don't knows any more numbers, I'm a cummin' t'find youse all now!"

Back at the table the moles were broaching a great new cask of October Ale, singing uproariously along with the Redwallers, showing the Long Patrol hares what good voice they were in.

"October Ale, 'tis brewed when summer's done,
From hops'n'yeast an' barley fine,
With just a pinch of dandelion,
A smidgeon of good honey, a taste of elderflower,
An' don't forget the old wild oat
Culled at the dawn's first hour.

We puts it up in casks of oak,
All seasoned well with maple smoke,
Then lays it in cool cellars deep,
Ten seasons long to sleep.

October Ale, no drink so good'n'cheery
In winter by the fireside bright
To warm your paws the whole long night,
Or after autumn harvesting, to rest an' take your
    ease.
Just sip a tankard nice'n'slow,
With crusty bread an' cheese.

'Tis wholesome full an' hearty
For any feast or party.
We'd tramp o'er forest hill an' dale
For good October Ale!"

Gurrbowl wielded her mallet, knocking the spigot through the bung with a satisfying thud. Skipper and his otters lined up with tankards and beakers as the foaming dark brew splashed forth. Sergeant Torgoch brushed his bristling mustache with the back of a paw, smacking his lips and clunking beakers with Galloper Riffle as they sampled the new barrel's contents.

Torgoch placed a coaxing paw around the Cellarmole's shoulders, saying, "Wot d'ye say, marm, 'ow about comin' to be Head Cellar Keeper at Salamandastron? Just think of all those poor hares who ain't never tasted yore October Ale. Take pity on 'em, I beg yer!"

The molewife was so flustered by the compliment she threw her pinafore up over her face. "Hurr, go 'way, zurr, you'm a turrible charmer, but oi wuddent leave this yurr h'Abbey for nought, so thurr!"

With a twinkle in her eye, Abbess Tansy chided Torgoch: "Shame on you, Sergeant, trying to rob us of our Cellar Keeper! But seeing as you like Redwall's October Ale so much, here's what I propose. You may take as many barrels back to Salamandastron as you can carry."

Rockjaw Grang placed his paws around a barrel. Grunting and straining, he was barely able to move it. The Sergeant pulled a mock mournful face. "Thankee, marm, yore too kind, I'm sure!"

Suddenly, Twingle the hedgehog Dibbun came stumbling up to the table, waving his paws wildly and shouting, "Come a quick, 'urry 'urry!"

Arven picked him up and sat him on the tabletop. "Now then, you liddle rogue, what's all this noise about?"

Twingle struggled down from the table, yelling urgently, "We was playin' 'ide-seek an' Sloey fell down d'big 'ole!"

Shad the Gatekeeper lifted the Dibbun with one big paw. "What, y'mean the pit under the south wall, Sloey fell down there?"

Breathless and tearful the Dibbun nodded. "All a way down inta the dark she gone!"

Like a flash the otters and hares were away, running headlong with Arven leading them.

Sloey's fall was broken by the rushing waters far below. The swift current was about to whip her off into the bowels of the earth when suddenly she was plucked from the roaring torrent by her apron strings and flung up on the bank. Half conscious, the mousebabe struggled upright and screamed with fright as a coil, heavy and scale-covered, knocked her back down. Something licked her paw, and she caught the dreadful waft of stale breath, hot against her quivering nostrils. A long, satisfied sigh sounded close to her face.

"Aaaaaahhhhhhh!"

32

Tammo was with Arven, Perigord, and Skipper as they hurried onto the platform over the chasm. Shad could be heard calling behind them, "Stay back, too many'll collapse the platform! Stay back, mates!"

Grabbing a rope, Major Perigord knotted it through the carrying ring of the lantern left there by the moles. He swung the light out into the gorge, paying the rope out. Everyone leaned over the edge, peering down as the lantern illuminated the abyss.

Arven bellowed down, "Sloey, can you hear me? Sloey?"

A wail of terror drifted upward as the lantern traveled lower.

Perigord grabbed Skipper's paw. "Great thunderin' seasons. Look!"

A big yellow river eel was menacing the mousebabe on the bank, its brown back and muddy umber sides rearing up snakily, the gashlike downturned mouth open, revealing glittering teeth. It swayed slowly, as if savoring the anticipation of a meal, while its eyes, amber circles with jet-black center orbs, focused on the helpless mite.

Skipper wiped a nervous paw across his dry lips, calling hoarsely, "Keep quiet, liddle 'un! Stay still, don't move!"

Arven stared anxiously down at the horrendous scene.

"Oh, mercy! What'll we do?"

Skipper of Otters acted swiftly. Grabbing the dirk from Tammo, he climbed up onto the rail of the platform. "I'll borrow yore blade, matey, speed's the thing now. One of you follow me down by usin' the rope. Rescue the Dibbun an' get 'er back up 'ere. Can't stop t'chat, mates, 'ere goes!"

With the long knife between his teeth, Skipper dove headfirst into the gorge.

Something flashed by Sloey and landed in the water with a booming splash. Instantaneously the big male otter surfaced and bounded clear of the rushing stream. The eel was about to strike down on its prey when Skipper hurled himself on the coiling monster.

"Redwaaaaaaalllllll!"

The eel struck, burying its teeth in the otter's shoulder and whipping its coils around his body. Skipper had sunk his teeth into the eel's back and was stabbing furiously with the dirk. Eel and otter went lashing and thrashing into the churning waters, locked together in a life-and-death struggle. In a flash they both were gone, swept away underground.

Arven and Perigord took hold of the rope together, but Tammo ducked between them and slid over the platform, clinging to the rope.

"I'm lighter than you chaps. Stand by t'pull me up when I get the Dibbun!"

Paw over paw the young hare descended, looking down to where the babe lay and shivered in the light of the bobbing lantern. Tammo dropped lightly beside Sloey and, taking off his tunic, he wrapped her in it, talking in a soft, friendly tone.

"There now, that nasty thing's gone, thank goodness. I know, we'll make you a nice seat so they can pull you up, wot!"

Sloey turned her tearful face to her rescuer. "I falled downa hole an' nearly got eated up!"

197

Tammo detached the lantern, knotted a fixed loop into the rope's end, and sat the mousebabe in it. "Yes, I know, but you're safe now, Sloey. You go on up an' have some more food at the feast, that'll make y'feel lots better."

He signaled and the Dibbun was lifted up in the makeshift sling, clinging tightly to the rope and calling back down, "Tharra naughty fishysnake, me 'ope Skipper smack its bottom good'n'ard!"

Lying flat on the rocks, Tammo allowed the waters to drench him as he held up the lantern and squinted away to where the boiling torrent raced off downhill into the darkness. Nowhere could he see sight or sound of Skipper or the yellow eel.

A pall had been cast over the golden afternoon. The feast lay abandoned as Perigord explained what had happened. In stunned silence the Redwallers heard the news.

Abbess Tansy stood by her chair, wide-eyed with disbelief. "Oh, poor Skipper, is there nothing we can do?"

Tammo wiped his wet paws on the grass. "I stayed down there an' took a good look, marm. The water goes straight down underground—'fraid Skipper's gone. What a brave beast he was, though. Never considered his own safety at all!"

Arven leaned against a table, his eyes downcast. "I saw his face before he jumped. I could tell that there wasn't anything he wouldn't do to stop little Sloey from being hurt. Skipper of Otters was a true Redwaller!"

Major Perigord gripped his saber handle tightly.

Some distance southeast of Redwall Abbey, the streams, brooks, and back channels became less rapid, flowing placidly through Mossflower Wood. It was here that they converged on the margins of a sprawling water meadow. Log-a-Log, the Guosim Chieftain, gave orders to ship oars and let the little fleet of logboats drift. He sat in the prow of the lead vessel, conversing with his friend

Frackle, their voices a low murmur, as if to preserve the sunlit peacefulness that hung over the flooded meadows like an emerald cape.

A half-grown dragonfly landed on the boat, close to Log-a-Log's paw. It rested, unconcerned by the shrews, its iridescent wings fanning gently.

"Hmmm, nothin' like a bit o' peace," the shrew leader sighed. "I never yet rowed through this place, always let the boat drift. See, Frackle, 'tis summer, the water lilies are startin' to open, an' look over there 'twixt the fen sedge an' bulrushes—yellow poppies sproutin' with the cudweeds. I tell you, matey, this is the place to take a picnic on a quiet noontide!"

Frackle let her paw trail in the dark water, swirling a path amid the minute green plants that carpeted the surface.

Then a white-fletched arrow hummed, almost lazily, through the still air, burying itself in the prow of the logboat, and a gruff roar rang out from somewhere behind the banks of fern and spikerush: "Thee'd ha' been dead now hadst thou been a foebeast!"

Log-a-Log stood up in the bows of his logboat, reassuring the other Guosim with a quick wave of his paw. Then, sitting back down, he pretended to stifle a yawn as he replied idly, "Yore brains are all in yore boots, Gurgan Spearback. If I'd been a foebeast I'd have spotted the smoke up yonder creek, from the chimneys o' those clumsy floatin' islands you call rafts!"

Hardly had he finished speaking, when one of the rafts came skirting the reeds and headed for the logboats. Propelled by six hedgehogs either side with long punting poles, the craft skimmed lightly and fast, belying the awkward nature of its construction.

There was a hut, a proper log cabin with shuttered windows and a door, built at the vessel's center, with a smokestack chimney sprouting from its roof. Lines of washing ran from for'ard to aft, strung between mast timbers. Between the rails at the raft's edges, small hedge-hogs, with safety lines tied about them, could be seen playing. It was obvious that several large families were living aboard.

The leader of the Waterhogs was a fearsome sight. Gurgan Spearback wore great floppy seaboots and an immense brass-buckled belt, through which was thrust a hatchet and a scythe-bladed sword. He had long sea gull feathers impaled on his headspikes, making him look a head bigger than he actually was. His face was painted white, with scarlet polka dots daubed on.

Gurgan leaned on a long-handled oversized mallet, its head a section of rowan trunk. As the raft closed with the leading logboat, the Guosim Chieftain sprang over the rail and hurled himself upon the Waterhog leader. They wrestled around the raft's deck, pummeling each other playfully while they made their greetings.

"Thou'rt nowt but an ancient blood pudden, Log-a-Log Guosim!"

"Gurgan Spearback! Still lookin' like a spiky feather-bed wid boots on, you great floatin' pincushion!"

More rafts joined them, sailing out from a creek on the far side. Soon they were joined into a square flotilla, with the logboats tied up to their outer rails. Food was served on the open decks, hogcooks bustling in and out of their huts, carrying pans of thick porridge flavored with cut fruit and honey, the staple diet of Waterhogs. This was accompanied by hot cheese flans and mugs of rose-hip'n'apple cider.

The little hogs wandered between groups, eating as if they were facing a seven-season famine. Big, wide-girthed fathers and huge, hefty-limbed mothers encour-aged them.

"Tuck in there, Tuggy, th'art nowt but a shadow, get some paddin' 'round thy bones, young 'og!"

Log-a-Log refused a second bowl, patting his stomach to indicate that he had eaten sufficiently. "Phew! I wouldn't chance a swim after that liddle lot, mate!"

Gurgan snatched the bowl and dug in with a scallop-shell spoon. "So, what brings thee'n'thy tribe around these 'ere parts?"

Log-a-Log patted a passing young one's headspikes and winced. "I could ask you the same question, mess-mate, but we're chartin' a course close to Redwall Abbey to warn the goodbeasts there. Did y'know there's Rapscallions on the move?"

Gurgan licked the empty bowl and hiccupped. "Aye, that I did. We've been four days ahead o' yon vermin since they burned their fleet on the southeast coast. Damug Warfang has o'er a thousandbeast at his back, too many for us. I was lookin' to avoid 'em someway."

Log-a-Log nodded gravely. "Perhaps the answer is to join forces and go after the vermin. We'd have a chance together."

Gurgan began licking his spoon thoughtfully. "Aye, that we would. But hast thou seen the number o' liddle 'uns we're rearin' now? 'Twould not be right to put their lives in danger."

The shrew sipped pensively at his beaker. "Aye, but think on this a moment, Gurgan. Warfang an' his army are like to sweep the whole land an' enslave all, 'less they're stopped. If Mossflower were conquered an' ruled by Rapscallions, wot kinda country would that be to bring young 'ogs up proper?"

Gurgan's paw tested the sickle-edged blade at his belt. "Thou art right, Log-a-Log. What's to be done?"

"We'll take yore young 'uns up to the Abbey an' lodge 'em there. That'll leave you free to fight!"

Paw met paw; Log-a-Log winced again as Gurgan's big mitt crushed his with right good will.

"Thee've an 'ead on thy shoulders, comrade. Thunder'n'snowfire! Ah'll give yon Warfang an' his ilk some death songs t'sing!"

33

Half the Guosim were left on the water meadows with the fighting crews, while the old and very young were conveyed toward Redwall in the logboats. Twilight was upon the land as they paddled upstream. Not too far off, Redwall could be seen, framed by Mossflower Wood on its north and east sides.

The logboats lay in a small cove, where the stream took a bend on the heathlands before turning back to the woodlands. Gurgan waddled ashore, leaning on a long puntpole he had brought along. "This looks as close as we'll hove to yon Abbey. Best leave the boats here an' walk the rest o' the way. Come hither, young Blodge, an' quit messin' about there!"

The young Waterhog Blodge had jumped ashore ahead of the rest and was poking about with a stick at the foot of a hillock by the stream bank. Waving the stick, she came scurrying along. "Look ye, I finded water comin' out o' yonder hill, sir!"

Log-a-Log and Gurgan went to investigate. Blodge had found a trickle of cold fresh water seeping out of the mound and flowing into the stream. She probed it with her stick until it became a tiny fountain, spurting from the hillside.

Log-a-Log took a drink. "Good water, sweet'n'fresh, cold too. It must be comin' from some underground stream, runnin' fairly fast, by the look o' it."

Gurgan Spearback placed his long pole against the water. It sprayed out either side of the butt. "Ah've ne'er seen ought like this," he said, shaking his great spiky head. "Stand aside there, I'll give it a good prod."

They stepped out of his way and he pounded the pole home into the hole with several powerful thrusts. Water squirted everywhere from the enlarged aperture, soaking them. A warning rumble from somewhere underground caused Log-a-Log to grab Blodge and leap back aboard the logboat, yelling, "Come away, Gurgan, mate! Quick!"

The rest of his warning was lost as the hill burst asunder with the awesome pressure of water building up inside it. Mingled with rocks, soil, pebbles, and sand, a mighty geyser of roaring water smashed sideways, demolishing the hillock and immediately swelling the stream to twice its size as it ate up the banks and the land close around.

Skillfully the Guosim oarbeasts rode the flood, turning their boats in midstream and beaching them on the farther side. Shouting and screaming, the young Waterhogs scrambled ashore, away from the danger. Gurgan Spearback was picking himself up and trying to wade upstream, when he was clouted flat by a mud-covered mass, shot from underground like a cannonball. Blowing mud and water from nostrils and mouth, the sturdy Waterhog fought to get the weight off him; it was pinning him down in the shallows, threatening to drown him.

Log-a-Log and several shrews came rushing to his rescue and grappled with the great muddy object, managing to free Gurgan.

Waist deep in icy water, Log-a-Log wiped his eyes and gasped, "Are you all right, mate? Yore not bad injured, are ye?"

"Ho don't fuss now, I'll be all right when I cough up this mud, matey!"

Gurgan looked at Log-a-Log. "Who said that?"

Skipper of Otters staggered to the bank, grunting under the weight of a dead yellow eel whose coils were still wrapped tightly around his sodden frame. He collapsed on dry land.

"I said that! Well, don't stand there gettin' wet an' gogglin', lend a paw t'get this slimy h'animal off me, mates!"

Log-a-Log was never one to panic. He took the situation in his stride. Relieving Skipper of Tammo's dirk, he began prising the stiff coils apart, talking to the otter in a matter-of-fact way.

"Ahoy, Skip, it's been a season or two since I clapped eyes on ye. So this is what yore wearin' these days, a serpent fish. What's the matter, ain't a tunic good enough for ye anymore?"

It was not often that the Abbey bells rang aloud once night had fallen, but Skipper's return proved the exception. Ginko the Bellringer swung on his bell ropes, sending out a joyous clangor across the land until his paws were numbed and reverberations hummed through both his ears.

The new arrivals were welcomed into Great Hall, while the heroic Skipper was carried shoulder high by the hares and his otter crew, down to Cavern Hole. He sat stoically as Sister Viola and Pellit cleaned, stitched, and salved his wounds, answering the volley of questions, of which Tammo's was the first.

"Did you bring my dirk back, Skip? How was it?"

With some reluctance, the otter returned Tammo's weapon. "I tell you, matey, that piece o' steel saved my life. 'Tis a blade t'be proud of an' I'd give ten seasons o' me life to be the owner of such a fine thing!"

The young hare polished his dirk hilt proudly before restoring it to his shoulder belt.

Shad poured hot mint tea for his friend. "I'll wager that ole snakefish kept you busy, matey?"

Skipper held his head to one side as the Sister ministered to a muddied slash the eel's teeth had inflicted. "Aye, he did an' all. A real fighter that beast was, a shame I had t'slay it. The snakefish was lost an' 'ungry; 'twas only his nature t'seek prey. Yowch! Go easy, marm!"

Sister Viola placed an herbal compress on the wound. "I'm sorry. There, that's done! It was extremely brave of you to act as you did, sir. Little Sloey owes you her life. I don't often say this to fighting beasts, but it has been an honor to treat your injuries."

Captain Twayblade pounded the table enthusiastically. "Well said, marm, we can't afford to lose a beast as perilous as the Skipper. I propose y'make him an Honorary Member of the Long Patrol, eh, what d'ye say, Major?"

Amid the roars of approval, Abbess Tansy entered. Smiling through her tears, she clasped the otter's paw affectionately. "So, you old rogue, you came back to us!"

Skipper stood slowly, flexing his brawny limbs experimentally. "Of course I did, Abbess, marm, an' I'll thank ye next time I'm gone that y'don't cancel the feast in me absence. Beggin' yore pardon, but y'didn't finish all the 'otroot soup, did ye?"

Shaking with laughter, Rockjaw Grang strode off to the kitchens, saying over his shoulder, "Sithee, riverdog, sit ee there, I'll fetch ye the whole bloomin' pot if y've a mind to sup it!"

Gurgan Spearback peeped around the door of the spare dormitory where the young Waterhogs had been billeted. "Hoho! There they be, fed'n'washed an' snorin' respectfully. My thanks to thee, goodbeasts."

Mother Buscol shuffled out, carrying a lantern, followed by Craklyn, who was holding a paw to her lips. "Hush now, sir, we've just got the little 'uns to sleep."

Gurgan carried the lantern for them as they went downstairs. "Thy Abbey be full o' babes—Dibbuns, my Waterhogs, three liddle owls, even a badgerbabe. How came you by him?"

Craklyn kept firm hold of old Mother Buscol's paw as she negotiated the spiraling steps. "That's our little Russano, he's very special to us."

Log-a-Log interrupted them as they entered Great Hall. "Council o' War's to be held in Cavern Hole straight away!"

34

Sneezewort and Lousewort, like the rest of the Rapscallion horde, were stunned by what they had witnessed. Both rats sat by their cooking fire in the late evening, discussing in hushed tones the terrible retribution Damug Warfang had inflicted on the ten runaway rebels whom Skaup and his hunters had brought back.

Sneezewort shuddered as he added twigs to the flames. "Good job you never went with 'em, mate. Nobeast'll ever think o' crossin' the Firstblade after the way 'e dealt with Borumm an' Vendace an' the eight who was left!"

Lousewort gazed into the fire, nodding numbly. "Er, er, that's true. Though if I 'ad gone wid 'em I'd 'ave sooner been slain fightin' to escape than . . . Wot was that word Damug used?"

"Executed, mate, that was wot 'e said an' that was wot 'e did. Ugh! Imagine bein' slung inter the water like that, wid a great rock tied around yer neck, screamin' an' pleadin'!"

Lousewort ran a paw around his own neck and cringed at the thought. "It was cruel, 'ard an' merciless an', an' . . . cruel!"

Sneezewort moved closer to the fire and shrugged. "Aye, but that's 'ow a beast becomes Firstblade, by bein' a cold-blooded killer. I was watchin' Damug's face—that'n was enjoyin' wot 'e did."

Damug Warfang was indeed enjoying himself. Everything seemed to be going his way. Not only had he brought the escapers to his own harsh justice, but his scouting expedition under the command of the weasel Gaduss had yielded a double result.

Rinkul the ferret, whom he had supposed long dead, was back with news of Redwall Abbey. Damug had never seen Redwall, though he had heard all about the place. What a prize it would be. From there he could truly rule. If all he had heard from Rinkul was true, then it would not be too difficult to conquer Redwall, seeing as the entire outer south wall looked like collapsing.

There was also the prisoner that Gaduss had brought in with him, an ancient male squirrel, but big and strong—one of those hermit types living alone in Mossflower.

Damug circled the cage that held the creature, idly clacking his swordblade against the seasoned wood bars. The squirrel lay on his side, all four paws bound, ignoring the Warlord, his eyes shut stubbornly.

Damug leaned close to the bars, his voice low and persuasive. "Food and freedom, two wonderful things, my friend, think about them. All you have to do is tell me what is the Abbey's strength, how many fighters, what sort of creatures. Tell me and you can walk free from here with a full stomach and a supply of food."

The reply was noncommittal: "Don't know, 'tis no use askin' me. I've never been inside the place. I live alone in the woodlands an' keep meself to meself!"

The swordblade slid through the bars, prodding the captive. "You saw what I did to those creatures earlier on. Keep lying to me and it could happen to you."

The old squirrel's eyes opened and glared scornfully at the Greatrat. "If you think that'd do ye any good yore a bigger fool than I took ye t'be. I've told you, I know nothin' about Redwall!"

The swordblade thrust harder at the squirrel's back. "There are ways of making you talk, far slower and more painful than drowning. Has that notion penetrated your thick skull?"

"Huh! Then try 'em an' see how far it gets ye, vermin!"

Damug knew his captive spoke the truth. The old squirrel would die out of pure spite and stubbornness rather than talk. Controlling his rising temper, the Firstblade withdrew his sword. "A tough nut, eh? Well, we'll see. After you've been lying there a day or two watching the cool fresh stream water flowing by and sniffing the food on our campfires, I'll come and have another word with you. Hunger and thirst are the greatest persuaders of all."

In a circle around a fire on the stream bank, the Rapmark Captains squatted, subdued by the memory of Damug's horrible executions, but eager to know more of the big Abbey whose wall was weakened to the point where it looked like falling. Rinkul sat with them, though he would not say anything until Damug allowed him to.

Damug Warfang strode into the firelight, flame and shadow adding to his barbarous appearance: red-painted features and glittering armor surmounted by a brass helmet that had a grinning skull fixed to its spike. Gathering his long swirling black cloak about him, he sat down, eyes flicking from side to side.

"Three days! Just three more days, then we march to take the greatest prize any Rapscallion ever dreamed of. The Abbey of Redwall!"

Beating their spearbutts against the ground, the Rapmarks growled their approval, until a glance from the Firstblade silenced them.

"In three days' time every Rapscallion will be rested, well fed, fully armed, painted for war, and ready to do battle. You are my Rapmarks; this is your responsibility. If there is any more desertion or mutiny in this army, one soldier unfit or unwilling to fight and die for his Firstblade, then I will look to you. You saw what happened to Borumm and Vendace today; they were once officers too. Let me tell you, they got off lightly! Should I have to make any more examples you will all see what I mean! Remember, three days!"

Damug swept off to his tent, leaving behind a circle of Captains staring in silence at the ground.

Mid-morning of the following day found the columns from Salamandastron marching under a high summer sun. Lance Corporal Ellbrig watched young Trowbaggs suspiciously. The youngster was actually skipping along, but still keeping in step with the rest, waggling his ears foolishly and twirling his sword. Ellbrig narrowed one eye as if singling out his quarry.

"That hare there, Trowbaggs, you lollopin' specimen, what d'you think you're up to?"

The Long Patrol recruit chortled in a carefree manner, "G'mornin', Corp, good t'be jolly well alive, wot?"

Ellbrig scratched his chin in bewilderment. "I was always a bit doubtful about young Trowbaggs, but now I'm sure. He's gone doodle ally, completely mad!"

Deodar, who was marching alongside Trowbaggs, reassured the Corporal: "He's all right, Corp, it's just that he's learned to march properly and his footpaws aren't so sore anymore. Sort of got his second wind, haven't you, old lad?"

Trowbaggs gave his sword an extra twirl and sheathed it with a flourish. "Exactly! Y'make the old footpaws go left right, 'stead of right left. A good night's sleep, couple of lullabies from the Sergeant, pinch some other chap's spoon an' fork, scoff a bally good breakfast, an' heigh ho, I'm fit for anything at all, wot!"

Drill Sergeant Clubrush had caught up with Lance Corporal Ellbrig and had heard all that went on. "Very good, young sir, fit fer anythin' are we?" he said.

Trowbaggs leapt in the air, performed a pirouette, and carried on skipping. "Right you are, Sarge, brisk as a bee, bright as a button, an' carefree as crabs on a rock, that's me!"

The Sergeant smiled and exchanged a wink with the Corporal. "Right then, we're lookin' for bushtailed buckoes like you. Fall out an' relieve some o' those ration pack an' cookin' gear carriers in the rear ranks. Look sharp now, young sah!"

The irrepressible Furgale stifled a giggle. "Poor old potty Trowbaggs. Serves him jolly well right for openin' his silly great mouth, I s'pose."

Sergeant Clubrush's voice grated close to Furgale's ear. "Wot's that, mister Furgale? Did I 'ear you sayin' you'd like t'join Trowbaggs? We're always lookin' for volunteers, y'know."

"Who me, Sarge? No, Sarge, I never said a blinkin' word Sarge!"

The Drill Sergeant smiled sweetly, an unusual sight. "That's the spirit, young sir, less o' the loosejaw an' more o' the footpaw, left right, left right, keep those shoulders squared!"

The columns did not break step until well into the afternoon. Halting to rest and take light refreshment, they sprawled gratefully on a high hilltop amid wide patches of scented heather. Lady Cregga Rose Eyes climbed onto a rock and surveyed the terrain ahead. Sighting two running figures, she summoned Clubrush.

"Runners coming back, Sergeant. We'll stop here until they report and rest. One of them's young Algador Swiftback, but I don't recognize the other, do you?"

Clubrush shielded his eyes and watched the Runners. "Aye, marm, 'tis one o' the Starbuck family. Reeve, I think."

Algador and Reeve put on an extra burst of speed for the last lap, running neck and neck uphill. The Sergeant dropped his ears flat in admiration.

"Look at 'em go, marm. Only Salamandastron hares can run like that. Ho fer the days o' youth an' t'be a Galloper again, eh!"

Dashing up with scarce a hairbreadth between them, the pair skidded to a halt in a cloud of dust, throwing up a joint salute.

"Found 'em, Lady Cregga, marm!"

"Rapscallion tracks, great masses of 'em!"

Leaping down from the rock, the huge badger confronted them, her eyes turning from pink to red as the blood rose behind them. "Where did you see these vermin tracks?"

Trembling under the Warrior's glare and still breathless, Algador and Reeve continued with their report.

"Comin' up from the south an' east, marm!"

"When we cut their trail 'twas about four days old, but it was Rapscallions right enough, travelin' north, marm!"

Cregga's mighty paw gripped the axpike haft like a steel vise. "Where would be the best place to cut their trail short?"

Algador stuck a paw straight out, turned slowly a few degrees to his right, and, narrowing both eyes, sighted on a location. "Right there, marm! If they're marchin' due north, the closest place we can cut trail would be between those two hills yonder."

Without waiting for anybeast, Cregga strode off downhill, headed for the distant spot. Sergeant Clubrush ruffled both the Runners' ears.

"Well done, you two. Rest here an' tell cooks to leave you food an' drink. Follow us when y'feels ready to go agin. Lance Corporal, get 'em up on their paws an' formed in marchin' order. Come on, you slack-pawed, famine-faced web-wallopers! Are you goin' t'sit around all day while yore good Lady Commander is off alone an' unprotected? Hup two three, last one in line's on a fizzer!"

Clubrush tugged Trowbaggs's ears as he passed by.

"Leave the carryin' to the carriers, Trowbaggs. Back up with the rest an' be'ave yoreself now."

Trowbaggs hurried along, saluting furiously many times. "Behave m'self, Sarge, yes, Sarge, very good, Sarge, thank you, Sarge!"

Clubrush and Ellbrig marched at the rear, helping and encouraging any stragglers. The Sergeant peered ahead through the column's dust. "I knows I shouldn't be sayin' this, Corp, but did you see 'er? She wasn't bothered whether or not she 'ad one or five 'undred at 'er back. Not Lady Rose Eyes, straight off she went, grippin' that axpike like she was stranglin' it, eyes blazin' red, jus' lon-gin' t'be destroyin' any vermin she catches up with!"

Ellbrig stooped on the march, retrieving a beaker some recruit had dropped, and continued without breaking step. "Well, you said it, Sarge, though you spoke for me 'cos I was thinkin' the same thing. We're led by a beast who's liable to run out o' control at any moment. But what can we do?"

The Drill Sergeant blinked against the dust, keeping his eyes straight ahead on the winding downhill path. "Our duty, Corporal, that's wot we can do. Obey Lady Rose Eyes's commands an' look after those who 'ave to obey us. Best thing we can do is the thing we do best. Turn these recruits into real Long Patrol hares who can take care o' themselves in battle. Teach 'em discipline an' com-radeship an' 'ope most of 'em come out o' this mess alive, experienced enough to teach those who'll come after them."

Clubrush raised his voice, bellowing out in true Drill Sergeant fashion so all could hear him: "Come on, me lucky buckoes, move those dodderin' footpaws, yore like a load of ole molewives out pickin' daisies! Pick up that step now! Shangle Widepad, you an' the older veterans, give 'em the 'Moanin' Green Recruit' song, see if'n these whippersnappers can keep up with the pace!"

The tough-looking hare who had helped Trowbaggs on

his first night by standing second guard for him struck up the tune Clubrush had requested. Shangle had a fine deep bass; his comrades joined in. Soon the entire column was moving faster, every young hare in the ranks not wanting to be identified with the object of the mocking air, the Moaning Green Recruit.

"O 'tis up at dawn every morn,
The flag is flyin' high,
Why did I join this Long Patrol,
O why O why O why?

I march all day the whole long way,
Me footpaws red an' sore,
If I get home I'll never roam
No more no more no more!

O watch that line, step in time,
Through sun'n'rain an' snow,
Would I sign up again to go,
O no no no no no!

The Corporal shouts, the Sergeant roars,
As like a snail I creep,
Just get me to that camp tonight
An' let me sleep sleep sleep!"

As a result of the quick-marching dogtrot, the column moved ahead speedily like a well-oiled machine, throwing up a dust cloud in its wake. Darkness was falling fast, and the twin hills were near. Lady Cregga would either be waiting for them in the valley between the hills, or she might have continued pursuing the trail of the Rapscallions. In any event, Clubrush had decided that was where night camp would be pitched.

Trowbaggs was marching directly behind Shangle Widepad when the veteran stumbled. The younger hare saved him as he fell backward. "I say, old bean, are you all right?"

Shangle grimaced, breaking into a hop to keep up with the pace. "Oofh, me flippin' footpaw, I just ricked it on a sharp stone!"

Trowbaggs supported him, nodding to Furgale. "What ho, Furg, lend a paw here, this chap's hobblin', wot!"

The two recruits took Shangle's weapons and pack, sharing them and bolstering up the veteran between them.

"C'mon, bucko, we'll get y'to camp, not far now."

"Rather, you just lean on me'n'ole Trowbaggs, that'll give us five footpaws between us."

Shangle threw his paws gratefully around their shoulders. "Thanks, mates, I'll do the same fer you sometime!"

Good-natured as ever, Furgale winked at the older hare. " 'Course y'will, old lad, when this is finished y'can piggyback both of us all the way home, wot!"

Lady Cregga was not at the rendezvous. It was a fine dry night, and the ground was still warm from the sun's heat. Lance Corporal Ellbrig was left in charge while Clubrush headed off alone after their leader.

Ellbrig watched Trowbaggs and Furgale staggering in with Shangle between them. "Well done, you two! Shangle, sit down there an' I'll take a look at that footpaw. The rest of you, cold supper, no fires, sleep on the ground with yore groundsheets as pillows, don't unroll 'em. We'll be movin' out sharpish at first light."

Deodar and a hare named Fallow were on first watch. They jumped up, weapons at the ready, as two figures loomed up through the gloom.

"Who goes there? Step forward an' be recognized!" Fallow ordered.

Algador and Reeve jogged out of the darkness.

"What ho the camp, 'tis only us Gallopers. Well, did y'catch up with Lady Rose Eyes?"

Fallow snorted. "You're jokin', of course. Sar'nt Clubrush has gone ahead to see if he can find her. You two best get some shut-eye; whole caboodle's movin' out at dawnlight."

Algador unshouldered his pack and let it drop. "Seasons o' slaughter, what drives Lady Cregga on like that?"

Deodar yawned, stretching languidly. "Search me, but whatever it is, we're bound to follow!"

35

Cavern Hole was packed tight for the Council of War. As Champion of Redwall, Arven sat at the Abbess's right paw, his weapon, the great sword of Martin the Warrior, laid flat on the table in front of him. As guests and experienced fighters, Major Perigord and his hares held the right side of the table, Log-a-Log and his shrews with Gurgan Spearback and the otter crew facing them.

The Guosim Chieftain had something to say before the main meeting got under way. "About that water runnin' beneath yore south wall, I think I've found the answer t'the problem. Today we found where the water comes out—good job we did, too, or Skipper woulda never been seen agin. So, I figgers that I knows the waterways of Mossflower better'n most. Any'ow, I put on me thinkin' cap about that stream. If'n it's got a place t'come out, stands to sense there must be a spot where it flows in. Heed me now, I think I knows where that very place is, 'tis on the river north an' west o' Redwall. I've sailed it a few times an' seen where it splits off. With yore permission, Abbess, marm, I'd like to take some o' yore otters an' molefolk with me to dam it off an' stop the water flowin' under yore wall. We'll go first light tomorrer, sooner the better!"

Mother Abbess Tansy signaled for her helpers to begin serving supper all 'round. "You have my permission and may fortune go with you and yours, Log-a-Log. The Guosim have always been special friends of Redwall. Skipper, Foremole Diggum, will you assist the shrews?"

"Aye, marm, my crew's willin' an' ready!"

"Bo urr, ee can count on us'n's, h'Abbess!"

Tammo was sitting between Perigord and Pasque. He sipped hot red-berry cordial and nibbled a wedge of heavy fruitcake, not feeling really hungry. Cavern Hole seemed overfull, rather muggy, warm, and distant. Tammo's eyes drooped, then he swayed slightly and settled back as the talk became a soothing murmur, as if it were echoes from far away. Then a butterfly flew gently by in his sleep-laden imagination; soft, delicate, and silent. It settled on the pink flowers of an almond tree, closing its fragile, pale gold wings. The flowers fell, drifting slowly through still noon air, lighting with scarcely a ripple on the tranquil waters of a shady stream. Catching a small eddy, butterfly and flowers together went 'round and 'round in lazy circles.

Both Log-a-Log and Gurgan Spearback had told the meeting of Gormad Tunn's death and everything they had seen of Damug Warfang and his Rapscallions. All eyes turned to Major Perigord and Arven, who were already deep in conversation. The squirrel Warrior, as Champion of Redwall, would naturally be consulted on the Abbey's defense. Finally Perigord leaned forward, nodding his head shrewdly. "Hmm, we've defeated those vermin at Salamandastron not s'long ago, but you'll forgive me sayin', we had the full force o' the Long Patrol an' Lady Cregga Rose Eyes full o' Bloodwrath when we did it. How many Rapscallions d'you estimate Damug has on call?"

Log-a-Log scratched his head reflectively. "Best ask Gurgan, he's seen 'em firsthand."

"Aye," said the Waterhog, "we've watched 'em on the

move and when they camped. Oft times they looked to number like leaves in an autumn gale. Hark now, 'tis not my wish to afright these gentle Redwallers, but my mate Rufftip, she counted 'em as they moved out from the coast. Damug Warfang has a few score o'er ten 'undred to do his biddin'."

A stunned silence settled upon Cavern Hole. Nobeast had envisaged a vermin army of more than a thousand on the march. Arven shot Major Perigord a quick glance. Something had to be done before panic set in. Perigord understood and rose to the occasion.

"Well now, chaps, that sounds like a tidy old bunch, wot! However, there was half that number again when they came at Salamandastron, ships too, but we still managed to send the rotters packin'. Main thing is not t'be scared by numbers, after all, 'tis quality that counts, not quantity!"

Pellit the dormouse challenged him. "You could stand 'ere all night talkin' like that, but it still won't stop all those Rapscallions attackin' Redwall. Point is, wot are you goin' to do about it besides talk, eh?"

Abbess Tansy glared frostily at Pellit. "Perhaps, sir, you would tell us what *you* propose to do?"

All the dormouse could do was bluster in his own defense. "I ain't no fightin' beast, marm, most of us Abbeydwellers don't know the first thing about battlin'. Wot d'you expect us t'do?"

Arven stood up slowly, frowning at Pellit, who cringed under the Redwall Champion's stern reproof.

"Major Perigord has pledged himself and his patrol to help us. I would expect that you have the good manners to give him a hearing, unless you have a better or more helpful suggestion to assist your Abbey in this crisis."

Pellit lowered his eyes and shrugged. The Abbess smiled apologetically at Perigord. "Forgive the interruption, Major. You were saying?"

But the hare had slightly lost track of his speech. To

gain time he stroked his whiskers thoughtfully and pursed his lips.

Suddenly all eyes turned on Tammo. He rose and walked 'round to stand beside Arven, gazing at the great sword that lay upon the table. In a calm, measured voice, he began speaking:

"Aye, Sire, it shall be as you say."

Arven could tell by the look in Tammo's eyes that he was still sleeping. The young hare moved toward the steps leading up to Great Hall. Placing a paw to his lips, Arven warned everybeast to hold their silence. Then he gestured with his other paw to clear a way. Redwallers fell back to either side as Tammo went by them, unaware of all about him. Craklyn uttered a single word as she followed in his wake:

"Martin!"

Lanterns burned dimly in Great Hall, casting shadows around the sandstone columns and recesses, and moonlight shone through the high windows onto a floor worn smooth by countless generations of paws. In complete silence the Redwallers grouped behind Tammo, who stood staring up at the tapestry on the wall. It was a marvelous piece of work, fashioned by Abbey creatures in the distant past. Martin the Warrior, Redwall's founder hero, was depicted there, standing armor-clad and leaning upon his sword.

"I brought you quill and parchment," Viola Bankvole whispered to Craklyn, passing her writing materials. "You may need them!"

The Recorder nodded her thanks as Tammo started speaking.

"Spring is done now, summer calls,
This season fraught with wartime's fear,
Fate says Damug will ne'er see our walls,
Battle must take place, though not here.

Manycoats will know the way,
So go with him, De Fformelo.
A soothsayer knows what to say,
Secrets Warfang longs to know.
One day Redwall a badger will see,
But the badger may never see Redwall,
Darkness will set the Warrior free,
The young must answer a mountain's call."

A vagrant night breeze waved the tapestry once, then all was still and quiet. Tammo sat down upon the floor. He rubbed his eyes and stared at his surroundings in bewilderment.

"What the . . . Who brought me here?"

Arven sat beside him, pointing to the figure on the tapestry.

"Martin the Warrior did, he had a message for us."

"Oh, y'don't say, an' what was the message?"

"You should know, friend, 'twas you who delivered it!"

"Me? I say, that's a bit blinkin' much. I don't remember a single thing. What did I, I mean he, say?"

Craklyn spread her parchment in front of the young hare. "Don't worry, Tammo, I recorded every word. Martin the Warrior is the guiding spirit of our Abbey. In times of trouble he will often choose somebeast to deliver his message to us. You must be a very special creature for Martin to single you out."

Tammo nodded absently as he scanned the parchment. "Hmm, never thought of m'self as jolly well special, marm. Hey, Midge, it mentions you here. It says, 'Manycoats will know the way.'"

Midge was far shorter than the other hares, but none the less brave. He laughed excitedly. "Hahaha! Wonderful! It's just come to me in a flash, yes, I certainly do know what t'do!"

"Well bully for you, laddie buck!" Perigord checked him hastily. "But there's no reason t'be worryin' our

221

friends with a lot o' balderdash. C'mon, chaps, all pop along an' get some shut-eye now, it's rather late y'know. Leave this to us, we'll sort out the details, wot!"

Abbess Tansy nodded in agreement. Some of the Redwallers looked rather reluctant, but one glance from their Abbess told them she was in no mood for argument.

Skipper, Foremole, Log-a-Log, Gurgan, and the hares followed Arven, Craklyn, and Tansy back down to Cavern Hole. Once there they made themselves comfortable by the fire embers.

Perigord stirred the logs with his saber tip, saying, 'Speak y'piece, Midge. Tell us what came t'you in a flash."

The small hare did so readily. "Listen, Martin said that the battle mustn't take place at Redwall, it's got to be fought elsewhere, see!"

Arven placed the great sword on the fireplace lintel. "That makes sense. We wouldn't stand much chance with over a thousand Rapscallions charging a collapsin' south wall. What do you intend t'do about it, Midge?"

"Here's the wheeze, old chap. Damug Warfang, like all Warlords, is prob'ly very superstitious. Well, what if an old ragged soothsayer puts a word in the ear of somebeast close to him?"

Perigord frowned. "What sort o' word?"

"Well, sah, the sort o' word tellin' where a battle might take place an' sayin' how unlucky 'twill be to look upon Redwall Abbey until the battle is won, an' how the chosen battle place'll be lucky for a certain Rapscallion leader . . ."

The Major shook his head at Midge's quick-wittedness. "Enough, enough, I've got the drift now. Well done, Midge Manycoats! Spot of action for you, young Tammo; the rhyme says you've got to go with Midge. Don't worry, he'll disguise you pretty well."

Eyes shining, Tammo clasped his dirk hilt. "Y'can rely on me, sah!"

Perigord ruffled Tammo's ears fondly. "Splendid! I knew I could. Y'know, you look the image o' your mother sometimes, not half as pretty, but somethin' about the eyes. However, can't let you two go alone. Rockjaw, you are our best tracker. Go with 'em, find the camp, and keep y'self close. We'll use you as a go-between. Very good! Sar'nt Torgoch, you an' Lieutenant Morio go right away at dawn an' scout out a good location for the battle. We'll get news of the chosen spot to you, Rockjaw. Taunoc, with his sharp eyes and knowledge of the woods, will be messenger. Meanwhile, Midge, you can be workin' y'self into the vermin's confidence. Shouldn't be too hard for a hare with a head on his shoulders like you have, wot. We'll get word t'you as soon as a good location's been staked out. That's all, chaps. Get some rest now, busy day ahead of us tomorrow. Dismissed!"

BOOK THREE

The Ridge

36

Two hours after dawn the next day, four logboats plied the waters of the broad stream north by west from Redwall. Foremole Diggum and his team crouched uneasily in the boats, some of them with cloaks thrown over their heads. Moles are not noted for being great sailors, preferring dry land to water.

"Boo urr, 'taint natcheral t'be afloaten abowt loik this!"

"Hurr nay, oi'm afeared us'n's moight be a sinkin' unnerwater!"

Log-a-Log dug his paddle deep, scowling at them. "Belay that kind o' talk, I ain't never lost a beast off'n a boat o' mine yet. Quit the wailin' an' moanin', willyer!"

Skipper stuffed bread and cheese in his mouth, winking at his otter crew as they gobbled a hasty breakfast. "Ooh, 'e's an 'eartless shrew, that'n is! Ahoy there, moles, come an' join us in a bite o' brekkfist, mates."

Gurgan Spearback, swigging from a flask of October Ale, noted the moles' distress.

"Hearken, Skip, yon moles were a funny enough color afore ye offered 'em vittles—don't go makin' 'em any worse!"

Log-a-Log's companion Frackle pointed with her oar-blade. "There 'tis, see, two points off'n the starboard bow!"

Part of the stream forked off down a narrow tributary. Steering the logboats into it, they followed the winding downhill course of the rivulet, wooden keels scraping on the bottom as they went. After a short distance, Log-a-Log waved his oar overhead in a circular motion.

"Bring all crafts amidships, sharp now, bow'n'stern broadsides!"

Four logboats were soon wedged lengthways against the flow, their stems and sterns resting on opposite shores of the narrow waterway. Gratefully, the moles scrambled ashore, kissing the ground in thanks for their safe landing. Skipper and his otters went ahead to the point where the stream disappeared into a hillside.

"This is it, mates," announced Skipper. "Spread out an' search for a big boulder!"

By the time the rest arrived, the streamflow had dwindled a bit, owing to the course being blocked by the logboats.

Gurgan waded through it and climbed the hill to admonish Skipper. "Thou'rt still hurted, thee shouldn't ha' come!"

The tough otter scratched at one of his wounds, which was beginning to itch. "Coupla scratches never stopped me doin' what I like, mate. Ahoy there, mates, that's a good ole boulder ye found!"

The stone was partially sunk into the earth, but Foremole Diggum and his crew soon dug it out. Using a smaller rock as a chock, the otters levered the roundish mass of stone uphill, using shrew oars to move it. Gurgan threw his added weight into the task, while Foremole marked out a spot on the hilltop, calling, "Bring ee bowlder up to yurr!"

Once or twice the heavy stone rolled back on them, but they were determined creatures. Otters, shrews, moles, and the Waterhog Chieftain gritted their teeth and fought the boulder, fraction by fraction, until it rested on Foremole's mark. Sighting with a straight twig, Foremole ordered the boulder moved a bit this way and a bit that way. Finally satisfied, he took an oar and gave the boulder one hard shove with the paddle end. The great rock toppled down into the stream, sending up a shower of water; then it rolled back downhill and lodged itself squarely across the spot where the flow vanished underground. Moles and otters dashed down to pack the edges with a mixture of mud, pebbles, and whatever bits of timber came to paw.

The flow of the stream halted and backed up on itself until it became a becalmed creek. A short celebratory meal at the creekside would have been appropriate, but the otter crew had eaten all the food, so they drank the last of the October Ale and plum cordial, then got the boats headed out. Log-a-Log called out to the moles, who had remained onshore, "Come on, mateys, back to the Abbey. 'Twill be a fine fast sail downriver, we'll be back afore ye knows it!"

Foremole wrinkled his nose, trundling off along the bankside. "You'm go, zurr Log, an' gudd lukk to ee. Us'n's be walkin' back even if'n it takes ten season t'do et. No more sailin' fur molers!"

Tammo watched, fascinated, as Midge Manycoats applied his disguise before a burnished copper mirror in Sister Viola's dormitory. The small hare explained as he went along.

"Alter the face first, that's half the trick. See, I roll my own ears down and put on this ole greasy cap with false ears stickin' out the side of it, one's only half an ear an' the other has a slice out of it, just like some smelly ole vermin. Now, I rub m'face with this oily brown stuff—pass me that candle, Tamm. Singe the whiskers down an' rub 'em 'til they're scrubby. Good! Put a patch over one eye, and paste a thin bit o' bark over the other, givin' it a nasty slant. Aye, that's more like it. Look, a little black limpet shell, stick it on the end of my handsome nose with a blob o' gum, an' presto! Snidgey pointed vermin hooter, wot! Few bits o' darkened wax over the teeth, two long thorns stuck in the wax just under the top lip. Haharr, fangs! Pass me that greasy charcoal stick, hmm, two wicked downcurved lines, one either side of the mouth, that's it! Righto, I throw this filthy tattered sack over me, belt it with a loose cob o' rope, crouch down a bit, hunch shoulders, shuffle footpaws. What d'you see, Tammo?"

The young hare gasped in amazement. Standing before him was an aged vermin creature, neither wholly rat, ferret, or stoat, but definitely vermin of some type.

"Great seasons o' soup! No wonder they call you Midge Manycoats!"

Midge adopted the whining vermin slang. "Harr, wait'll yer sees yerself when I'm done wid ye, cully!"

Rockjaw Grang was having what he figured would be his last good hot meal for a while, working his way through an immense potato, mushroom, and carrot pastie oozing rich dark herb gravy. Dibbuns surrounded the big hare, watching his throat bob up and down as he polished off a tankard of dandelion and burdock cordial. Gubbio the molebabe pushed a steaming cherry and damson pudding in front of Rockjaw, and Sloey, none the worse for her adventure, poured yellow meadowcream plentifully over it.

"Whoo! A you goin' to eat alla dat up, mista G'ang?"

Rockjaw sat the mousebabe up on the table. "Sithee, jus' you watch me, liddle lass, but keep out of t'way, else I'll scoff thee an' all. Aye, y'd be right tasty wi' a plum in yore mouth an' some cream o'er yore 'ead!"

Clapping their paws and jumping up and down, the Dibbuns chortled, "Goo on, mista G'ang, eat Sloey alla up!"

The giant hare set Sloey back down on the floor. "Only if she's very naughty. 'Ey up, wot's this?"

Two thoroughly evil-looking vermin shuffled into the

kitchens and began dirtying their blades by coating them with vegetable oil and soot from the stovepipes. The Dibbuns shrieked and leapt upon Rockjaw, clinging tearfully to his neck. He patted the tiny heads soothingly.

"Shush now, liddle 'uns, 'tis only Midge an' Tammo actin' at bein' varmints. You go an' play with the babby owls an' Russano now. I'll eat those two up if'n they frightens any more Dibbuns."

Shad the Gatekeeper took Abbess Tansy and Craklyn down to the platform beneath the south wall. They lowered two lanterns on a rope and saw that the water had dwindled away to a mere trickle.

Shad grunted with satisfaction. "Y'see, marms, they found the stream an' likely blocked it off. Soon it'll be dry down there. May'aps then we'll go down an' take a look around. I don't mind tellin' you, I'm real curious t'see wot 'tis like. I know you are too, miz Craklyn."

The old Recorder peered down at the drying stream bed. "It's my duty to see what's down there. Everything has to be recorded and written up for future generations of our Abbey. Which leads me to think I've been looking in the wrong place to find out more about this—the answer might lie in your gatehouse, Shad. I suspect that if we look through Redwall's first records, the truth about all this may emerge."

Tansy kissed her old friend's cheek. "But of course! What a clever old Recorder you are, Craklyn."

The Recorder of Redwall turned away from the pit, signaling Shad to escort them aboveground. "You're no spring daisy yourself, Mother Abbess. Come on, we've a long dusty job ahead of us."

Shad hastily excused himself from the task. "Beggin' yore pardons, but I got other chores t'do. You ladies 'elp yoreselves to anythin' y'need in my gate'ouse. I can't abide the dust an' disorder when you starts unpackin' those ole record books'n'scrolls off the shelves, miz Craklyn."

Tansy watched the otter hurrying off across the Abbey lawns. "Other chores to do, indeed, great wallopin' waterdog!"

Craklyn chuckled as she took her friend's paw. "Don't be too hard on poor Shad. Otters never made good scholars. He's probably off to play with little Russano and the baby owls."

232

37

The south wallgate had been jammed shut by the subsidence, so Tammo, Midge, and Rockjaw were leaving by the little east wallgate. Major Perigord and Pasque Valerian saw them off. Perigord was none too happy about Tammo going.

"Now remember, you chaps, keep y'heads down an' don't attract too much attention to yourselves. Normally I would have sent Tare or Turry with Midge, but as the rhyme names you, Tamm, well it seems you're the one to go. So take it easy, young bucko, an' report back to Rockjaw whenever you can. We'll get news of the battleground to you as soon as we hear back from Torgoch and Morio. Look after 'em, Rock. I've no need to tell you of the danger they'll be in."

Rockjaw Grang saluted the Major. "Never fear, sah, y'can rely on me!"

The soft brown eyes of Pasque looked full of concern. Tammo winked roguishly at her from beneath his vermin disguise. "Don't fret, chum, we'll be back before you know it!"

Perigord watched them threading their way south through the woodland until the three figures were lost among the trees. He locked the east wallgate carefully, then, turning to the dejected Pasque, he chucked her gently beneath the chin. "C'mon now, missie, you'll bring on the rain with a face like that, wot! Your Tammo'll be back in a day or two, full o' tales of how he outwitted the Rapscallions. Cheer up, that's an order!"

Midge Manycoats had done an excellent job of disguising Tammo, making him look old and thoroughly evil by giving him shaggy beetling brows to hide his eyes and a matted straggling beard. To this he added a greasy flop hat, lots of jangling brass ornaments, and an old dormitory blanket that was literally in frayed tatters, after he had finished trouncing it about in the orchard compost heap. Tammo not only looked villainous, but smelled highly disreputable.

Both hares found themselves gasping for breath under their camouflage. Leaning against an oak tree, they pleaded with the long-striding Rockjaw.

"I say, Rock, ease off a bit, will you, you've got the pair of us whacked with that pace o' yours!"

"Aye, slow down, mate, or we'll perish long before we find the vermin camp. Whew! I'm roasted under this lot!"

The big fellow turned and retraced his path, halting several paces from them and wafting a paw across his nostrils. "By 'eck, you lads don't mind if'n I stands well upwind of ye?"

Tammo leered nastily and tried out his vermin accent. "Ho harr, me ole matey, you don't expect us t'go sailin' inter a Rapscallion camp smellin' like dewy roses now, do yer?"

Beneath his disguise, Midge winced at the pitiful attempt. "I think you'd best keep your lip buttoned an' pretend to be my dumb assistant, Tamm. That vermin accent o' yours is awful!"

Rockjaw agreed with Midge's assessment. "Aye, yore too nice-spoken, Tammo, prob'ly 'cos you was well brung up!"

Young Friar Butty brought a tray to the gatehouse that afternoon because neither Tansy nor Craklyn had been back to the Abbey building for anything to eat. Both windows and the door were wide open to counteract the dust. Butty blinked as he entered, and looked about for somewhere to set the tray down.

"I was beginnin' t'get worried about you, marm, an' you too, miz Craklyn. So I brought you a snack. There's turnip an' carrot bake, cold mint tea, some blackberry tarts, an' a small rhubarb an' strawberry crumble I made special for you. They're fresh strawberries from the orchard, nice an' early this season."

Tansy looked up over the top of her tiny glasses. "Thank you, Friar Butty, how thoughtful. Just put the tray on that chair, please. Let's take a break, Craklyn."

While they ate their food, Butty looked around at the piles of books, ledgers, scrolls, and charts piled everywhere, lots of them browny-yellow with age.

Craklyn watched him as she sipped gratefully at a beaker of cool mint tea. "Those are our Abbey records going right back to when Redwall was first built. Unfortunately they're mixed in with lots of old recipes, poems, songs, herbalists' notes and remedies. Help yourself to any recipes that you like—they may come in useful when you get stuck for cooking ideas."

Butty, however, was looking at the latest piece of writing, the parchment on which Craklyn had recorded the words sent via Tammo from Martin the Warrior. He read aloud the second part of the verse.

"One day Redwall a badger will see,
But the badger may never see Redwall,
Darkness will set the Warrior free,
The young must answer a mountain's call."

Abbess Tansy glanced up from her seat in a deep arm-chair. "Why did you pick that part of the poem to read, Friar?"

The young squirrel tapped the parchment thought-fully. "Well, it seemed to me at the time that the first part of the thing was all that you were interested in, that bit about the battle taking place elsewhere and Tammo goin' along with Midge Manycoats. Nobeast took an interest in the second part. What d'you suppose it means?"

Craklyn pointed out the first two words of the ninth line. "See here, this line begins with the words 'One day.' So we take that to mean at some distant time in the future. All we were looking for in the poem was Martin's imme-diate message to save Redwall from danger. But you're right, Butty, it is a very mysterious and interesting part you read out. Alas, we cannot see the future, so we will just have to wait for time itself to unroll the message it contains."

Friar Butty put the parchment down and riffled through the mass of papers piled on a nearby shelf. He withdrew a thick and aged-looking volume, blowing the dust from it. "Aye, I suppose you're right, marm, time reveals all sooner or later, probably even the secrets that this old volume contains."

Tansy liked young Butty; he was a fast learner. "My word, that is an ancient-looking thing. Does it say who wrote it? The name will be inside the front cover."

Butty opened the book and read the faded script therein. "'The journal of Abbess Germaine, formerly of Loamhedge.'"

Mint tea spilled down Craklyn's gown as she jumped upright. "The architect of the Abbey! That's the very volume we're looking for! Well done, young sir!"

Hurrying out into the sunlight, the trio seated them-selves on the broad stone steps leading to the gatehouse threshold. Craklyn turned carefully to the first page. "I'll wager an acorn to a bushel of apples that the answer to what lies beneath our south wall is in these pages some-where!"

The crews of the logboats strode into the kitchens, refreshed by their fast trip downstream and hungry as hunters. Skipper whacked his rudderlike tail against a big pan. "Ahoy, Friar Butty, any vittles fer pore starvin' creatures?"

Mother Buscol waddled from the corner cupboard, waving a threatening ladle at the otter. "Look, you great noisy riverdog, Butty ain't 'ere, see. So don't you come with yore rough gang a shoutin' an' hollerin' 'round these kitchens when we just got the owlbabes takin' their noontide nap!"

Gurgan Spearback touched his headspikes respect-fully. "Thee'll 'scuse us, marm, we'll be well satisfied t'sit out in your dinin' room an' wait t'be served by one as pretty as yoreself."

Taken by surprise at the Waterhog's courtly manner, Mother Buscol smiled and dipped a deep curtsy. "Indeed to goodness, sir, I'll just warm up the pasties and heat some soup. Would you be takin' gooseberry cordial with it?"

Gurgan bowed, sticking one of his immense boots for-ward as he made what he considered to be an elegant leg.

" 'Twould be more'n sufficient, m'lady, 'specially if it were served by yore own fair paws!"

Chuckling, the old squirrelmother set about her task.

Log-a-Log nudged Gurgan. "You fat ole flatterer, all she was about t'give us was a swipe with 'er ladle. 'Ow d'you do it, matey?"

Gurgan led them out to the tables, winking slyly. "A smidgeon o' sugar's worth ten barrels o' rocks, friend. Lackaday, who did that to yore nose, Shad?"

The burly otter Gatekeeper was seated at the table, feeding candied chestnuts to the little badger Russano. He touched the dock leaf wrapped tenderly 'round his snout. "Never lean too close to owlchicks, matey, they got beaks on 'em like liddle scissors. I just found that out when I was playin' with 'em. Savage beasts they are, they'll eat anythin' at all!"

Skipper laughed and tickled the badgerbabe's foot-paws. "An' 'ow's my liddle mate 'ere behavin' 'imself, eh?"

Shad patted Russano proudly. "I just taught 'im a new word. Watch!"

He held a candied chestnut up, just out of Russano's reach. The tiny fellow reached out his paws, uttering the word gruffly. "Nut! Nut!"

The otters and shrews thought Russano's new word was a source of great hilarity. They gathered 'round him, chanting, "Nut! Nut! Nut! Nut!"

The two Little Owls, Orocca and her husband, Taunoc, came flying out of the kitchens. They landed on the table-top, contracting and dilating their massive golden eyes and flexing their talons.

"Whichbeast is making all the noise out here?"

"Waking our eggchicks with that silly nut-nut call!"

Straightfaced and serious, all the otters and shrews pointed at the badgerbabe Russano, who lay innocent and smiling. " 'Twasn't us, it was him!"

38

Skaup the ferret and a dozen or more Rapscallions were out foraging, roaming farther than they usually did. Skaup was pleased: they had slain several birds and in addition had two clutches of waterfowl eggs and a fat old perch they had found floating dead in a stream. They were seated in a patch of shrub that had a blackberry sprig growing through it. Although the berries were only partially ripe, the vermin crew readily picked and ate them, the reddish-purple juice staining their paws and mouths.

Suddenly a stoat pointed to the left. "Over there, three beasts. Look!"

Rockjaw Grang dropped swiftly out of sight at the sound of the stoat's shout. He scurried off backward, bent double. "I ain't sure they got a proper glimpse o' me. You'll have to bluff 'em, Midge. Good luck, you two!"

Swords drawn, the Rapscallions advanced on the pair. Midge muttered urgently to Tammo, "Remember, you're dumb. Leave this t'me!"

A moment later the tip of Skaup's blade was touching Midge's throat. "Who are yer an' where'd you come from?"

Midge stood his ground fearlessly, curling his lip at the

239

ferret. "I could ask you th' same question, bucko!"

"You ain't in no position to ask questions, rag'ead," Skaup sneered back at him. "There was *three* o' yer. Where'd the other one go to?"

Ignoring the swordtip, Midge shook his head pityingly. "If you seen three of us then you've either bin swiggin' grog or yer eyes are playin' tricks on yer. I'm Miggo an' this is me matey Burfal. There ain't nobeast with us."

The stoat who first sighted Rockjaw scratched his head. "I'd swear I saw another, a big 'un 'e was, I'm sure of it!"

Midge pushed Skaup's blade aside and grabbed the stoat, pulling him close. "Ho, so yore the one seen three of us? Well wotta useless lump you are! I wager yer don't even know there's a chestnut in yore ear, do yer?"

Reaching out quickly, Midge gave the stoat's ear a sharp tug. The vermin yelped in pain, but his companions stood goggle-eyed, staring at the candied chestnut which the stranger had apparently pulled from the stoat's ear.

Tammo caught on right away to Midge's trick. Sliding a candied chestnut from the pouch under his blanket, he hobbled past Skaup, who had lowered his sword. Midge noted what Tammo had done, and gave the ferret a snaggle-toothed grin. "Look at yer swordpoint, mate!"

Skaup lifted the sword level with his eyes and found himself gazing at a candied chestnut impaled upon it. "But . . . 'ow did that get there?"

Midge cackled as he performed a shuffling little jig. "Heeheehee! An' how did two of us turn up 'ere when we're supposed ter be three? I dunno, do you, mate?"

Midge looked so comical that some of the vermin started laughing. Tammo joined in with his friend's dance, the pair of them whirling and stamping, rags and tatters jouncing and twirling. Soon all the vermin were laughing at their antics, even Skaup.

From his hiding place behind a stately elm, Rockjaw smiled. Midge and Tammo were safe for the moment. Keeping a safe distance, the big hare shadowed the party as they made their way back to the Rapscallion camp.

Skaup trudged alongside Midge, eyeing him curiously. "Yore a clever ole beast, Miggo. Let's see yer pull a chestnut out o' my ear, go on!"

Midge's unpatched eye twinkled slyly. "No need to, bucko. Look, there's one stuck to yer cloak!"

Skaup shook his head in wonderment as he pulled the sticky nut from the cloak across his shoulders and munched happily on it. "Yore pal there, Burfal, why don't 'e never say anythin'?"

Midge passed a paw across his throat, grinning wickedly. "We 'ad an argument when we was both young 'uns. Burfal called me some bad names, so I cut 'is throat. Haharr, 'e lived through it, but 'e ain't never spoke a single word since that day. Heeheehee! Ole Burfal won't call anybeast bad names no more!"

It was getting toward evening when they reached the Rapscallion camp on the hillside above the stream. A shudder passed through Tammo as he followed Skaup's party. There were countless vermin crouched around fires, cooking, resting, squabbling, and arguing with their neighbors. Drums throbbed ceaselessly, and hideously painted faces glared curiously at the two disguised hares. Everybeast was armed with an ugly array of weaponry, from cutlasses and spears down to what looked like sharpened hooks set on long poles.

Smoke from the fires swirled around them as they reached the stream bank. Skaup halted his party in front of a tent with four rats guarding the entrance, and laid the supplies they had foraged for on the ground.

Tammo and Midge were pushed forward. Suddenly the tent flap was thrown back and they found themselves face-to-face with Damug Warfang, Firstblade of all Rapscallions. Though the fur on his back stood rigid with fright, Tammo could not help being impressed by Damug's barbarically splendid appearance. The Greatrat was wearing the helmet with a skull on its spike, and his slitted feral eyes glared at them out of a scarlet and blue painted face. He wore a close-meshed tunic of silver mail, belted about with a broad snakeskin band. Sandals and gauntlets of green lizard skin covered his paws.

Damug Warfang leaned forward, his powerful frame like a coiled steel spring as he pointed at the hares with his symbol of office, the sword with two edges, one straight, the other like the waves of the sea.

"What do you want here? You are not Rapscallions!"

Midge nodded his head knowingly as he spoke out boldly, "I was a Rapscallion long afore you was born. I served under yore father, Gormad Tunn. Wait now, don't tell me, you'll be Damug the youngest son, or was it the eldest? I forget. Didn't you 'ave a brother? Haharr, I remember now, 'twas Byral. Where's 'e got to these days?"

Damug's eyes glinted dangerously. "You ask a lot of questions for a ragged old creature. Silence is the best policy for one such as you when I am holding a sword!"

Midge sat down on the ground. He pulled an assortment of colored pebbles and some carved twigs from beneath his sacking gown, and tossed them in the air. Totally ignoring the Warlord, he studied the jumble of wood and stone on the grass in front of him. Then in a sing-song voice he said, "I got no need to ask questions, my signs tell me all. The moon an' stars, the wind in the trees, an' water that runs through the land, all these things whisper their secrets to me."

Midge could tell by the look in Damug's eyes that he had captured the Warlord's interest. The Greatrat sheathed his sword. "You are a Seer, one who can look into the future?"

"Somebeasts have called me Seer. Maybe they're right, who can tell?"

"Who is that beast with you, is he a Seer also?"

"Not Burfal. He is called the Silent One an' must be allowed to roam free an' unhindered. Burfal, go!"

Tammo sensed that Midge was giving him an excuse to find Rockjaw and report to him. Smiling foolishly he wandered off.

Damug turned to Skaup. "Let nobeast harm Burfal; he may go where he pleases. Seer, what do they call you?"

"My name is Miggo. 'Twas given to me on the night of the dark moon by a black fox."

Damug stared at Midge for a long time, then beckoned to him, "Come into my tent, Miggo. You there, bring food and drink for this creature. The rest of you, get about your business."

Tammo's footpaws shook as he made his way through the camp. He could feel Skaup watching him, so instead of traveling in a straight line he wandered willy nilly. The aim of his walk was to take him over the hilltop, away from the camp, where he would seek out Rockjaw Grang.

Night had fallen now, and all over the hillside the vermin campfires burnt small islands of light into the darkness. Tammo was threading his way 'round one fire when he stumbled awkwardly. A hardwood stick had been thrust between his footpaws by one of the vermin seated at the edge of the fire. It was the ferret Rinkul. As Tammo tried to pull himself upright, Rinkul kicked him flat.

"Wot are you doin' skulkin' 'round our camp, yer dirty ole bundle of smells? Well, speak up!"

Tammo shook his head wildly, pointing dumbly to his mouth.

One of Rinkul's friends, a wily-looking vixen, snatched the dirk from Tammo's rope belt and held it to the firelight. "An ole slobberpaws like you shouldn't be carryin' a blade like this'n 'round. Bit o' cleanin' up an' this'll make a fine weapon fer me."

Suddenly Skaup was on the pair of them, whacking both Rinkul and the vixen heftily with his spear haft. "Don't y'dare put a paw near Burfal again, either o' ye!"

Tammo retrieved his dirk from where the vixen had

dropped it, then he staggered off into the night as Skaup continued beating Rinkul and the vixen.

"Owch! Yaagh! We was only 'avin' a bit o' fun. Yowch! Aargh!"

"Fun, was it? I'll give ye fun! Firstblade's orders is that nobeast is to bother ole Burfal. Either o' ye lay paw on 'im agin an' Warfang'll slay yer good'n'slow. See!"

Skaup thwacked away with the spearhaft until he decided they had been punished thoroughly.

Tammo was relieved to be away from the Rapscallion camp. It was calm and peaceful on the other side of the hill; only the distant throb of drums on the night air reminded him of the vermin encampment. Suddenly a big dark figure detached itself from a clump of boulders and waved to him.

"Sithee, Tamm, over here, mate!"

Good old Rockjaw Grang. They crouched together in the outcrop, and Rockjaw dug oat scones, cheese, and cider from his sizeable pack. He shared the food with Tammo as the young hare made his report.

"Midge has got his jolly old paws well under the table there. Damug thinks he's some kind o' Seer. Any news of the battleground yet, Rock?"

The giant hare demolished a scone in one bite. "Nay, 'tis too early yet. May'aps the Major'll get word to me on the morrow."

Tammo squinted uncomfortably from beneath his odious rags. "Sooner the better, wot. I don't want t'stay in that foul place a moment longer'n I have to, chum."

"Aye, well, that's wot y'get for runnin' with Long Patrol, young Tamm. You'd best finish up vittlin' an' get back afore yore missed. I'll be here tomorrow night, same place."

39

Midge knew he was playing a risky game. Damug was no fool. He sat staring at the disguised hare across a small fire, which was laid in a pit at the center of his tent.

"Speak to me, Miggo, tell me something."

Midge stared into the flames awhile, then he spoke: "I see a mountain and a badger Warrior with eyes like blood. I see Gormad Tunn and a fleet defeated there."

Damug Warfang rose and, reaching across the fire, seized Midge around the neck. Lifting him high, Damug shook him like a rag. "Anybeast could have told you that, you sniveling wreck. Tell me of my future and tell me quickly, before *your* future ebbs away as I strangle you!"

Fighting for breath and with colored lights dancing before his eyes, Midge Manycoats dangled above Damug's head. Grabbing what he needed from beneath his ragged garb, he planted the object, at the same time kicking out with a footpaw and catching the Warlord in one eye.

Midge managed to shout hoarsely, "I see! I see your future!"

Damug dropped him, squinting hard, and pawed at his eye to make sure no damage had been done. Midge sat up, massaging his throat. Damug was sitting in his former position, the eye watering and smarting slightly. He stared unruffled at Midge, unwilling to let him see that he had been hurt.

"Well then, what do you see? Tell me."

Midge went back to his former seat at the other side of the fire. Again he took out his pebbles and twigs, tossing them in the air and watching how they fell. He spoke like one in a trance.

"Here are ten twigs, each of them represents one hundred Rapscallions; this means you command a thousand. These stones are red, the color of blood, the color of a red sandstone Abbey. Only one stone can rule that place, that is your stone, the brown one. Brown, the color of the earth and the symbol of the Firstblade who will conquer all the earth."

Midge closed his eyes and lapsed into silence. After a while, Damug became impatient, wanting to know more.

"Where is this brown stone? I see only twigs and red stones on the floor. Tell me quickly, Seer, where is the brown stone?"

Reaching into his rags, Midge cast a pawful of powder into the fire. The flames gave forth smoke as they burned blue.

"Aaaahh! 'Tis up to ye to find it, Firstblade. The stone cannot be found in yore heart. Allbeasts know that a Warlord's heart is made o' stone, so how can a stone be found within a stone? But 'tis also known that you are wise—mayhaps the stone is in yore brain. Can you look inside yore skull, Damug Warfang?"

Mystified, the Greatrat took off his helmet and placed it on the ground. He touched his own head, back, front, and beside both ears, all the time glaring through the firesmoke at Midge.

"Find a brown stone inside my own skull? Do you take me for an idiot? Let me warn you, Miggo, if you think you're going to pull something from my ear, I've seen that done before—try it and you're a deadbeast!"

Midge folded his paws, staring back at Damug. "I'll sit over here, Sire. If I tried anythin' you'd say it was a trick. My voices tell me the brown stone is inside yore skull; more'n that I cannot say."

Damug touched his head again, this time more carefully—running both paws along his jawline, around his eyes and the base of his skull. Suddenly he jumped up angrily, shaking his head. "This is stupid! You talk in riddles. How could there be a brown stone inside my skull? Rubbish!"

He kicked the war helmet to one side. From the mouth of the rabbit skull impaled on its spike, a brown stone rolled forth.

Trying not to show his immense relief, Midge pointed. "See, the skull belongs t'you. Did I not say the brown stone could be found inside yore skull?"

Midge Manycoats had guessed correctly. Damug Warfang was like any other conqueror, superstitious and ready to believe in omens and signs.

Damug picked up the simple brown pebble and gazed in wonder at it. "You spoke truly, Miggo. You have the gift of a Seer. What is my future? Tell me—I must know!"

Midge knew now that he had his fish well hooked. Closing his eyes, he sat back, remote and aloof. "I need food and drink now, rest too. Have quarters prepared for me and my friend, Burfal the Silent One. Tomorrow we will talk."

Rinkul the ferret was smarting from the beating he had received, but that did not stop him. He limped about the Rapscallion camp, looking for the one called Burfal. There was something about the dumb creature that disturbed him. Using the hardwood stick to aid his walking, he crisscrossed the hillside, checking the creatures around their campfires. Maybe it was something in Burfal's eyes, in the way he had looked at him.

"If yer after vittles, we ain't got none 'ere, mate!"

Rinkul ignored Sneezewort and questioned Lousewort. "May'aps you've seen a raggy ole beast about, one o' the two who came inter camp earlier on? Did 'e pass this way?"

Lousewort sucked on a fishbone and thought for a moment. "Er, er, y'mean the Silent One? Stay away from 'im, matey, Firstblade's orders. Did you 'ear, Cap'n Skaup knocked the livin' daylights out o' a few smartychops that tried interferin' wid that dumb beast. Stupid fools, serves 'em right, I say!"

Rinkul's hardwood stick rapped Lousewort's nose viciously. "When I wants yore opinion I'll ask for it, mudbottom. Now, which way did the dumb beast go?"

Sneezewort pointed toward the stream. "Went by us a moment back, 'eaded thataways."

Supported by his stick, Rinkul hobbled off to the stream. Lousewort hugged his nose tenderly as he watched the ferret go. "There wath no need for him to do that, wath there!"

Tammo had seen the caged squirrel on the stream bank. Pulling faces, and pushing the two stoats guarding the cage, he made it clear that he did not want them around. The guards retreated a distance to the nearest fire, where they sat warming themselves. Word had got around regarding the Silent One, and they were careful not to offend him.

Drawing his dirk, Tammo pushed it through the bars and began prodding the old squirrel, pretending to have some cruel fun with him. Moving to the cage's far side to avoid the blade, the old creature cast a withering glance at his tormentor.

"Do yore worst, vermin. I ain't afeared of ye!"

Tammo's whisper barely reached his ears. "Sorry, old chap. Can't speak up, they think I'm dumb, y'see. I'm no vermin, this is a disguise. Really I'm a hare of the Long Patrol. I'll help you if I can."

Lying flat, the squirrel rolled over, closer to Tammo so that he could whisper back. "Get me some food an' a blade!"

"I'll try, but don't attempt anything on your own. Leave this to me an' my friend—he's disguised like me."

Before he spoke further, Tammo took a swift look about and saw Rinkul leaning on his stick, watching him. Throwing caution to the winds, Tammo dashed at the ferret and dove on him. They went down together. Tammo grabbed Rinkul, pulling him on top of himself and uttering little mute squeaks of distress.

A Rapmark stoat named Bluggach, who was seated by the fire with the two guards, grabbed his cutlass. "Lookit that, the addle-brained oaf, don't 'e know no better? Damug gave orders not t'touch the dumb 'un! Cummon, mates!"

Rinkul found himself roughly hauled off Tammo, his protests lost among the angry roars of Bluggach and the two guards as they thrashed him with the flats of their blades.

"Git off that beast. Wot d'yer think yore doin'?"

"We've all been ordered to stay clear of 'im!"

"You wanna dig the soil out'n yore ears, ferret!"

"I ain't gonna report this or Lord Damug'd kill yer, but you gotta learn to obey orders. Teach 'im a lesson, mates!"

Gathering his rags about him, Tammo fled the scene.

Midge stuck his head out of a canvas shelter that had been erected between a bush and a rock. He peered into the night at the lumpy figure ambling aimlessly about.

"Tamm, over here, pal! We've got our own special quarters!"

Tammo scrambled gratefully into the shelter and crouched by the fire. Midge passed him some rough-looking barleycakes, a piece of cooked fish, and a canteen of strong grog, but Tammo put it aside, saying, "Thanks,

Midge, but I've already eaten. I contacted Rockjaw and he gave me supper. But tell me your news first—how did y'get on with old thingummy Warface?"

The friends exchanged information, telling each other all they had experienced since arriving at the Rapscallion camp. Tammo tightened his paw 'round the dirk handle, gritting his teeth. "Those vermin we were tracking—remember the one that got away? I've seen him, the ferret they call Rinkul. He was the last of the murderers who slew the old badgerlady and my friend Russa; the scum still carries her stick. First chance I get I'll make him pay for them!"

Midge shook his head. "That's not what we were sent here for, Tamm. You'll get your chance at Rinkul, but not here—it could cost our lives an' the safety of Redwall. Let's rest up a bit, then when all's quiet we'll take food to the squirrel. I've got a small blade with me, we'll deliver that to him as well. Rest awhile now."

Long after the midnight hour had passed and the sprawling Rapscallion camp lay silent, two figures made their way carefully down to the prisoner in his cage by the stream.

40

Redwall's twin bells had tolled out the midnight hour, but their muted tones were heard only by the three creatures who were still awake. Abbess Tansy, Friar Butty, and Craklyn the Recorder sat around a table in the kitchens, studying the journal of Abbess Germaine. It had been written countless seasons ago when the Abbey was actually under construction. The Little Owl Orocca had watched them awhile, waiting for Taunoc, who had gone off under the command of Major Perigord. When it became apparent he would not be returning that night, Orocca retired to care for her three owlchicks in the kitchen cupboard.

Butty selected some hot muffins, which his helpers had baked for next morning's breakfast, took a bowl of curds, flavored it with honey, and stirred in roasted almonds. He brewed a jug of rose-petal and plum-flower tea and set the lot on the table, inviting his friends to help themselves.

"It's sort of half breakfast an' half supper, suppfast, I calls it, when I'm up very late cookin' down here. Tell us more about this place called Kotir, marm."

Craklyn opened the journal at an illustrated page. "This is what it must have looked like, an old crumbling castle, damp, dark, and ruled over by fearsome wildcats, backed by a vermin horde. Martin the Warrior and his friends destroyed it and defeated the enemy, long before Redwall was built. They diverted a river and flooded the valley in which Castle Kotir stood. It sank beneath the waters and was never seen again. Redwall was built from the north side first, I think the south wall was to have been bordered by the lake that had covered Kotir. But our Abbey was not built in one season, nor ten, nor even twenty. You can see by these sketches farther on that by the time the north wall was erected, the lake had begun to dry up. Abbess Germaine states that all the soil and rock dug up for the Abbey foundations was dumped into the lake. Well, over a number of seasons the lake became little more than a swamp, the only trace of it being a spring that bubbled up in a hollow some distance from the original lake site. This kept throwing up clear water until it became incorporated in the Redwall plans as an Abbey pond."

Tansy blew upon her tea and sipped noisily. "The very same pond we have in our grounds today, how clever! But carry on, Craklyn. What happened next?"

"Hmm, it says here that by the time the main Abbey building was in progress, a drought arrived after the winter. Spring, summer, and autumn were intensely hot and dry, not a drop of rain throughout all three seasons. Even the Abbey pond shrunk by half its length and breadth. What had once been swamp became firm and hard ground, with tree seedlings taking root on its east side. So they ignored the fact that Castle Kotir, or a lake, or even a swamp had once been there, and carried on to build Redwall Abbey."

Craklyn closed the journal and dipped a hot muffin in the sweetened curd mixture. Friar Butty flipped through the pages; yellowed and dusty, they seemed to breathe ancient history. He paused at one page with a small illustration at its chapter heading.

"Here 'tis, see! A sketch of the completed Abbey with a

dotted line representin' Kotir an' where it once stood. There's the answer!"

Abbess Tansy brushed muffin crumbs from the parchment. "Well, I never. They built the south wall right over the part where Castle Kotir's northwest walltower stood. So after all these seasons the ground has decided to give way, and that hole we were looking down must be the inside of Kotir's walltower. It would be fascinating to climb down there if it was dry and safe enough."

Orocca's head appeared around the partially open cupboard door. "You'll beg my pardon saying, Abbess, but I wish you'd stop all your noisy yammering and go now. These eggchicks need their sleep!"

Tansy began gathering up the remains of the meal carefully. "I'm sorry, Orocca. Right, let's away to our beds. We'll take a look down there first thing in the morning. Shad and Foremole will go with us, I'm sure."

As dawn shed its light over the flatlands west of Redwall, Major Perigord sat up in the dry ditch bed where he had passed the night. Captain Twayblade was balancing on a thick protruding root, scanning the dewy fields in front of her.

Perigord reached up and tugged her footpaw. "My watch I think, old gel. Any sign of 'em yet?"

Twayblade climbed down from her perch. "Not a bally eartip. Where d'you s'pose they've got to, sah?"

The Major drew the rags of his once-splendid green velvet tunic about him and yawned. "Who knows? Torgoch an' Morio are a blinkin' law unto themselves when they're on the loose together. I say there, come on, Taunoc, you jolly old bundle of feathers, up in the air with you an' scout the terrain, wot!"

Taunoc peered from under his wing, then struggled from beneath the ferns where he had been sleeping, and blinked owlishly.

"Strictly speaking, I am a nocturnal bird, not widely

given to flapping about in dawnlight like a skylark. What is it you want?"

With a flourish, Perigord drew his saber and poked at the sky. "I require your fine-feathered frame cleaving the upper atmosphere, lookin' out for any sign of our friends. That too much trouble?"

With a short hopping run the Little Owl launched into flight. "After a night in a ditch, nothing is too much trouble."

He soared high, wheeling several times before dropping like a stone. "Your Sergeant and Lieutenant are coming now, west and slightly south of here. I suggest you wave to denote your presence, Major."

Perigord climbed out of the ditch and waved his saber. It glittered in the early sunlight as he hallooed the two hares. "What ho, you chaps, what time d'you call this to come rollin' back home? Come on, Torgoch, on the double now!"

Sergeant and Lieutenant came panting up to the ditch. Throwing themselves flat in the damp grass, they lay recovering breath.

Morio raised himself up on one paw, his normally saturnine face glowing with pride. "We found the place, sah, day an' a half's march sou'west o' here. There's a rock stickin' up like an otter's tail top of a rollin' hill range, and beyond that a valley with a gorge runnin' through. Looks somethin' like this." In the bare earth of the ditch top he scraped out a rough outline with his knifepoint.

Twayblade nodded approvingly. "Well done, chaps, looks a great spot for a picnic, eh, wot?"

Perigord studied it, obviously pleased by what he saw. "Aye, we could shell a few acorns there! Stretch our forces along the ridge and send out a decoy party t'lead 'em into the valley from the south side. If we can get 'em with the gorge at their backs and the hill in front, 'twill be an ideal battleground. Taunoc, time for you t'do your bit, old lad. Fly out an' scout this place. When you're satisfied as to its location, seek out Rockjaw Grang and tell him exactly where the battlefield is to be. Got that?"

Once again the Little Owl heaved himself into the air. "I think I am reasonably intelligent enough to understand you, Major. After all, I am an owl, not a hare!"

When the owl was well away, Sergeant Torgoch grinned at Twayblade. "Well curl me ears, marm, there goes an 'uffy bird if ever I saw one. Bet 'e counts 'is feathers regular!"

"You, sir, would find yourself counting your ears after an encounter with me, I can assure you!"

Torgoch almost leapt with fright as the owl landed beside him. The bird stared accusingly at Perigord. "You gave me the location and told me to whom I should deliver the information, but you did not mention when the battle is to take place."

The Major bowed courteously to Taunoc. "Beg pardon, I stand corrected. Shall we say three days, or however long after that the Rapscallions can be delayed? We need to play for all the time we can get. My thanks to ye, sir!"

Long after the owl had flown, Sergeant Torgoch looked mortified. "I really opened me big mouth an' put me foot-paw in it there!"

41

Abbess Tansy and her party were ready for the descent into the pit beneath the south wall. Friar Butty was armed with a stout copper ladle, his chosen weapon. Foremole Diggum and Shad the Gatekeeper had lengths of rope, lanterns, and a fine rope ladder that Ginko the Bellringer had loaned them. Tansy and Craklyn had donned their oldest smocks, and between them they carried a hamper of food.

It was a good hot summer morning. Tare and Turry of the Long Patrol were pushing a wheelbarrow about on the lawn. Three little owlchicks and the badgerbabe Russano sat on a heap of dry straw in the barrow, taking their daily perambulation.

Tansy waved to them as they passed. "See you later. Bye bye!"

Waving back, the babies repeated the word they used most often. "Nut! Nut!"

Craklyn fell about laughing. Shad opened the food hamper and tossed a pawful of candied chestnuts into the barrow for them. "Bye bye, hah! These liddle tykes know wot's good for 'em!"

Having lit the lanterns, Friar Butty strung them at regular intervals upon a long rope and lowered it into the depths, providing illumination all the way down. Shad secured the rope ladder and let it unroll into the void. "I'll go first," he said. "Butty next, then Abbess an' Craklyn. Foremole, you follow last. Remember now, take y'time an' step easy!"

One by one they descended into the silent pit, lantern light and shadows dancing eerily around the rough rock walls that surrounded them. Scarcely a quarter of the way down, Foremole pointed a digging claw at the wall in front of him.

"Yurr, thurr be's ee writin' that Bunto see'd!"

Foremole Diggum had remembered that Bunto, one of his mole crew, had seen writing carved upon the wall.

Craklyn studied it. "See these broken rock ends and bits of shattered timber? There must have been a spiral stairway running from top to bottom of the walltower once. There's a space that may have been a window, all blocked with earth now. This carving is beside it—probably some vermin soldier did it while he was idling away the hours on guard duty at that very window."

Tansy tweaked at her friend's footpaw, which was directly above her head on the ladder. "Never mind the architecture, what does the writing say?"

The Recorder's voice echoed boomingly as she read out aloud.

"Turn at the lowest stair,
Right is the left down there,
Every pace you must count,
At ten times paws amount,
See where a deathbird flies,
Under the hunter's eyes,
Radiant in splendor fair,
Ever mine, hidden where?

Verdauga, Lord of Kotir."

Clinging to the ladder, Tansy looked up at her friend as

the echoes faded to silence in the strange atmosphere. "Sounds like some sort of riddle to me. Craklyn, what are you doing up there—writing?"

"Scrap o' parchment and a stick of charcoal always come in useful," the old Recorder muttered busily as she scraped away. "I never go anywhere without them. This won't take long. Hmm, Verdauga, he was mentioned in Abbess Germaine's journal, some sort of wildcat who ruled Mossflower before Martin the Warrior arrived. There, I've got it!"

Foremole Diggum, who was last on the ladder, grunted impatiently. "Ho, gudd for ee, marm. Can us'n's git down thurr naow? Oi'm not gurtly pleased 'angin' 'round up yurr!"

It was a long and arduous descent. When they touched ground at the pit bottom, Friar Butty peered upward to the platform. It looked very small and far off.

"Phew!" he said, nodding in admiration. "Just think, Skipper dove from up there, what a brave an' darin' beast! I think if I tried it I'd prob'ly die of fright halfway down."

Shad tapped his tail against the mud-coated rocks. "Since the waters dried up, mate, you'd die fer sure if you landed 'ere. Right, let's git the lay o' the land."

He lit another lantern and they moved gingerly on the slippery stones of the dried streambed, staring at their surroundings. It was little more than a stone chamber, with a gaping hole at eye level where the water had flowed in from the right, and another hole beneath their paws to the left, where the stream had exited downward.

Tansy found a dry rock and sat down. "It's very smelly and cold. We'd best watch we don't slip and fall down that hole—goodness knows where we'd end up. Well, anyone got some bright ideas? This place looks like a dead end."

Craklyn studied the verse she had copied, then took a careful look around. She pointed to a spot not far above their heads. "Look there, up to the left. There's a hole in the wall, but it's blocked by rubble and old timbers. I think that was where the stairs finished originally. We must be standing below the old ground level now, where the water carved the floor away."

Shad climbed back up the ladder, swinging it inward until he could reach the hole in the side of the wall. He secured the rope ladder to a splintered wood beam that stuck out. "Aye, yore right, marm, this is where the last stair was. I think we might've found a passage 'ere. Stand clear while I try an' unblock it."

Huddling beneath an overhang at the cave's far side, they watched rock, timber, and masonry pouring from the hole as the husky otter cleared away the debris. It was not long before he called down to them, "Haharr, 'tis a passage sure enough—dry, too. C'mon up, mateys!"

One by one Shad helped them from the rope ladder into the passage. Foremole discovered a shattered pine beam and, using a dash of lantern oil, soon had a fire burning cheerily.

"Thurr ee go. Oi thinks us'ns be 'avin' a warm an' summ vittles afore us do ought else, bo urr!"

Abbess Tansy warmed her paws gratefully. "What would we do without a good and sensible Foremole?"

Friar Butty unpacked a latticed fruit tart, some nut-bread, and a flask of elderberry wine, which he set by the fire to warm. As the friends ate they discussed the verse that Craklyn had copied.

"So," said Tansy, "it wasn't an idle sentry who carved those words, it was the Lord of the castle himself. But why put it there in plain view?"

Craklyn explained what she had seen. "It wasn't exactly in plain view, though. I noticed some spike holes in the stone; there must have been a wall hanging or a curtain hiding the verse. Maybe Verdauga was getting old and he carved it there to remind himself."

Foremole sliced the tart evenly, shaking his head.

"Hurr, 'tis a gurt puzzlement tho', marm. 'Roight is ee left daown thurr,' wot do that mean?"

"I know it sounds odd, but it's not really. Creatures who hide something and write about it usually try to trick others by arranging the words so they sound strange. 'Right is the left down there' means that the left passage is the right one to take. I could say that two ways; either the left is the right one to take, or as Verdauga put it, right is the left to take. See?"

Butty poured out small amounts of the warm wine for them. "I'm with you, miz Craklyn, 'tis right to take the left passage, an' that's the one we're in now, lucky enough. I think I've got the next two lines as well. 'Every pace you must count, At ten times paws amount.' Everybeast has four paws, so add ten to that an' it makes fourteen paces we must count."

A smile hovered on the Recorder's lips as she challenged the Friar. "Is that right? Go on then, young Butty, take the lantern and walk fourteen paces down this passage. Tell us what you find."

The young squirrel marched off, counting precisely. He was lost to sight at the count of eight, where the passage took a bend. Shortly he returned to sit by the fire, scratching his chin. "Hmph! Wasn't a thing there, nothin' except stone walls!"

Craklyn shook a paw at him in mock severity. "That's because your arithmetic was wrong, Friar. Work it out properly now. You have four paws, and the line says 'Ten times paws amount.' *Times!*"

The answer dawned upon Butty suddenly. "Of course, ten times four is forty—it means take forty paces!"

Tansy passed him a slice of tart. "Well done, sir, but let's have our meal, then we'll all go and count it out together."

Beyond the turn a long passage stretched before them, dark and gloomy, layered with the dust of untold ages. So intense was the silence that they paced on tip-paws, whispering out the count. Tansy looked left and right at the forbidding bare stone walls and the worn paved floor. What sort of creatures had walked them in the distant past? How long had it been since a living beast set paw down here?

"Thirty-eight, thirty-nine, forty!"

"Well wallop me rudder, look at this, messmates!"

A great shuttered window stood before them, broad and high, its lintel, sill, and corbels intricately carved with sinister designs. Shad unlatched the shutters, announcing jokingly, "Wonderful view o' Mossflower countryside from 'ere. Take a look!"

Cobwebs parted as Shad drew back the creaking shutters, revealing the entire frame, packed solid with stone and dark earth. He shut them again and pushed the rusty latch into place.

"Too far down even for roots or worms to travel. Question is, wot are we supposed t'look for now?"

Craklyn repeated the fifth and sixth lines of the verse:

"See where a deathbird flies,
Under the hunter's eyes."

Tansy shuddered as she held up the lantern to inspect the sill. "These carvings are skillfully done, but they're horrible. See here, there's a snake swallowing a little mouse, and here, two rats are cutting up a skylark with curved knives. Everywhere you look there's cruelty and murder being done. No wonder Martin and his friends fought so hard against the vermin who lived here. But where's the deathbird and the hunter?"

Piece by piece they went over the grisly scenes until Shad, being the tallest, stood on the sill and held up the lantern to view the lintel overhead.

"Is this wot yore lookin' for, marm?"

He was pointing to a picture of a raven. The big black

bird was trying to fly away, but it was trapped by a leaping wildcat that had bitten deep into the raven's back.

Craklyn clenched her paws tightly, fascinated yet repulsed by the dreadful image. "Yes, that's it, Shad! The wildcat is the hunter, and the raven has long been known as the deathbird for the way that it feasts upon carcasses of dead creatures. I'm sure that is it!"

They sat upon the windowsill, looking at one another in the flickering lamplight. Tansy read out the final two lines:

> "Radiant in splendor fair,
> Ever mine, hidden where?"

Young Friar Butty hunched his shoulders, shivering slightly. "I couldn't imagine anythin' radiant or splendidly fair down here, but if there is I'll bet 'tis behind the carvin'!"

Shad took out his knife and stood up on the sill. "Well, let's see, shall we!"

He tapped with the knife handle, rapping the corbels and the surrounding wall, finally hitting the lintel several smart raps. "Aye, yore right, Friar. Sounds as if there's a cavity wall above this lintel. Pass me the lantern."

The light was passed up to Shad. He dug and scraped away with his blade until they were forced to vacate the sill beneath him.

"You'm sendin' daown a turrible dust, zurr. Wot be you'm a doin'?"

"Oh! Sorry 'bout that, mates, but there's a big stone that's stickin' out a bit up 'ere. I'm just diggin' out the mortar wot's holdin' it in. I reckon wot we're after lies be'ind it."

"Yurr, oi'll coom up an' 'elp ee. Lend oi yore young shoulders thur, Butty, let oi git moi diggen claws worken on et."

Butty stood on the sill, grunting as Foremole Diggum

clambered up onto his shoulders.

Shad and Foremole blinked mortar dust from their eyes as they dug, tugged, and probed. The otter grasped the lantern ring in his mouth to leave both paws free.

Craklyn watched them anxiously. "Do be careful now, mind your paws don't get jammed in the cracks."

"Stan' asoide, lukkee owt naow, yurr ee comes!"

With a few mighty heaves the two creatures pulled the big oblong wallstone free and dropped it.

Boom!

It shattered a section of the paved floor as it fell, sending up a choking dust cloud, through which Shad could be seen, one paw rummaging deep in the hole as he held out several glittering objects with the other.

"Ahoy there, hearties, lookit wot I found! Owowooh! Me paw!"

There was a rumbling, crumbling sound as the stones above collapsed down, trapping the paw Shad had buried in the wall space. He hung there awkwardly, gritting his teeth against the pain. Then everything happened without an instant's notice.

Foremole slipped from Butty's shoulders and fell backward as, with a dull roar, the entire wall and ceiling disintegrated in an avalanche of stone, mortar, and thick choking dust!

42

Vermin snored and muttered in their sleep, fighting imaginary battles, some of them even singing snatches of songs as they lay around their campfire embers in the warm summer night. The guards of the cage were still at the fire of the stoat Bluggach, within easy distance of the prisoner they were supposed to be watching. Like Bluggach, they too were flat on their backs, mouths open wide to the sounds of their painful rasping snores.

The old squirrel watched the two ragged figures' silent approach to his cage. He grabbed at the food they pushed through the bars to him, and his throat moved up and down as he gulped water from a canteen, drinking until the vessel was empty. With his head bent low he gave a long sigh of satisfaction, then began chewing the food slowly, while Midge whispered questions at him.

"What do they call you, and how did y'come to be here?"

"My name is Fourdun. I live alone in Mossflower. They took me by surprise—I must be gettin' old."

Midge passed the small knife through to him. "We're both Long Patrol hares. I'm Midge, he's Tammo. Listen to me, old feller—don't do anythin' silly. We'll get you free. Maybe tomorrow night or the night after, but we'll do it. So watch out for us an' don't try escapin' by yourself."

Nudging Midge, Tammo hissed urgently, "Look out, that big stoat Cap'n's awake!"

Bluggach woke with a throat that was both sore and dry from snoring. Coughing hoarsely several times, he staggered down to the stream. Crouching in the shallows, the stoat pawed water into his mouth until he had drunk enough, then he straightened up and belched.

There was no place for Tammo or Midge to hide—one movement from either of them and they would be discovered. Midge shoved Tammo toward the stream, muttering to him, "Sit by the water an' look as if you're meditatin'—hurry!"

Tammo walked straight for the stoat, bumping into him as he slumped by the shallows, and stared intently into the water. Bluggach was about to say something when Midge strolled up.

"Pleasant night to ye, Cap'n. Take no notice of ole Burfal, 'e goes off doin' odd things any hour o' the day or dark."

The stoat drew his cutlass, eyeing Midge suspiciously. "Wot are yew doin' 'round 'ere?"

Midge produced the flask of grog he had been about to give Fourdun. "Oh, jus' keepin' an' eye on Burfal, seein' 'e don't disturb nobeast. 'Ere, take a pull o' this, sir, Warfang's own private grog. 'Twill put a throat on ye like a cob o' velvet."

Bluggach was still not quite convinced by Midge, but he took a good swig of the fiery grog as he weighed the ragged beast up. "You'll be the Seer, then? Some sez yore a magic creature."

Smiling craftily, Midge moved close to the stoat and reached out. "I ain't magic, Cap'n. You are, though. Wot's this candied chestnut doin' in yore earlug?"

Grinning widely, the big stoat tossed the nut into his mouth and gave Midge a friendly shove that almost

265

knocked him flat. "I knew you was magic the moment I clapped eyes on ya, haharrharr!"

Midge laughed along with him, urging Bluggach to drink some more. "Bein' magic ain't as good as bein' a Rapmark Cap'n like you, sir."

The stoat warmed to the tattered Seer. Throwing a paw about him, he said, "Ho, ain't it though? I tell yer, matey, sometimes I wish I c'd magic some discipline inter this lot. Lookit those two, snorin' like weasels at a weddin', an' they're supposed t'be on guard! But tell me more about yore magic. Y'know wot I like, haharr, I likes beasts like yerself who know clever riddles. Go on, do a riddle fer me. 'Tis ages since I 'eard a good 'un."

Midge tapped a dirty paw against his stained teeth. "Hmm, a riddle, now lemme see . . . Ah, 'ere's a riddle fer ye. Wot goes gurgle gurgle snuffle trickle blubber ripple scrawf scrawf? D'yer know the answer to that one, Cap'n?"

Bluggach took another good pull at the grog and sat down, narrowing one eye and scratching his head. Midge beckoned Tammo silently, and together they began moving away. The stoat Captain drank some more, halting them with an unsteady wave.

"Er, burgle sniffle truckle sprawl, wot goes like that? Hah! That's a good 'un, mate. I dunno, tell me the answer."

Midge pointed at the two sentries sleeping by the fire at the water's edge. "There's yore answer, Cap'n. Two fat lazy guards sleepin' their 'eads off by a stream all night. C'mon, Burfal, time we was goin'."

They departed as the joke's punch line dawned on Bluggach, and made their way back to the shelter and their own fire with the stoat Captain's laughter ringing out behind them.

"Oh harrharrharr, that's a good 'un, hohohoho! Wake up, you two, an' lissen t'this. Harrharrhohoho! Wot goes grungle snirtle, worf worf an' sleeps like youse two by the stream all night? Yarrharrhahaha! Betcha don't know the answer, do yer?"

Sitting beside their own fire, the two hares discussed their plans.

"If Rockjaw gets a message from the Major tomorrow, we'll be able to quit this place once I've worked more of my magic on Warfang."

Gathering his rags about him, Tammo lay back to rest. "Aye, but we'd best wait until late night to make our escape. That'll be a good time to break Fourdun out, too—we can't leave him there for the vermin to starve an' torment, he must go with us."

Midge smiled at the determination on his young friend's face. "Of course Fourdun's goin' with us, wouldn't have it any other way, Tamm. But it ain't goin' to be easy, by the left it ain't!"

By mid-morning of the following day, Rockjaw Grang had shifted his hiding place. Moving farther downhill, he settled himself in a dip, surrounded by rock and bushes. Not knowing how long it would be before he could once more sample the good food of Redwall, the giant hare ate sparingly. Munching on a russet apple, he checked his weapons. He laid out his heavy arrows and counted them, then rubbed beeswax on the stout string of his great yew bow. Rockjaw tested his sling, refilled the pebble bag, and set himself to honing a long dagger on a smooth stone.

Taunoc appeared beside him suddenly. Without raising an eye, the big fellow continued whetting his blade, commenting drily, "Sithee, bird, where'st thou been? Much longer sittin' 'ere alone an' I'd be talkin' to mahself!"

The Little Owl folded his wings rather moodily. "Continue with that attitude and you *will* be talking to yourself, sir! My late arrival was due entirely to the tardiness of your own compatriots. However, I am not here to bandy words with you. I bring important news, so listen carefully."

Lady Cregga Rose Eyes was lost in strange country. She had plunged forward in the darkness, driven by the Bloodwrath, running all night until she could go no farther. Now, with her massive axpike clutched in both paws, the Badger Warrior lay amid the ferned fringe of an ash grove. She slept a fevered sleep, shivering, with her tongue lolling out and eyes half open, but unseeing.

From the grove, a colony of rooks watched, hoping the badger was so ill that she would soon be weak and dying. A young rook made as if to hop forward, but the leader, a hefty older male, buffeted him flat with a single wingsweep.

"Chakkarakk! We wait, take no chances with a stripedog. When the sun sets we will fall on that one. Never have we tasted stripedog; there will be plenty there for all!"

The Long Patrol had risen at dawn. Picking up Sergeant Clubrush's trail, they pressed forward on the double. The Drill Sergeant was sitting cooling his paws in a brook. He watched them approach, gnawing his lip in disappointment. Ellbrig halted the column in front of Clubrush, who shook his head.

"Must be gettin' old lettin' 'er give me the blinkin' slip. I lost Lady Cregga's trail sometime in the night. But even if I 'adn't, what beast can keep up with a badger travelin' at 'er speed?"

"Sah, beg t'report," Trowbaggs called out from the back ranks. "Lady Cregga's tracks are here to the left, travelin' due west by the look of it!"

The veteran Shangle Widepad inspected the torn-up grass and scratched rocks. "Well spotted, young 'un. She's well off course, though."

Clubrush limped slowly over to the spot. After a quick

glance he gave his verdict to Ellbrig in an undertone.

"Bad news for us, Lance Corporal. Looks like the Bloodwrath's full on 'er. Take four with you an' find 'er. We'll wait 'ere."

Trowbaggs, Deodar, Furgale, and Fallow jogged in a line abreast with Ellbrig. In broad daylight the trail of Rose Eyes was clear: ripped-up moss, flattened bushes, and trampled heather all told the story of the badger's flight.

The irrepressible Trowbaggs chatted constantly as they forged on. "I say, looks like a flippin' herd o' badgers passed this way, wot? This Bloodwrath thing, Corp—what's it all about?"

Ellbrig eyed the grinning recruit, about to tell him to mind his words, then he thought better of it. "You've as much right as the next beast t'know, I suppose. Bloodwrath is more a sickness than anythin', 'tis a terrible sight t'behold. I think 'tis mainly Badger Warriors suffer from it, though I 'ave 'eard o' otherbeasts taken by the Bloodwrath. Imagine hatin' an enemy so much that even if he had ten thousand at his back, y'd charge at 'im, aye, an' destroy many to get at 'im. They say a beast taken in Bloodwrath can fight on, even though wounded almost to death. Aye, they battle on still, as if they was fresh as a daisy, slayin' anybeast that stands afore 'em. Red-eyed, full of the lust for death, an' scornin' fear, that's Bloodwrath. Worst thing that c'n happen to a creature, I think!"

Trowbaggs was subdued by the Corporal's statement, but only for a moment. He nudged Furgale, saying, "Hard luck on the foebeast, I'd say, but blinkin' useful to have a hefty dash o' the Bloodwrath on our side. Wot, wot!"

In the late afternoon, Ellbrig stopped to scan the weaving, meandering trail. "Hmm, the fires appear t'be dyin' down. These tracks are all over the place, willy nilly. She can't be far ahead."

Fallow pointed to the distant ash grove, set in a vale

between three low-lying hills. "I'll wager we find her there, 'tis where I'd make for if I was tired'n'weary. What d'you think, Corp?"

"Aye, I'd say you made a good bet. Let's get a move on. I think there's big birds flyin' low over that way."

They increased the pace. Drawing closer to the grove, Ellbrig put on extra speed, roaring out an order. "Out slings, it's rooks, they're attackin' somethin'!"

Yelling Eulalias and loosing off stones, the five hares leaped to the fray. Shrieking harshly, the rooks fled from their prey in a dark flapping mass, beating at one another with wing and talon in an effort to regain the safety of their grove.

A few bold ones remained, sticking out their necks and menacing the hares with their pointed beaks. Charging into the ferns, Ellbrig and his companions battered at the birds with loaded slings. Several rooks were slain before the birds finally fled.

Cregga Rose Eyes was surrounded by dead and dying birds. The big badger was ripped and pecked in a dozen places. Using her axpike for support, she staggered from the ferns with the hares assisting her. Ellbrig watched her carefully as she drank from a small canteen he had brought along, and he noted that her face was calm and her eyes had returned to their normal rose pink.

"Sar'nt Clubrush sent us, said you'd lost y'way, marm."

Cregga looked slightly bewildered. Wiping a heavy paw across her eyes, she blinked at the Lance Corporal. "Lost? Yes, I suppose I was, in a way. Where are all the others?"

Ellbrig pointed in the direction they had come from. "Nearly a full day's march back that way, marm. Can y'make it?"

The badger set out slowly, her head bowed wearily. "Yes yes, you carry on, Corporal. I'll be fine."

Drill Sergeant Clubrush sat finishing a fine supper of forager's stew, washed down with some good mountain cider. He wiped his platter with a chunk of rye bread.

"By the fur'n'feather, that was a better meal than I ever knocked together in my recruit days. Top marks to you'n' yore crew, young Algador, there's hope for ye yet!"

As Algador saluted he cast a quick glance to the huge form of Lady Cregga, fast asleep on a pile of ground-sheets by the fire. "Thanks, Sarge. Will we be movin' out at dawn?"

Clubrush continued wiping his already clean platter. "Y'move when I say, laddie buck, an' I move when she says. Though the seasons only knows when Lady Cregga'll waken. She looked fair done in. Thank the fates that she's normal agin."

43

Rinkul was festering with hatred for the ragged pair of mystics who had entered the Rapscallion camp. He gathered a dozen of his cronies about him and issued secret orders. "Let me know every move that pair make, see. An' the dumb one, keep a keen eye on 'im, 'specially once it gits dark!"

Tammo managed to give Rinkul's cronies the slip. He slid off at twilight, while the hillside camp was still teeming with Rapscallions going about the business of cooking, fishing, and foraging for supper.

Rockjaw Grang was awaiting his arrival. He fed the young hare from the last of his supplies and passed on the information Taunoc had vouchsafed to him. Getting back was more difficult. Tammo could see Rinkul and his band searching for him as he peered over the hilltop. There was only one thing for it. Keeping bent double, Tammo shuffled into the camp, trying hard to look inconspicuous. He was doing fine until a heavy paw descended upon his shoulder. It belonged to the big, slow-witted rat Lousewort.

"Er, er, tell me a funny riddle like you tol' Cap'n Bluggach."

His companion Sneezewort shook his head in disgust.

"Oh, belt up, seedbrain, that 'un can't talk—that's the dumb 'un!"

Lousewort was not convinced. "But he's magic like the otherbeast. Maybe he kin put a spell on hisself so that 'is voice comes back!"

Lousewort's voice was so loud that he attracted the attention of Rinkul and his gang. Immediately they spotted Tammo and began making their way toward him. The young hare acted quickly. Moaning and uttering dreadful croaking sounds, he waved his paws wildly at Lousewort and Sneezewort. Unsure of what the ragged creature was about, the two rats backed off nervously. Rinkul and his vermin tried to shove past them and seize Tammo, but he pushed Sneezewort and Lousewort into them and ran off. Extricating themselves from the tangle, Rinkul and two others gave chase.

Tammo threw himself into the shelter, where Midge was waiting. He barely had time to gasp out the information when Rinkul appeared. Ducking his head under the canvas awning, the ferret drew an ugly-looking blade.

" 'Tis time ter settle up wid you two ragbags!"

Midge gave an evil cackle and raised his paws dramatically. "Beware o' my magical powers, fool. Raise that blade at me an' I'll turn yer into a toad, right where y'stand!"

Sneeringly, Rinkul began raising the blade. Midge also raised his paws higher, threatening his adversary. "Don't say I didn't warn ye. Snakeblood an' lightnin' come strike this abode, an' turn yonder ferret into a fat toa—"

"What's going on here?"

At the sound of Damug Warfang's voice, Rinkul swiftly sheathed his blade. Lowering his eyes humbly, he shrugged and said, "Just a bit o' fun, Sire. The ragged one was gonna show me'n'my mates a few spells an' tricks."

Damug strode between them, eyeing Rinkul suspiciously. "Get out of here and leave these creatures alone!"

Rinkul and the other two vermin bowed and hurried

off, relieved that the Firstblade had not sensed their intentions. Damug bade the two hares to be seated. He stared at Midge for some time, then asked, "Could you have turned Rinkul into a toad?"

Cocking his head to one side, Midge returned the stare boldly. "That's my business, Warlord. Now I'm really goin' to show yer some magic. D'you want to know where t'meet the Redwallers?"

Damug leaned forward eagerly. "Aha! Your voices have spoken to you, Seer! Tell me!"

Midge shook his head knowingly. "Not so fast, Damug Warfang. Answer my questions an' you'll find that you already know, the information'll come out by itself."

For the first time, Damug looked puzzled. "You speak in riddles, Miggo. What do you mean?"

"Be silent, an' speak only when I ask you a question!"

Tammo was as mystified as Damug. He feared that Midge had gone too far with their dangerous game. But as he listened, Tammo was surprised by his friend's skills.

Midge tapped the patch that covered his eye. "Tell me, Firstblade, 'ow many good eyes 'ave you'n'I got between us?"

The Greatrat answered without hesitation "Three."

Midge cackled knowingly. "Haharrharr! You said it. Three! That's the time you'll meet those Redwallers, three days from now!"

Damug's voice quivered with excitement. "What are their numbers—how many will they be, Seer?"

Midge Manycoats eyed him scornfully. "What if they 'ad twice yore number? Redwallers are peaceful creatures, they toil at growin' things in earth. Yore a Warlord wid a thousand at yer back, all warriors. But 'earken t'me, Damug, if we're talkin' in hundreds, then three is still yer lucky number."

Damug thought about this a moment, then grinned wickedly. "Three hundred peace-loving beasts!"

Midge nodded. "You said it, Warfang, an' 'tis little use lyin' to yerself. Wot's three 'undred farmers agin a thousand soldiers?"

Damug drew his sword, pointing it at Midge. "If there's only three hundred, then why can't I just march on Redwall Abbey and take it, tell me that?"

Midge brushed aside the swordpoint contemptuously. "Go if ye will, fight 'em there! Wreck the place, smash it, burn Redwall t'the ground. What'll ye have then, mighty one? Go on, you tell me that!"

Sullenly the Warlord sheathed his weapon. "Mayhaps you are right, it is difficult to control a thousand when they sense plunder in battle. So, where is the place to be?"

Squatting by the fire, Midge tossed in a pawful of salt. Blue flames rose from it. "Beneath a blue sky west o' here lies a valley. I see a hill with a rock like an otter's tail atop of it, and three 'undred standin' by, waitin' for yore blades to bring 'em death. Now I see yore father, Gormad Tunn, tellin' you t'make the Rapscallions great again. Keep the rift at yore back, my son, that's wot 'e says, keep the rift at yore back!"

The blue flames from the salt died down, and Midge shrugged. "That's all, I see no more."

Damug continued staring into the fire. "So why should the whole of Redwall be waiting for us in this field?"

Midge smiled. "Think, great one. The Redwallers have friends throughout Mossflower. They have been informed that a great army is gathering to attack. They will not risk allowing you to reach their sacred gates. Tomorrow they will hold a Council of War, this I have seen. The quickest route to Redwall is through that field. The next day they will decide upon an ambush there. The third day they will set forth. All this I have seen."

Damug sneered. "Well, what's to stop us taking Redwall when the fools are all away playing soldiers in this field?"

Midge toyed with his cap while he rapidly thought of

an answer. "Think again," he said finally. "You are destined for complete victory, to be the unchallenged ruler of all Mossflower. Do you really want to deal with bands of insurgents, resistance fighters who know these woods better than their own right paws? No! Better to slay and take prisoners for slaves to serve you and your great army. True victory only comes through conquest, great Lord!"

Convinced at last, the Greatrat recounted the information. "Three days from now I will face the Redwallers west of here. They will be on a hilltop; I must keep the rift at my back. What does my father mean—keep the rift at my back?"

Midge closed his eyes, as if exhausted. "I can't tell yer, that's all I know."

"Hmm," Damug grunted. "Well, I will field a thousand, but the Redwall creatures number only three hundred. Are you sure you can tell me no more, Seer?"

Midge shook his head several times. "Nothin' except a certain victory for you an' yore army."

Damug strode to the entrance of the dwelling and summoned two guards; then he turned to Tammo and Midge. "So be it. Pray to the fates that you have seen truly. These two guards will watch you and never leave your side until Redwall is mine. If you have tried to play me false, I will have you both skinned, roasted, and fed to my army."

He fixed the two guards with a cold stare. "If either of you let these two out of your sight for a moment, I will make you curse the day you were born. Is that clear?"

Sneezewort and Lousewort (whose turn it had been to stand guard duty) bobbed their heads vigorously as they croaked, 'Er, er, yes Sire!"

Immediately after Damug had left, the two rats leveled the heavy guard spears they had been issued with at Tammo and Midge. "Sit still an' don't bat an eyelid, you two, or yer deadbeasts!"

The two hares sat with spearpoints almost touching

their throats, knowing that the nervous rats were capable of anything in their highly strung state. Tammo stared beyond them. Outside he could see Rinkul and his gang lurking. In a barely audible whisper, he said to Midge, "Touch an' go, old chap, wot?"

Midge blinked his eyes in agreement. The situation was extremely dangerous. If they escaped the guards it would be like jumping out of the frying pan into the fire. Yet they had to escape and take Fourdun with them before dawn, when the Rapscallion army would break camp and march west.

"Time t'put the old thinkin' caps on, bucko!" he murmured back to his friend.

44

Spitting pebbles and dust, Foremole Diggum worked furiously in the darkness. When the tunnel collapsed, he had been thrown partially clear, but he was trapped below the waist by the mountain of debris that stretched from floor to ceiling. The mole's powerful digging claws tore at the rubble, showering stone and mortar either side until he pulled himself free. His head struck the lantern; it had gone out. Grabbing the cover off, Foremole blew gently on the smouldering wick, and a spark showed. Slowly he coaxed the flame back to life.

"Ahoy there, mate, move aside, I'm comin' down!" Shad the otter emerged from the top of the pile and slithered carefully over the slope of the cave-in, favoring his injured paw. "C'mon, let's git diggin' fer the others!"

Glittering pieces of booty sparkled in the lantern light. Shad seized a heavy gold platter and, using it as a scoop, he attacked the pile.

Foremole dug alongside him, calling out, "Whurr are ee, you'm gennelbeasts? Call out naow!"

A muffled but urgent cry came back at them from inside the pile: "Go easy, there's only a beam protectin' us. Dig careful, friends!"

Shad grunted as he tunneled into the jumble of earth

and stone. "Take care o' miz Craklyn an' the Abbess, young Butty—we'll soon have ye out o' there!"

They hauled aside a block of masonry between them, and pulled and tugged at timbers and rock slivers. Foremole flinched suddenly. "Yowch! Oi be stabbed in ee tail!"

Shad held up the lantern to see what it was. An ornate silver spearhead, studded with peridots and tasseled with silk, was poking out of the debris, its point waving and shaking.

"In here, we're in here! Hurry, the air's runnin' out!"

Shad held on to the spearhead while Foremole dug swiftly around it. The good mole was an expert digger, and he soon had a small tunnel through to the three trapped creatures. Shad began enlarging it, scooping aside earth with his gold platter.

There was an ominous creaking of timber, then the sound of Abbess Tansy's voice calling to them, "You'd best be quick—Craklyn's been knocked senseless and I think this beam is about to break under the weight of rubble!"

Shad thrust the lantern through and squeezed in after it. Bent double, he sized up the situation.

The cave-in had fallen around a huge baulk of timber, leaving a small space. Butty and Tansy were crouched in it, supporting the limp form of Craklyn. Suddenly, unable to bear the weight of collapsed material, the beam gave a splintering crack, showering them with soil and mortar dust.

Foremole scrambled in alongside Shad. Moving Tansy aside, he took her place so that he and Butty were supporting Craklyn. "Hurr, et be gurtly bad in yurr, marm. Do ee get owt quick loik!"

Shad assisted Tansy into the escape tunnel, and the timber beam began to groan like a living thing as it shifted. The hefty otter threw caution to the wind. Wedging his back beneath the beam, he strained upward and took the weight upon himself.

"Get 'em out, Diggum, mate. Don't argue. Go!"

They scrambled out, dragging Craklyn between them, through choking dust and a rain of pebbles.

Foremole and Butty grabbed the silver-headed spear, thrusting the pole back toward Shad, who had been forced almost flat. Butty shouted instructions: "Grip tight to the spearpole, mister Shad. You push, we'll pull. Ready, one, two, push!"

Shad held the spearpole like a vise as, forcing himself free of the beam, he gave a mighty shove. Foremole and Butty heaved on the other end, knowing their friend's life depended on it.

Covered in earth and battered by stones, Shad flew out of the tunnel as the beam broke and everything collapsed inward behind him. He was practically shot out of the hole like an arrow from a bow, landing in a heap atop his rescuers.

Butty found the remains of a flask of elderberry wine, which had been thrown clear. While Tansy bathed Craklyn's brow with it, Shad took stock of their situation. "Well, messmates, that's wot we get fer goin' treasure 'untin'. We're blocked in this passage better'n if we'd been walled in by builders. Still, we're alive, an' the air is fit to breathe."

Licking her lips, Craklyn came back to consciousness. "Mmm, I taste like elderberry wine, that's strange. What happened? Is everybeast all right?"

Tansy breathed a sigh of relief and hugged her old squirrel friend fondly. "Everyone is fine, though you were knocked out when the tunnel collapsed. How do you feel?"

Craklyn stood up and dusted off her gown. "Fine, never felt better! Dearie me, looks as if we're trapped down here, though. What in the name of seasons are you up to, young Butty?"

The squirrel Friar pointed proudly to the small heap of glittering objects he had gathered from the rubble.

"Collectin' treasure, marm. "Tis rare pretty stuff!"

Foremole wrinkled his snout at the precious trove. "Phwurr! Pretty is all et be. Us'n's caint eat et, hurr no, so 'tis of no use at all down yurr!"

Craklyn ignored the mole. She dug out of her pocket the rhyme she had copied, shaking her head knowingly. "I thought so. Treasure, that's what we missed. Look at the first letter of each line, reading downward.

> "Turn at the lowest stair,
> Right is the left down there,
> Every pace you must count
> At ten times paws amount,
> See where a deathbird flies
> Under the hunter's eyes,
> Radiant in splendor fair,
> Ever mine, hidden where?"

She folded the scrap of parchment triumphantly. "So that's the riddle solved. Treasure! And we've found it!"

Shad picked up the empty wine canteen. "Well good fer us, marm, but Foremole's right, treasure ain't goin' to feed us or get us out o' this mess. So, wot next?"

Craklyn and Butty gathered up the treasure and wrapped it in a cloak—having found it they were not about to leave it behind. The young Friar gazed at the heap of debris blocking the passage. "We'll take this with us. Hmm, bet there's lots more of it buried in there, pity we can't dig it out."

Abbess Tansy tweaked Butty's ear playfully. "You greedy young wretch! Come on, let's explore farther down this passage and see where it leads. Bring the lantern, Shad."

There was neither dawn nor dusk far beneath the earth; time had no meaning. It was only by hunger and thirst that the five companions could judge how long they had been down there. Long, dark and dreary, dry, dusty, and silent, the passage wound on a downward slope. Occasionally they arrived at a cave-in that had not quite blocked the way, and then they found themselves scrambling up hills of broken stone, forcing their way through narrow apertures close to the tunnel ceiling.

Foremole tapped the walls regularly and probed the tight-packed earth at window and door spaces, but without any great success. Being the strongest of the party, he and Shad forged ahead in front of the others, to make sure the way was safe.

The big otter was wearied from his exertions fighting the crushing beam. "I don't like it, Diggum," he murmured in a low voice to Foremole. "Looks like we're goin' nowheres down 'ere. We ain't got food nor drink, only the air we breathe, an' that lantern light ain't goin' to last forever."

Dust rose from his back as the mole patted it. "Hurr, oi knows that, ole riverdog, but us'n's be bound t'put ee brave face on, lest ee froighten an' scare ee uthers. Coom now, let's set an' rest awhoile."

They waited for the others to join them, then all five sat with their backs against the wall, tired and dispirited, each with his or her own thoughts, which were rather similar. Green grass, sunlight, fresh air, clear water, and the happy world of Redwall Abbey, so far above them that it all seemed like a dream.

45

Major Perigord stood in the gap of the south wall with Captain Twayblade. Together they watched the shrews and Waterhogs from the water meadows being led up the slope by Log-a-Log and Gurgan Spearback to join the Redwall army. Perigord attempted a rough head count as they turned west to the main gate.

"About a hundred an' ten, maybe twenty, not many really. Let's go an' see what Morio has mustered up."

Lieutenant Morio was seated in the orchard with quill and parchment on an old tree stump. Pasque was assisting him in compiling the figures on what number of fighting beasts were available.

Perigord looked questioningly at the two hares. "Make y'report, be it good or ill. Speak up, chaps."

Morio wiped an inky paw against his tunic. "Well, it ain't good, Major, but they all seem fit'n'able. There's fifty Redwallers, and thirty squirrels come in from 'round Mossflower, all pretty fair archers an' good slingers, well equipped too. Skipper's rounded up a few more otters, bringin' his strength up to twoscore. Wish we had more otters—they look like they know their way 'round a fight."

Perigord straightened his green velvet tunic, now

283

practically in tatters after all it had been through. "Wishes don't win wars, Lieutenant, we make the best of what we've jolly well got. Have y'counted all the shrews'n'hogs?"

"I have, sah. One hundred an' sixty-three all told, and if you add our twelve, well, that's the total strength. Always providin' that Tammo, Midge, an' Rockjaw make it back from the Rapscallion camp in one piece."

Perigord did a quick mental calculation. "Well, that makes nearly three hundred we can put in the field. Pasque, me pretty one, how's the jolly old armory?"

Pasque Valerian had slightly better news. "Top o' the mark, sah. Everybeast carries their own weapon, an' there's a chamber in the bell tower crammed full of arms, all manner of blade, spear, and bow. Ginko the Bellringer says you're welcome to 'em all, sah!"

Twayblade drew her rapier, and flicking an apple from a nearby branch, caught it deftly and polished it on her sleeve. "Three hundred, eh. Wish I'd told Midge to let the Rapscallions know there was only two hundred of us, but I said three, hopin' we might have had four. Always nice to keep a hundred as a surprise reserve. Ah well, no use worryin' over spilt cider, wot."

Perigord took the apple from his sister and bit into it. "Indeed, we'll just have t'give ten times as good as we get off the vermin. Hello there, what's amiss here?"

The Galloper Riffle was trying to restrain Viola Bankvole from reaching Perigord.

"Sorry, marm, y'can't see the Major right now, he's busy."

Viola thrust her jaw out belligerently. "Stand aside, young sir, or I'll take a stick to you. I must see your officer right now!"

Perigord gestured Riffle to one side. "At y'service, marm. You wanted to see me?"

Viola shot Riffle a haughty glance before addressing the Major. "It's our Abbess. She's missing, and so are Shad the

284

Gatekeeper, Foremole Diggum, Craklyn the Recor . . ."

Perigord cut her off with a wave of his paw. "Enough, marm, enough! Just tell me how many altogether."

"Well, there's five of them. They're nowhere to be seen, I've searched the Abbey grounds high and low. Now, what do you intend doing about it, sir?"

Perigord answered her gently, seeing that Viola was upset. "Beggin' y'pardon, lady, but there ain't a lot I *can* do. We're about to march off an' fight a war. So as y'see, I can't spare anybeast to go off searchin' for your friends."

Viola Bankvole's paw waved under the Major's nose as she ticked him off. "Well, that's a fine how d'ye do. But mark my words, sir, I will gather more reliable searchers and look for them myself. Good day!"

She flounced off through the orchard, calling to the older ones. "Gurrbowl, come here! I need you to search with me, and you, Mother Buscol, you too, Brother Ginko. Follow me!"

Captain Twayblade chuckled as she rescued the apple back from her brother. "I say, chaps, I think we'd best stay here an' search. Send *her* off to face the vermin. She'd soon send 'em packin', wot!"

Perigord nodded admiringly as he watched Viola bullying half the Abbey elders into service. "Aye, she's a bold perilous creature right enough. But to business now. Pasque m'dear, would y'be good enough to assemble the leaders? We'll have to get geared up an' movin' shortly."

The last full meal had been produced in Redwall's kitchens by Guosim shrew cooks. They had filled six huge cauldrons with a thick stew of leeks, mushrooms, carrots, turnips, water shrimp, onions, potatoes, and lots of herbs, enough to feed an army. October Ale casks were broached and served in beakers with rough batch loaves and wedges of autumn nut cheese.

As the Redwall force ate, Perigord consulted with their Chieftains: Skipper of Otters, Log-a-Log of the Guosim,

Gurgan Spearback of the Waterhogs, and Arven, Champion of Redwall, bearing with him the great sword of Martin the Warrior. There was not a lot to say that had not already been said; they all knew what they had to do, and even in the face of overwhelming odds they were prepared to do it, or go down fighting.

Mother Buscol had evaded Viola. She stood on the sidelines, with Russano the badgerbabe and Orocca's three young owls in the straw-lined wheelbarrow, enjoying the sun. The rest of the Abbey Dibbuns crowded 'round, hanging on her apron strings, in the absence of anyone else to mind them. Together they listened to the Major address his troops.

"Right ho, chaps, for those who don't know me, let me introduce m'self. I'm Major Perigord Habile Sinistra of the Salamandastron Long Patrol, commandin' this entire operation, though your orders will prob'ly reach you through your own leaders an' chieftains. Now I'll make this as short as possible, wot! There's a thousand Rapscallions sweepin' upcountry, an' Redwall Abbey's in their path. So to save the place I've . . . ahem . . . arranged for the jolly old fracas to take place elsewhere. According to Taunoc the blighters are on the move, and we've found the ideal place to meet 'em head on. So that's what we'll jolly well do, if y'follow me. As you know, we'll be outnumbered by more'n three to one, but by jingo we won't be outclassed! We won't be outfought! An' as long as I can stand with a saber in me paw, we won't be driven backward a single pace!"

Every creature listening leapt up cheering and brandishing their weapons.

"No surrender! No retreat!"

"Eulalia! 'S death on the wind!"

"Boi 'okey they'm furr et!"

Perigord gestured for silence. "Thank you, friends. But as you know, not all of us will come marching home. War is war, and that is a fact. So if there are any of you with families or young 'uns to look after, well, nobeast will think less of ye if you go home to them now."

A rough-looking otter stood up. "Beggin' yore pardon, Major, but I got a wife an liddle 'uns, an' if I didn't go with ye then I'd think less of meself. 'Cos we ain't fightin' the vermin just to protect Redwall, we're facin' 'em to make the land safe an' rid of their kind."

Mother Buscol trundled her barrow of babes through the army ranks, followed by a flock of Dibbuns. She halted in front of the Major and presented him with a cloth bundle. "Indeed to goodness, sir, you can't 'ave an army without a flag to march under, oh dear no you cannot!"

Skipper and Arven unrolled the bundle. It was a dark green tablecloth with a big red letter R embroidered upon it. Inside the bundle was another smaller package, which Buscol gave to Perigord. "It ain't velvet, sir," the old squirrelmother said, shrugging awkwardly, "but may'ap 'twill be of service."

Arven grabbed a long pike and began fastening the flag to it. "Here, Skip, lend a paw, you can tie better knots than me." The banner was lashed to the pikestaff, and Arven waved it high over the crowd. Back and forth it fluttered in the sunlight as the massed shouts rose to a concerted roar:

"Redwaaaaaalll! Redwaaaaaalll! Redwaaaaaalll!"

Major Perigord slipped out of his tattered tunic and donned the one that Mother Buscol had made for him. It was blue linen, homespun, but beautifully fashioned from an ancient bed quilt. Fastening on the medals from his old tunic, he bowed gracefully and kissed the squirrelmother's paw. "My thanks to ye, lady, I'll wear it with honor an' pride. Mayhap I'll even return here with it unharmed."

The Dibbuns dove upon the Major's old tunic.

"Me wannit, 'smine, gitcha paws offen it, Sloey!"

Perigord eyed them sternly. "Silence in the ranks there, you fiends! Y'can wear it a day each at a time. Sloey first."

Even the search party led by Viola left off their task to see the Redwall army on its way. Elders and Dibbuns alike lined the path to the main gate as the warriors marched past four abreast, every creature well armed and carrying provisions. Arven and Perigord stood to one side, each drawing his blade to salute the flag, which was being borne by Skipper. The stout otter dipped the colors, awaiting orders as the columns formed up on the path outside.

It was a high summer day, and the sun shone out of a sky that appeared bluer than it had ever been. They stood waiting in silence, listening to grasshoppers chirruping and skylarks singing on the western flatlands. Many Redwallers straightened their backs, breathed deeply, and blinked to prevent a tear appearing, wondering if they would ever see the old Abbey on such a beautiful day again.

All the good-byes had been said, though Major Perigord bowed to Sister Viola and spoke a last few words. " 'Tis always hard to leave a place, marm, particularly when certain friends are not there to wish you farewell. I wish you every good fortune in your search for the Mother Abbess and her companions. In happier, more peaceful times, myself and the patrol would have been at your disposal to help find them, but alas it was not to be. I hope you bear me no ill will, marm. I must bid ye good-bye."

Sister Viola smiled at the gallant hare. "How could any true Redwaller bear ill will to a brave soldier marching to defend our home and our very lives? Never fear, sir, I will find our lost friends. I bid you success and good fortune along with my good-bye. You are a perilous creature, Major."

Sergeant Torgoch's stentorian roar rang out through gateway and path: "Flagbearer three paces forward! All offisahs to the vanguard! In the ranks . . . Atten . . . shun! Corporal Rubbadub—beat the advance! By the right . . . quick . . . maaaaaarch!"

Shouldering blades, Perigord, Arven, Gurgan, and Log-a-Log formed the first rank of four behind Skipper's banner, with Rubbadub behind them setting up a fine, paw-swinging drumroll.

"Barraboom! Barraboom! Drrrappadabdab! Buboom!"

Galloper Riffle called out through the rising dust cloud, "Permission for the Company to sing 'O'er the Hills,' sah!"

"Permission granted, Galloper," Perigord's voice rang back at him. "Sing out with a will!"

"O'er the Hills" was a famous marching song, and close to three hundred voices roared it out lustily:

"O'er the hills an' far away,
'Twas there I left my dearie,
An' as I left I heard her say,
'Come back to me d'ye hear me,
Y'may eat cake an' drink pale wine,
But come back home at autumn time,
An' on fresh bread'n'cheese you'll dine,
For no one brews good ale like mine.'

O fields are green an' skies are blue,
Ole woods are high an' full o' loam,
But hearken friend I'll tell you true,
Ain't no place in the world like home.

O'er the hills an' far away,
'Tis there my home's awaitin',
The season's shorter by a day,
Whilst I'm anticipatin'
A logfire made from cracklin' pine,
An' washin' dancin' on the line,
As blossoms 'round the door entwine,
Hurrah, for there's that dearie mine!"

Redwallers old and young stood out on the path

waving kerchiefs, aprons, and headscarves until the marchers diminished to a faraway dust cloud, with their song a faint echo on the hot air.

Viola could not help sniffling into a lace kerchief, "Oh, they made such a brave sight going off like that!"

Ever the practical creature, Gurrbowl Cellarmole shooed the Dibbuns back inside, remarking, "Hurr aye, they'm did, an' let us'n's 'ope they'm lukk ee same on ee day 'em cumms back!"

46

The two rats Sneezewort and Lousewort kept their weapons firmly centered on Midge and Tammo, suspicious of their every move. It was a stalemate that was lasting far into the night, with little hope of the two hares escaping.

Eventually the fire inside the canvas-and-brush shelter began to burn low. From beneath his heavy disguise, Midge Manycoats winked significantly at his friend. It was time to make their move. Tammo edged slowly around until he judged that Rinkul the ferret and his cronies, who were hovering outside, could not see him.

Midge stood upright. Sneezewort's spearpoint menaced him, a fraction from his throat. "Siddown, ragbag, where d'yer think yore goin'?"

Midge stood his ground, nodding at the guttering flames. "Need more wood fer the fire, matey."

The rat considered Midge's request, then jabbed with his spear so that his prisoner fell back in a sitting position. "I'm not yore matey, an' you ain't goin' nowhere. Lousewort, keep an' eye on 'em. I'll get the wood."

Once Sneezewort had gone outside, Midge turned to his slow-witted partner. "You ain't afeared of us, are yer, bucko?"

A slow smile spread across the rat's dull features. "Er, er, scared? Huh, why should I be scared o' two rag-bottomed beasts like youse? Yore no bother at all t'me."

Midge moved closer to him, chuckling in a friendly manner. "Of course we ain't, a dumb ole vermin like me mate there, an' a pore one-eyed wreck like me. Fat chance we'd 'ave agin a fine big strappin' beast like yerself, armed wid a great spear like that 'un. But lookit, yore spear shaft's cracked right there!"

Lousewort lowered his head, following Midge's pointing paw. "Where? I don't see no crack."

Midge's other paw came swinging over, clutching a stone he had picked up from where he had been sitting.

Whump!

He hit Lousewort a hefty blow between the ears. The rat's body wobbled, and he staggered dazedly. Using the handle of his dirk, which he had kept well hidden beneath his cloak, Tammo sprang forward and dealt Lousewort a smart rap between the eyes.

Midge caught the spear, lowering the senseless rat quietly down. "Quick, Tamm, put that fire out and get this spear!"

Tammo kicked earth over the embers, then, grabbing the spear, he stood to one side of the entrance. Midge positioned himself on the other side, holding the fallen rat's cloak at the ready. Almost as they did, Sneezewort ducked inside, carrying a few twigs. "Hoi! 'Taint arf dark in 'ere, wot's go—*Mmmmffff!*"

Midge had flung the cloak over the rat's head. Tammo gave him two good hard knocks with the spearhaft to make sure he went out.

Then they lay still, peering outside at Rinkul and his band, who had made a fire some distance away—careful after Damug's warning to stay away from the prisoners. Tammo watched them until he was sure they had noticed nothing amiss. Midge passed him Sneezewort's cloak and spear, and donned Lousewort's cloak himself.

"Get rid o' those rags now, Tamm. We'll have to shift pretty fast!"

Discarding their disguises, they slid under the rear of the canvas shelter and wriggled off into the night, hugging tight to the ground until they were well away. Midge threw the hood of his cloak up. "Now t'get old Fourdun free. Right, Tamm, straighten up there! Make it look as if we're two sentry-type vermin takin' a duty patrol 'round the camp, wot."

Picking their way boldly 'round Rapscallions sleeping by campfires, the pair made their way down to the stream. Bluggach the Rapmark Captain was snoring next to his companions by the water's edge, their fire untended and burned to white ashes.

Tammo crept up to the cage and identified himself to the old squirrel. "It's Tammo an' Midge. C'mon, old chap, time to go!"

A few swift slices of Tammo's dirk severed the ropes on the cage door, and Fourdun crawled out, having already freed himself of his bonds with the small knife they had given him earlier.

Positioning themselves either side of Fourdun, the hares gripped his paws and marched him off quietly, Midge whispering to him, "If anybeast stops us, leave the talkin' to me. We're two Rapscallion guards takin' you to Damug 'cos he wants to question you. I'll bluff us through, don't worry."

Lousewort had two things going in his favor: an extra-thick skull and remarkable powers of recovery. Staggering from the dark smoky shelter, he sat on the ground, nursing his head and grunting with pain.

Rinkul, who had been watching the darkened shelter suspiciously, came bounding over. "Where's the two prisoners? 'Ave yer still got 'em?"

Shaking his head gingerly, Lousewort peered up at him. "Er, er, I dunno, it went dark all of a sudden!"

Rinkul ran back to his fire and snatched a blazing

brand. Kicking Lousewort aside, he rushed into the shelter, and seizing Sneezewort cruelly by one ear, he struck him several times with the burning stick until the rat came 'round with a yelp.

"Bunglin' idiot," Rinkul snarled into Sneezewort's frightened face. "Y've let 'em escape, 'aven't yer! Best thing you can do is take off fast afore the Firstblade learns they're gone, or Damug'll slay you'n'yore mate fer sure. Go on, beat it, an' don't raise no alarms. Leave those two t'me, I'll settle wid 'em!" He signaled to his waiting band. "Arm up an' let's go, they've escaped. Don't go shoutin' an' roarin' all over the camp. I wants those two ragbags fer meself. We'll catch 'em an' take 'em somewheres nice'n'quiet where I'll do that pair 'ard an' slow afore dawnbreak. Now go silent!"

Lousewort staggered upright, and Sneezewort leaned on him for support. "That's us finished wid the Rapscallions, mate. Let's be on our way afore Warfang wakes an' decides to 'ave us fer brekkfist!"

Without another word, they stumbled off, south, as far as they could get from Damug Warfang's vengeance.

The three escapers made their way uphill through the still-sleeping camp. Tammo felt that all was going well, too well, and that worried him. Fourdun peered around into the darkness and suddenly saw Rinkul and his band striding through the camp, coming in their direction.

Thinking swiftly, the old squirrel pulled his two friends down beside half a dozen vermin lying 'round a fire, and scrambled beneath Midge's cloak. "Lie still, some o' the scum are comin' this way!"

Hardly daring to breathe, they stretched on the ground amid the slumbering Rapscallions. Rinkul actually trod on the hem of Tammo's cloak as they went by, and Tammo heard the ferret murmur to one of his companions as they passed, "I've got a feelin' they'll be down by the stream where that ole squirrel's caged up!"

Raising his head carefully, Midge watched them from the back as they headed toward the water. The trio rose slowly, avoiding the outstretched paws of a stoat who was acting out a dream. The stoat snuffled and turned away from them, kicking out with a footpaw that came into contact with a glowing log.

"Yowch!"

At the sound of the creature's yelp, Rinkul and his party turned.

Midge saw they were discovered. He took off at a run, hissing to his friends, "Fat's in the fire, chaps, make a dash for it!"

Silently and grimly the chase of death began as they shot off uphill.

The stoat was clutching his scorched footpaw, hopping about. One of Rinkul's band whacked him with a cudgel as he passed, and snarled, "Go back ter sleep, mate!"

Though Fourdun was a strong old beast, he was not half as fast as the two hares, so they were forced to run at his pace. With the enemy hard on their heels, they got clear of the encampment and made the brow of the hill. Midge turned and threw his spear, and it pierced a vixen who was running alongside Rinkul. This slowed their pursuers momentarily and bought them a second's time.

Breasting the hill, Tammo called out as they ran, "Rock! Rockjaw Grang!"

Lower downhill, the giant hare heard Tammo. Leaping from cover, he bounded uphill to meet them. Rinkul was first over the hilltop. He had pulled the spear from the dead vixen; taking aim at Midge, he threw the weapon skillfully.

"Sithee, Midge, look out!"

Rockjaw flung himself in a flying tackle, bulling into Midge and knocking him sideways. The spear took Rockjaw through his side.

Hatred welled up in Tammo. He heaved his own spear straight at Rinkul. It struck the ferret through his middle, snapping off as he fell and rolled downhill toward them.

Rockjaw brushed Midge and Fourdun aside as they tried to lift him. Close to a dozen vermin were dashing down upon them now. The big hare unslung his bow, crying, "Get goin', I'll hold 'em off!"

The lifeless carcass of Rinkul the ferret halted its downhill roll in front of Rockjaw. He forced the hardwood stick from its death grip and tossed it to Tammo. "Good throw, young 'un. Russa woulda been proud o' ye. Now leave me an' run fer it, I'm bad hit!"

Fourdun ducked an arrow as he inspected Rockjaw's side. He looked up, shaking his head at Tammo. "'Twould kill him to pull the spear out!"

The big hare sat up and sent two arrows in quick succession at the vermin. Notching another shaft to his bow, he glared angrily at the two friends standing either side of him. "Sithee, 'tis not yore night to die. Now get out o' here an' don't stand there wastin' my time. Leave me t'my work!" Ignoring them completely, he fired the arrow and selected another.

Fourdun tugged at their paws, whispering urgently, "Can't y'see he's dyin'? If we stay here we'll all be slain. That beast doesn't want or need yore 'elp. Come on!"

Attracted by the shouts of their comrades, the vermin from the camp edges near the hilltop appeared. Rockjaw laughed wildly. "Hohoho! Come t'the party, buckoes, the more the merrier! Tammo, Midge, tell the Major I took a few wid me. Good fortune, pals—run straight'n'true an' remember me!"

Tammo, Midge, and Fourdun had to run for it before the Rapscallions encircled them. They ran like the wind into the night, shouting, "Give 'em blood'n'vinegar, Rock!" Soon they were lost among the groves and knolls, charging headlong across darkened country until there was no sound save the thrumming of their paws against the earth.

Rockjaw Grang sat on with his back against a jutting

boulder, the arrow quivers of two dead vermin beside him, his sling and stones ready for when he ran out of shafts. Completely surrounded, and wounded in four places, he fought on.

"Come on, thee cowardly scum. Ah'll wager nobeast warned ye about Goodwife Grang's eldest son. Eulaliaaaaaa!"

As the foebeasts closed in on him, Rockjaw drew the spear from his side and hurled himself upon them like a creature taken by the Bloodwrath.

"'S death on the wind! Eulalia! Eulalia! Eulaliaaaaaaa!"

He bought the time for his friends to escape safely, for even within sight of Dark Forest gates, Rockjaw Grang was a perilous hare.

47

Lady Cregga Rose Eyes sat bolt upright from the bed of grass and soft mosses she had been laid upon for a day and a night. It was but a few hours to dawn as the great badger roared out, "Eulaliaaaa!"

Corporal Ellbrig and Sergeant Clubrush, wakened from their sleep, rushed to her side.

"Lady Cregga, what is it?"

Her strange eyes looked all 'round before settling on Clubrush. "A bad dream, Sergeant, a very bad dream!"

She rose and stared over his shoulder in a northwesterly direction. The Drill Sergeant was very concerned. He watched Cregga's eyes carefully, though it was still too dark to see them clearly.

"Are you all right, marm?"

She moved to the nearest fire, nodding to reassure him. "I'm fine, Sergeant, but very hungry. How long to breakfast?"

Corporal Ellbrig busied himself at the fire. "Right now if y'like, marm, you h'aint eaten in two days."

Deodar and Algador had just finished their sentry watch, so they joined the trio at the fire. Young hares are always willing to eat an early breakfast when they smell it being cooked. Lady Cregga seemed in a rather mild, thoughtful mood, which was unusual for her. She passed scones and honey to Deodar, followed by a beaker of hot mint and dandelion tea.

"Breakfast tastes good after being on sentry, eh?"

Through a mouthful of scone, the young hare sipped her tea. "Rather, marm, 'specially when you can have an hour's sleep before reveille an' join the jolly old queue for more."

Lady Cregga smiled at Deodar's honesty. "Tell me, young 'un, do you ever have dreams?"

"Dreams, marm? Well, yes, I s'pose I do."

The badger stared down at her huge paws. "I had a dream just now, and I believe it to be true."

Algador paused from ladling honey onto a hot scone. "Really, marm? May I ask what it was about?"

The Sergeant was about to upbraid Algador, when Cregga spoke. "I'm afraid I couldn't tell you the parts that aren't clear, but I know a brave creature died. I shouted Eulalia with him as he went down. Somewhere over there to the northwest. And the more I think of it, the more certain I am. That is where the army of Rapscallions is at this very moment. I can feel it!"

The two young hares exchanged puzzled glances with the Corporal and Sergeant until Lady Cregga caught their attention once more. "When the sun is up and my hares are fed, we will go there."

Trowbaggs spooned hot oatmeal in at a furious rate, eyeing a last scone that lay between him and Furgale. "Well lucky old us, it's heigh-ho for the northwest on the strength of a bally dream, wot! I think I'll dream tonight that I've been sent back to Salamandastron to take up the blinkin' job of head food-taster. D'you think it'll work?"

Drill Sergeant Clubrush tweaked the cheeky recruit's ear. "Strange y'should say that, young sir. H'I've just 'ad a dream that you was on pot-washin' duty an' you volunteered to carry my pack all day. Wot d'you say to that, young Trowbaggs?"

"Er, haha, silly beastly things dreams are, Sarge, er, that is unless Lady Cregga dreams 'em up, wot!"

The Sergeant's pace stick tapped Trowbaggs's shoulder lightly. "Right y'are, bucko, an' don't you forget it!"

The Long Patrol hares assembled after breakfast for their final orders before marching. Lady Cregga and Corporal Ellbrig looked on from the sidelines as Drill Sergeant Clubrush lectured them.

"Listen carefully now. From this moment we march silent an' quick. An' when I say silent—Trowbaggs an' some o' you other young rips—I means it! Foolish an' thoughtless noise or playactin' could get us all ambushed or slain. Shangle Widepad, you an' the other seasoned veterans keep an eye on our recruits, 'tis yore duty to show 'em the ropes. Everybeast, make sure yore weapons are in good order—slings, javelins, swords, bows'n' quivers. Soon we'll be in enemy territory an' you may need 'em. Right, that's all. Unless you got anythin' t'say to 'em, Lady Cregga, marm?"

For the first time, the Badger Warrior addressed the five hundred hares who formed her traveling army. "So far you have all proved worthy and well, my thanks to you. Soon we will be facing Rapscallions in battle. Make no mistake about them—vermin they may be, but they are trained killers. To bring peace to these lands we must slay them, or be slain. From this moment you are hunters and warriors, and there will be no marching songs, Eulalias, or campfires. That is all."

They marched then. No commands were called; a nod, the wave of a pace stick, or a signal from the Sergeant's paw was all that they required. They kept to grassland, ferns, and rocky terrain wherever possible, so that a tell-tale dust cloud would not betray their position. Trowbaggs strode silently alongside Shangle Widepad. After a while the irrepressible young hare found himself humming a little ditty called the "Fat Frog's Dinner," and he winked at Shangle and grinned. The glare he received from the grizzled veteran silenced him immediately. Grim-faced and determined, the five hundred pressed on.

Rapscallion drums pounded savagely, throwing out their wild challenge to the summer skies. Pennants and war banners fluttered in the breeze, bedecked with tails, skulls, and hanks of animal hair. The little rat informant Gribble slunk about outside the Firstblade's shelter, waiting for him to emerge.

Damug Warfang strode out, his face streaked purple and red for battle. Unsheathing his sword, he cast an approving eye over the ranks of snarling vermin before turning to the rat groveling on the ground in front of him.

"Speak your piece quickly, Gribble, then get out of my way!"

The rat was already shuffling backward to avoid a sudden kick. "Great Lord, the Seer and the dumb one are gone, so are the two guards you left to watch them. Also the ferret Rinkul and several others are missing from camp."

Damug faced west across the valley slope and nodded curtly. "Well, let's hope they catch those two, for their own sakes. If they've deserted I'll find them when this is all over. But now I march west, to find out what these Redwallers are made of. Stand aside—death waits on anybeast barring my way!"

The Greatrat hurried to the forefront of his vast eager army, with their roars drowning out the pounding drums: "Warfaaaaang! Warfaaaaang! Warfaaaaang!"

Away to the west, a green valley basked in the warm sun. Light breezes rippled the vale ferns and stirred the blossoms of gorse and pimpernel on the broad hillslope. A single rock with moss and lichen clinging to its sides stood out on the long high ridge like a raised ottertail. Far below, wispy tendrils of mist arose from where the sun's warmth penetrated a deep rift that ran like a jagged scar along the valley's far edge. Small birds, redstart, stonechat, and wheatear, chirruped and chattered, perching on gorse thorns with sure-clawed skill, bright beady eyes constantly searching for minute insects. Butterflies and bumblebees visited the flowers of the vale, and sunlight glinted off the iridescent wings of hoverflies seeking aphids.

The life of the valley hummed peacefully on, lulled by summer's warmth, unaware that three armies were marching toward it.

48

Trapped in the tunnels of old Castle Kotir, far beneath Redwall Abbey's south ramparts, five creatures sat dozing fitfully in the gloom. Giving off an occasional flicker, their lantern warned that its light would soon be out.

Abbess Tansy gazed ruefully at the small golden tongue of flame as it gently swayed. "I should never have encouraged you to come on this silly venture, friends. I'm sorry."

Craklyn snorted, wagging a paw at her old companion. "*You* encouraged us, *you*? Hah! Let me tell you, Tansy Pansy, we're all down here because we wanted to come. We encouraged ourselves!"

Tansy clasped the old squirrel Recorder's paw affectionately. "Dearie me, 'tis some long seasons since anybeast called me Tansy Pansy. D'you remember when Arven was a Dibbun, he was always saying that name? Now what was it he used to chant at me?"

Craklyn thought for a moment, then chuckled. " 'Tansy Pansy toogle doo.' Hahaha, he was a proper little wretch."

Foremole wrinkled his nose severely at the pair. "Beggin' ee pardun, but do you'm be soilent, oi can yurr summat."

There was a moment's silence. Young Friar Butty

looked around. "Aye, I c'n hear somethin' too. Sounds like water drippin'."

Shad pressed his ear to the tunnel wall. "That's water, all right, on the other side o' this 'ere wall. I can 'ear it drip-drippin' away. Sounds like 'tis fallin' a far way down. Wot d'ye think, Abbess, marm, shall I 'ave a go at breakin' through the wall?"

Foremole Diggum waved a digging paw hastily. "Ho no, zurr, you'm'll be a bringen ee tunnel topplin' on us 'eads agin fur sure!"

Shad scrambled upright and retrieved the lantern. "P'raps yore right, mate. You all stay 'ere an' I'll scout about further down this tunnel t'see wot I can see."

While Shad was gone, the remaining four creatures sat in complete darkness without the lantern. To keep their spirits up, Tansy sang a simple little ditty.

"If I were a leaf upon a tree,
Then I would live right happily,
I'd grow up flat and green and big,
Unless of course I was a twig,
A twig with a leaf upon its end,
And then the leaf would be my friend,
I'd grow to such a wondrous length,
And from my branch I'd take my strength.
If I were a branch upon a tree,
With leaf and twig for company,
I'd grow so round and fair and trim,
Sprouting from a great stout limb,
But if I were a limb all thick and wide,
Branch, twig, and leaf I'd hold with pride,
And they would all depend on me,
And the mighty trunk of my big tree.
Then if I were a tree with bark for husk,
I'd stand up firm from dawn 'til dusk,
And limb, branch, twig, and leaf would be,
All through the season part of me!"

She had barely finished singing when Shad's voice boomed up the passage and they saw the welcome glow of the lantern. "Ahoy there, mates! Come an' see this—I've found a way down!"

Stumbling through the half-light behind the fading lantern, they followed Shad down the corridor. He halted in front of a heavy wooden door, swinging it open with a jarring creak to reveal its other side, covered in fungus.

"Welcome to the ole castle cellars, me hearties, though I don't see wot good they'll do us. We should be goin' up, not down'ards!"

Dropping his bag of treasure, Friar Butty pushed past the otter. "Look, torches!"

From rusted iron rings in the wall he pulled four hefty wooden bundles, their ends coated thick with pine resin. Tansy took one and lit it from the last dying lantern flame. "Of course, it makes sense to leave torches at the entrance to cellars. By the seasons, they do burn brightly!"

Brilliant yellow light radiated around, revealing their position. Far larger than Great Hall, the cellars stretched above and below them. Water dripped from long stalactites hanging from a high-hewn rock ceiling, falling down from a great height to splash far below where they stood. The five questors were on a narrow step jutting from the wall. Other steps wound their way downward, hugging the wallsides until they ended in the depths below.

Shad lit another torch from the one Tansy carried. "Only one way t'go, mates: down. C'mon, foller me."

Placing their backs to the wall, they descended carefully, step by step, each holding the other's paws. The stone stairs seemed never-ending, and by the time they had covered three-quarters of the distance, wet moss and slime made the going treacherous.

Shad stopped and rested by crouching against the damp walls. "Phwaw! This place is enough t'give a crab the creeps. You got any rope left, Diggum?"

The Foremole unwound a coil from 'round his waist. "Yurr, oi gotter liddle len'th."

Shad took it and knotted it 'round his middle, then passed it back. "Best rope ourselves together fer safety— *Yaaaaar!* Gerraway, yer filthy scum!"

A large, gross toad with sightless eyes was trying to gnaw the end of the otter's tail. With a swift flick of his rudderlike appendage, Shad tossed the amphibian in the air and batted it off the step. The toad whirled in an arc, then hit the liquid below. It vanished with a squelching plop, leaving a small dimple on the surface.

Tansy held her torch out over the stair edge. "That isn't water down there, 'tis more of a swamp!"

Other toads were crawling upstairs toward them, the dreadful creatures apparently attracted by Shad's cry and Tansy's voice.

Craklyn hid behind Foremole, shuddering. "Ugh! Horrible monsters, keep 'em away from me!"

Butty had been carrying his treasure slung on the end of the silver-headed spear he had found in the rubble. Untying the bundle, he passed the spear along to Shad.

The otter Gatekeeper began clearing the toads off into the ooze below. Some spread their webs to prevent themselves from sinking instantly, and these were set upon and torn to shreds by creatures not half their size, who appeared in packs. At the same time they were being devoured, the toads began eating their tormentors.

The five friends watched, revolted but fascinated by the sight.

"Yurr, they'm all a h'eatin' each uther!"

"Aye, those small 'uns look like some kind o' mudfish, they're blind as the toads!"

"So they all live down here in this slimy darkness, feeding off one another. What an awful existence!"

"Yukk! What are we doin' in this terrible place? Let's get out!"

Foremole Diggum tugged against the rope as they

began moving. "Hurr no, us'n's mus' gotter stay. Lookee!"

They followed the direction his paw was pointing, across the underground morass to a dark hole in the wall at the cellar's far side.

Tansy held the torch high. "What is it, Diggum?"

The mole's reply was prompt and confident. "That thurr's a tunnel dugged boi moles, oi'd stake moi snowt on et, oi surrtinly would, 'tis a mole tunnel, 'twill lead oopward!"

Shad shook his head doubtfully. "Are you shore 'tis a mole tunnel, mate? 'S a long way off."

Diggum Foremole would not be shaken from his belief. "Oi said 'twurr, din't oi, oi'm ee Foremoler, oo'd know better!"

Friar Butty stared unhappily across the expanse of cannibal-infested bog.

"If that's the way out, then how do we get to it?"

A small meeting was being convened in the kitchen at Redwall Abbey. It was for elders, though the Dibbuns had invited themselves along too, because there were always plenty of tasty bits to nibble at in the kitchens.

Viola Bankvole presided. "Mother Abbess always appoints me in her place when she isn't here, so if you don't mind I'll take charge. Gubbio, get your head out of that oven, please!"

Mother Buscol shooed the little mole from the oven, nipping back to the table just in time to stop Russano the badgerbabe grabbing a bowl of soup. "Indeed to goodness, Viola," she said, passing a paw across her flustered brow, "what is it you're wantin' now? Can't you see we've got our paws full as it is?"

Viola shook her head primly at the old squirrel. "Abbess, Craklyn, Foremole, Shad, and young Butty are still missing. Sloey! Put that ladle down this instant! Now, have you all searched properly?"

Pellit the dormouse tried to wrest the ladle from Sloey's grasp. "Well, I searched the entire orchard and down as far as the gatehouse, Sister. I don't think Ginko was looking very hard, though."

Ginko the Bellringer glared across the table at Pellit. "I done my share o' searchin'. Found *you* asleep 'neath the stairs in my bell tower, didn't I!"

Gurrbowl Cellarmole, who was sitting with Taunoc and Orocca, tending the owlchicks, ventured a suggestion: "May'ap they'm losed theyselves unner ee gurt 'ole at south wall."

An owlchick fumbled itself loose from her and lumbered into the bowl of soup that lay nearby. Viola leaned over and fished the little bundle of downy feathers out. "Good job that soup was cold. Under the south wall, you say? Ridiculous! What would our Mother Abbess be doing grubbing about down there? Personally I think she may have gone up into the Abbey attics to look for something, and taken the others with her. Barfle, stop pulling Sloey's ears. She'll end up looking like a hare. What do you think, mister Taunoc?"

"About what, madam, the Abbess in the attics, or Sloey looking like a hare?"

"Silly! I'm talking about the Abbess in the attics!"

The Little Owl ruffled his feathers and blinked at her. "Silly yourself, madam! All this meeting has achieved is to get one of my chicks soaked with soup. Wherever the Abbess is at this moment, it will be exactly where she wants to be. Your Abbess is a hedgehog, old and wise. She will return in good time."

Russano looked at Taunoc and spoke the only word he knew. "Nut!"

Sloey the mousebabe managed to hit Pellit a good whack on his nose with the ladle he was trying to take from her. Reaching over to assist Pellit, Viola Bankvole upset the bowl of cold soup, and it spilled all over Mother Buscol's apron. An owlchick fastened its small sharp beak on Ginko's paw, who yelped with pain and woke the remaining owlchick, who had been sleeping. The owlchick set up a din. The meeting dissolved in disarray, with Viola Bankvole struggling to maintain her dignity in the position of deputy Abbess.

"Er, continue the search. I will inform you later of when the next meeting is to be held. Be about your business now!"

Viola was about to make a stately exit, when she slipped on a patch of cold soup that had dripped from the table, and sat down hard on the stone floor.

The molebabe Gubbio tried pulling her upright by the apron strings, lecturing the bankvole severely: "Doant ee play abowt onna floor, marm, you'm get drefful dusty!"

The meeting ended with everybeast of the opinion that without a Mother Abbess to run things, Redwall Abbey would grind to a halt.

Underground, young Friar Butty made his way back up to a dry step, where he sat nursing his rumbling stomach. "Ooh, am I 'ungry, I've never been so 'ungry in all me life!"

Abbess Tansy sympathized with Butty, but she could not show it. "We're all hungry, but sitting complaining about it isn't going to do us any good. Look at Shad. He's bigger and hungrier than the rest of us, but he isn't moaning, are you, Shad?"

The otter, who was perched on the bottom stair amid the mud, called back up to Tansy, "No I ain't, marm. I think I've got a plan t'get us across to yonder mole tunnel!"

Picking their way carefully down the muddy steps, Tansy and the others joined Shad. He shifted a big venturesome toad off into the swamp with his spearbutt before explaining. "See, about halfways along the wall there, 'tis a chain, hangin' from a ring set high in the stone. If'n we could get hold o' that chain, I reckon we could swing across to the ledge over yonder an' make our way along it to the mole tunnel."

Craklyn studied the scheme, looking doubtful. "It'd be a mighty big swing needed to get onto that ledge, and look, the ledge itself is piled high with those loathsome creatures. But the main difficulty would be getting hold of the chain. It's much too far away for us to reach."

The thin, rusty chain hung down into the mud, well out of reach by about eight spearlengths. Shad scratched his chin thoughtfully. "Hmm, yore right, marm. I could soon clear those ole toads off'n the ledge when I got there, but 'ow t'get the chain over 'ere, that's the problem. Any ideas, mates?"

"Burr aye, farsten summat to ee rope an' try to snare ee chain!"

Shad's hearty laugh echoed boomingly 'round the vast cellar space. "Haharr, leave it to our ole molemate. Good idea, Diggum!"

Knotting their own belts and habit ropes together, they fastened them to the rope Foremole had brought with him. Shad coiled it up. "That should be long enough fer the job. Now, wot we needs is an 'ook to tie on to our line. Let's 'ave a look at yore treasure trove, young Butty."

The squirrel Friar tipped a glittering heap of precious objects from their cloak wrapping and began sorting through them. "Nothin' here that looks like a hook, mister Shad."

Craklyn selected a long thin dagger. It was a beautiful thing, more ornament than weapon, with a hilt crusted with seed pearls and blue john stones. Its slim, elegant blade was made of solid gold. "Here, this should do. Gold is soft metal, it'll bend."

Shad took the dagger and, setting it in a crack between the stair stones, he bent it double with a few powerful shoves. The rope was tied tightly to the dagger handle, and Shad twirled it like a sling.

"Right, mates, let's go fishin'!"

310

The first few throws went short. Hauling the line back through the watery mud, the otter winked broadly. "I've got the range now, this time does it. Redwaaaaaallll!"

Mud splattered all 'round as he swung rope and hook in a circle above his head. Shad let go, paying out the coil as his hook streaked out. It landed with a splodge, slightly beyond where the chain hung. Crouching down, he began drawing the rope slowly in.

"Easy does it, messmates. Come t'me, you liddle beauty . . ."

The chain moved toward them. Butty waved his paws wildly, crying, "Good throw, Shad, you've got it!"

It was indeed a good, or a lucky, throw. As the chain appeared from beneath the surface of the swamp, they saw that the point of the hooked dagger had actually passed through the center hole of a chainlink, snaring the chain securely. But Shad took no chances; he continued drawing the line in carefully until he could reach out and seize hold of the rusted and muddied object.

"Gotcha!"

Craklyn backed off, surveying the risky venture with a jaundiced eye. "Er, who's going to go first?"

The otter Gatekeeper tugged boldly on the chain to test it. "Bless yer 'eart, marm, who else but me, seein' as I'm the biggest an' 'eaviest? If the chain 'olds fer me, 'twill be safe fer all."

Without further ado Shad climbed up five stairs and stretched his paws high, holding the chain as far up as he could. Abbess Tansy had a sudden thought. "Here, Shad, you'll need the spear to clear those toads from the ledge. Stay there, I'll bring it to you!"

Shad bit down on the spearhaft and nodded, and the Abbess stood aside. He took a short run and launched himself from the stairs. Tansy watched the gallant otter swing out in a huge semicircle over the vast lake of liquid mud, with a spear clenched in his teeth and his tail standing out straight behind him, and knew she would never forget the sight. She held her breath. It looked as though the wide, arcing swing was about to dip downward and plunge Shad into the swamp. But on the final stretch he kicked out and up with both footpaws, jerking himself onto the ledge. The four friends on the steps cheered heartily. Shad held the chain in one paw and thwacked at the fat revolting toads that had already crawled up onto the ledge with his spear handle, sending them flying high and wide with dreadful hisses and croaks of protest.

"Shove off, ye great blobs of blubber, g'wan, jump fer it!"

The oozing surface boiled with writhing mudfish tearing at the toads who, in their turn, gobbled down as many mudfish as they could.

"Stand ready wid the 'ook an' line," Shad yelled across to Diggum Foremole. "'Ere comes yore chain!" He swung the chain out in a wide arc. Foremole threw the line, hooking it as it came within range.

"Oi got 'er. Coom on, miz Crakkul, doant ee be faint'earted!"

Craklyn went next, aided by a mighty shove from her friends. She wailed and yelled the whole way across the ledge as she swung over the toads, mudfish, and deep morass.

"Whoooooeeeeeeeaaaaaaa . . . Heeeeeeelp!"

"Well done, marm. Never fear, I've got ye, yore safe now!"

The old squirrel Recorder ceased her din, smiling sweetly at Shad. "There, it didn't hurt a bit. Send the chain back to Tansy now, mister Shad. I've never heard an Abbess scream, have you?"

Tansy was next to go, but when Foremole and Friar Butty pushed her from the step, she did not scream at all. Instead she clung on like grim death and closed her eyes tight. Shad and Craklyn caught her. She wagged a mischievous paw across at the Foremole. "Guess who's next, Diggum?"

When he had hold of the chain, Foremole looked pleadingly at Butty. "Oi 'opes they toadyburds an' muddyfishes doant get oi!" As it was, Foremole probably had the best crossing of all, coming in to land so fast that he almost hit the wall.

Young Friar Butty was last to go. His was the most difficult trip, because he had nobeast to give him a good starting push. The fat little squirrel launched himself off, only to swing in a faint halfhearted circle and land back on the steps.

Abbess Tansy roared across at him, "Oh, come on, Friar, you can do better than that. Imagine twenty hungry hares are chasing you to cook dinner for them, and run."

Butty went at his task with a will; grabbing the chain high, he dashed from the step and leapt out, yelling, "Go an' get yore own dinneeeeeer!"

He flew across the swamp, but halfway across his paws began slipping down the muddy chain. Butty was still traveling inward towards the ledge when he plowed into the swamp and vanished.

49

Immediately the surface of the swamp began wriggling and roiling with toads and mudfish.

Shad seized the spear close to its blade. "Quick, you three, grab the other end tight an' don't let go!"

Hanging on to the spear with one paw, Shad dipped daringly outward and grabbed the chain with his free paw. "Pull me in, pull me in quick!"

They hauled him from his almost horizontal position back onto the ledge. Wordlessly they all took the chain and pulled it in paw over paw, heaving madly at the rusted, mud-coated links. Butty was dragged forcibly to safety, practically unrecognizable. He was coated from head to tail in reeking sludge, roaring and spitting mud as toads and mudfish clung to him, gnawing.

"*Blooaargh!* Gerrem off me, the filthy dirty swamp-scum!"

They brushed and wiped at him, cleaning him up as best they could.

"There y'are, matey, you'll live. The worst bit's over now!"

Butty winkled mud from both his eyes and glared at Shad. "How do you know?"

Toads proved the only problem on the narrow rock

ledge. They congregated there in droves, perching on one another's backs, standing on the heads of those beneath them, blocking the way, sometimes five and six high. Sightless, filmed eyes, bulbous heads, damp spreading webs, and fat slimy bodies barred the path of the five Redwallers. The cavernous space echoed to the sound of venomous hisses and croaks.

However, Shad was made of stern stuff. He headed the party, battling a path for them along the slippery rock strip. Buffeting left and right with the spearhandle, he thrashed the creatures unmercifully until they were forced to flee into the swamp. Toads plopped and flopped in scores to the waiting mire below.

The four creatures walking behind Shad kept their backs firmly against the wall. Gripping one another's paws, they edged slowly along to the mole tunnel, encouraging their champion.

"Get that big scoundrel, Shad—that 'un there!"

"Watch out for that fat 'un, he's tryin' to slip past you!"

"Burr, you'm give 'em billy oh, zurr, 'ard'n'eavy!"

The hole was not too high up. Shad could see into it by pulling himself up tip-pawed, but it was dark inside.

Foremole Diggum produced one of the torches from the cellar. "Oi brung this'n o'er with me. Can ee set flame to et?"

With a few threads of Tansy's habit, a piece of flint which Friar Butty always carried, and the steel blade of Craklyn's quill knife, they improvised spark and tinder. Tansy set the smouldering threads on the resin head of the torch, and blew gently until it ignited.

Shad boosted them all into the mole tunnel, where they sat and took a breather. They all were tired, thirsty, and with grumbling, rumbling stomachs.

Friar Butty picked drying mud from his paws and spat out grit from between his teeth. "Ah well, we might yet see daylight if this tunnel goes anywhere."

Foremole wrinkled his nose and sat back confidently.

"Lissen yurr, Butty, if'n summ mole digged this tunnel, then you'm can lay to et thurr be a way out. Ho aye!"

It was a steep uphill climb, slippery at first, but growing easier once they encountered deep-sunk tree roots, which they could hold on to.

Craklyn explained the tunnel's origin to Tansy as they went. "From the journals of Abbess Germaine, I gather that this is one of the original passages that the moles dug to flood Castle Kotir. They diverted a river down several tunnels and flooded the place out."

The Abbess, who was traveling behind Craklyn, smiled wryly. "Very interesting, I'm sure, marm, but will you try to stop kicking soil down the back of my neck!"

Friar Butty, who was traveling up front with Foremole, shouted, "Fresh air! I can taste the breeze!"

Foremole, who was carrying the torch, suddenly backed up on to Craklyn's head, pulling Butty with him. "Coom quick, zurr Shad, thurr be a surrpint up yurr!"

Scrabbling soil and bumping past the others, Shad, who had been bringing up the rear, fought his way to the front. "A snake, ye say, matey? Where?"

The torchlight showed a sizeable reptile, coiled around a mass of roots, hissing dangerously. Butty was petrified by it. "Sh . . . Sh . . . Shad, look, 'tis an adder!"

The otter seized the torch and thrust it at the bared fangs and beaded eyes. The snake's coils bunched as it backed off.

" 'Taint no adder, that's a smooth snake. It don't carry poison in its fangs, but it can bite an' crush ye!"

"Hurr, you'm roight, zurr. Oi see'd ee smoothysnake once. Moi ole granma, she'm tole oi wot et wurr. Gurr, boitysnake!"

The fearless Shad stripped off his tunic. "A bitin' snake, eh? Then we'll just 'ave to give it summat to bite on, mates. There y'go. 'Ow's that, me ole scaley foebeast!"

He hung the tunic on his spear and jabbed it in the snake's face. Instinctively the smooth snake struck, biting

316

deep into the homespun material. Shad was on it like lightning. He bundled the snake's head in the tunic, wrapped the garment tightly, and thrust it forcibly into the crossed forks of some thick-twisted roots. The snake thrashed about madly, but only for a brief time. It settled down into a steady twitch as it tried to pull itself free of the encumbering tunic.

Shad pointed upward. "Come on—I can see a twinkle o' starlight up ahead there!"

They followed him, hugging the far side of the tunnel cautiously as they passed the slow-writhing reptile.

Even though they were sore and weary, the five companions leapt about gladly once they were aboveground in the moonlit woodlands.

Friar Butty was ecstatic. "O sweet life! O fresh fresh air! O green pretty grass!"

Foremole was used to being underground. He sat back and grinned at the young squirrel's antics. "Hurr hurr hurr! Wot price ee treasure naow, young zurr? Oi'll wager ee wuddent loik t'go back an' lukk fer it."

Butty shook his voluminous Friar's habit and the cloakful of treasure fell out upon the grass. "I wasn't leavin' that behind! Why'd you think I slipped down the chain— it was the weight of this liddle lot!"

Shad tweaked the young squirrel's nose. "Yer cheeky liddle twister, we shoulda left you fer the toads an' mudfishes!"

Butty pulled loose and jumped out of the patch of moonlight they were standing in. His four companions looked shocked for a moment, then they started laughing uproariously.

He pouted at them indignantly. "What're you all laughin' at? I don't see anythin' funny."

Craklyn wiped tears of merriment from her eyes. "Oh, don't you? Well, take a look at yourself, you magic green frog!" Swamp mud, dried and crusted, and the dust on Butty's paws, was shining bright green in the darkness.

He gazed at his small fat stomach in anguish. "I'm green, shinin' bright green!"

Craklyn patted his back sympathetically, and a cloud of green dust arose. "It must be some mineral in the mud that does it, phosphorus or sulphur, I suppose. Heeheehee! Lead on, Butty, we won't need a torch to show us the way, my small green-glowing friend!"

Butty waved a bright green paw at the Recorder. "One more word outer you, miz Craklyn, an' I'll give yore share o' the treasure to Sister Viola, so there!"

Two old moles, Bunto and Drubb, were sleeping in the gatehouse at Redwall Abbey when they were wakened by banging on the main gate. Bunto blinked from the deep armchair he was settled in. "Oo c'n that be a bangin' on ee gate inna noight?"

Drubb rose stiffly from the smaller of the two armchairs by the fire. He yawned, stretched, and said, "Us'll never know 'til us'n's open ee gate. Cummon, Bunto."

Stumbling out into the darkness, they unbarred the big gate and opened it a crack to see who required entrance to the Abbey. The other four had hidden themselves; Butty stood there alone. The two moles took one look and scooted off toward the Abbey building, roaring in their deep bass voices, "Whuuuooooh! Thurr be ee likkle green ghost at ee gate, an' ee'm lookin' loik pore young Butty. Murrsy on us'n's!"

A half of a dandelion wine barrel cut lengthways formed the badgerbabe Russano's cradle. Mother Buscol rocked it gently with a footpaw as she dozed on a pile of sacks in the dark, warm kitchens of Redwall. Only a faint, reddish glow showed from the oven fires, where the scones were slowly baking for next morning's breakfast. From his cradle, the little Russano sat up and pointed at the strange apparition that had appeared. He smiled at it and uttered the only word he knew.

"Nut!"

Mother Buscol half opened her eyes, inquiring sleepily, "Nut? What nut, m'dear?"

Then her eyes came fully open and she saw Butty standing there. "Waaaoooow! 'Tis young Butty, come back to 'aunt me! Ho, spare me, green spirit, don't 'arm me or the liddle one!"

The glowing phantom answered in a hollow, moaning voice, "Bring scones from the ovens, enough for five, honey too, an' woodland trifle if'n there be any about. Some strawberry fizz an' October Ale. I'll be outside. Remember now, enough for five!"

The specter faded slowly away to the small canteen outside the kitchens. Mother Buscol busied herself, complaining to a cockleshell charm she always wore around her neck, "Indeed to goodness, fat lot o' good you were. Lucky charm, indeed. I was nearly eaten alive in me bed by an 'ungry ghost. Fifteen scones, that'll be three apiece, now where's that woodland trifle got to? Oh, dearie me, don't you fret, my liddle babby, I won't let 'im 'ave you!"

Russano stood up in his tiny nightshirt, chuckling. "Yeeheehee. Nut!"

Accompanied by Taunoc and Orocca, the old squirrel-mother brought out a heaped tray. Shad had to take it and put it on the table, as she almost dropped it. In the lantern-lit area, Butty appeared normal.

Tansy waved at her. "Hello, Mother Buscol, Orocca, and Taunoc, my friends. How are your eggchicks? Well, I hope?"

Taunoc bowed courteously and alighted on the table. "We are all healthy, thank you, Abbess. Welcome back to Redwall!"

50

Major Perigord Habile Sinistra looked around the high ridge in the dawn light, sizing up the hillside and valley below.

"You an' Morio did well, Sergeant Torgoch. This ridge could be held against many by a few. Top marks, wot!"

Morio threw a languid salute. "Best place we could find, sah. Looks like we're first here."

Brisk as ever, Torgoch was issuing orders. "Scout around now, see if y'can find stones, any kind, from pebbles to blinkin' boulders. Put 'em in piles along the ridge—always useful t'chuck down on the vermin."

Perigord nodded approvingly. "Good show, Sar'nt, make use of the terrain, eh, wot. Chief Log-a-Log, what can I do for you, old lad?"

The Guosim leader nodded, shrews not being in the habit of saluting. "Thinkin' about food fer the troops, Major. Shall we risk lightin' cookin' fires?"

"Why not, old chap, why not, we want the blinkin' enemy to see where we are. Light some whackin' great bonfires, if y'please."

Log-a-Log took Perigord at his word, and soon three huge fires were alight and blazing out like beacons in the gray of dawn.

Gurgan Spearback had a stroke of luck. His Waterhogs reported they had found a great, fallen pine trunk on the ridge's other side.

"Thee did well, 'ogs. Fetch rope an' wedges. Methinks I'd like yon timber atop o' the ridge—'twill come in useful."

Everybeast joined in to roll the big dead trunk uphill. Gurgan, painted for war, wearing his club and ax, supervised the job. "Put thy backs into it, thou slab-chopped ne'er-do-well rabble! A liddle twig like yon should give thee an appetite for when we breakfast. Worry not about gettin' lily-white paws dusty, by me spikes, come on, move it, afore I move *ye* to bitter tears!"

Captain Twayblade levered hard at the pine with a pike, smiling in high good humor at the fat hedgehog's insults. One of Skipper's crew working alongside her gritted his teeth as he threw his weight against the massive log, and muttered, "Wot's so funny, Cap'n?"

Twayblade leaned on the pikehaft, taking a short breather. "That Waterhog, old chap, Gurgan thingummy. I'd like to put him in a contest against our Sergeant Torgoch. I wager they could insult a regiment for a full day without jolly well repeatin' themselves. That Waterhog's a born Color Sergeant!"

Pasque Valerian sat alone near the tall standing rock at the ridge center, her breakfast untouched, watching the daybreak. Rising from behind a bank of dusky cream cloud, the sun appeared reddish-hued like a new copper coin, burning the morning dew into tiny wraithlike tendrils. It was the start of a high summer's day, but the young hare was downcast.

Arven, the Champion of Redwall, had already eaten. He wandered across to where Pasque sat, and, leaning against the rock, he watched her. "Gracious me, there's a long face! D'you want it to rain?"

The young hare looked up into the squirrel's kind features. "No sir, I hope the day stays fine."

"Lost your appetite too, I see?"

"Oh, I'll get 'round to eatin' it, sir."

"What is it, then? Are you afraid of the battle to come?"

"Not really, sir. I've seen quite a bit of action with Long Patrol."

Arven drew the Sword of Martin from its sheath across his back. He touched Pasque's paw lightly with the tip, smiling secretly. "D'you see this sword? Did you know that it has the power to make pretty hare maidens happy?"

Pasque cast her eyes over the legendary blade. "I've never known a sword do that, sir, but if you say it does, then I'll have to take your word."

Arven snorted impatiently and flourished the blade. "Hah! I see y'don't believe me. Right, I'll show you, missie. C'mon, up off your hunkers and see where my blade is pointing!"

Pasque arose with a small sigh. She did not feel like being forced to laugh at sword tricks.

Arven pointed the blade out and downward to the back of the ridge. "Place your eye level with my sword and look carefully."

The young hare did as she was bid, and in an instant she was wreathed in smiles, jumping about excitedly. "It's Tammo, he's coming! He's coming here!"

Arven watched the small figure below on the plain, running in front of two others like a true Long Patrol Galloper. "Y'see, I told you this is a powerful sword!"

Major Perigord had to lower his brows and glower a bit to prevent himself from smiling. "I say, Pasque, old thing, d'you mind lettin' go of young Tammo's paw, just while he makes his blinkin' report t'me, wot!"

Tammo flushed to his eartips and gave a smart salute. "Midge'll be here soon, sah, our mission was successful. Damug Warfang is headed this way with the Rapscallion army. Sorry to report that we lost Rockjaw Grang . . ."

Tammo's voice broke for a moment. "He . . . he gave his life so we could escape. Brought a squirrel with us, name o' Fourdun; he was a prisoner, y'see. I cut your trail 'twixt here, south o' Redwall, and we've been runnin' like mad-beasts all night t'get here. Sah!"

The Major turned aside and, taking out a spotted ker-chief, he wiped his eyes. After a moment he faced Tammo again, his face pale. "Big Rockjaw Grang, eh? A good an' perilous hare. By my blood an' blade, we'll make the ver-min pay heavily for him! Go an' get y'vittles, Tamm, you look quite done in. I'll get the fine details from Midge. Thank ye, y'may dismiss."

Bluggach, the big stoat Rapmark, made his way to the head of the marching Rapscallions, pointing as he came level with Damug Warfang.

"See, Firstblade, fires burnin' on that ridge in the distance!"

The Greatrat kept his gaze locked on the trio of smoke columns rising against the distant sky. "I saw them a while back. Send Henbit to me."

Henbit was a wily-looking Rapmark officer. He appeared at Damug's side with scarcely a sound. "Mightiness, you wanted to see me?"

"Aye, listen now. Take a score of trackers, good ones who are able to hide and run silent. Get over to that ridge, look for a rock like an otter's tail, and see how many are waiting for us there. Then check the valley, it should have a rift running along the far side of it. Take care that you are not seen. Go!"

Damug was confident that he could win. Who else could put an army of a thousand in the field? Where in all the country east of Salamandastron was any serious force of fighters to be found? As he strode at the head of his powerful force, Damug planned ahead.

He had learned the lesson of over confidence from his father, Gormad Tunn, when they attacked

Salamandastron with disastrous results. Though this battle would be different and his opponents fewer, that was no reason not to take precautions. He would split the army into two groups, sending them into the valley from both ends in a pincer movement. This would catch any of his enemy who were lying in wait on the valley floor and prevent the Rapscallions being outflanked.

Those Redwallers had a harsh lesson in death coming to them. Redwall—when the Abbey was his he would change its name. Fort Damug! That had a good sound to it. His name would live forever when the place was mentioned in far seasons to come. Fort Damug. Tales would be told of how he defeated the foe on open ground and took the Abbey without disturbing a stone.

A keen-eyed squirrel, one of the friends from Mossflower Wood, stood erect on top of the standing rock. Shading both eyes with a paw, he scanned all 'round. The way in which he halted, tail erect and head thrust forward, told Lieutenant Morio that he had spotted something.

Morio hailed him. "What ho there, Lookout, any sign o' movement?"

Holding his position, the squirrel called back, "Dust cloud comin' out o' the southeast, too faint yet t'see much!"

Morio's long face lit up momentarily. "Keep your eye on it, bucko, looks like our visitors are on their flippin' way. Report if you note any change!"

The big pine trunk had become a kind of social gathering place; hares, mice, hedgehogs, shrews, moles, and squirrels grouped about it when they were off duty. Perigord sat scratching his initials into the wood as he listened to Morio's report.

"That sounds like the blighters right enough. When d'you think we can expect them to arrive?"

"Can't say, sah, have t'wait on the Lookout's report."

The Major winked at his waiting warriors. "Well, whenever it is, we'll give the blackguards a warm welcome, eh?"

Ribald comments greeted this statement.

"Aye, we'll feed 'em a nice 'ot supper o' cold steel!"

"Haharr, we'll rap their scallions for 'em!"

"Give the villains rock cakes served with spearpoints!"

Perigord looked down to the thick end of the trunk. Several creatures were throwing weapons at a shriveled leaf, which they had pinned to the trunk. A selection of axes, knives, and javelins quivered from the wood all 'round the leaf.

A shrew called Spykel held up a ribbon of crimson silk. "First to pin the leaf dead center wins this!"

Log-a-Log balanced his rapier and threw it like a javelin.

"A hit! The Guosim Chief's hit it!"

Gurgan Spearback inspected the leaf. "Nay, 'tis not dead center, a touch left, I'd say. Stand away now, yon ribbon'd look fetchin' in my wife, Rufftip's, spikes!"

Gurgan stood on the ten-pace mark. Closing one eye, he licked the blade of his ax, sighted, and flung it spinning. It struck the leaf, slicing it neatly in half through its middle. Gurgan pulled his ax loose and wound the ribbon on to his paw. "See, that's how a Water'og learns to cast his blade!"

Midge Manycoats stopped Gurgan strolling off with the prize. "If a chap could send his blade spot into the cut your ax made, would you give him that nice fancy ribbon, old feller?"

Gurgan chuckled so that his oversized boots quaked. "Hohoho! Hearken to this 'un! 'Taint possible, master 'are! Nobeast can cast a blade good as that in one throw!"

Midge winked at Tammo, who was standing nearby with Pasque. "Show the Waterhog how our patrol chuck a blade, Tamm, go on!"

The young hare blinked modestly. "Oh, really, Midge, I don't go in for showin' off."

From his perch on the trunk, Perigord interrupted. "Go

to it, Tamm, win the ribbon for young Pasque!"

Three paces farther out than the mark, Tammo drew his dirk. "Oh, well, if you say so, sah . . ."

The weapon shot from Tammo's paw like chain lightning. It hissed through the air and thudded deep into the center of the split made by Gurgan's ax. A roar went up from the onlookers.

Bewildered, the Waterhog Chieftain inspected the throw. "Lackaday, I never seen a beast sling steel like that, young sir! What manner o' creature taught thee such a skill?"

Tammo grunted as he used both paws to tug the dirk free. "One called Russa Nodrey, a far finer warrior than I'll ever hope t'be. Keep your ribbon, Gurgan, 'twas you split the leaf."

But the Waterhog would not hear of it. He draped the crimson silken ribbon on Tammo's paw and bowed formally. "Nay, I'd like t'see thee give it to thy pretty friend!"

Tammo felt his ears turn bright pink as he draped the silk about Pasque Valerian's neck. Everybeast cheered him, and Perigord shook him warmly by the paw.

"Your mother'd be rather proud if she could see you now, Tamm!"

51

Furgale and Algador Swiftback had been out scouting the land ahead of the Salamandastron contingent. They returned at mid-noon and made their report to Lady Cregga and Sergeant Clubrush.

"I'm afraid we haven't sighted the ridge you described, marm. It must be further than you estimated."

The badger leaned on her fearsome axpike. "No matter, 'tis there somewhere, I know it is. Did you sight vermin or anything else of interest?"

"Well, m'lady, about two hours ahead there's a dip in the land, sort of forming itself into a windin' ravine. It goes north and slightly west . . ."

Cregga exchanged a knowing glance with the Sergeant. "Good work! We'll camp there tonight and follow the course of this ravine you speak of. That way we won't betray our presence; 'twill keep us well hidden as we march."

Drill Sergeant Clubrush winked at the two recruits. "Top marks, you two, that's wot I calls usin' the old h'initiative. Go an' join yore pals in the ranks now."

Twilight was falling as they entered the ravine's shallow end. Within moments nobeast within a league's distance could tell there were five hundred hares on the

327

march. The columns were reduced to three wide in the narrow gorge; they pressed forward with the rough earthen walls rearing high either side of them.

Trowbaggs accosted Corporal Ellbrig in quaint rustic speech. "Hurr, 'ow furr be et afore us'n's makes camp, zurr?"

Ellbrig looked at him strangely. "Wot're you talkin' like that for, y'pudden-'eaded young rogue?"

Trowbaggs continued with his mimicry. "Hurr hurr hurr! 'Cos oi feels just loik ee mole bein' unnerground loik this, zurr, bo urr!"

The Corporal nodded sympathetically. "Do you now? Well you keep bein' a mole, Trowbaggs, an' when we makes camp you kin dig out a nice liddle sleepin' cave in the ravine wall fer yore officers."

Trowbaggs did a speedy change back to being a hare. "Oh, I say, Corp, why not let old Shangle do the diggin'? He looks a jolly sight more like a mole than I do."

Shangle Widepad fixed the young recruit with a beady eye. "One more squeak out o' you, laddie buck, an' y'won't be either mole or hare, y'll be a dead duck!"

It was chilly sleeping in the ravine. After a cold meal of thick barley biscuit and apple slices, the hares settled down for the night, wrapped in their groundsheets. However, Lady Cregga Rose Eyes felt her blood run hot as she lay there, dreaming of meeting Rapscallion vermin in a valley beneath a far-off ridge.

Standing as high as he could on the pine trunk at the ridgetop, Arven watched the Rapscallion campfires. They dotted the far plains like tiny fallen stars. Skipper of Otters climbed up beside him and passed the Redwall Champion a beaker of vegetable soup, steaming hot.

"All quiet down there, mate?"

Arven blew on the soup and sipped gratefully. "Aye, Skip. If they break camp just before dawn, I figure they'll arrive in the valley below at midday tomorrow. By the fur'n'fang, though, there's going to be a lot of 'em facin' us!"

The big otter set his jaw grimly. "Mebbe, but there'll be a lot less of 'em by the time we're done! Wot makes 'em act like that, Arven? Why can't they just be like ordinary peace-lovin' creatures an' leave us alone?"

Paw on swordhilt, the squirrel Champion shrugged. "Hard to say, really, Skip. There'll always be vermin of that kind, with no respect for any creature, takin' what they please an' never carin' who they have to slay, as long as they get what they want. Peaceful creatures to them are weak fools. But every once in a while they come up against beasts like us, peace-lovin' an' easy-goin' until we're threatened. Win or lose then, we won't be killed, enslaved, or walked on just for their cruel satisfaction. No, we'll band together an' fight for what is ours!"

Far away from the ridge, in the safety and warmth of Redwall Abbey kitchens, the badgerbabe Russano lay in his barrel cradle, his soft dark eyes watching a chill blue mist forming across the ceiling. From somewhere, slow muffled drumbeats sounded, sweet voices humming in time with them.

A scene appeared out of the mists. The army from Redwall lay in slumber amid shattered spears, broken swords, and a tattered banner. Other creatures came then, warriors he had never met, yet a voice in the babe's mind told him he knew them. Martin, Matthias, Mattimeo, Mariel, Gonff, all heroic-looking mice. There were badgers, too, great fierce-eyed creatures with names like Old Lord Brocktree, Boar the Fighter, Sunflash the Mace, Urthclaw, Urthwyte, Rawnblade, and many more. They wandered the ridge, and each time they touched a creature he or she stood and went with them.

Finally they stood in a group together, pale and spectral, and another joined them. It was Rockjaw Grang, the big hare who had carried and nursed Russano on the long trek to Redwall Abbey. Though he did not speak, the little badger heard his voice.

"Remember us when you are grown, Russano the Wise!"

Mother Buscol was awakened by the babe's unhappy cries. Not knowing what he had witnessed, she laid him on her lap and stroked his head, whispering soothingly, "There, there, my liddle one, sleep now, 'twas only a dream."

Back and forth she rocked the little badger until he drifted back to sleep, far too young to tell her what he had seen. Russano had witnessed the Redwall army upon the ridge in the aftermath of battle; he had beheld all those who lived, and the ones who did not.

52

Dawn brought a mad bustle of activity to the army on the ridge, with fires being relit, Corporal Rubbadub beating all creatures to stations, and Chieftains roaring commands.

Damug Warfang had stolen a march on them. Perigord listened as the squirrel Lookout reported what he had seen at daybreak.

"Major, those fires last night were nought but a bluff. Damug must've lit 'em an' carried on marchin' forward. They split into two forces, and right now they're lyin' in the rift at both ends o' the valley, waitin' on some kind o' signal to move!"

On the right flank, half of the Rapscallion army crouched, led by the Firstblade himself. He sat motionless as the rat Henbit, who had headed the scouting expedition, told what he had discovered.

"Mightiness, there can't be more'n three 'undred creatures atop of that ridge—a few hares'n'otters an' some Water'ogs. The rest ain't much: squirrels, mice, an' moles, wid a scatterin' o' those liddle raggy beasts that sail the streams, shrews I think they call 'em. They got plenty of weapons, but no chance o' winnin' agin a thousand of us.

Back side of the ridge is too steep an' rocky—you'd be best advised to attack from this side, Sire."

Damug Warfang peered upward, noting the piles of rock heaped along the heights and the big tree trunk positioned at its center. "A thousand won't be needed to conquer three hundred. Bluggach, you take half of this five hundred. Gribble, take word to Rapmark Skaup that he will send half of his force with Captain Bluggach's fighters. Between them they should take the ridge. That is my command. Go now."

The little rat scurried along the defile to where the ferret Skaup lay waiting on the left flank.

Tammo stood with Pasque on one side of him and Galloper Riffle on the other. He leaned slightly forward and looked down the line. Tight-jawed and silent, the front rank waited, while behind them the second rank, mainly archers, checked shafts and bowstrings.

The young hare felt his limbs begin to tremble. He looked down and noticed that the footpaws of Pasque and Riffle were shaking also. Behind him, Skipper drummed his tail nervously on the ground.

"Me ole tail's just bumpin' about for the want o' somethin' t'do," the otter leader chuckled encouragingly. " 'Tis all this waitin', I s'pose, mates. Can y'see 'em, miss Pasque?"

Gripping the cord of her sling like a vise, Pasque nodded. "Indeed I can, Skip, they're lyin' in the rift down there, waitin' the same as we are. D'you suppose they're nervous too?"

Sergeant Torgoch was pacing the ridge, keeping an eye on the front rank. He winked as he halted in front of her. "Nervous, missie? I can see 'em quakin' in their fur from 'ere!" He waved his pace stick to where Perigord was perched on the pine trunk, leaning nonchalantly upon his saber. "Wot d'ye think, sir, shall we tell 'em wot we thinks o' vermin?"

Waving back with his blade, the Major smiled. "Capital idea, Sar'nt, carry on!"

Swelling out his chest with a deep breath, the Sergeant roared in his best drill parade manner at the Rapscallion army, "Nah then, you scab-tailed, waggle-pawed, flea-ridden excuses fer soldiers! Are ye sittin' down there 'cos yore too stoopid t'move, or are yer afraid?" Then he turned his back on the foebeast and waggled his bobtail impudently. Laughter broke out from the Redwallers' ranks.

Gurgan Spearback clumped up in his oversized boots, wielding the massive mallet that was his favorite weapon. "Hearken t'me, all ye vermin wid half a brain to lissen. Remember what thy mothers told thee about climbin'. If you come climbin' our hill, we'll spank thee right 'ard an' send you away in tears!"

Hoots of derision from the ridge accompanied this announcement. Then Lieutenant Morio's deep booming voice called out a warning: "Stand to arms, here they come!"

Five hundred Rapscallions clambered out of the rift from both flanks, and charged. They made a blood-chilling sight: painted faces, bristling weapons, and blazing war banners. Drums pounded as they screamed and howled, racing like a tidal wave across the valley floor toward the slope of the ridge.

Nobeast could stop it now. The battle was begun.

Captain Twayblade held her long rapier point down. "Steady in the ranks there, let 'em come! Stand by the first three rockpiles! Slingers, wait my command! Steady, steady now, chaps!"

The vermin pounded up the slope, increasing their pace until they were running at breakneck speed, spearpoints, pikes, and blades pointing upward at their adversaries.

Tammo stood his ground, deafening noises thrumming in his ears, watching the hideous pack draw closer until he could see their bloodthirsty faces plainly.

Sergeant Torgoch's voice rumbled across the first rank. "Wait for it, buckoes, wait on the Cap'n's command!"

A barbed shaft whistled past Twayblade's jaw. "Front rank, let 'em have it," she shouted. "Now!"

Slings whirled and a battering rain of stone struck the leading Rapscallions. Tammo saw the look of shock on the face of a lean scarred weasel as his round weighty river pebble struck it hard on the forehead. The creature toppled backward with a screech, rolling downhill, still clutching a broken bow. Loading the sling swiftly, Tammo swung out and hit a rat who was almost upon him.

Now Major Perigord was standing with the front rank, whirling his saber and calling to the moles who were behind the hills of stone. "First three rockpiles away!"

Boulders, rocks, soil, dust, and stones showered down on the advancing Rapscallions. The vermin were seasoned fighters, giving as good as they received. Ducking and dodging, they battled upward, thrusting with pike and spear, slinging, firing arrows, and hurling anything that came to paw.

Tammo was on his third sling when he heard Sergeant Torgoch bellowing, "Down flat an' reload slings, first rank. Second rank, shoot!"

Tammo and Pasque threw themselves down side by side, fumbling to load up their slings. Skipper and the second rank stood forward, shafts drawn back upon tautened bowstrings, and sent a hail of arrows zipping down into the massed vermin. From where they lay, the first rank twirled their slings and added to the salvo.

Then everybeast in the Redwall army grabbed for the spears lying on the ground between the ranks. Tammo, Pasque, and Riffle, like many others, did not have a proper spear, but the long ash poles with fire-hardened points served just as well. Staves, spears, pikes, and javelins bristled to the fore all along the line.

The Rapscallions were completely taken by surprise. They had expected their opponents to stand and defend the ridge, not to mount a counter charge with spears. Many a vermin heart quailed then as the war cry of Salamandastron's Long Patrol cut the air.

"Eulaliaaaaa! 'S death on the wind! Eulaliaaaaaa!"

The Redwallers' charge broke the Rapscallion advance. Drums from below in the rift pounded out the retreat, calling the vermin back.

Damug Warfang estimated that he had lost threescore in the first assault; the Redwallers had lost about half that number. Slightly more than he had expected, but the Greatrat was satisfied. Now that he had tested his enemies, he knew their strength and also their weakness. However, the Firstblade was surprised at his adversary; for peaceful Abbeydwellers they showed great ferocity in fighting and much cunning in their maneuvers. Despite this he was confident they would be unable to resist the might of his full army.

Arven sat still as a mole plastered boiled herbs to a deep graze in his side, lifting one paw up to allow the healer better access to his wound. The mole stopped bandaging, blinking at the sight in the valley below.

Damug Warfang was standing on the grassy sward with his entire army formed up behind him.

"Bo urr an' lackaday, zurr, lukkee, 'tis a turrible soight!"

It was indeed terrible, and impressive. Almost a thousand well-armed vermin, lined in columns, flags streaming, drums beating, with the Greatrat in full armor, sword drawn, out in front.

Log-a-Log stopped sharpening his rapiertip on a whetstone and glanced quizzically at Major Perigord. "Wot d'you suppose Warfang's up to now?"

The hare viewed the scene below dispassionately. "Tryin' to frighten us with a show of force, what else? That was only half their blinkin' number he threw at us in the first charge."

Sergeant Torgoch saluted with his pace stick. "Shall I stand the troops ready for action again, sah?"

Perigord sheathed his blade and started downhill. "I think not, Sar'nt, the blighter obviously wants to parley. Huh! We're all supposed t'be tremblin' in our fur at the size of his force. I expect he wants us to jolly well surrender."

Arven's voice echoed the Major's final word incredulously. "Surrender?"

Tare and Turry, the Long Patrol twins, helped Arven upright. "Hah, fat chance of that, old lad!"

About a third of the way downhill, Perigord halted, calling out, "I take it y've got somethin' to say, rat. Well spit it out an' be quick about it, a chap can't dally here all day, wot!"

Damug Warfang waved his sword eloquently at the massed Rapscallions backing him. "What need of words, hare, when we could destroy you in a single sweep!"

Perigord shook his head and smiled mockingly. "Oh, is that all you've got t'say? Wasted your breath, really, didn't you? Still, what else can one expect from vermin?"

The Greatrat smiled back as if he were equally at ease. "Just think for a moment what we will do to the ones you left behind at Redwall Abbey. I imagine they're the creatures not fit to fight, babes and oldbeasts. Have you considered them?"

Perigord seethed inwardly, but he did not show it. "Oh, if it comes t'that, old thing, I wouldn't worry if I were you. Y'see I fully intend slayin' you, so y'won't be 'round to see it."

Damug was still smiling as he played his trump card. "I'm a bit ahead of you there, because I intend killing you. Now!" He let his sword blade drop and nodded.

The rat Henbit had lain near the ridgetop, concealed among the dead vermin that littered the slope. He sprang up, poising himself to hurl the javelin he held, not three paces from the Major. Suddenly he sighed, as if tired of it all, and let the javelin slide carelessly backward as he fell, an oak shaft in his back.

Perigord stepped distastefully over the fallen rat. "Don't like that sort o' thing. Sneaky. Well shot, Corporal!"

Rubbadub twanged a chord on the empty long-bow string, grinning from ear to ear at his officer's compliment.

"Drrrrrubadubdub!"

Then the Rapscallion army charged. As it swept across the valley, Tammo left off helping Pasque Valerian to bind wounded heads and paws and took up his position in the first rank, feeling slightly detached from it all.

Gurgan Spearback nudged him with a rough paw. "Art thou all right, friend?"

The young hare shrugged in bewilderment. "Strange, isn't it, but here we are facin' almost a thousand an' all I can think about is the time o' day. Look, 'tis almost evening, yet it only seems a moment ago it was mornin'. Can't get it off my mind, really. What's happened t'the rest o' today? Where'd it go?"

Gurgan stumped the ground with his mallethead like a batsman at his crease. "Aye, I know what thou means. All I can think of is my wife, Rufftip, an' our seven liddle 'ogs, 'avin' a pickernick on our boat in the water meadows. Silly wot a body can think of at times like these —Oofh!"

An arrow protruded from Gurgan's shoulder. Tammo stared, aghast. "You're hit!"

The Waterhog pulled the shaft out, snapped it, and flung it from himself bad-temperedly. "Tchah! When a beast's as full o' spikes as I am, one more don't make much difference, though 'tis a great displeasure t'be shot!"

Before Tammo could reply, Sergeant Torgoch was bawling out orders. "First rank, sling! Second rank, stand ready! Keep 'em off the slope!"

At the point where valley met hillslope, the Rapscallions took the full force of the first stone volley. Owing to their numbers, Major Perigord had taken the decision to strike early and save his Redwallers being speedily overrun. He turned to the moles, saying, "How's the fire comin' along under that log, chaps?"

"Ee'm a burnen broight an' reddy t'go, zurr!"

"Capital! Splash all that vegetable oil over the trunk now, quick as y'like!"

Dry timber and resin gave a great whoosh as the oil buckets were hurled upon it. The evening sprang to light, sparks and flaming splinters crackling as they leapt from the blazing tree. Skipper and his otters rolled it forward using spearpoints and ash staves. It teetered a moment on the brow of the ridge, then took off with a crash, rumbling, rolling, bouncing, and spinning.

Lady Cregga Rose Eyes and the Long Patrol army had been plodding all day. The going was awkward and rough in the narrow rift; it seemed to stretch on forever. They had waded through mud and water, squeezed through narrow gorges, and climbed over collapsed debris.

Deodar was first to see it. "Look, Sergeant, up ahead, that light!"

A sudden bright glow lit the evening sky from a ridgetop in the distance. It flared brightly then disappeared, leaving the hares blinking against the gathering darkness. Sergeant Clubrush placed himself in front of Lady Cregga, blocking her way.

"Deodar, Algador, drop y'packs but 'old on to yore weapons. Scout up ahead, close to that ridge as y'can get. We needs h'information quick as to wot's goin' on up yonder. So make all speed there an' back. Run lively now, young 'uns!"

As he spoke, the Sergeant had pulled Corporal Ellbrig and several others past him to barricade the rift. Both

Runners hared off.

Lady Cregga glared fiercely at Clubrush. "Stand out of my way, Sergeant!"

It would be said in later seasons that this was the first time a hare openly disobeyed a Badger Ruler. Sergeant Clubrush drew his sword.

"Sorry, Lady, but we got to wait 'ere 'til the Runners gets back. If you goes chargin' off now, not knowin' wot lies ahead, you could get y'self an' all these slain, recruits an' veterans. We must know wot's goin' on at that ridge first afore we goes at it. Now I know y'could snuff me out like a candle, marm, but I'll try to stop ye if'n I can, for the good of all 'ere!"

Lady Cregga Rose Eyes raised the terrible axpike high over her head with one paw. She brought it smashing down into the rift wall, knocking out a great quantity of soil-bound rock.

"So be it, we wait! But those hares of yours had better be quick, Sergeant, because I won't wait long!"

339

53

Vermin screamed and wailed as the blazing pine trunk cut a swathe through the Rapscallion ranks. It thundered off the hillside, over the valley, and disappeared with a crash of loose earth into the rift, where one side of the defile fell in on top of it.

This was followed by a frightening silence.

Galloper Riffle rubbed both his eyes, peering into the fallen night. "What's happenin'? Why's everythin' so bally quiet—I can't see a flippin' thing!"

A shrew standing by Riffle blinked hard several times. "Neither c'n I, matey, all's I see is colored lights, poppin' all round. 'Twas that burnin' tree wot did it."

Most of the Redwallers were grouped at the center of the ridge, in the place the otters had launched the trunk from. A shout from the far side of the ridgetop alerted them.

"Help! They're attackin' this end!"

With their sight growing clearer, the Redwallers rushed to defend that end of the summit, only to be hailed by another distress cry. "Yurr, on ee t'uther end, they'm up 'ere too!"

Damug had not been slow. Even as the burning trunk was launched from the crest of the ridge, he had issued

340

orders for his army to split up again and attack the summit from both ends. Now the Redwall army was in deep trouble. Damug's plan had worked; he had gained the precious moments he needed to put his Rapscallions on the ridge summit.

Tammo fought back-to-back with Pasque, sling in one paw, dirk in the other. Vermin came at them in mobs. Lieutenant Morio was surrounded and alone; gallantly he battled away, hacking at the encroaching Rapscallions with a cracked pike. Tammo and Pasque began forcing their way through to Morio's aid, but too late. The brave Lieutenant went down, fighting to the last.

"Eulaliaaaa! 'S death on the wind! Eulaliaaaaa!"

Captain Twayblade, too, was ringed by the enemy. Her long rapier darted and flickered as she wove it around cutlass and spear, slaying every vermin she touched. "Saha! Come an' meet me, sir vermin, I'll have ye crowdin' at Dark Forest gates this night!"

Tammo glimpsed a fox working his way behind Twayblade, and as the fox raised his sword, Tammo let fly with the dirk.

"A hit!" Twayblade laughed. "Over here, Tamm, come on, Pasque!"

They were joined by Skipper, and between them they smashed free of the crowding foebeasts. The otter pushed them toward the standing rock. "Over there, mates—get our backs agin somethin'!"

Perigord and Gurgan had been outnumbered and driven back along the ridge. Striving valiantly with what was left of their group, they too managed to reach the standing rock. The Major's saber decimated the ranks of vermin swarming to get at them. Blood ran from a cut above his eye as he stood shoulder-to-shoulder with Gurgan.

"Whew! I keep choppin' 'em down, but they're still comin'!"

The Waterhog's huge mallet hit the Rapmark Skaup,

wiping him out. "Aye, there's nought left but to take as many as we can with us. Hearken though, I'd like t'get yon Damug atwixt my paws!"

Log-a-Log gritted his teeth, bringing down a weasel with his heavy loaded sling. "Y'won't get close to that scum, mate. Damug's the kind who leads his army from be'ind, like the true coward he is! Tamm, did they get ye, bucko?"

Tammo almost collapsed as Pasque drew the pike from his leg. "Aaaagh! He got me, but I made sure I got him, the blackguard!"

They ringed the pair, fighting off the attackers as Pasque stuffed herbs into the awful gash and bound it with the red silken ribbon. "There, that'll hold you, sir. Lean on me. I knew that ribbon'd come in useful. Good job you won it for me, wot!"

Deodar and Algador slumped on the rift floor, gasping for breath after making their report.

Lady Cregga acted instantly. "Sergeant, take the right flank; Corporal, you take the left. I'll hold the center. Let's get out of this ditch and form up in a skirmish line, ten deep, fifty long. Double-quick speed, weapons out and ready. We'll come at that ridge from the back. Rapscallions haven't got the brains to think we'd attack that way!"

Still fighting for air, Algador and Deodar drew their blades. "We're comin' too, Sergeant!"

Trowbaggs nodded to Shangle Widepad. "Grab old Algy there, chum, we'll help him along. Fallow, Reeve, lend a paw to Deodar, there's good chaps!"

The night air thrummed to the paws of five hundred Salamandastron hares. Silent and determined, they sped off into the darkness.

Damug Warfang was delighted beyond measure. He stood back from the fighting, leaning on his sword by a fire. The Rapscallions had suffered heavy losses, but nothing to what the creatures of Redwall had sustained. From his position he viewed what he considered to be the last stages of the battle. His enemy would soon be soundly defeated and the famous Abbey of Redwall his for the taking.

Rapscallions crowded in on every side around the standing rock, but there was a space at the center between them and their opponents. The Redwallers had fought more fiercely than anybeasts they had ever encountered, and now, at this final part of the battle, many vermin were growing cautious, not wanting to be on the lists of the slain while their comrades enjoyed the spoils of victory.

The stoat Captain, Bluggach, was a bigger and more reckless beast than his confederates. Pike in one paw and a wicked steel hook in the other, he swaggered into the open space between the armies and began taunting his beleaguered enemy.

"Haharr, so yore the bold crew who were gonna spank us an' send us off in tears, eh? I wager the one who shouted that is 'idin' somewheres at the back now, prob'ly in tears hisself!"

Mass laughter and cheering from the Rapscallion horde prompted Bluggach to become bolder. He leered at the Redwallers, licking the tip of the hook he carried. "C'mon out an' face me, 'tis my turn t'do the spankin'!"

Gurgan Spearback was already out as he spoke, wielding his tree-trunk-headed war mallet. "Stoats be windy braggarts. Come an' spank me if thee thinks thou art warrior enough to do it!"

Bluggach gave a wild yell and charged the big Waterhog. Gurgan sidestepped and swung the mallet once. Just once.

Bluggach slumped to the ground, never to rise again.

But Gurgan's sidestep had carried him close to the Rapscallion mob. A crowd leapt upon him, overwhelming the Waterhog Chieftain.

The Redwallers could not leave their friend in enemy paws. They charged forward into the vermin pack, roaring, "Redwaaaaallll! Redwaaaaaallll!"

They were hopelessly outnumbered, but prepared to sell their lives dearly. Strangely, though, it was Damug Warfang who saved them.

The unpredictable Warlord strode among his vermin, lashing out with the flat of his swordblade. "Halt! Enough, I say! We will take these creatures as prisoners. Nobeast must touch them. I will keep them as captives to serve me!" The Greatrat halted in front of Perigord. "All except you, hare. Nobeast talks to me as you did and lives!"

Held fast by four Rapscallions, the Major still struggled to break free and get at his enemy, even though he was twice wounded. "So be it, foulface. Give me back my saber an' I'll fight you, blade-to-blade. Come on, vermin, let's have at it, wot!"

Damug looked Perigord up and down. Dried blood was caked over the Major's brow, covering his right eye, while the Redwall tunic hung from him in shreds, revealing a ragged scar on one shoulder. The Greatrat sneered contemptuously. "Your fighting days are over, fool. I'm going to make an example of you in front of your friends. Conquered beasts always learn to behave better when they see their leader executed. Get him down in front of me and bend his head!"

A massive roar shook the night air, chilling the blood of every Rapscallion on the ridge.

"Eulaliaaaaaaa!"

Thundering forward, fifty paces ahead of her command, Lady Cregga Rose Eyes hit the vermin ranks like a lightning storm.

Tammo saw vermin actually fly through the air as the huge badger, her eyes blazing red with Bloodwrath, swung her axpike into them. Then she was upon Damug Warfang. Casting her weapon away, she seized the

Firstblade with both paws and teeth.

"Spawn of Gormad Tunn! Evil murderer's kin! Come to me!"

Hacking furiously at the Badger Warrior's head with his sword, Damug gave an unearthly screech. Locked together, the pair hurtled into space from the ridgetop.

"Eulaliaaaa! 'S death on the wind! Eulaliaaaaaa!"

Booting aside a rat, Major Perigord grabbed his saber. "Hares on the ridge, hundreds of 'em! Eulaliaaaaaa!"

54

The army from Salamandastron charged into the Rapscallions' midst to join the Redwallers. Galloper Riffle was down; a snarling weasel who was about to dispatch him with a dagger thrust fell forward, slain by a saber swing. Riffle felt himself pulled upright; he stopped a moment in the thick of battle, recognizing his rescuer. "Algador! My brother!"

The young Runner blinked, smiling and crying at the same time. "Riffle, thank the seasons you're alive!"

"Logalogalogalogaloooooog!"

The shrew Chieftain, at the head of his remaining Guosim, tore into a pack of vermin and chased them the length of the ridge.

"Redwaaaaaalll! No surrender, no quarter, me buckoes!"

Skipper of Otters and his ragged band threw themselves headlong at another group of foebeasts, javelins forward.

Tammo had formed foursquare with Pasque, Midge, Twayblade, and Fourdun, battling madly against the desperate Rapscallions. They pushed their way with blade, sling, and tooth to where Corporal Rubbadub lay stretched on the ground, limp and trampled. While the others fought, Pasque stooped to inspect the big lump and the awesome cut across the back of Rubbadub's head. She looked up sadly at her friends. "I think poor old Rubbadub's gone!"

"Nonsense!" Twayblade kicked Rubbadub's paw roughly.

Turning over, the drummer rubbed his head, grinning widely. "Dubadubadubb! B'boom!"

Sargeant Torgoch found himself fighting alongside Drill Sergeant Clubrush. The pair fought like madbeasts but chatted like old pals.

"By the left, Sar'nt, yore young 'uns are shapin' up well!"

"They certainly are, Sar'nt—they pulled yore chestnuts out o' the fire!"

Tare and Turry had formed up with Trowbaggs and Furgale. They pressed forward in a straight line, driving Rapscallions off the edge of the ridge. Determined to distinguish himself in this his first action, Trowbaggs pulled away from the others and began taking on four vermin single-pawedly. "Have at ye, y'scurvy rascals, Trowbaggs the Terrible's here!"

He managed to slay one before another got behind him and put him down with a dagger in his side. Corporal Ellbrig and Shangle Widepad rushed in to his aid, slaying two and sending the other one running.

Holding on to his side, Trowbaggs managed a weak smile. "Chap got behind me. Wasn't very sportin' of him, was it, Corp?"

Shangle provided cover while Ellbrig ministered to the recruit. "Trowbaggs, wot am I goin' t'do with you, eh? War isn't no game—there ain't no such thing as a vermin bein' sporty. Good job that dagger only took a bit o' fur'n'flesh. You'd be a goner now if'n that was an inward stab instead o' a sideways one. Come on, up on yore hunkers, me beauty, stick wid me'n'ole Shang."

Furgale and Reeve Starbuck were in difficulties.

Heavily outnumbered, they fought gallantly. Tammo's party saw they were in a fix and dashed over to help, but too late. Both the recruits went under from vermin spear thrusts before they could be reached. Others came running to avenge their comrades, exacting a terrible retribution on the vermin spear-carriers with swords and javelins.

Clubrush saw Furgale twitch, and he knelt by him, supporting his head. "Y'did bravely, young sir. Be still now, we'll git you some 'elp."

Furgale tried to focus on Clubrush, his eyes fluttering weakly. "Get my old job back, servin' you an' Colonel Eyebright in the mess . . . won't shout too loud though, Colonel doesn't like that . . ."

The young recruit's head lolled to one side, his eyes closed. Drill Sergeant Clubrush hugged him tightly, tears flowing openly down his grizzled face. "I 'ope you've gone to an 'appier place than this blood-strewn ridge."

The tide of battle was turned. What was left of the mighty Rapscallion army fled from the hill, pursued by the hares and the Redwallers. Major Perigord and Captain Twayblade limped their way down the hill and across the valley, with Tammo and Pasque following them. They found Lady Cregga in the rift, clutching the mangled remains and broken sword of Damug Warfang.

Pasque Valerian was the only one of the four who was still fit and active. She climbed down to the bottom of the rift. Perigord peered over the edge, watching her inspect the badger.

"I say, Pasque, get a chunk o' that smoulderin' wood t'make a torch."

The young hare snapped off a billet of pine from the charred trunk and blew gently upon it until the flame rekindled itself. She looked closely at the still form of Lady Cregga, checking her carefully.

"Good news, sah! Though you wouldn't think it to look at her. Lady Cregga's alive, but Warfang must have slashed an' battered at her with his sword somethin' dreadful. Her face, head, an' eyes suffered terrible injuries, but as I say, she lives!"

The Major winced as he straightened up. "Well, there's a thing! Our Badger Lady must be jolly well made of iron. Tammo, see if y'can hunt up stuff t'make a stretcher and find some able-bodied beasts to carry it. Tamm, are you all right, old lad?"

Tammo sat at the edge of the rift, his head in both paws, shaking and weeping uncontrollably. "No, I'm not all right, sah. I've seen death! I've been in a battle, I've slain other creatures, seen friends cut down before my eyes, and all I can think of is, thank the fates *I'm* not dead. Though the way I feel right now I don't know if I want to go on living!"

The Major sat down beside him. "I know what y'mean, young 'un, but think for a moment. Think of the babes at Redwall and the oldsters, think of all the families, like your own, who will never be frightened or harmed by the bad ones we fought against. You've done nothin' t'be ashamed of. The Colonel an' your mother would be proud to know they had a son like you. What d'you say, Pasque? Tell this perilous feller."

Pasque Valerian paused from her salves and dressings, capturing Tammo with her soft voice and gentle smile. She pointed skyward. "I don't have to tell you anything, Tamm. Just look up."

Tammo felt the other three staring upward with him.

Fading from dark blue to light, dawn was breaking, with threads of crimson and gold radiating wide. Pale, cream-washed clouds lay in rolls to the east, their undersides glowing pink with the rising of the sun. Somewhere a lark was singing its ascension aria, backed by waking curlews on the moor, and wood pigeons in the copses.

The spell was broken abruptly as the Little Owl Taunoc swooped out of nowhere to land at the rift edge. "I see by your returning warriors and the vermin carcasses lying everywhere that you won the battle."

Perigord wiped his saber blade with a pawful of dewy grass. "Aye, we won!"

Taunoc nodded sagely, preening his wings, ready for flight. "I will carry the good news back to Redwall Abbey. Is there anything else you wish me to add?"

Tamello De Fformelo Tussock dried his eyes and smiled. "Tell them . . . tell them we're coming home!"

55

Extract from the writings of Craklyn the squirrel, Recorder of Redwall Abbey in Mossflower Country.

Healing the wounds of war takes a very long time. It is four seasons since the victorious warriors returned to us, but still the memory of that terrible time is fresh in all our minds. When Lady Cregga was brought to our Abbey, we feared greatly for her. She spoke little and ate even less, lying in the Infirmary with her whole head swathed in bandages. Pasque Valerian and Sister Viola both knew Cregga would be blind, even before the bandages were removed.

Alas, when we did unbandage her, the rose-colored eyes were no more. They had been replaced by tightly shut eyelids. She no longer had the desire to slay, the Bloodwrath, they call it; all that was gone. Throughout the winter she remained in an armchair by the fire in Cavern Hole.

It was pure accident that a miraculous change was wrought in her. One day the baby Russano got loose and crawled off, and we found him perched in Lady Cregga's lap, both badgers entirely happy. Since then she lives only to rear and educate Russano. He is her eyes, and now that he can walk in a baby fashion, they are seen everywhere together. Tammo reminded me of the second half of the rhyme Martin imparted to him:

> One day Redwall a badger will see,
> But the badger may never see Redwall,
> Darkness will set the Warrior free,
> The young must answer a mountain's call.

After the battle, the Warriors buried the Rapscallions in the rift and our own on the ridgetop. When spring arrived, they returned to the Ridge of a Thousand (for that is what it is known as now). Major Perigord took Lady Cregga's big axpike. Moles chiseled a hole into the top of the standing rock on the summit, and they cemented the axpike in it, upright, with the old green homemade flag that bears the red letter R fluttering proudly from the piketop. There it will stand until the winds of ages shred the banner and carry it away with them.

The moles are good stonemasons; they carved Pasque Valerian's poem to the fallen on the rock.

> Slumber through twilight, sleep through the
>   dawn,
> Bright in our memory from first light each
>   morn,
> Rest through the winter beneath the soft snow,
> And in the springing, when bright blossoms
>   show.

> Warriors brave, who gave all you could give,
> Offered your lives so that others would live.
> No one can tell what my heart longed to say
> When I had to leave here, and you had to stay.

Aye, there are memories that die hard and others that we want to keep forever. What courageous creatures they were; as the Long Patrol would say, perilous!

I wish that little Russano would never grow up, but that is an idle and foolish thought. One day he will have to take his place on that mountain far away on the west shores; he will be Lord of Salamandastron. Lady Cregga is certain of this. He is a quiet youngster, but he seems to radiate confidence, understanding, and sympathy to all about him. Already the hares call him Russano the Wise.

The owlchicks of Orocca and Taunoc are big birds now. My goodness, how quickly they grew and learned to fly! They chose the names Nutwing, Nutbeak, and Nutclaw, because "nut" was the only word they spoke for a full season. All three are fine birds, though not as well-spoken as their parents and inclined to be a bit impudent at times, but they are still young.

I am the official keeper of the medals, did you know that? I'll tell you about it. The treasure we brought up from sunken Castle Kotir was melted down by order of my good friend Abbess Tansy. She decreed that a solid gold medal, each set with a separate gem, would be made for everybeast who fought at the Ridge of a Thousand. Redwallers get a ruby, Waterhogs and otters a pearl, shrews a peridot, and hares a blue john, every one set in a small gold shield attached to a white silken ribbon. But I am left in charge of them all because they will not wear them to work!

What work, did I hear you say? Why, the rebuilding of our south wall, of course. Major Perigord, Skipper, Log-a-Log, Gurgan Spearback, and our own Arven all agreed that they cannot abide idle paws. So we have a veritable army working on the south wall, filling holes, tamping down earth, and relaying the massive red sandstone blocks. It will soon be completed, and then there will be double reason, nay treble, for festivities. One for the new wall, and two to celebrate the lives of those lost in the battle last summer. The third reason is so exciting that I can scarce bring myself to write about it.

Tammo and Pasque are to be wedded!

It's true! Taunoc flew off some time back to bring Tammo's family from Camp Tussock to attend the celebrations. Mem Divinia was very proud of her son, and even old Colonel Cornspurrey had to admit that his son was a true Long Patrol warrior. Abbess Tansy saved enough gold and three beautiful emeralds to make a paw bracelet for Pasque. She is the prettiest hare I have ever seen, and I personally think that she knows more of healing wounds than anybeast. But don't tell Sister Viola I said that. Alas, even Pasque can do nothing for Tammo's limp, which the spear wound in his leg caused. But Tammo just laughs when asked about his injury. He says that he never intended being a Runner and gets about better than most. I agree with him, the limp is hardly noticeable.

When the sad day arrives that Russano has to leave us, our Abbey will not be without a badger. Lady Cregga has decided to live at Redwall as Badger Mother. The Dibbuns adore her, and though she has massive strength, her gentleness toward them is touching to see. And talking about seeing, Mother Cregga is learning to see more without the use of her sight than most of us can see with two eyes!

The Guerilla Union of Shrews in Mossflower, or the Guosim, as they are known, have faithfully stayed at our Abbey to help rebuild the wall, as have the Waterhogs. Redwall is full of fast-growing Dibbuns with even faster-growing appetites. Log-a-Log has been hearing the call of the streams and rivers of late, though he says he will wait until Russano is ready to go, then the shrews can accompany him.

Gurgan Spearback keeps his houseboat on the water meadows, merely for the pleasure of his large family. What a quaint beast Gurgan is. He has relinquished Chieftainship of the Waterhogs to his eldest son, Tragglo. Gurgan's great interest now is being Abbey Cellarhog; he was so enthusiastic about brewing October Ale that old Gurrbowl has retired and passed the job on to him.

You will forgive me, but I am about to put aside my quill pen and scrub the ink from my paws. I have an appointment with Friar Butty. Together with the Friar and Captain Twayblade, I will help to plan the triple feast. There will be ten kinds of bread, from hazelnut and almond to sage and buttercup loaves.

Cheeses, well, last autumn's cheesemaking was the best ever. We have some huge yellow ones, with celery and carrot pieces in them, and all the different cheeses in between, ending with tiny soft white ones.

Friar Butty has drawn up a recipe for a South Wall Cake, it will be the centerpiece of the tables. Though if you could see the recipe and the amount of fruit, honey, and meadowcream the cake will take, you would wonder how any other food could find room on our festive board. The seasons have been kind; there will be more than enough for everybeast, but then they deserve it.

What more is left to say, my friend? Redwall Abbey is as it has always been, basking in the shelter of Mossflower Wood, the gates ready to open any old sunny day to weary travelers, friends, and visitors, all good honest creatures like yourselves. Please come and feel free to stop for a season, any time. You are always welcome.

Craklyn Squirrel, Recorder of Redwall Abbey

Epilogue

Many a long season passed since Major Perigord Habile Sinistra had set eyes upon the mountain of Salamandastron. Straightening his scarlet tunic and brushing his slightly graying whiskers, he touched the long-healed scar line upon his brow and gazed up at the fortress on the far west shore.

"The old place hasn't changed a bit, wot!"

Captain Tamello De Fformelo Tussock and his wife, Lady Pasque Valerian, detached themselves from the throng of travelers. Standing to one side, they too viewed the mountain.

"So this is Salamandastron, m'dear. 'Tis all you said it would be."

"Wait until you see inside, Tamm—it's even more impressive. Oh, look, there's a welcoming party coming out to greet us!"

Old Colonel Eyebright headed the reception group, leaning heavily upon the paw of Garrison Captain Cheeva. Tammo was reminded of his own father as the old hare popped in his monocle and peered closely at the lines of shrews, Waterhogs, and Redwallers, led by Arven, who carried the Sword of Martin.

Then Colonel Eyebright's gaze shifted to the hares, and

356

the monocle dropped from his eye to dangle on its string. "Well, 'pon my life. Perigord!"

The Major clasped paws warmly with his old friend. "Colonel Eyebright, sah, you're lookin' remarkably chipper. Brisk as a blinkin' barnacle on a big boulder, wot!"

Eyebright chuckled, shoving Perigord playfully. "Away with you, base flatterer! I'm as old as I feel and twice as jolly well old as I look. The owl Taunoc told us you were comin', but I didn't expect you until the start of winter. 'Tis still autumn!"

Drill Sergeant Clubrush and his companion Sergeant Torgoch saluted the Colonel smartly. "Beg to report, sah, we made good time, mostly by water with our pals the Guosim shrews an' the Waterhogs. Sah!"

"Aye, we remembered what you taught us, sah, save the old footpaws wherever possible. No doubt the owl gave you our message, sah, 'fraid we didn't bring 'em all back, two score an' a half lost in action . . ."

Colonel Eyebright nodded sadly. "So I heard, Sergeant. Perilous beasts, they'll live in our memories forever, wot. Your friends from Redwall will have to stay with us until spring—no good makin' that long trek back in wintertide. We'll make them welcome to share all Salamandastron can offer. You there, young chap, c'mere. What name d'you go by, eh?"

"Tamello De Fformelo Tussock, sah!"

"Hmph! No need t'shout, sir, I'm not deaf, well not completely. So, you'll be the laddo who stole the prettiest hare on the mountain. Wed to our Pasque, if I'm not mistaken. Hmm, Tussock, knew your father well, your mother too, she was as pretty as your wife."

Tammo and Pasque bowed respectfully to the Colonel as he gestured Cheeva to assist him walking through the ranks. The Colonel halted near the rear markers and, slowly bending his knee, bent his head down until he touched a massive footpaw with his forehead.

"My life and honor are yours to command, Sire!"

Immediately he was raised up by a gentle paw.

The old hare found himself gazing into a pair of dark hazel eyes. He knew instinctively that they held more wisdom than he could have gathered in two lifetimes. The badger was tall, young, and slender, but his paw and shoulder structures dictated that in maturity he would be a beast of mighty girth and boundless strength. Shifting aside his homespun green traveling cloak, he walked toward the mountain entrance, with Eyebright leaning upon his paw for support.

Holding her Colonel's other paw, Captain Cheeva glanced across at the tall young badger, curiosity overcoming her. "Sire, it is said that Badger Lords always carry a great blade, spear, or mace, yet you carry no weapon. Why is that?"

Such was the calm and dignity radiated by the badger that everybeast was attracted to his presence. They all craned forward to hear him speak for the first time. His voice was deep and mellow.

"I have no need of a blade, nor any kind of great weapon. This is all I carry. You would be surprised what a creature can do with this. I have been brought up by good friends and instructed in its use." Smiling quietly, the badger drew forth from his cloak a short hardwood stick, well used and polished to a dull sheen. "It once belonged to a warrior, formidable and perilous."

Old Colonel Eyebright tightened his grip on the badger's wide paw. "It was written in the stones of Salamandastron that you would come here one day to rule. Truly you are named Russano the Wise, Lord of Salamandastron!"